SWEET CHAOS

KALI SWEET URBAN FANTASY, BOOK 2

MISTY EVANS

Beach
Path
Publishing
LLC

Sweet Chaos, Kali Sweet Urban Fantasy Series, Book 2

Misty Evans

©2010 - 2024

ISBN: 978-1-964028-05-7

Cover Art by Fanderclai Design

Formatting by Beach Path Publishing, LLC

To you, the readers and fans of Kali and Rad.
Rock on.

ACKNOWLEDGMENTS

Thank you to the readers and reviewers who enjoyed getting revenge along with Kali in the last book. I hope you enjoy her new adventures in Sweet Chaos.

I've included a glossary of terms at the end of the book as well as
the full version of Rad's song for Kali, *Whisper in the Dark.*

ONE

I'm the best at what I do, but what I do isn't nice.

Unless you're a human I'm saving from a demon. Then you might appreciate my enforcer skills. For those who step on the wrong toes, however, my vengeance services will probably leave you in pain or dead.

The biggest lesson I've learned after three hundred years of being a vengeance demon has nothing to do with justice or revenge. It has to do with love.

Love changes every game. Human or demon, once you love someone, they become your Achilles' heel.

Bass music thumped a hard tempo against the plexiglass windows of the VIP booth upstairs at club Fright Night. Lights flashed across the dance floor, throwing a jagged spotlight on pole dancers dressed in triangles of green and red fabric. Various supernaturals moved to the rhythm of a Christmas classic remixed with a Euro trance beat.

I couldn't decide whether to plug my ears or tap my foot.

On the table, my cellphone buzzed, a text message lighting

up the ID display with Maddy's favorite moniker for my Achilles' heel: *Rock God.*

Translation: Radison Beaumont.

The VIP booth had to be rocking eighty degrees, yet seeing his name made goose flesh rise on my arms and down my back.

Achilles' heel was an understatement.

Beside me, sipping Jack Daniels from a squat glass, my bodyguard, Cole, glanced at the phone before returning his gaze to the club below. His eyes swept the bar and the customers, scanning every one for weapons, magical or not. There were plenty of those, but few supernaturals who would attack us unprovoked. After all, Cole is a War demon, and I'm Kali Sweet, the best damn vengeance demon on earth. Tangle with either of us, and you'll be eating your intestines for breakfast.

The phone buzzed again. I slipped it off the table, going for discreet, and opened the text.

I need to see you.

Ignoring the text and the second shiver running down my spine, I set the black phone back on the table and tapped my foot more from nerves than the beat. "I'll give Dru one more minute, and then we're out of here."

Cole and I loathed sitting in a strip club in downtown Chicago, loathed being kept waiting by a pack of vampires. But when you're the queen of the region's Undead population—even if it's in name only—duty sometimes calls.

My phone buzzed once more, this time vibrating like an angry bee. I wondered if Rad had sent extra chaos juice through the invisible airwaves. Being discreet seemed like a lost cause, but I slipped the phone into my lap anyway before opening the message.

Tonight.

Demanding, that one.

I hate demanding.

Rad's chaotic energy flowed from that simple word, reaching me even through the damn phone. I slammed it down on the table and sighed, the sharp breath lifting my bangs.

"Guitar Boy harassing you?" Cole sipped his whiskey, gaze lingering momentarily on a redheaded witch wearing enough crystal bling to rival a Vegas showgirl. She caught Cole watching her, swiveled her hips, and blew him a kiss. Cole's gaze moved on.

Harassing was a good word for Rad's constant demands. He was my blood slave—thanks to the city's previous vamp king —and needed to drink from me once a week. Lately, it seemed once a week wasn't enough. I'd set up a well-guarded blood supply for him and my other slave, Arman, in the blood bank run by the Tempter demon Chloe. It was under the club, but Rad preferred drinking directly from the source.

Truth was, I preferred the direct route, too. Usually, we ended up doing more than sharing blood.

That was a significant problem. Being a vengeance demon who worked for the Bridge Council to protect humans from supernaturals, I was breaking Bridge law by having blood slaves since Rad and Arman were half-human.

Worse, I couldn't afford to get involved with a guy who tangled my emotions into a knotted mess, even if he was a sexy half-demon, half-human rock star and the love of my pathetic, three-hundred-year-old life. Every time I got close to Rad, I got hurt. Others got hurt. Hurt as in *dead*.

Not to mention he was a Noctifector—a demon hunter— and my name had a bright red bull's-eye around the number one spot on the Noct kill list.

Hence, Cole was my constant bodyguard these days, and our boss Damon, head of the Bridge Council, had insisted I move into the Bridge Institute for security reasons.

Being a hermit by nature, I found living in the supernatural equivalent of a massive college dorm with my boss and his council cronies watching my every move akin to my worst nightmare.

Pocketing the phone in my red cape, I stood. "I have three cases for Sweet Investigations to take care of tonight. I can't wait any longer."

Cole tossed back the last of his whiskey and stood alongside me, his gaze continuing to scan the club for possible trouble-makers. "Dru and his brothers already hired you to hunt down Toel and take revenge for their father's murder. What's with this theatrical performance?"

"They want to send a message to reestablish their place in the supe world. You kill Vlad the Impaler, and you end up with Kali Sweet on your ass. No better place than here to assert their position against Toel and make sure every supe in Chicago knows I'm gunning for him."

A warm tingle ran through my veins as if our discussion generated Dru's appearance. I wasn't a vampire—thank the devil—but I'd been injected with the previous vamp king's blood, making me sensitive to the Undead. The more time I spent around the Chicago vamps, especially Alexandru, the House Master, the more sensitive I became. When my blood warmed, I knew Dru and his brothers had arrived.

First through the door was a petite female vamp dressed in body-hugging black leather. Her blonde hair was secured in a high ponytail, and she'd flipped up the collar of her trench coat.

As Dru's security detail, she looked harmless enough, but I knew better. She'd spent the past two weeks at the Institute training with me and Cole. Brianna Ann Mullins had been turned by Alexandru—son of the ultimate master vamp, Vlad the Impaler—and carried his ancient royal blood in her veins.

So far, she'd been the toughest vamp to come through the Institute.

Her round baby doll eyes searched the balconies and landed on me in the VIP booth. Blood red lips moved in a tight smile, and she tilted her head to me—her queen—in a show of respect. Amidst the act and the over-glossed lips, her contempt was obvious.

The demon inside me laughed. Demons and vampires don't play well together. My appointment to queen and the subsequent exchange of training favors at the Institute had done little to improve relations between the two camps. Although Damon insisted I go the extra mile in treating the vamps with courtesy and respect, I had limits. Brianna had proven adept at pushing me to them.

One of these days, I promised her with my return smile, *you'll poke this demon and get more than you bargained for.*

Her gaze shifted to the ground in mock subservience before rising again and landing on Cole. He tensed, the movement so slight, I wouldn't have noticed it if we hadn't spent every waking hour in each other's presence for the past month. Hell, he practically lived in my skin these days. It had gotten to the point I could tell when he was hungry before he realized it himself.

"If you and Miss Mullins need to talk, you know, about bodyguard" —I searched for the proper term, came up blank— "*stuff*, while Dru and I have our meeting, there are plenty of private rooms down the hall. I can arrange one for you."

"Nothin' to talk about."

"You sure?"

Bottled annoyance. "I don't do dead girls."

Since he'd been chained to me, he hadn't been doing *any* girls. He was even grouchier than normal, and I was pretty sure the abstinence had something to do with it. "She's not dead.

Undead, yes, but I sparred with her yesterday, and believe me, she's very alive and talented in hand-to-hand combat. She's learned a great deal from you."

Cole snorted at my backhanded compliment. "I hate vamps."

"I hate Noctifectors." I lifted the phone and waggled it in his face. "And I'm still fucking one."

Another snort, this one laced with genuine humor. "You are so damaged."

My gaze fell on the crowd. Miss Sparkles was trying to catch Cole's attention again. "What about a witch?"

"Hell, no."

"She's a natural redhead."

"You can't tell that."

"Wanna bet?"

Brianna touched her ear, where she kept a small two-way communication device just like Cole always wore, and said something, probably giving the all-clear to Dru and his brothers. Two seconds later, the five of them came through the front door, looking like escapees from The Matrix. Brianna parted the crowd before them with the ease of Moses parting the waters.

Dru, in full Master Vamp mode, led the procession, his schiavona sword banging against his thigh as he strutted through the onlookers. Four oversized bad-ass vamps followed.

The power radiating off the pack sent a fresh wave of tingles coursing through my system. I resisted the sensation, the demon inside my chest skittering against my heart. A sharp pain sliced through my stomach without warning, burning like holy water. Everything inside me—including my inner demon—suddenly froze.

"Damn," I said on a heavy exhale, bending at the waist and gripping my stomach.

"What is it?" Cole grabbed my arm and placed a supportive hand on my back. "What's wrong?"

The agony diminished as fast as it had come, and I straightened, watching the vamp pack make its way to the stairs leading to the booth. Having witnessed my sudden spasm, Dru's brows dipped in concern. "I'm fine. Just hungry."

"You haven't eaten red meat in a couple of days. We get done here, we'll hit Rush Street for food. Vitali's, maybe." Cole resumed his stance beside me as the door opened. He checked his shirt, smoothing it down before Brianna entered.

"Offer still stands," I said *sotto voce*. "About you visiting a private room."

Brianna locked eyes with my bodyguard as she held the door for her Master and his brothers. Cole lowered his voice to match mine, sexual tension and magic pouring off him. "And leave you in a room full of vampires? What kind of half-assed bodyguard do you think I am?"

"I can take care of myself."

"Damon would crucify me for leaving my position, and like I said, I'm *not interested*."

Crucify. I cringed at the term and the image of my family it called up.

Cole, realizing his poor choice of terms, squeezed my arm. Brianna, who gave me a jealous glance, did not miss the gesture. Dru swept in, his dark eyes immediately locking with mine and then searching my face.

Down below, groups of supernaturals paused in their drinking, dancing, and drugging to watch. Dru held out a hand to me. "Kali, are you all right?"

Vampires are a mix of blood lust, sex, and power. Demons are a mix of the seven deadly sins. Put the two together and sparks fly whether we want them to. Because I had vamp blood in my veins and Dru was a Master vamp born from the Prince of Darkness, his power felt like the North Pole magnetically dragging me toward him.

The demon in me bared her teeth, but the rest of me went willingly toward his outstretched hand. The instant our hands touched, fireworks exploded under my skin. His blood lust was well contained. His sex lust, not so much.

But Dru was my friend and my friend only. While I was no less of a demon in his presence, I seemed to be less evil. "Your blood called to mine and I resisted." I made a dismissive gesture with my free hand. "No biggie."

One side of his mouth lifted in a cocky grin. "Still trying to resist, are you?"

I sensed Cole rolling his eyes behind me. "Always."

"Why would she resist?" One of Dru's brothers, French from his accent, gave me a curious once-over. I had the feeling he didn't think much of what he saw. "She is queen, yes?"

Dru released my hand. "Kali Sweet, my brother, Stephen."

Stephen reached for my hand. Well-coiffed hair, bushy eyebrows, goatee. Check, check and check. Definitely a Frenchman. I folded my arms across my chest, returning his assessing gaze. "*Je suis la reine. A la mort.*"

I am the queen. Until death. The statement made my stomach tighten, but with vamps, politics could make or break you. I needed to take a firm stand with this group, for my sake as well as Dru's, since he would be held accountable for me. "I'm also a vengeance demon whose services you need. Shall we get down to business?"

TWO

Properly snubbed, Stephen chuckled and nodded. The others smiled and shook their heads, and we all moved to the table—all except Cole and Brianna. Brianna stayed at the door, and Cole stood behind me in the shadows. On the dance floor, the glittering witch continued to stare into the booth.

Poor Cole. So many females who wanted him, and he was stuck with me.

Dru introduced his brothers, who represented the five continents. Vlad the Impaler, the first vampire to ever live, had made the most of his six centuries of life until one of his sons, Toel Chase, had ended it here in Chicago after my crowning ceremony. While all of Vlad's offspring were biologically sterile, Vlad procreated with human women all over the world and produced hundreds of baby vamps. Those seated at the table in the Fright Night's VIP lounge were first-generation family members, most of whom were older than me and more than a little shocked that Toel—a young vamp by their standards—could have killed their father.

I removed a contract from my cape, spread it on the table.

"Just so we're all clear, I'm working as Kali Sweet, owner of Sweet Investigations. Not as Kali Sweet, employee of the Bridge Council." I pointed to a highlighted paragraph on the first page. "The Bridge Council is in no way involved nor has jurisdiction over this revenge mission. You will not hold the Bridge Council or the Institute accountable for anything I do, say, or otherwise indicate on this job. Do you understand?"

Separating my two jobs was of utmost importance. As owner of Sweet Investigations, I could get away with much more than I could as enforcer for the Bridge Council. In turn, the things I might do as investigator and vengeance demon for this mission had to not reflect poorly on the Council or Institute. This job wasn't connected to the Bridge Council, although they had a keen interest in the outcome, and that's how I planned to keep it. Damon could look over my shoulder but couldn't tell me how to run the job.

If there's one thing vamps understand, it's politics. Each vamp at the table nodded in turn. Dru took the pen I offered, scanned the rest of the contract. Apparently, I wasn't the only one who was thorough. "We don't want him dead," Dru said. "We want to exact our own revenge. We only want you to find him and bring him to us. Then, as Undead Queen of the Central United States, you'll have a say in his punishment."

Worked for me. So far, Toel had proven to be a worthy adversary because I'd underestimated him and let myself get distracted by Rad and the whole blood slave fiasco. In three hundred years, I hadn't found too many supernaturals who could outwit me, but Toel had done it. Should have let my demon kill the bastard when I'd had the chance. "I'll even wrap him up and stick a bow on top if you want."

My snark wasn't lost on Dru. He smiled and made a production out of signing our agreement so the club's onlookers were satisfied. "Glad to see you're in the Christmas spirit."

"Hunh," I grunted, sounding like Cole. "More like the vengeful spirit. I don't do Christmas, but I love seeing justice done. It will bring me no greater pleasure than to capture Toel and hand him over to you, although exactly what shape he'll be in, I can't guarantee." On my arm, Volante, my whip, trembled with the thought of violence against the arrogant vamp. I petted her, a promise she would taste Toel's blood soon.

Dru wagged a finger back and forth. "No personal vengeance, remember, demon?"

How could I forget? "I'll offer Toel the easy way out—to come peacefully—but he won't take it."

"And you prefer the hard way."

"More fun for me."

We exchanged a smile. Dru had told me there was a lot of posturing between the five brothers for their father's head position of the Undead, but they were in total agreement on this subject.

"We have a deal." Dru took my hand, lifting it to his lips. All eyes in the club were on us, the crowd seeming to hold its breath as one entity. Staring directly into my eyes and moving with slow deliberation, Dru turned my hand over, bent his head, and kissed my palm.

The trance music skipped a beat. Or maybe that was my own heart.

"A source in California reports a thousand vampires have left the West Coast and are headed this direction." The words were murmured against my skin, and I shivered. Dru raised his head but held onto my hand. "We'd like Toel's head on a stake before they arrive."

"You think Toel has called in reinforcements to claim Vlad's position as his own?"

"Most likely."

A vampire army headed toward Chicago. Damn. The

Bridge Council would shit a hailstorm when they heard that. "How long before they arrive?"

"They're coming by foot to not bring attention to themselves. Could be a week, could be a day."

"Kali." Cole stepped to my right, his voice cutting through the heavy coating of power floating through the room.

I followed his gaze and my breath caught. There, on the stairs headed my way, his golden eyes blazing directly at me, was a gorgeous specimen of male. Half-demon, half-human, Rad Beaumont looked like a fallen angel. A dance floor spotlight zoomed from a stripper humping a pole and followed Rad's ascent up the stairs. Maybe it was the focused illumination, but he looked pale, and even the light on his face couldn't bleach out the smudged shadows under his eyes.

At the sight of him, everything in me rejoiced, including my demon.

He took the stairs two at a time, and in his wake, chaos erupted. Glasses on the bar shattered, random objects flew through the air, chairs flipped over, and people screamed and ran for the doors.

Chaos demons. Always the life of the party.

Because he was half-human and my blood slave, his stormy energy coursed through my body. Wild, unsettled, and definitely volatile. And all of it directed at me.

Probably should have answered his texts.

I motioned at Cole, and he went into full War demon mode, a hell and damnation doorstop intercepting Rad. Brianna looked startled, and then her lust spiked, flooding the room with another layer of emotion as she stepped back and acceded the door to my bodyguard.

I extracted my hand from Dru's, folded the contract and stood. "Nice doing business with you, boys. I'll be in touch."

All five vamps rose, either because they were gentlemen or

because the chaos below made them antsy. "We haven't discussed your fee," Stephen said.

"You'll owe me one."

Stephen didn't look happy about the arrangement, but Rad came crashing through the door at that moment, chaos following him.

I touched my ring fingers to my thumbs. Too late, my defenses weren't sufficiently raised when his energy hit me like an ocean wave. The scent of a briny storm filled my nostrils as air swirled in the room. The invisible wave sucked me under, making me stagger and gasp for oxygen.

Dru grabbed me to stop my fall. Cole stood his ground, and Rad hit him like a hurricane. The two tousled, the vamps looking on with something between amusement and scorn. Maybe a touch of concern. After all, I was the vamp queen, and Rad was obviously a threat.

"Let me at her," Rad said, shoving Cole back a few feet.

Cole lunged and punched him solidly in the stomach. Rad "harrumphed" but didn't so much as bend over. The chairs the vamps had been sitting in careened wildly across the floor, smacking into the plexiglass. One flew at Cole's head. He ducked and it skimmed his hair.

Though most of the crowd had vanished, a few brave stragglers cowered around the bar below to watch the unfolding drama. The glittering witch was one of them. All that glitter, combined with the waves of chaos and vamp power, made my vision blurry. Her features faded out for a split second, and new features formed under a ghostlike mist. The new face was familiar. I gasped, my heart stuttering for a second.

She looked like Queen Maria, the female succubus who'd practically raised me in the Italian court. The woman who'd turned me into a sadist.

Dru's fingers dug into my upper arm. "Kali? What is it?"

I shook my head and blinked my eyes. When I looked again, Maria was gone, and the redheaded witch was back.

Drawing a deep breath to steady my overworked nerves, I withdrew from Dru's grasp and pulled myself together. "Let him through," I said to Cole. Then I motioned at Brianna. "Blinds."

A flick of her fingers at the window control panel on the wall and a coppery-brown film slowly rolled down the plexiglass, creating a two-way mirrored effect. We could see the club. Those below, however, saw their reflections.

"Are you crazy?" Cole stopped a punch Rad threw at his face, and I heard bones break. "Guitar Boy's out of control."

Exactly. And I was the only one who could give him back that control. I wasn't sure why he was so angry, why he needed to drink again so soon, but I had to find out.

Dru's protective energy had revived me. I touched my fingers and thumbs together and raised my magic. A cool blue light engulfed me, and my senses cleared. I took a deep breath. "I can take him."

Across the room, Rad's gaze snapped to mine and held. There was more desperation than anger in his eyes. Why? Was he *that* hungry? Usually when he needed to feed, he lost his strength, not dissolved into a chaotic mess.

Losing control of his demon side, breaking into my meeting with the vamps, and calling attention to our relationship was dangerous for both of us. Dangerous and completely unacceptable. "Control yourself, slave."

The nasty moniker got him—or maybe it was the look in my eyes. His jaw tightened, but he did as commanded. The chairs righted themselves, and the breeze he'd created died.

Everyone's focus turned to me. "If you'll excuse us," I said to Dru and the vamps.

Dru gave my arm a slight squeeze. "You're sure?"

Another of those sharp pains hit my stomach, but I gritted my teeth and held still until it passed. Unable to speak, I gave him a curt nod.

The vamps filed past Rad, Cole keeping his body planted between us. Brianna was the last to leave, giving Cole a meaningful glance over her shoulder. "See you tomorrow night," she said, her focus doing a direct and open appraisal.

He didn't respond, but I again sensed the tension in his muscles ratcheting up. As soon as the door shut behind the vamps, Cole gave Rad a solid push against it. I had to give Rad credit for not fighting back. The two demons stood there, breathing heavily and staring each other down.

"Do that kind of shit again, Guitar Boy, and I'll rip your head off, regardless of what Kali says."

Cole might as well have said chaos demons were angels. Rad laughed, no more intimidated by Cole than a mongoose facing down a cobra. "Any time you want to try..."

Cole made to hit him. "Don't," I said. He dropped his fist, shook his head, and moved aside.

I wanted to go to Rad and touch him, but I stood my ground. "Why are you here?"

His voice shook. "I need to feed."

"So soon?"

All he did was nod, his Adam's apple bobbing as he swallowed. There was pain in his eyes and profound privation.

The cells in my body did a little dance. They knew that look and responded to it like a dog to the scent of a juicy bone. But I stopped myself from stepping toward him. "You cannot interrupt my business dealings and make a spectacle of our relationship in public. Next time, go to Chloe and get a damn bottle of blood to hold you over."

He stalked toward me, the pained look morphing into something more animalistic. "I don't drink from the bottle."

It took all my willpower not to step back. He sent the table between us sliding out of the way with one hand. With the other, he grabbed me and yanked me to him. His body was hard and hot and demanding, his emotions and magic swirling around both of us.

My cool blue light struggled to stay intact. At the same time, my inner demon struggled to free herself from the leash I had on her. She wanted Rad with a—dare I say it?—vengeance, and she urged my blood and inherent magic to lose control just like he'd done.

I held my breath as Rad lowered his lips within an inch of mine. "Feed me, Kali," he whispered against my lips.

Damaged demon that I was, I didn't say no.

THREE

Two hours later, Cole and I consumed juicy rare steaks, fries, and sides of spaghetti from Vitali's, our favorite restaurant on the South Side. We left the place sated, hauling out a plastic carryout box filled with cannolis for a midnight binge.

Sweet Investigations is a small office anchoring one end of a strip mall complex near U.S. Cellular Field. The other end is a coffee shop, and in between is a bail bonds office. I walked in through the back entrance and opened my senses.

Being a demon, I can tap into the flow of dark magic in the ground, stones, and trees. As I entered my business, I tapped into the magic coming up from the floor and ran my hand over the doors and wood casings. A familiar drone seeped into my skin. Nothing amiss, although the energy seemed weighted, heavier than usual.

The holiday season brought out nutcases in the supernatural world just like it did in the human one. My desk was piled high with blue and pink file folders, cases divided into male and female by my office manager and best friend, Aphrodite.

Di, as she preferred to be called, was the goddess of love. She looked at and categorized the world much differently than I did.

Along with the files sat a national gossip magazine, its pages open to a story on Rad. In bold headlines read, "Who is Little Red Riding Hood?" Underneath the headline were several paragraphs speculating about Rad's secret girlfriend, a no-comment quote from his PR manager, and several more quotes from distraught female fans—aged fifteen to forty-five—that the woman hiding behind her red cape was bad for him. "He looks so sad these days," one lamented. "She can't be making him happy."

A grainy picture accompanied the short story, and sure enough, the main focus was me, caught from the side on Halloween night, the night I'd joined Rad and his bandmates at a party. Someone had shot it with a cell phone. Luckily, I'd had my hood up at the time, and all the camera caught of my face was my Italian nose.

"What did you bring me?" Di eyed the white carryout box in my hands and sniffed the air as she set a stack of pink message slips on top of the files. Her gaze darted to the magazine article, and she opened her mouth to comment but thought better of it and switched gears. "You smell like greasy fried food, so it better be good."

I handed her a cannoli and another to Maddy, my teenage vamp friend sprawled on the office's leather sofa, watching a cheesy Christmas movie on a cable channel that had gone all Christmas, all the time on the first of November.

Maddy's attention didn't leave the TV as she took the cannoli and stuffed one end in her mouth. Di plopped down next to her and turned up the volume. "Jobs are on your desk."

I untied my cape and hung it up, blew out an exasperated sigh at the stack of messages and files. Toel was up to something, and I didn't have much time to find him to see if Dru's source was right about the vamp army headed this way.

Shutting off the TV, I tossed the remote on the coffee table and sat at the big wooden desk that once belonged to my father. "I'm reshuffling the job assignments. Maddy, I need you and Arman to get back on finding Toel."

She groaned, still chewing, and reached for the remote. "We've already been over the entire North side and turned up zilch."

"And now you'll work the South Side. Try sniffing out Victoria as well. She may be easier to locate and, in turn, lead us right to him."

I filled her and Di in on the possible vamp army headed for Chicago. "I promised Neve I'd help her take care of Fielder Benson's ghost issue tonight, but Di, you'll have to handle the Stewart investigation. I'll chastise Dalinda, and you'll visit the Stewarts."

If anyone could get Mr. and Mrs. Stewart back together after a member of the dark Fae had split them up, it was Aphrodite. Instead of me taking revenge on Mr. Stewart for his inhuman affair, I thought it might be better for Di to counsel the couple while I reminded Dalinda that the Institute frowned heavily on supernaturals tinkering with humans. Besides, Dalinda was a repeat offender. With the Bridge Council reminder, I could slap her wrists a little harder this round and make her think twice about Mr. Stewart or future human diversions. Dealing with the Stewarts might take hours, and I was no good at advising anyone on love issues.

Di finished off her dessert and rubbed her hands together. "I'm on it."

Maddy had turned on the TV and was again engrossed in a story about a guardian angel in love with the human woman he was supposed to guard. If only all supernatural-human relationships ended as happily as the made-for-TV versions. "Maddy, focus. Go find Arman and get your sniffers on the ground."

She rolled her eyes, did a heavy sigh that only a teenage girl could properly deliver, and flipped off the television. Kicking up her feet and resting them on the coffee table, she slumped back against the sofa. "Why do you care if Toel takes over the vamp kingdom? It's not like you don't dream of staking all of us."

Somebody woke up on the wrong side of the coffin. "Toel won't stop with taking over the Undead. You know that. He wants to wipe out humans. Use them for blood slaves and kill any who resist. Besides, he's a dick who needs his ass handed to him, and believe it or not, there are a few vamps I *do* care about. You're one of them, so even if stopping Toel only saved you, I'd still do it."

My usually upbeat sidekick didn't even look at me. She gave another drama-filled sigh, rose from the sofa, and trudged out of the room.

Cole and I exchanged a look. He shrugged. I dittoed. Who understood the mood of a fifteen-year-old female vamp? I just hoped she wouldn't be like this for the rest of her Undead life.

Di came bustling back in and pointed at the stack of pink slips. "Did you call Chloe back? She was quite upset."

"About what?"

"She wouldn't say. Probably because it had something to do with Rad and Arman and your blood."

Merde. "I need to talk to her anyway. I'll call her now."

Di looked over her shoulder and lowered her voice. "What about Maddy?"

"What about her?"

Frowning, Di approached my desk and lowered her voice even further. "Christmas time? Her first one without her family? She misses them, and she can't exactly show up on their doorstep and shout, 'Hey, I'm a vamp. Merry Christmas!'"

"Why not?" Cole said.

Di and I both shot him a *shut up* look. He knew as well as we did that Maddy's human family had no idea she'd been turned. She'd gone to a concert, ended up a vamp, and never returned home. Her parents believed she'd been kidnapped or murdered, and in some ways, that's precisely what had happened to her. And since the 'rents were of the hell-and-damnation group of humans who went to church and didn't believe in vampires, her hesitation to reveal the truth was understandable. Her parents *did* believe in demons, angels, and witches. Bet you can guess which group would get a prominent seat at the dinner table versus those they'd exorcise or burn at the stake.

"I don't know what you want me to do, Di. I don't do Christmas."

"But you know what it's like to lose your family. You may be an island, Kali Sweet, but Maddy isn't. She needs a family."

"I'm an island?"

"You think you are. You don't need anyone, yada, yada. But Maddy isn't like that. She needs closure with her real family and to believe we're her new one. You know what she's going through."

Maddy's family was still alive. Mine wasn't—they'd been murdered. I started to mention that small but pertinent fact, but the look on Di's face made me bite my tongue. I'd taken Maddy under my wing, and she was now my responsibility. "I'll think of something, but I refuse to watch those awful Christmas movies with her."

Di smiled, turned on her heel, and passed JR on the way out.

My office was Grand Central Station all of a sudden. So much for being an island. "What is it, JR?"

"I got a hit on Victoria," my tech guru said. "You know how she likes black magic? Even though Maddy changed her into a vamp, I figured she'd still be messing around with raising demons."

Good call. Victoria had managed to raise Lilith, the Queen of Hell, before I broke their connection and forced Maddy to change her from witch to vamp. Then the ungrateful bitch ran off with Toel. "Where?"

"Occult Arts on West Thomas near St. Mary's."

Witches and saints. Interesting spot for an occult shop.

"She bought ingredients for a spell and some kind of spell book. Paid with a credit card."

"Doesn't help me find her."

JR shuffled his weight and stared at my chin. He never looked me or anyone else directly in the eye. "Unless she comes back. In the past week, she's attended a potluck and a spirit board night at the shop."

"What is she up to?" I mused. "Put Maddy on it. See if she and Arman can spot Vicky and follow her to Toel's hideout."

"You got it, boss." JR left.

I had a good crew. Now, if I could just catch up on the stack of pressing jobs.

Cole had his gun out and was double-checking the chamber and its stash of holy water bullets. "You think that's a good idea? Sending Maddy and Arman after Victoria?"

"They're not going to do anything except follow her."

"And maybe that's what Toel wants." Cole glanced up, his liquid brown eyes boring into mine. "Bargaining chips."

War demons...always strategizing. I sat back in my chair and rocked, letting my brain follow Cole's thought process. "Vicky's been off the grid since the coronation, and suddenly, she shows up three times in a week. Toel wants me to find him." I rubbed a spot on my father's desk, an indentation he once banged into the wood with an angry fist. The wood hummed under my fingers. "Maddy?" I called.

"What?" came a curt, almost angry reply from the kitchen across the hall.

She strolled in, the air around her vibrating with challenge. What was *with* her? Seemed overkill for the whole Christmas-without-parents thing.

"I'm going with you. First, I have to meet Neve at Shadow Hill and take care of the ghost stalker. Then, you, Arman, and I will check out the occult shop and see if you can pick up Vicky's scent."

She cocked a hip. "I can handle it without you."

Definitely challenging. "It's most likely a trap. Toel wants us to follow her back to him. I don't need you and Arman falling into Toel's hands."

She started to retort but JR swung into my office, one hand holding on the doorframe. His gaze skittered across mine and landed on the top of my desk. "Um, Kali? There's someone in the parking lot I think you should get a look at."

JR's surveillance system was top-notch. His paranoia equaled mine. "Who is it?"

"Not sure. But it looks like a...a priest."

Maddy lost the angry air and smiled. "Finally something interesting happens around here."

"Noctifector?" I asked.

He didn't answer, just disappeared, heading for his cubby-hole of electronics.

Maddy nearly skipped out of my office. Cole and I rose, exchanged another look, and followed her.

FOUR

O n the security camera's screen, the priest looked harmless enough. He wore the black cloak of priests and scholars, the hood up and his hands hidden in the bell sleeves. He stood under a tall street light in the parking lot— one of the few vandals hadn't broken. Light poured down on top of his hood but seemed to be sucked up by the black garment like a black hole. Odd shadows fell over his face and across his shoulders.

He stood motionless, and even though I couldn't see his eyes, I would have sworn he was staring directly at the camera. Directly at me.

My demon hissed and scrambled deeper inside, searching for cover.

"Noctifector?" Cole echoed my previous question over my shoulder.

A silver chain encircled the priest's waist, the ends dangling down to his knees. On both ends were plain silver crosses with four sharp tips each. Tips, I was sure, could do some wicked damage to a demon. "Probably."

But Noctifectors didn't work alone. They were human, and although highly trained and skilled at defeating supernaturals, they couldn't do it singlehandedly. They traveled in groups in order to overwhelm their target and even the playing field.

I scanned the other dozen screens in front of JR. Six boxes of equipment were stacked off to one side. Apparently, my computer guru was setting up a new system. Again. "Any sign of others?"

He pecked at the keyboard. A list of security devices around the building flashed on a separate screen. "No breaches, no unusual activity. All systems green."

My own magical security system registered the same.

Maddy fidgeted off to the side, biting one of her fingernails. "Maybe he's just a priest."

And I was just a demon.

"What does he want?" Di asked.

Question of the hour. The only answer I had was too simple, but after three hundred years of experience with the Catholic Church, it also seemed the most likely. I fingered Volante, where she hung on my waist. The whip trembled under my ministrations, eager to be put to use. "Me."

Maddy dropped her hand from her face. "Because everything is about you."

She marched out of the room and I let out a strained sigh.

Cole leaned out the doorway. "Mouse, where are you going?" He called her by her nickname when he was trying to get her attention.

Her voice echoed down the hall. "I'm going outside to meet the nice priest and find out what he wants."

Cole raised an eyebrow at me. "Not a good idea."

"No shit, Captain Obvious." I barreled past him and jogged down the hall to the back door. Maddy had grabbed the handle and paused there.

I sensed her fear of following through. "Wait up, Mad."

She faced me, one hand still on the door. "I can handle this."

Of course she could.

Not. We didn't even know what *this* was. "Just because we don't see other priests doesn't mean this one's alone. He could be the bait to draw me—us—out."

Her eyes were hard, determined. "Bring it on. I've been itching for a fight."

Stress has led me into a lot of fights over the years. Stupid fights that could have gotten me killed. "Look, I know you're having a tough time with this vamp-at-Christmas thing, but challenge Cole to fight if you want to burn some pent-up shit. Not a priest who can stake you and end your life."

Opening the door an inch, she peered through the crack into the poorly lit parking lot. I inched closer to peer out with her. Shadows danced on the edges of what we could see, lifting the hair on my arms. Maddy, however, didn't seem to be fazed. "Would a priest ever grant a vampire absolution?"

That was a left turn I hadn't expected. Stumped for an answer, I searched for a response that wouldn't come out as incoherent babble. "I'm probably not the demon to ask, but I'd guess no." Always sucked to be the bearer of bad news.

I touched her arm, trying to channel Di. "Maddy, you haven't committed any mortal sins. You were turned against your will."

"But I'm a vampire." Her attention focused on me. "Do I still have a soul? Am I going to hell when I die?"

Che cavolo. How had I managed to step in this pile of shit?

Popular culture said vamps—outside of Buffy's Angel— didn't have souls, but I knew differently. They had 'em, and when they went poof, their souls went to purgatory. Not hell, granted, but close enough. Quite a few of them were there, thanks to my favorite cherry wood stake. Which wasn't info Maddy would appreciate hearing. "Damon's the expert in this area. What do you say we go see him after we locate Vicky and you can ask him?"

That would give me time to send Damon a heads-up text and for him to figure out a way to let Maddy down easy about her potentially awful afterlife. Better yet, I could come up with a distraction, and we could all have this extremely uncomfortable conversation at a later date. A much later date.

Maddy seemed to consider my offer. Then she did the typical Maddy thing, throwing open the door and stomping out to the parking lot to confront the priest.

Had to admit, I admired her style.

Cole, who'd come up behind me, swore under his breath and grabbed his gun from its holster.

Taking a deep breath, I took Volante off my belt and ran out after Maddy.

FIVE

T he priest was gone.

"What the hell?" Maddy swiveled in a circle in the deserted parking lot, searching the area for the missing man. An empty cup from the coffee shop blew across her feet. "Where did he go?"

I kept Volante in hand, scanning the nearby buildings, snow-filled culverts, and trees. Cole was at my back, gun raised and in full bodyguard mode. Car noises from the street out front met my ears. No sign the priest had been there except for the faint scent of Catholicism...a mix of wax candles, ancient artifacts and guilt. Along with that, I smelled unrefined wool. The priest's robe must have been made of it. No wonder it seemed to absorb the light like a black hole.

My brain niggled uncomfortably. When was the last time I'd seen a priest wearing unrefined sheep's wool? The nubby, scratchy stuff had generally been used in Italy when I was a girl, but in the past two centuries, I'd only seen that type of robe on a monk, and never in America.

Keeping an eye out, I grabbed Maddy's arm and guided her back toward the building. "So much for that."

Once we were inside, I questioned JR. "Where did he go?"

"He knew you were coming." JR pointed at one of the screens showing a ditch filled with overgrown weeds, untrimmed trees, and dead vegetation, all covered with an inch of snow. "Glided off there and disappeared."

Cole returned his gun to the holster. "What d'ya mean, *glided*? Is he some kind of supe?"

I shook my head. "He smelled like the Catholic Church. Sanctimonious. Had to be human."

JR shrugged, but excitement rode his voice. "He had a red cross embroidered on the back of the robe."

"Big deal. Priests and crosses go hand in hand."

JR was an expert in religious studies. "It was a Templar knight cross."

Templar knights? Either JR was indulging in fantasies, or the priest was. "Why would a human priest wear an ancient robe with a Templar cross woven into it?"

Cole shrugged. "Halloween costume gone wrong?"

Maddy chewed on another fingernail. "Will he come back?"

For all our sakes, I hoped not. "With my luck, he'll be back with reinforcements." I checked my watch. "I'm late to meet Neve. JR, text me if the priest comes back. Otherwise, keep things locked up. Di, go ahead and tackle the Stewarts, but keep your guard up. Toel's out there, and this priest could also be trouble." I glanced around at my group. "As always, everyone watch your back. No one get hurt tonight, okay?"

Nods of agreement circled me. "Maddy, I'll call you when I'm ready to meet you and Arman at the occult shop. Until then, hang out here with JR."

Without answering, she trudged off to my office. A second

later, the sound of a Christmas movie filtered into the cubicle. Di gave me a *you have to talk to her* look.

Yeah, like that had gone so well a few minutes ago. "I'll hit Dalinda before dawn and make her see the error of her ways with Mr. Stewart."

Di drummed her fingers on JR's desk. "And then you'll have a heart-to-heart with Maddy, right? She can't spend the whole holiday season in this funk."

"Sure." I motioned for Cole to follow me out, ignoring the way he snickered at my easy lie. We took a good look around the parking lot for the priest again but saw nothing out of place. The air was filled with normal Chicago night smells. As we climbed into my TT Roadster—a car built for much warmer climates— I slipped Volante into my lap for easy access. "What's your gut say about the priest?"

Cole, as cautious as I was, kept his gun in hand. "Templar knights and the priests who blessed them for battle have been extinct for seven-, eight-hundred years."

"So he's not a Templar priest."

"Didn't say that." He shrugged. "Secret orders still exist throughout the world."

I started the car, and she growled under my fingertips. "For what purpose?"

"The knights were servants of God, securing safe travel for those journeying to the Holy Land, and wiping out infidels. They also established an effective banking system, built temples, and acquired land."

"Medieval Donald Trumps."

"The Templar priests were business savvy too. A few stood in place of the Pope at various locations and during battles. The rest amassed wealth for the Church and persecuted demons."

I left the parking lot and joined the other late-night drivers heading north. "You one of the demons they persecuted?"

"I tangled with a few of them."

Best not to prod him for details about those entanglements. Cole kept his past behind a solid mental door, and I respected that. Another thing we had in common. He'd tell me about his experiences with Templar knights and priests if he wanted to. "And the priest from tonight? You think he's part of some secret order that still exists?"

"What I think is that your computer whiz spends too much time with his head in books. He needs to get out more and quit spending all your profits on new computer systems you don't need. Did you see all that shit he bought?"

"Yeah. Not sure what's up with that, but he just spent his year-end bonus."

We drove in silence, and I put my questions about the priest on hold. I needed to focus on the job with Neve, tracking down Victoria (and therefore Toel) and handling Dalinda. The ghost exorcism would be a snap. Finding Vicky and Toel, dangerous. But it was more of a scouting mission than a take-down. So it looked like Dalinda, the succubus, would be my most formidable challenge for the night. Succubus Fae could chew you up and spit you out, and instead of running from them, you'd beg for more.

I had experience on my side, though. I'd lived under the rule of the toughest succubus on the planet and killed her when the time came. "Any suggestions on how I get Maddy out of her funk?"

"God's balls, I hate teenagers. Always so full of themselves."

"Is there anything you don't hate right now?"

He looked at me, and one corner of his mouth tipped up. "Fighting, sex. You know. The basic vices."

I did know. Fighting and sex fed our demon bodies and let

our minds rest. "I suggested Maddy see you for a sparring match."

"Sure, shove her whiny ass off on me. She sucks at hand-to-hand, but she's good with a bow and arrow. I'll give her some training exercises for that."

"Bow and arrow, huh? Pretty cool. How come she didn't tell me?"

"Jesus, Kali, stop mothering her and let her live a little. Take her to a concert, get her drunk, get her laid, let her have some fun. That'll cure this woe-is-me shit."

"She's fifteen."

"She's a vamp. Outside of a stake in her heart, nothing can hurt her."

He had a point. "I think I'm offended that you're accusing me of mothering her."

"Good. Maybe you'll stop with the overprotective bullshit."

I was overprotective? "Classic example of the bodyguard pot calling the demon kettle black."

"It's my job to protect you."

And in Cole's mind, it *wasn't* my job to protect Maddy.

Nope. Not buying that one. "Nudra turned her. I should have staked him before he had the chance."

"Blah, blah, blah. You can't save the whole damn human world."

I could try. "It's what I do, pot."

He made a dismissive noise in the back of his throat.

Fine. I punched on my satellite radio, and, to Cole's vexation, turned up Megadeath.

SIX

Neve Lucrezia Vaselli is a combination of *yidde'oni* and *baal'ob*—one who talks to ghosts and helps them cross over. The Bible and other religious books refer to these ghost whisperers as witches, but they aren't witches or supernaturals of any kind. They're humans who can detect and interact with earthbound spirits.

An accident left Neve paralyzed from the waist down and able to talk to ghosts. According to her, the physical challenge was nothing compared to the psychological one. Trying to convince people she could communicate with spirits was harder than accepting she would never walk again.

A decade after the accident, she's estranged from her family and most of her friends. She feels more comfortable hanging around entities like me, a demon, and Di, a forgotten goddess, than other humans.

Our mutual client that night was a professional basketball player who'd once been on the Chicago Bulls. He was half Ludio demon, meaning his natural inclination was to excel at sports. Not exactly a badass unless his competitive nature got out of hand or his obsession required him to win at all costs. Drugging, injuring competitors, working magic in order to win a game...it happened most often with Ludio demons.

Fielder Benson wasn't giving into his inner demon...at least not that I could see. His problem was a ghost of a pro-basketball wannabe who'd latched onto him and wouldn't leave him alone. At first, the ghost rider simply tried to take over Fielder's jump shot and free throw and did a hellaciously lousy job of it, getting Fielder benched. Then he was fired. And then, he ended up in Shadow Hill Psych Hospital along with a whole bunch of other wackos. Most of them, like Fielder, some form of supernatural.

Neve, a clinical psychiatrist along with being a ghost whisperer, thought Fielder had had enough. If she didn't get rid of Marvin, the ghost, soon, she was afraid Fielder would completely lose touch with reality.

Marvin had also been a supe in his earthly life. A short, overweight trickster demon who would've given his soul, if he'd had one, to be a superstar athlete. Hence, Neve's request I be present during her confrontation with him was smart. She was going to encourage him to go into the light—in his case, the fires of hell—and if he refused to crossover peacefully, I was going to exorcise his ass into the afterlife.

If he refused was a misnomer. Without a doubt, I would have to kick Marvin across the great divide. He would refuse, sure as shit, and I would, too, if I had the choice of ghost-riding my role model or spending eternity in the equivalent of a demon prison. Dropping the soap is the least of your worries down there.

As the guard waved us through the gated entrance, I smacked the steering wheel. "I forgot to call Chloe before we left."

Cole pointed at the front of the hospital where Neve sat

behind the glass doors in her wheelchair, impatiently tapping her fingers on the arms. "Better save it."

"You're late," Neve said in greeting as she buzzed Cole and me into the building. Her once dark brown hair was as milky white as the ghosts she helped cross over. It had turned white after the accident. Another thing we shared...mine had bleached out the night I had my first nightmare about Rad stabbing me in the heart with a silver dagger. After two hundred eighty-three years, I doubted it would return to its original color.

Cole glanced around with nervous eyes. "You're lucky we're here at all."

Shadow Hill was initially a military training school built at the end of the Civil War. Since then, it had been a vet hospital, a compound for a religious sect whose members had offed themselves on Y2K, believing it was the end of the world, and now, a hospital for mental supernatural patients. Foreboding and depressing? Check.

Somewhere in the deep recesses of the building, an eerie cry rang out, followed by another.

Creepy horror movie sound effects? Check.

The buzz of Neve's motorized wheelchair echoed in the quiet air as she rolled forward, nearly clipping Cole's toes. She eyed my face. "You're stressed."

"What's new? Come on, let's get this over with."

Neve wore a Wiccan robe, complete with a hood, dreamcatcher earrings, and a Celtic knot pendant at her throat. A bible rested in her lap. She liked to cover all her religious bases. The only thing on her that looked remotely Italian was her snapping dark brown eyes. In the low lighting of the foyer, they looked black. "You're sure you want to be here?"

Was it that obvious?

Bone-deep cold seeped up through the floor and into my

boots. The earth magic here was strong and unnerving. The building had undergone major renovations to ensure its insane supernatural population stayed put. Inside the brick was some serious iron and refined steel, creating a magical barrier to keep the inmates inside and unwanted outside magical forces from entering. "Marvin won't go peacefully, Neve. And he's a trickster demon. You can't trust him, no matter what he says or agrees to."

"*Was* a trickster demon. Now he's a spirit."

A demon is a demon. I headed for the elevators. "Follow my lead, and we'll be done in fifteen minutes—maybe less."

She grabbed one of my hands, jerking me to a stop. "We do this my way first. If it doesn't work, you can take over."

This was her gig, not mine. I'd agreed to be her backup, and even though I knew she would fail, I had to honor that agreement.

Nodding, I motioned her into the lead. Cole chuckled under his breath as he fell into step beside me. He knew it was damn hard for me to play sidekick when it came to annoying demons. "We don't have to chant or anything, do we?" he asked.

Neve ignored him, stopping at the elevator and punching the down button. We rode in silence to the basement, and a weird energy rippled over my skin. Down there, the dampening barrier was even more substantial. I wondered if it would dampen my magic when the time came to use it.

Stopping in front of a metal door with the number six affixed to it, Neve raised her hands in the air. "Divine will be done through me for the highest good of all and for the true manifestation of my purpose here tonight."

Dropping her arms, she leaned forward and unlocked the door with a keycard.

The room was dark. Fielder sat on the floor in the corner, a darker shadow inside the unlit room. Here and there, tiny lights flickered around him as if miniature fireflies surrounded his body.

Hello, Marvin.

But something was off. Another shadow outlined his legs where they sprawled on the floor and ran toward the door. Blood. The metallic scent was heavy with decay.

Bye-bye Fielder.

"Oh, no," Neve said. "Tell me he's not dead."

Wish I could have. "His life energy is gone, Neve. He bled out."

"But how? Why? He was in this room to protect him from himself as well as others. This isn't possible. No one but me has been in or out of the room all day, and I saw him right before you arrived. He was fine. Well, not fine, but you know. *Alive.*"

Even with my hot demon body temperature, I felt cold to the bone. The earth magic was still strong but tempered. I laid my palm against the concrete wall and reached for it, drawing it to me to try and find some answers.

Since demon magic comes from the ground, I imagined my booted feet connecting with the earth under the building and waited for it to respond.

Out of nowhere, a flash bang went off in my mind. Blinding light, spurting blood, waves of sharp, terrified pain. My body seized, even as I tried to jerk my hand back and break the connection. The magic wouldn't let go. It seared into my system with the force of a hot branding iron.

My demon awoke and bellowed. Volante tightened where she was wrapped around my arm.

Outside the agony, I heard Cole and Neve call my name. I mentally reached for that lifeline, reached for each of them. If I could latch onto their energies, I could break the connection...

It wasn't enough. A darkness that I hadn't felt in nearly

three hundred years swamped my mind. The sensation caressed my demon even as it filleted my psyche.

Maria.

Couldn't be. I'd killed the queen bitch, decapitated her, and burned her body. Her earthly link had been severed, her soul sent back to hell where it belonged.

Twice in one night, my pain-filled brain reminded me. That was no coincidence.

A brittle thickness clogged my throat. Or maybe it was the memories Maria evoked. My demon roared her anger, forcing me to cry out. That cry broke the hold the building held on me, and I staggered backward.

Cole caught me and half-carried me from the room. "Holy hell, Kali. What was that?"

My legs wobbled uncontrollably, and I couldn't remain upright on my own, falling against his chest when he released me. My eyelids refused to stay open, and my teeth chattered so hard I couldn't speak at first.

"Evil," I heard Neve say. Her voice sounded like it was floating far away. "That was pure evil."

"Get Neve....out...of here." I grasped Cole's arm and squeezed. "Now."

"We're all getting out of here." He started to pick me up to carry me to the elevator.

I struggled out of his grasp, forced my eyes open. "I have to...go back in. Have to...figure out what happened."

"*Madonna mia!*" Neve's voice was stronger now, even though she was stage whispering. "What happened in there? Just touching the wall gave you a stroke! You go back in there, you could die."

Walking away wasn't an option. I could still smell the tang of Fielder's blood, could still see the images touching the wall had invoked.

There had been a lot of blood, both on the floor and in the image I'd seen.

Maria.

"Fielder was murdered." I rubbed a shaky hand over my face, took a deep breath to clear my head. "I have to know who did it."

"The trickster ghost?" Cole asked. "He could do that?"

I shook my head. "Whoever killed Fielder was a demon, not a ghost."

But I wasn't sure about that. The sparkling witch's features morphing into Maria's earlier that night flashed in front of me.

Maria's gone. Not just dead, but roasting in hell. Right?

Neve glanced at the door, back at me. "Earthbound spirits are amazingly innovative with what they can do. Especially those who were demonic or even half-demon on Earth. When they lose one body, they can possess another as easy as sneezing. But murder? That takes a spirit of incredible power."

The night I'd killed Maria, there were no other bodies around for her ghost to sneak into. I made sure of that. "Neve, at the club tonight, I thought I saw the ghost of a powerful demon I killed..."

I trailed off, my brain cells arguing, *it's not her. It can't be.* "A long time ago. Long, *long* time ago. I cut off her head and burned her body, and there were no other bodies around for her spirit to possess. It's not possible that she could still be hanging around, is it?"

Neve fixed me with her penetrating brown eyes. "Not unless she possessed you when you killed her."

There was an uplifting thought.

"Can we take this conversation upstairs?" Cole grabbed Neve's wheelchair without waiting for her consent and pushed her toward the elevator. "Freezing my damn demon balls off down here."

Apparently, I wasn't the only one feeling the cold. But was it from Marvin, who was still hanging around Fielder's lifeless body, or was it coming from something darker and more sinister?

A minute later, we sat in the first-floor cafeteria, each trying to figure out what had happened below our feet.

The evil seemed to be contained inside that room. I couldn't feel any signs of it coming up through the floor. I still wasn't certain what had happened, but there was nothing I could do for Fielder now, and I had a lot of questions about Maria running rampant in my head. "The spirit of the demon I killed couldn't have possessed me. I would have known it."

Neve nodded, her hand toying with the Celtic knot at her throat. "I agree. You're not one to let others in, spirit or otherwise. Your blocking defenses are the strongest I've ever encountered."

Her tone made it sound like veiled criticism. "Is there any other explanation for why I think I saw that demon's ghost?"

She fiddled with the knot, face set in thought. "What happened at the club to stress you out? Were you with Rad?"

Boy, was I. "There was a lot going on tonight. Dru and his brothers were there, and we discussed Toel and the possibility of him raising a vampire army to attack Chicago. I was worried about Cole, and Rad made a most chaotic appearance."

"Me?" Cole said. "Why the hell are you worried about me?"

Neve dropped the knot and gave me a relieved smile. "Crisis apparition. That's all it was."

"What's that?"

"It's a common phenomenon. Under extreme stress, people sometimes report seeing a spirit. Doesn't mean there wasn't a real ghost, but like most people, you attached a familiar face to it. And often there is no spirit; it's just a figment of your over-worked and tired brain."

"Oh." For some reason, I felt let down. Not that I wanted Maria back on earth in any shape or form, but a crisis appari-tion? Nah. Not after what I'd sensed in Fielder's room.

"Guess I better report Fielder's demise." She backed up her wheelchair. "Although how I'm going to explain it is beyond me."

"Can you give me ten minutes down there before you report it?"

Shock contorted her face over me wanting to return to Fielder's room. "You can't think that's a good idea."

I stood and straightened my cape. "I'm fine. I wasn't prepared last time, but you know me, I'm Chicago tough. Southside tough."

"Maybe you should call Damon and have him check it out instead."

Cole, who was already heading to the kitchen exit, snorted. He knew I would never run to our boss and ask him to hold my hand.

But I saw the worry in Neve's eyes and knew I needed to reassure her. "I'm the best one to handle this, and I can handle it now that I'm prepared."

She shook her head but conceded. "Ten minutes. No longer."

Back downstairs and standing in front of door number six, my demon gnashed her teeth. The brutality of the magic done inside had ruffled her feathers, and she was itching to lash out. But what exactly had been done? It made me antsy and ready to take out the entire building. Since I would need my demon when I entered the room, I didn't try to calm her, only dug down and kept a tight hold on the magical leash I had around her neck.

Volante's handle slid into my palm, cool and reassuring. I nodded to Cole. "Let's try this again."

"I hate this freaky shit. Your demon under control?"

"No promises. If I do go dark side, get out and call Damon."

"Your demon comes out to play," —he waggled his brows— "I'm staying."

We stared at the closed door, neither of us wanting to go inside. Another of those skin-crawling cries rent the air off to my left. Touching my ring fingers and thumbs together, I raised my protective magic, which I should have done before touching the wall the last time. Volante vibrated from the charge, practically jumping out of my hand with eagerness. The barrier resisted my magic as I laid a hand on the door, but the resistance was easy to overcome.

"Is it Maria?" Cole whispered. He knew about my past with the queen, knew I'd taken revenge on her for all the six-hundred and sixty-five humans and supernaturals she'd made me torture and kill. I was a kid then, living at the Italian court under her reign.

The door gave up nothing but a wailing energy, as if it wished it could run from the building. "Guess we're about to find out."

SEVEN

Someone had tortured Fielder before killing him and done so with exacting deliberation.

Once I tapped into the energy on my terms, I found the air vibrated with the presence of the one who'd done the nasty work, but the evil was dissipating as quickly as a fox. Whatever demon had hacked Fielder's insides to pieces was long gone.

That thought didn't excite me. First, the lingering magic had still been strong enough earlier to trap me just from touching the wall, and second, the demon was now cruising Chicago for its next meal.

Third—if I let myself go there—was the fact this was a classic Maria move. Carnage that seemed directed at me, as if she knew I was headed to see Fielder that night and had left me a present.

Or maybe Maddy was right, and I was paranoid or self-centered enough to think everything had to do with me. But I'd seen Maria's face behind the sparkling witch. I'd felt her unique brand of magic when I'd reached into the ground to get a read on Fielder's death.

"Do you think I'm paranoid?" I asked Cole as we walked around the body, avoiding the spreading blood. "You know, in the *hey, the world revolves around me* kind of way?"

"You're a demon. Comes with the territory." He flipped over the mattress on the bed to look under it. "Paranoia keeps us alive."

True fact, that. I had Nocts and vamps who wanted to kill me and an assortment of other supernaturals who would be pretty happy if I was dead and off their asses.

The room's lack of light made it difficult to find obvious clues. I flicked my fingers at the high ceiling, and a caged fluorescent light sprang to life.

"Look." Cole pointed at the far wall.

Blood dotted the concrete in a poor imitation of a Jackson Pollock canvas.

As we both stared at the seemingly random splatters, the dots started to form patterns. At least to my eyes. Patterns that created ancient runes I was all too familiar with.

My demon gnashed her teeth some more, and Volante strained in my hand.

After another minute of staring, I stepped as far back as possible to assess the bigger picture the blood splatters created. I pointed at the outline. "That's the witch from tonight."

"What witch?"

"The one at the club making googly eyes at you. Apparently, our killer is an artist, rendering the witch's features here in blood."

Cole stepped back with me, tilting his head from side to side. "All I see is blood."

And then my overactive imagination made the witch's features come to life and look right at me.

Maria, my brain insisted. Volante shivered, wanting to

strike out at the picture and wipe the smirk off the face depicted there.

Maria or not, that witch was in a world of trouble, and she probably didn't even realize it. Or maybe she was happy to house Maria's spirit. The powerful ancient succubus could be making it worth her while.

She'd been at the club eyeing Cole. Who was she, and what was she up to? "Snap a picture of the blood splatter and send it to JR."

Cole played around with his cell, doing what I'd asked. A minute later, my phone rang, and JR asked, "What do you want me to do with this, boss?"

"Can you make out a face or anything else from the blood splatter? Runes, maybe?"

"I can see some sort of rune here and there, but I'm not seeing a face. I'll connect the dots digitally and see what comes up."

"Once you get a face, find out who it belongs to and where she lives. I may need to pay her a visit."

"You got it."

Cole examined the wall again. "You want me to call Damon with this?"

The killer was supernatural, not human, but Fielder had been a well-known basketball player. Neve couldn't cover up what had happened, only control what was reported. If we weren't all careful with this one, Fielder's death would make national headlines, and a whole lot of humans would be sniffing around. Neve could get into trouble. Cole and I could as well.

The Bridge Institute had friends in the police department. Some were supes who covered for us when this sort of thing went down. In all my years in America, I'd never had to report a crime with so many repercussions. While I was determined to find the killer myself and exact justice, I was equally eager to stay out of the human investigation.

I nodded at Cole to call Damon. While he gave our boss the deets, I noticed Fielder's body was no longer glowing with Marvin's spirit. Damn it. One more problem to add to the list.

I left the room and wandered down the hallway, which had plenty of doors lining both sides. Marvin had probably found a new body to possess.

"Marvin?" The evil inside Fielder's room was not from Marvin's spirit. If anything, the ghost was hiding, scared witless.

A single light lit the end of the hall, along with the glow from an exit sign above a door. Opening my senses in hopes of picking up on Marvin or any other nonhuman entity hanging around, I noticed nothing but a small reception desk with a scattering of holiday decorations.

Focusing on each of the doors as I walked down the hallway, I felt more than saw a presence out of the corner of my eye dart from shadow to shadow. "Marvin?"

Nothing.

And then, a faint wisp of air crossed my right cheek. The scent of old paper, like the kind that drifted out of Damon's ancient books in his personal library, tickled my nose. Hmm. "Marvin, or whoever you are, if you saw what happened here tonight, you need to talk to me."

Silence. A creeping silence, as if someone was closing in on me one slow footstep at a time.

I turned in a circle, scanning and searching, but I could only see dense shadows and dark shapes. The scent grew stronger and gooseflesh rose on my arms. Volante reacted to my increased anxiety, tightening on my arm. I released her into my hand, preparing for what I wasn't sure.

Was Marvin playing with me, or was there something else

here? Was there some leftover evil from the killer? I stood in place, closed my eyes, and let my demon rise.

Before she climbed up my spine, my phone blared much too loudly in the silence. I flinched, then cursed myself for being so jumpy.

Digging the phone out of my cape, I punched the connect button without looking at the caller ID. "What is it? I'm a little busy."

Chloe's syrupy-sweet Southern Tempter demon voice poured through the receiver into my ear. "Well, sugar, you better get *un*busy. We got a problem on our hands."

"Chloe, I'm sorry I didn't call you earlier..."

Something hard and unforgiving whacked me in the back of the head. Fireworks exploded behind my eyes. I pitched forward, but before I could lock my knees, a second heavy whack sent me sprawling to the floor.

"Kali?" Chloe's voice sounded miles away as I lay there, fighting the pain and trying to get my hands and feet under me. I'd dropped the phone and Volante. My ears rang, and I couldn't focus.

My eyes fluttered closed, and I forced them open. I called for Cole, my voice sounding weak and childlike.

He didn't hear me, and before I passed out, the shadows came for me.

EIGHT

When I woke, I had one hell of a headache. So bad, in fact, that I whimpered when I tried to open my eyes, a mew that sounded like a scrawny day-old kitten.

How embarrassing.

Smells accosted me: Damon's warm wood smoke, Yasmin's sharp, acidic scent, and Kirill's dead mouse smell. I was back in my room at the Institute, drowning in Egyptian cotton sheets and a heavy blanket, while my boss sat next to me on the bed and the other two Bridge Council directors stood staring down at me.

Damon touched my arm. "Kali?"

Forcing my eyes open, I pushed onto one elbow, and a sharp pain attacked my frontal lobe. At the same time, the back of my head throbbed so hard I thought it would explode right out of my skull. With another sickly whimper, I slid back down into the sheets and closed my eyes.

"Where's Cole?" The sound of my voice vibrated inside my head. This was the worst hangover I'd ever had. Only, being a demon, I never suffered from alcohol abuse, and I couldn't remember having a single drink, much less enough to cause this. But Cole's absence sent alarm bells ringing in my head along with the throbbing. "Is he okay?"

"He's fine." Damon touched my forehead. "Are you in pain?"

Gee, ya think? "My head." I wanted to lift my hand and rub my temples, but moving hurt too much.

"What happened?" Yasmin's voice rapped against my ears. "Cole said he found you passed out on the floor right after he called Damon."

"Don't shout." I peeled one eye open. She stood next to Damon, arms crossed, looking pissed off. Nothing new there. "I was hit in the head by something heavy. And really hard. I think. I'm a little hazy on details."

Damon glanced at Kirill. He frowned and shook his head.

"Twice," I emphasized, lifting one hand and pointing to the back of my head. Gingerly, I touched the spot at the base of my skull where the injury had occurred. There was no bump, no open gash, or bleeding wound. Not even a tender spot. What the hell?

The pain was all inside. And from the looks on the Council's faces, they thought I was making it up.

Damon's brows pinched together. "Do you remember what you were doing before you were hit?"

The details were fuzzy, mainly because it was hard to concentrate on anything besides the throbbing. "Talking to a ghost. No, wait. I was talking to Chloe. She was upset. Something happened..."

Adrenaline fired through my system. Once again, I attempted to sit up. The pain increased, but I gritted my teeth and refused to give in. "I have to call her. She'll think I blew her off again. And I need to call Di and Maddy, too. They're all waiting for me."

Slow down. As his voice slipped into my head, Damon put a restraining hand on my shoulder. The fact he'd planted his *Psuhke* demon seed in me after my run-in with Nudra so he could read my mind and talk to me telepathically pissed me off. Tonight, however, his deep voice was soothing to my brain. The throbbing eased.

Do that again.

What?

Talk to me. In my head. It feels good.

His fingers settled against my temple. *Never thought I'd hear you say that.*

Ahh...

"What's going on?" Yasmin pushed closer to Damon, pressing a hip against his shoulder as if to remind him she was there. "Are you doing that mental thing with her?"

Already bored with the show, Kirill stalked to the room's window seat. The sun had just started its morning rise, forcing the dark December night back. Could have been my wonky brain, but I thought I saw lightning flash in the distance, breaking into a dozen different white streaks over the gray waters of Lake Michigan. "What or who exactly do you think hit you in the head, Kali? The entity that killed Fielder? The ghost you were talking to?"

Damon's fingers were still massaging my temples. My demon purred contentedly. I closed my eyes and eased deeper into the pillow, trying to recall who my attacker had been.

Marvin had been hiding in the shadows, afraid to talk to me, and probably for good reason. Whatever had filleted Fielder's internal organs might have still been in the building. I hadn't felt it, but something had been there. Something strong enough to knock me out and not leave even a measly bruise.

Maria. The thought surfaced without any help. *But it can't be.*

Maria? Damon's fingers stopped working their delicious magic. My demon stopped purring.

With one hand, I prompted him to continue massaging. *Crazy, right?*

He sat back in the chair, taking his talented archdemon fingers with him. "You saw Maria?"

"Maria, who?" Yasmin demanded.

I sighed and opened my eyes. "I didn't see Maria. I...felt her. Or something like her. Whatever killed Fielder was evil to the nth degree. Sick. Bloodthirsty. But it wasn't feeding on the body. It fed on his fear, I think. On Marvin's fear, too. There was definitely a fine degree of torture exacted on Fielder before he died."

Kirill turned from the window. "Maria, huh? Interesting. Haven't seen her in, oh, three-, four-hundred years?"

"Because I killed her, Kirill. Cut her body into parts and burned them. Remember?"

"Right, right." He tapped a finger against his chin. "So who then?"

I looked at Damon. So did the others. When in doubt, the boss was supposed to have the answer, right?

Wrong. "I have no idea. I've never seen another demon like her."

Yasmin made a face. "I thought Queen Maria was half succubus, half human. Big deal."

Big deal? The hybrid had forced me to torture and kill hundreds of humans and quite a few supes while I'd lived at her court between the ages of nine and seventeen. She'd brainwashed me into believing it was my nature to torture. When I rebelled because I'd fallen in love with Rad, she killed my family, sicced the Noctifectors on Rad, and would have killed me, too, if she could have.

She took a nine-year-old demon from her earthly family

and turned her into a weapon of mass destruction. I became the most formidable vengeance demon on earth under her tutelage. And in the end, this WMD took her down.

Maybe Damon's fingers had done the trick, or perhaps it was thoughts of Maria that got my adrenaline pumping. Either way, my head stopped throbbing and started humming with determination. I had work to do. "The big deal is Yasmin, if it is Maria in some new form, she's coming after me, and innocent people will get hurt in the fallout. And if it *isn't* her, we still have a major problem because it's just like her, which means it will feed on humans and supernaturals alike."

Damon rose from the bed, brushing past Yasmin. "I'll make a few calls to the other Councils and see if they've noticed anything similar in their countries."

Councils existed all over the world in various large cities. They were run by archdemons and employed demons like Cole and me to protect innocent humans from supernatural bad guys, but their ranks were as thin as ours. Few demons cared about humans beyond what they provided—souls, blood, sex, and money.

Kirill followed on Damon's heels. "I'll see if breakfast is ready."

I flipped off the covers and sat up. Someone, hopefully Yasmin, had changed me into my pajamas before putting me to bed. My stomach tilted when I stood, but the previous evening's meal stayed down. A low buzzing set up shop at the base of my skull.

Yasmin looked me over, and a mocking smile appeared. "Must have been something pretty powerful to knock the great Kali Sweet off her feet."

Snark was my go-to recourse, especially with her, but I had bigger things on my plate than verbal sparring with Damon's groupie. "If it had been really powerful, it would have confronted me head-on. And it would have lost." I let my demon peek through my eyes as I met her gaze. Her eyes widened ever so slightly at my direct challenge. "There are very few things in this world that can knock me off my feet" — Radison Beaumont being one of them—" but there is nothing that can keep me down."

NINE

Cole caught up with me on my way out of the Institute. Morning had dawned with a temperature in the low teens, and light snow fell from the overcast sky. Normally, I'd be going to bed for a full eight to twelve hours of sleep, but the three I'd had after getting knocked out would have to do.

I'd managed a hot shower, a full breakfast, and another short session with Damon's fingers, easing the last of the lingering pain in my head while he coached me on what to do if I came across anything that hinted at Maria. Too late. Everything I'd encountered didn't just hint at Maria—it screamed her name. But denial is a wicked, strong force of nature, and Damon was embracing it.

So I tuned out his instructions while soaking up his healing magic and warm, caressing voice. Meanwhile, I planned out my day. My first stop would be Chloe's.

"Already been there," Cole said, reading my determined walk and handing me a paper sack with my favorite fast-food chain's logo on the front. He looked tired. The scent of bacon, scrambled egg, and English muffin wafted past my nose.

I'd already eaten a dozen of Kirill's chocolate chip pancakes, but a demon needs her energy, especially when facing homicidal queens, warring vamps, and whatever craziness Chloe and her blood bank had goin' on.

I unwrapped the paper and bit into the breakfast sandwich. "And?" I said around a mouthful of egg and bacon heaven. "What was the emergency?"

Cole stuck the keys to my TT cruiser into his jeans pocket and leaned against the doorframe. His tired eyes scanned the parking lot and the front of the Institute. "Your slaves are causing problems. Drinking up the Kali Sweet inventory and throwing hissy fits when there isn't enough to go around."

I continued inhaling my food and shook my head. "Rad's drinking directly from me most of the time, and I'm donating three bottles of blood every week for Arman. No way should he need more than that."

"After we left the club last night, Guitar Boy went down to Chloe's for more of your blood. Arman was there picking up the last bottle. They got into a fight and damaged a bunch of Chloe's prized inventory. She says you owe her..." He pulled a wadded-up piece of paper from his pocket. "Two thousand, six hundred and fifty-two dollars. And some blood."

"Holy shit." I nearly choked on a bite of sandwich. "What the hell is wrong with those two?"

"Beats me." He stepped closer, scanned my face. "What happened to you last night? You look like hell."

What every female wants to hear. "Something hit me in the back of the head twice but left no visible injury."

Like usual, I'd put my hair in a high ponytail for work. Cole turned me around, slid one of his hands up my neck, and ran his fingers over the back of my skull. Damn, every male in my life had skilled fingers that immediately made me sigh with contentment.

His fingers probed, rubbed, and outlined my entire head, and then he made a *hunh* sound.

I turned back to face him. "What do you think?"

His fingers lightly tapped my facial bones while he checked my pupils. "You're not nauseous. Any dizziness? Vision problems?"

"I had a bitch of a headache when I woke up."

"It's gone now?"

"Damon did something to my temples. Worked like a charm."

A muscle jumped under Cole's right eye. "You think it was the ghost? Maria?"

"Those are the going theories, but since when can a ghost take out a demon, and how could it possibly be Maria?"

"How did it knock you out without leaving any wound?"

I shrugged. "I need to go back to the scene. See if I can figure it out."

"Cops are all over it. Better wait until they clear out. Let's get some sleep, then we'll hit it tonight."

"No time for sleep. I still have Toel to chase and Dalinda to stop."

"You're pale as the snow." He stepped closer—so close that his nose was practically in my hair. My demon took notice and sat up. "You smell off."

"I showered with the vanilla latte body scrub Di gave me. An early Christmas present, she said. She knows I don't do holidays."

He shook his head. "It's not that. Your demon. She smells... weird."

The demon in question hissed at the criticism. "So I look sick and smell weird. Any more shots for my ego?"

His nose grazed my neck below my earlobe, and a tickle of electricity sent a shudder down my spine. "Your iron is low.

Way too low for a demon. You've got to quit feeding Guitar Boy all your blood."

Demons, in general, have high mineral counts. Our magic comes from the earth, so our bodies are natural sources of iron, zinc, magnesium, etc. We can bleed to death, but it's a rarity because we heal fast, and the minerals give us extra fortification. "Let's not forget Arman's drinking his fair share as well."

Cole sighed, sounding older than his gazillion-odd years, stepped back, and leaned one hand on my car. "It's like they're addicted to your blood."

"They're blood slaves. Of course they're addicted. Not *my* blood so much as Nudra's. If he hadn't injected me with his in the first place, neither Arman nor Rad would have been able to drink from me. It would have tasted like gasoline."

"This is beyond normal blood slave addiction, Kali."

Okay, but what could I do about it? "I don't know what's going on with them, but I have bigger issues to worry about right now. I'll ask Dru next time I see him and see what he thinks."

Another tired sigh escaped Cole's lips. The sun was higher in the sky, and a few weak rays cut through the gray clouds, emphasizing his hazel eyes and five-o-clock shadow. "So where to first?"

I balled up the now empty wrapper and shoved it in the bag. "When was the last time you slept?"

Cole straightened. "I don't need sleep."

Dire o sparare. "Don't bullshit me. You haven't slept in a week, you haven't screwed anyone in six. You're an absolute bear to be around right now, so get some sleep, and I'll call Hone and have him meet me at the office. He can play bodyguard."

Fishing the keys from his pocket, he motioned me to get in the car. "Forget it, toots. You're stuck with the bear. Although, I don't know what you think you'll pull off during the day. Vicky and Toel will be in their coffins, Chloe is closed until five, and Dalinda won't pop her head up until sunset."

I peeked up at the filtered sunshine. Usually, I worked nights and slept days. The tug of warm covers and a few more hours of shut-eye called to me. Especially since I hadn't been having the Rad nightmare. Since he'd come back into my life, my subconscious seemed appeased by his real-life threat, so he stopped showing up in my dream world carrying a silver knife. "Tell you what, I need to pick up some things at my house. After that, we can come back here until sunset. I'll regroup with Maddy, JR, and Di on my cases while you catch a few hours of dream time."

"And you'll call Dru and see what he knows about your blood slave freak show."

If Cole was pushing me to talk to the Master vamp, he was well and truly concerned. "I'll call Dru."

Turned out I didn't have to. A second before his black BMW pulled up to the Institute's double iron gates, my stomach clenched hard, and I doubled over. "*Che cavolo*, what is wrong with me?" I bit out between clamped teeth.

The clouds overhead suddenly blotted out the weak sun, casting shadows dark as night over us. A cold wind kicked up, blowing flakes of snow in my face. The gates swung open, and Dru's Beemer roared onto the grounds. Meanwhile, Cole grabbed me to stop me from falling.

His well-muscled arms held me against his body, one of his chiseled thighs sliding in between mine to steady me. "I've got you."

Boy, did he, and thank Satan for warrior bodyguards with overprotective instincts. There's not much better to hold you tight—all that solid muscle and steady demon—when your own body seizes so hard, you nearly crack your spine.

Brianna exited Dru's car first, her eyes lit with happiness to see Cole. That happiness died the instant she saw him embracing me. She opened Dru's door, and he extracted his long, lean frame from the sports car, his attention also drawn to Cole and me as snow blew into my eyes.

A shark seemed to be eating my intestines, and I sucked my lips between my teeth to keep from letting out any sound of distress. Cole hefted my butt up onto the hood, steadied me against him, and stuck out a hand to Dru. "Stay back. You're causing her pain."

"What?" Dru and I spoke simultaneously, his voice carrying much more weight than mine.

I hated being weak. There'd been a time in Maria's court when pain didn't exist for me. She'd conditioned it right out. Or maybe I should say my demon lived for pain back then. Reveled in it.

After hundreds of years of repressing my demon, however, I'd begun to feel again. I'm no wimp, but this pain—and the earlier one in my head—was at a level I hadn't felt since my early days under Maria's torture. It made me feel vulnerable...a sensation I was determined to slay as effectively as I did super-naturals who crossed my vengeance path.

To overcome my weakness, though, meant letting my demon rise. Giving her more headroom than I had since the night I let Toel egg her out for a fight. She's a tough one to control, and in this situation, an unnecessary risk, but I had to do something to salvage my pride and not look weak.

Inside me, she gladly responded to the invitation, and it took me a moment more of gritted teeth and warring emotions to get her on a sufficient leash.

"She's sick," Cole said to Dru. "And you're making it worse. You need to leave."

I swallowed hard, looked at Dru, and realized Cole was

right. Again. Damn, even exhausted and strung out, he was thinking on his feet better than I was. But what the hell was going on? Why was Dru's vamp blood making me react like this? "This is more than my demon resisting the call of your family's blood, Dru. I don't know what's happening, but Cole's right. You need to leave."

Dru looked as pained as I felt. He started to step forward but instead backed up a few feet. "It's Nudra's blood, Kali. It's at war with your demon blood, and it's losing. You need more of it."

I pushed Cole back and slid off the hood. "I'm having withdrawal?"

Dru's gloved hand tapped against his trench coat. "That's why I'm here. It's been bugging me all night. This demon-vamp thing is new to me, but I saw your reaction in the club last night, and I knew it wasn't normal. I did some research, and it's a possibility that Nudra's death didn't stop the effects of his blood on your system. You need more vamp blood."

Hell with that. I almost felt relieved. "If it's withdrawal, all I have to do is ride it out."

He shook his head, eyes studying me intently. "You can't ride it out, Kali. I know you hate our kind, but in a sense, you're one of us now. If you don't drink, you'll die."

Sick joke. That's what this was. "But I'd have to drink from Nudra, and he's dead."

Everyone was quiet as realization sunk in. If Nudra was dead and I needed his blood to live...

Then, I was one dead demon.

TEN

"Drink mine." Dru held up a hand, revealing his wrist under the glove. "I'm a royal. I can save you."

"Oh, hell," Cole swore under his breath. He turned his back on Brianna and Dru, stepped in my line of sight, and blocked them out. "Be careful, Kali. This smells like a trap."

Lot of those around. I stewed it over, my brain feeling as heavy as the circling clouds and wet snow. I lowered my voice. "I'm already vamp queen. What would making me his blood slave gain him?"

Cole's dark brows drew together, and the tic under his eye started again. Snow dotted his hair and stuck on his whiskered cheeks. "He's wanted you in his bed since the first time he saw you."

Dru was a big flirt, and while I was sure he wouldn't turn down a roll in the coffin with me, I sensed he wasn't offering his blood for that reason alone. We were friends. I'd helped him with Toel, and he'd made my transition to queen of the Undead reasonably easy.

On the other hand, vamps traded blood and sex as readily

as I downed copious amounts of spaghetti and meatballs. Being the political creatures they were, they used blood and sex to get what they wanted. And unfortunately, the two went hand in hand.

I was a demon, not a vamp, and a strong, three-hundred-year-old demon at that. I struggled to control the seven vices that made up my entity—and occasionally, I gave into those vices with wild abandon—but I could control them if I wanted to.

Shifting to look around Cole, I asked Dru, "How long do I have?"

Dru lowered his hand. "The longer you go without vamp blood, the weaker you'll become. Could be weeks. Could be days. There's no precedent, only a few legends older than I am that talk about this crossbreed sort of thing."

Crossbreed. A conversation I'd had with Lucifer in November pinged my brain. *You are one of the vitiums of Mary Magdalena.*

Mary Magdalena had been possessed by seven demons. They were exorcised from her by Jesus Christ. She then became the most beloved disciple Jesus had on earth.

Or so Lucifer claimed. He also claimed I wasn't a demon in the usual sense. I was a freak—some weird crossbreed of good and evil.

I glanced at Cole and saw the tension on his face. Dru had the same expression. This wasn't either of their decisions, though. It was mine. "I need more information about this process and what it's doing to me. About what I really am. And if I do decide to go through with it, I need your word that you won't use this against me or the Council."

Hope lit Dru's eyes. "Of course. I'm offering this out of friendship, nothing more."

Cole made a rude noise in the back of his throat, took my arm, and prompted me to get into the car.

He held open the car door, but I stood a moment longer, letting my demon read the Master of Chicago's Undead. He was strong, physically, mentally, and psychically—precisely the type of strength I would need to fight Maria if and when the time came. And I had no doubt it would come.

The wind lifted the end of my ponytail and blew it across my eyes as if an invisible force was trying to break the connection between us. Dru sensed it, tilting his head but not breaking eye contact with me. Brianna tensed, whether from his sudden awareness filtering to her or her sensing the presence on her own. She shifted closer to her Master, put out a protective arm.

A second later, Cole was at my back, weapon drawn. "Kali? What is it?" he murmured in my ear.

I was afraid to speak and scare it away, so I held utterly still and carefully transferred my attention from scanning Dru to scanning the air in front of my face.

Calina, a voice whispered in front of me. *Bambina*.

My earthly mother never called me my given Italian name. She'd always called me *bambina*. Daughter.

So had Maria.

The smell of thick, heady perfume filled my nostrils. *Roses*, I thought. And then, *ancient paper*. The swirling snowflakes became a tornado, flying faster and faster into a human form, the white flakes glowing, iridescent.

A ghost from my past that defied all reason.

My heart clenched. "What do you want?"

A throaty laughter came from the tornado shaped like a woman. Fingers of dark magic reached for me, pricking my skin right through my cape wherever they touched. Punching through my resistance and grasping onto my emotions. The world around us faded, and Maria came into sharper contrast, her striking blue eyes piercing, red hair flying around her head resembling Medusa.

Familiar feelings of anger, pride, and the deep-seated need for revenge rose inside me. Then were sucked away as she absorbed them. My body swayed, the magic whirlwind carrying me off. Drawing my demon out. *Calina...*

For a second, I let my demon succumb, but it was only in order for me to get a good look at the entity in front of me. She smelled like Maria, laughed like Maria, even had the queen's features. She exuded a special brand of dark magic I'd only ever felt while around her, and she was definitely a succubus. But there was something not right about this entity. Something that didn't match.

Maria had never glowed.

Was it the fact she was a ghost? I'd have to ask Neve. Never in all my years had I seen a ghost light up. Didn't mean it wasn't possible.

A demon as evil as Maria, though? Far stretch for me to believe her ghost would glow with something akin to angelic light.

My demon struggled to break free from her leash, snapping and clawing at me and straining my hold over her to the breaking point. The clouds pressed down around us, ominous and suffocating.

No. Bringing my fingers and thumbs together, I raised my protective magic. "Vengeance is mine," I yelled into the wind and pushed my hands out from my body.

My shield was weak but it held as I shoved a wall of magic at the entity, at the clouds, at the snow storm trying to engulf me. My heart thumped hard at the strain to push the evil away, and at the same time, contain the evil inside fighting to free itself and join her.

Magic flowed, rising and falling, pushing and pulling. I

held on, and from somewhere outside my wall, a new thread of magic flowed toward me. Like a strand of DNA, it locked with my magic, curling around me and renewing my strength. Together we succeeded at slamming her back.

And just like that, the wind died, the ghost disappeared, and the clouds lifted.

Snow fell in gentle spirals, and a salty ocean scent teased my nose. My demon slunk back into her hole and a gentle calm settled in my bones. "Rad?" I looked around, but only Cole, Dru, and Brianna were there, staring back and asking if I was okay.

Shaking from head to toe, I nodded and leaned on the car, my eyes continuing to scan the parking lot, buildings, and front drive. Rad was nowhere to be seen, but I was sure I'd sensed him.

My phone buzzed inside my cape. Loud, bee-like.

Rad.

I checked my messages, and sure enough, Rock God had sent me one. More than one. They all asked the same question: *R U OK?*

With shaking fingers, I texted back. Y

Dru rushed toward me, and a new pain ripped through my stomach. As I wrapped an arm around my waist and bent over, Cole once more stepped between the two of us. "Back off, bloodsucker."

Angst creased Dru's forehead and face, but he did as commanded, moving far enough back that the pain eased. Cole's hands rubbed my back, my arms, my neck. "Fight it, Kali. Whatever the hell *it* is."

I straightened, blew my bangs out of my face. "I'm okay." And I was until I looked up and saw Damon watching out one of the Institute's windows.

"Was it Maria?" Cole asked.

If it walked like a duck and quacked like a duck...or in this case, a succubus demon ghost...it probably was. Though the light show I'd just seen gave me pause. "I'm still not sure what the hell it is." I gave Dru a weak wave, slid into the car. "Let's get out of here before Damon goes archdemon on us and confines me to my room. I need to think and I can't do that with him in my face."

Cole didn't need any prompting. He jumped in the driver's seat and gunned the engine. We took off, and as I looked back, Dru watched with his sexy, sad eyes and his face set in grim lines.

ELEVEN

"How do you kill her?" Cole said as we took the Dan Ryan heading north.

"I don't know." Three words I hated when strung together. They made me feel like there was a solution, but I couldn't find it.

"You killed her before."

"She was a physical being then. Not a ghost."

Traffic was moderate, most of the morning commuters already at work. As always, Cole drove way above the speed limit and gave me whiplash as he jerked my car in, out, and around other vehicles. "Must be your worst nightmare, huh? To have her come back to haunt you?"

My worst nightmare involved all the ghosts of the humans I'd tortured and killed coming back to haunt me, but having Maria running around in any form was a close second. My mind turned over thought after thought, playing through my memories, looking for an easy solution. Any solution.

I came up blank.

And that, I realized, was my worst nightmare. My deepest

fear. Not that the ghosts of my past would materialize, but that I wouldn't know what to do with them if they did.

Cole glanced at me, worry over my silence knitting his brow. "You and Neve will think of something to send her back where she came from."

"Neve's human. I can't involve her in this. Maria, or whatever this thing is, gets one whiff of a human trying to take her down, and Neve's life will be forfeit."

"I'll protect you, Kali. Neve, too, if necessary."

I fiddled with the edge of my cape. "You're already protecting me from Toel and the Noctifectors. You're good, Cole, but you're not Superman."

"Superman's a joke. I'm Batman."

"Okay, how are you going to protect me from a ghost, Batman?"

He took the off-ramp to my house. "I don't know, but I'll figure it out. I screwed up letting you meander away from me at the schizo circus. Won't happen again."

My house is inside an old, abandoned Gothic church way off the beaten path. Behind the behemoth castle-like structure, an ancient graveyard is hidden by overgrown trees, shrubs, and some of my protective magic. The graveyard contains a portal between worlds, and as Cole and I walked to my back door, my mind churned once more. I'd used the portal to send the queen of hell packing. Maybe I could also use it to send this queen on her way.

With Cole covering my six, I laid a hand on the church's stone wall. Familiar magic buzzed against my skin. JR had installed a hefty security system, but I'd also embedded protection magic deep in the walls, floors, windows, and foundation after my latest run-ins with Lilith, Toel, and other bad supernaturals. A girl couldn't be too safe.

Which is why I live at the Institute these days. Damon had

insisted, and I'd rebelled against the idea until I'd taken a minute to actually think through the logic. Not only was the Institute one of the safest locations in Chicago, it was also full of Bridge employees. If a dangerous entity did somehow break through the high-tech and magical fortress of security systems, a small army of equally dangerous supernaturals like Cole had my back.

But the Institute wasn't home. Feeling the waves of cool earth magic flowing into my hand and welcoming me home, I breathed a slight sigh of relief. The tension in my shoulders ebbed. The church was potentially less safe, but it was mine. I belonged here.

I held my hand on the stone a moment longer, absorbing the feeling of rightness. Just before I dropped my hand, a different magic tickled it.

"Everything okay?" Cole asked, his back to mine as he kept his gun up and his gaze scanning the area.

I hesitated a second too long for his liking. He swung around, gun aimed at the door. "Kali, what is it?"

The new magic tickled me again, winding its way around my fingers, caressing my hand. There was a bit of vibration in it, as if it wanted to hold onto me and, at the same time, divide itself and run amok along the rest of the stones, dive into the ground, and fly up to the sky.

Drawing my hand away, I smiled to myself and put a restraining hand on Cole's gun. "It's Rad."

"What's he doing here?"

I unlocked the door. "Rad?" My voice echoed through the entryway. I opened my senses...and felt nothing. His lingering stormy ocean smell was present, but he was gone.

Disappointed, I nevertheless rallied. "I'm calling Hone. He can give us extra protection while we're here."

"We don't need him."

"Yes, we do because you're taking a nice little nap while I make phone calls and research ghosts." I took off my cape, grabbed my cell from one of the pockets, and hung it up before I headed toward my office to check the security monitors.

As I passed my sunken living room, I stopped short. Cole, right behind me, did the same. He whistled low under his breath as we surveyed the damage together. "Guitar Boy is one big freakin' Chaos demon."

Rad had pushed the furniture to the edges of the room and set up a mini recording studio in the center. A keyboard sat in front of the fireplace, a sound system to its left, and a computer to its right. An assortment of acoustic and electric guitars lay on the couch and chairs. Cords snaked all over the floor, various speakers were stacked on top of each other.

Take-out boxes, plates, cups and condiment packages littered the area. Heaps of manila-colored papers covered the coffee table. Loose papers were also piled on every other viable surface. Dozens of them, strewn on the floor, across the speakers and furniture, caught in guitar strings.

Bending down, I picked up one of the papers. Musical notes and words ran across both sides in reckless abandon. I picked up another and saw the same thing. "They're songs." An odd sinking sensation filled my chest as I scanned the living room again. "There must be hundreds of them."

"What's he writing them here for? They kick him out of his fancy suite at the Blackstone?"

Cole was missing the point. "This isn't normal."

"Living like a pig? He's part Chaos demon. That's totally normal."

A trail of Rad's clothes led from the living room to the stairs. Following the black T-shirt and ripped jeans breadcrumbs, I climbed the steps to my loft and stepped over more scattered sheets of music on the way to my bedroom. Cole followed.

When Damon forced me into the Institute, he'd moved my bedroom furniture to the apartment across from his. Guess he figured I'd feel more at home if I had my own stuff. While I appreciated the sentiment and sleeping in my bed, I had missed this room most of all. Two floor-to-ceiling windows gave the room light. One was clear, the other a stained-glass illustration of Christ's temptation. I'd missed my bathroom and the enormous walk-in closet filled with clothes and shoes I had collected over the years.

Now, the hardwood floor echoed my footsteps back to me as I stepped entered. A couple of blankets lay on the floor where my bed had been. Another guitar and more food boxes sat beside it.

Once again, dozens of music sheets covered the floor, along with the blankets and the two lonely pieces of furniture Damon's movers had left behind.

A dozen pencils, some worn down to nubs, others broken, were strewn around the room. Some next to the blankets, others thrown at the walls before breaking and falling to the floor.

A single sheet and pencil lay on the pillow. The title of the song was *Unquenchable Need.* I read the first set of lyrics, written in Rad's familiar flowing script.

There is no hope
Only thirst
It's never enough
Only driving desire
For more of her, more of her
She's never enough
But she's all I need.

Randomly, I picked up other songs from around the room. Their subjects concerned curses, star-crossed lovers going down in flames, soul mates carving out each other's hearts. One talked about the gates of heaven being forever closed to the singer and his lover holding the only key. Another about the singer refusing to bow to love and the forces tearing him inside out. Yet another about sending his enemies to blood-soaked graves.

Just the usual rock songs.

Not.

Well, maybe they were. Most songs I listened to had similar angst-riddled verses, and the Chaos Demons had won Grammys for Rad's gritty lyrics. But just like the sensation I'd had when watching Maria's ghost light up, something about this was off.

"This is beyond chaos." I turned a circle, thought about Rad and Arman's blood lust. The sinking sensation ratcheted up a notch. I handed the music to Cole, let him read a few lines. "This is mania. There's something in my blood driving him crazy."

Cole shifted his weight, read the lyrics to *Unquenchable Need*. "More like something *not* in your blood that he needs. He's starving."

I lifted my gaze to his. "Nudra's blood."

He gave a quick downward tilt of his chin. "My guess, too."

Fucking Nudra. Even in death, he was making my life hell.

If Rad was coming unglued, Arman had to be, too. According to Dru, there was only one way to save us all.

I shook my head, let out a frustrated chuckle. "What the hell am I going to do, Cole?"

Never one to bullshit me with meaningless reassurances, my bodyguard shrugged and said the words I hated. "I don't know."

TWELVE

Jesus stared down at me as I phoned Dru. *What would Jesus do* ran through my head.

Rad wasn't the only one losing it.

Dru answered on the first ring. "I've been waiting for your call. Where do you want me to meet you? Or would you prefer we do the blood exchange here?"

"Whoa, vamp Master. Back up the Undead cart a minute." While I was considering his proposal more seriously, I wasn't ready to join the ranks of true bloodsuckers just yet. I hit the speaker phone button so Cole could hear our discussion. "I need some information."

Dru's voice sounded polite and patient but a touch irritated at my reluctance. "I'm at your service, Queen."

Hell save me, I hated that moniker more and more. Whether he'd used it to remind me of my station among the Undead or simply in reply to my reference to his Master status, I couldn't be sure. Didn't matter. Dru's agenda aside, hidden or not, he was my friend and one who could help me figure out my options. "If I die, will the bond to my blood slaves break like it does with your people? Or will my slaves die too?"

The restrained patience cracked. "You'd rather die than drink my blood and save yourself?"

"I'm a fucking demon, Dru. Quite honestly, up to the time I met you and Maddy, which was barely six weeks ago, I hated the Undead. Every one of them. Forgive me if I'm reluctant to jump on the let's-drink-blood-together-like-one-big-happy-vamp-family bandwagon."

There was a strained and unfriendly silence from the other end. I rolled my eyes up in my head to the brink of giving myself a concussion and forced my voice not to convey my frustration. "I'm exploring options. That's all. I can't make an informed choice until I know all the consequences of becoming your blood slave."

"You won't be a blood slave to me in the usual sense of the term. We would still be equals, as we are now. My blood would simply be a...supplement...to your current diet."

Cole quirked one eyebrow. He wasn't buying it.

I was. Maybe because Rad's life was now on the line along with mine. Maybe because after two-hundred-eighty-three years of going through the motions, I wasn't afraid of dying, but I'd only just started living again with Rad back in my life.

I tamped down the emotions that idea raised and firmed my resolve. "Your word, Master Dru. I want your word that you won't use me the way you use your other slaves. That I make the calls in our relationship, no matter what desires you have or political stakes our sharing blood might create."

Another long pause greeted me. A suspiciously long pause.

Did Dru have a hidden agenda like Cole believed, or was he simply pissed that I dared to demand he swear fidelity to me?

Cole made an *I told you so* face, the silence seeming to

confirm Dru's agenda was less about us being friends and more about us becoming lovers. I faced Jesus and let the silence hang between me and the vamp Master. It was his move, whatever that move was.

"I'll consider your request," he said and hung up.

For a second, I stared at the square cell phone, the dial tone mocking me. Then I blustered. "He hung up on me."

"I heard." Cole smirked. "He's a spoiled vamp who's full of himself and his power. You didn't think he'd give you equal footing on his turf, did you?"

Yeah, I did. In the short time we'd known each other, Dru and I had built a solid friendship. Or so I thought. Shows you what I know about friendship. Which is probably why I don't have many friends.

I'd had a lot of bad days in three hundred years. This one was creeping its way into the top one hundred. I blew out a depressed sigh and headed back downstairs. The kitchen was as messy as the rest of the spaces Rad had been occupying, so I skirted the worst piles to get to the pantry. Inside, I pulled out a stylish, flat bottle of Woodford whiskey. I set up two glasses on top of some empty pizza boxes on the kitchen counter and poured three fingers of the beautiful liquid into each. Cole and I clinked the glasses together and drank the shots straight down.

I carried the bottle to my office, checked the security system and sat back in my chair. The to-do list in my head was growing, and busy work would give my brain time to stew on my situation with Maria's ghost and my predicament with Nudra's blood. In between shots of whiskey, I called Hone and hired him for a day's worth of protection services, texted Rad and told him to get his rocker butt to the church, and then I phoned Di.

Maddy and JR worked nights like me and slept during the day. Di, being a goddess, didn't need sleep. She liked a big bed and expensive satin sheets, but those were props for her endless string of boyfriends.

She didn't need to eat either, but she loved carbs as much as I did. Only on her, they looked infinitely sexier. "Kali," she answered her phone. Slurping noises interrupted before she continued. "Cole said you passed out at the hospital. Are you okay?"

"Fine. What are you eating?"

"Wesley made me a fruit smoothie. It's healthy and surprisingly good."

"Wesley? Have I met him?"

"Thank goodness, no. I don't need you scaring another one off."

True, I didn't take to many of Di's boyfriends. However, her blaming me for their hasty departures was stretching the truth. At the first sign any of them wanted to hang around for more than a week or two, she'd turn up the super diva personality, and bingo, another boy would bite the Aphrodite dust. The goddess of love was an expert in sabotaging her own love life.

"What's your worst nightmare, Di?"

"My worst nightmare?" She slurped more smoothie. "Hmm. I suppose it's to love someone and not have them love me back. Most people fear that you know. Love drives everything else. All our emotions. Our self-confidence, our destiny, our successes and failures."

Don't get Di started on the virtues of love. "That's your deepest fear? Not being loved?"

Cole muscled my leather lounge chair into the office, made himself comfortable, and put his eagle-eyed bodyguard stare on me. I gave him five minutes, tops, before he fell asleep.

"Why? What's yours? I assume there's a good reason we're playing this game."

At least Di's reason explained why she never let any man

get close to her. If she let them in and she fell for them, they had the power to break her heart. "You don't worry about any of the guys you've dumped coming back for revenge?"

"Did that jerk Danny hire you to take revenge on me?"

Danny? I couldn't remember a Danny in the lineup. "No, I'm just curious if you ever worry about the past coming back to bite you in the ass."

"Nope. The past is the past. Love is all about the future."

Right. But I wasn't dealing with love. I watched Cole's eyelids dip to half-mast. "Any change in Maddy's outlook?"

Di made a belligerent noise in the back of her throat. "Thought you were going to talk to her."

An image of Maddy with her heart in her eyes asking me about redemption flashed in my mind. I'd never seen her so scared. "I'll talk to her, I promise."

The image continued to plague me. Her voice rang in my ears. *Do I still have a soul? Am I going to hell when I die?*

Guess I knew *her* deepest fear.

Di was still talking, but I'd missed what she'd said. Something about JR. "What?"

"JR. Instead of going home this morning, he headed to the box store to buy more tech stuff. He's already got the whole control room filled with boxes. Laptops, gaming systems, those tablet thingies he's been trying to get me to use. He's maxed out the company credit card, Kali. You need to talk to him, too."

Merde. Had everyone around me gone flat-ass crazy? I frowned at Cole, whose head was now tipped back, eyes closed. The Unquenchable Need sheet sat on the desk in front of me. Fear, obsession, pride—my friends weren't crazy, just giving into their vices.

I sat up straight. Di seemed immune, but as a goddess, she was immune to almost everything. "How did your meeting with the Stewarts go?"

"Oh, goddess, be sweet. Those people are whacked. Dalinda was there. With them. Apparently, Mrs. Stewart has had a change of heart, and they're...well, having a nice little three-way with D."

Closing my eyes, I sighed. "Dalinda's using her magic on the wife now, too."

"Seems like it. They asked if I wanted to join them."

A four-way? Eww. "I so don't have time for this."

"You should try hooking that Toel character up with Dalinda. She might divert his quest for world domination long enough for you to stake him."

Not a bad idea, except that, "Vampires are often immune to succubi."

"But they're not immune to sexual gratification. Or love, for that matter."

Di's motto: love will save the world.

My motto: love is what screws up the world.

"See you tonight." If I lived long enough. I hung up before she could respond and dialed Neve. "Is it possible for a demon ghost to infect the living with sin?"

"Hello to you, too, dear." Her sarcasm rang more with worry than actual derision. "How are you after last night's escapade?"

"I'm fine. What about demon ghosts infecting the living with various sins? Is it possible?"

She sighed. "I have no idea, but from my experience, anything's possible in the world of earth-bound spirits."

Not exactly the unequivocal answer I'd hoped for, but good enough. "Thanks. I gotta run, but I'll call you with more questions soon."

Tossing the cell phone on the desk, I scribbled notes on a blank piece of paper. Probably the only one left in the house after Rad's explosion of creativity. On screen, I saw Hone arrive, locking up his car and waving at the security camera. I slipped out of the office so as not to wake Cole and met the humongous human at the front door.

Hone looks like a defensive back for the Bears. He's as broad as he is tall, with a hefty dose of Hawaiian king in his DNA. He rarely swings his fists. All he has to do is look at most people, and they run the other way.

Inside, he's a gooey mass of sweetness. He's also a bonafide psychic. Those bad guys who do stay to tangle with him, instead of running like good sense would dictate, get their asses handed to them on a Hone-sized platter.

"Kali Sweet, how are you doin', sweetheart?" He clasped my hand and embraced me.

"Thanks for coming, Hone," I said into his hulking chest. He set me back and smiled. "Think you can keep an eye out here on my perimeter? Cole's inside, and the electronic security system is on high alert, but I trust human intel more."

One of his large, beefy hands patted my cheek. "You know I'd do anythin' for you, Kali."

"Haven't seen any invite to you and Renee's wedding yet."

The smile widened, showing off his pearly whites. "Soon enough, I promise. Givin' my lady a diamond for Christmas big enough to sink one of them fancy party barges always cruising the lake in the summer."

I clapped him on the shoulder. "Good deal." I handed him one of the earbuds Cole used for all his security details. "I'll be inside. If you need anything or see anything, holler."

"You got it."

The big man started a circuitous route to the right. I went back to my office.

My cell display showed a graphic of a message envelope. I'd missed a call, and it had gone to voicemail. My overprotective bodyguard had slept right through the phone's ringing, which was good, I guessed. Regardless of his insistence that he was fine, I needed him at maximum fighting capacity, and there was no way he could be if he was chronically sleep-deprived.

I grabbed my phone, my heart squeezing at the thought that the message might be from Rad. He might be a perfectly capable half-demon and my enemy lover, but I was still worried about him.

When I heard Damon's demanding voice in my ear, my heart stopped acting stupid and my nerves bristled. "Alexandru has informed me of your illness. Although I'm sure you'd rather ignore this problem to focus on Maria, it is of utmost importance we deal with your health first. Return to the Institute so Kirill can do a full physical evaluation. We will then discuss treatment possibilities and proceed with the most promising one."

Damon made it sound like I had cancer. While demons couldn't contract human diseases, we had a wide and varied assortment of our own, many of them similar to their human counterparts. They rarely killed us, preferring instead to prolong the pain and suffering. The demon way of life...and death.

Demon diseases affected our magic and minds and threw our vices into overdrive. Kirill might have been the top disease archdemon around, but he was more adept at spreading infections, maladies, and disorders than curing them. Putting myself in his hands was hardly a reassuring idea.

Plus, I might be dealing with more than one type of *health issue*, as Damon referred to it. My capital sin had always been *superbia*, pride, with a few others thrown in for good measure. Maria's succubus nature had *gula*, gluttony, and *fornicatio*, lust, at the forefront. Her strongest skill was manipulating and escalating others' vices so she could feed on them.

With me, she'd played on my ego in order to create the most

proficient and accomplished vengeance demon the world had ever known. For a time, nothing was more important to me than doing everything she wanted and doing it so well, she loved and respected me more than the other demons in her court.

Of course, that meant spreading pain and fear everywhere I went. Reveling in the blood and suffering of humans and supernaturals alike. Turning my back on the tiny seed of humanity my earthly parents had instilled in me until Maria snatched me from them the day I turned nine.

Remembering that day brought a flood of old, ugly memories to mind. I sat in my office chair, swallowed down the lump in my throat, and forced myself not to push those memories away. If I were dealing with Maria again, I would have to delve deep into the past, whether I liked it or not. That's where the answers were.

Hand shaking, I poured a shot of whiskey and sank into my office chair. Recalling those memories hurt as much as my body's withdrawal from the lack of Nudra's blood in my system. As much as being whacked on the head had the previous night. If I let them, they'd consume me, and I'd drown in guilt and self-loathing, but I had to examine them again for clues. Clues that might tell me how I could defeat Maria again, even if she was a ghost.

One shot of whiskey wasn't enough. As Cole snored and I dredged up my three-hundred-year-old past, I picked up the bottle and let the liquid coat my tight throat, filling the void in my cold, hollow stomach. If there was one advantage to accepting Dru's blood offer—besides possibly saving my life and that of my slaves—it was the fact I'd be even stronger when facing Maria. At least, that was one theory my brain had tossed up. Dru was the son of Vlad the Impaler, a born vampire, not one that was made. He'd lived longer than I had, and his eminence in the Undead world equaled mine in the demon world. Surely the intermixing of our bloods would increase my already superior skills to unmatched heights.

But would it be enough to handle a ghost? A spirit I couldn't face head-on? One who only possessed a physical body when she wanted to and who couldn't be killed by simply cutting out her heart or beheading her.

"Early to be drinking, isn't it?"

Rad stood in the doorway, the collar of his wool coat flipped up, his gold eyes peering from underneath dark bangs. His French Mediterranean coloring and thick lashes didn't hide the shadows lingering under those beautiful eyes and my heart gave a hard squeeze.

Tight lines bracketed the corners of his mouth. The cheekbones above the coat's collar stood out too much for my liking. His dark hair was a tangled mess, like he'd just gotten out of bed.

I'd been so absorbed in thoughts of Maria that I hadn't noticed him on the security screen or heard him enter the church. But just like when I was seventeen, his presence lifted me out of my nightmare and reminded me I could be benevolent and merciful, as well as vindictive and cruel.

I set the nearly empty bottle down, picked up Unquenchable Need, and hustled him out of the office and into the living room so we wouldn't wake Cole. "We need to talk."

He unbuttoned his coat, and that's when I noticed the pack of paper and box of new pencils in his hand. "Conversations that start with those words never end well for me."

Handing me the paper and pencils, he shrugged off the coat and tossed it on a nearby chair, the buttons raking across the strings of a guitar. A harsh, discordant *twang* came from them, seeming to emphasize his point. He motioned at a mound of trash. "Sorry about the mess. Didn't think you'd mind me hanging out here since you're living with Damon now."

Was that jealousy lacing his voice? "I'm staying at the Institute under Damon's orders, not because I *want* to live there." I handed the paper and pencils back to him. "What's going on with you?"

I'd said it quietly, gently. It didn't matter. I saw it in his eyes—that defiance that swam under the surface of our relationship, as if I was always accusing him of something.

Which, in general, I was. He'd left me at the altar—a scared but determined young female demon who'd been willing to sacrifice everything to marry him— and I'd lived the past several hundred years believing he'd abandoned me that night. The very night I'd needed him the most. The night I'd defied Maria to be with him and found my parents and little sister crucified.

I hadn't known until recently when Rad came back into my life what had happened to him that night or the years that followed. How he'd been kidnapped by the Noctifectors, tortured, and blackmailed into becoming one of them in order to infiltrate demon families and find their weaknesses so the demon slayers could wipe them off the face of the earth.

He lobbed the paper and pencil supplies onto the coffee table and sunk into the fancy, padded leather chair stationed at the keyboard. "A *furor poeticus* wind blew. I needed a quiet space to let the inspiration flow."

Furor poeticus. Divine frenzy. Poetic madness. The gift of gods. Writers, musicians, and artists craved inspiration, begged their muses to produce it, and often went through elaborate rituals to seek it out. The Greeks called it ecstasy.

Rad's angular face did not show ecstasy. Exhaustion, yes, but the type of exhaustion that was soul-deep, not just physical. I wanted to touch him—calm the crazy hair, kiss the shadows under his eyes, massage the tension from his forehead.

"You're welcome to stay here as long as you want." I

stepped closer to him, studying the three-day growth of beard along his jawline and the tight set of his lips. Even in the throes of obsession, he was perfect. Beautiful, his humanness flowing off him like sweet, dark syrup.

I envied his creativity with words and instruments. Envied the way he embraced his demon side, succumbing to the chaos rather than fighting it all the time. "How many songs have you written this week?"

His gaze bounced around the room at the dozens of scattered songs before locking with mine. "Two hundred sixty-seven. Maybe more. I lost count."

My eyebrows shot up and my jaw dropped. "Is that normal when you have a burst of inspiration?"

Running a hand over his face, he shook his head and looked down at the floor as if embarrassed.

I held out the song in my hand. "Is this about me?"

Defiant eyes raked over me, going from my feet to the top of my head. "They're all about you."

He said it so softly I almost didn't hear him. Not knowing the proper protocol for having two-hundred and sixty-seven songs written about you in a week, I held his gaze and mentally flipped through potential responses. *Thank you? Holy crap, that's weird?*

Why me?

"Rad, I…"

One second, I was looking down into his eyes, and the next, I was up against his body. He came out of the chair so fast I didn't even see him move. His arms wrapped around me, his mouth closing over mine. Pure carnal desire poured out of him. His lips were hot, warmer than the whiskey I'd downed earlier, and the kiss sucked the oxygen from my lungs.

Salty air stirred my nose, the ends of my hair lifting. I couldn't breathe, but I didn't want to. All I wanted was Rad.

Not just the beautiful, creative human, or the wild, stormy chaos demon. I wanted the mysterious, intangible thing that made him who he was. The one thing I could never touch.

His soul.

Two months ago, my world was stable, and my life was good. I'd left the past behind and made plans for the future. I'd been helping humans rather than hurting them and had found peace with my past mistakes.

Now, I was dying. I had two half-human blood slaves who were dying as well. I was the vamp queen of Chicago's Undead, and a rogue vampire I'd failed to kill wanted to wipe out the city's entire human population. I was Rad's sworn enemy, and he was duty-bound to sink a silver dagger in my heart.

On top of all of that, a ghost from my past was infecting my friends with mortal sins, driving them crazy. She'd found my Achilles' heel and was getting revenge for what I'd done to her.

I should have pulled back and pushed him away. If I gave in, he'd want to feed as well as have sex, and I couldn't afford to lose any more blood. Not until I decided what I was going to do about accepting Dru's offer. Since my decision affected Rad and Arman, I needed to lay the cards on the table for them, too.

But when I broke away from Rad's lips, he said, "I need you, Kali," and the hedonist in me rose to the task of quenching his unquenchable need.

THIRTEEN

I'm such a sucker. I never should have given into Rad's desire or my own. My life was already screwed up enough, and the timing was wrong on many levels, but I didn't care. The chance to stop things between us came and went in the blink of an eye. A single beat of my heart. I could no more control the lust pumping through my veins than I could make the sun set in the East.

So when Rad dragged me down into the chair, positioning me on his lap, I ground my pelvis against the swell of his jeans. When he slid his hands under my turtleneck and tickled my skin with his callused fingers, I raised the hem over my head, shucked the shirt, and then unhooked my bra. I wanted his mouth and skilled fingers touching me everywhere, and I wanted his skin bared to me.

Selfish and greedy, I ripped off his shirt, sunk my hands into his hair, and tugged his mouth to my breasts. As he locked on the first one, teasing it with his tongue and teeth, I took a choppy breath. "No drinking my blood today."

He murmured a response against the mound of flesh, his

rich voice sending a shocking vibration through to my heart. I shuddered and nearly orgasmed right there on the spot.

I hated to do it, but I disengaged my breast from his mouth. "What did you say?"

His attention stayed locked on my nipple, and one hand pressed at the small of my back, forcing my upper body closer. "Why not?"

Clamping onto his hair to keep his mouth off my breast, I shifted my hips and rocked back and forth on his lap, the ache between my legs nearly unbearable. I wasn't thinking straight and blurted, "Because I'm dying, and I can't afford to lose any more blood today."

He froze, those defiant eyes meeting mine, but now they were filled with shock and concern. "What the hell?"

Oops. I probably should have dropped that bomb later. "It's no big deal." The devil took me. I was such a liar, but at that moment, consumed with lust, I couldn't think straight. "I'll get it figured out, and we'll all be fine. I promise."

"Kali..."

I shushed him by putting a finger to his lips. "I said I'll figure it out." I replaced my finger with my mouth and kissed him hard, wanting to forget everything but the feel of his body against mine.

Each time he tried to talk, I launched a new attack. Good thing he was consumed with lust and snowballing desire, or I'd never gotten him to satisfy me. As it was, he would bring me to the brink of climax, regain control of his lust, and back off, trying to get me to cough up the facts about the blood problem. Just when I thought I was going to have to pin him to the floor and shove my panties in his mouth to keep him quiet, his will broke.

I'd always wanted to be human, to feel what humans felt. Being he was my blood slave, I felt what he felt. His emotions hit me in one magnificent sucking wave after another, pulling me under. Sure, I had emotions, but not like these vast, sweeping groundswells of sensation. Excitement, passion, hunger, anger...impressions of a million seeds of consciousness and awareness that had nothing to do with magic. The very essence of being human.

Naked and sweaty on the floor, papers clung to my damp skin as well as Rad's, wrapping us in his music. A strong breeze twisted through the room in conjunction with Rad's emotions, lifting songs from the furniture and keyboard and swirling them like paper versions of dust devils. At one point, Rad snapped his fingers, turning on the makeshift studio's computer. A song he'd recorded flowed through the speakers, volume rising with the movements of our bodies.

It was the song he'd started shortly after we'd gotten back together. He still hadn't finished it but had switched lines around and added another verse. The deep, gritty baritone of his voice filled my head while he finally knelt between my thighs and sunk, hot and enormous, inside me.

Listen to my music
Listen to my heart
Find the good within
The past no longer ripping us apart

I finally found my way
No words of mine can ever say
How much I miss you

He pulled back, sunk deeper, trailing kisses down my neck and whispering the words against my skin. A flash fire of heat and desire shot from the apex of my thighs, up my torso and right through my heart.

After all this time
After all the wrongs
I still care...

I opened my mouth to tell Rad I loved him, but the words died in my throat as he slammed into me over and over. Pain and pleasure mixed together as he worked me across the floor.

Listen to my music
Listen to its heart
Listen to the whisper
Hiding in the dark

Finally, he groaned deep in his chest, and we both came in a searing tidal wave of carnality and decadence. He locked his golden eyes with mine, and I saw heaven reflected inside them.

FOURTEEN

In the aftermath, we lay boneless, entangled in each other and remnants of Rad's chaotic inspiration. The song coming from the speakers ended, and the wind stopped, papers fluttering down on us like confetti.

Cole, rubbing sleep from his eyes, strolled in, stopped, and planted his eyes on the ceiling. "You two are worse than rabbits on Red Bull."

"Sorry we woke you," I said, not feeling one bit sorry. My nerve endings danced and hummed a sweet melody, the words of Rad's love song playing over and over in my head. Rad's emotions ebbed and flowed around me, and I might have floated away on them if his solid body hadn't been anchoring me to the floor.

Cole turned on his heel and, as he left, scratched the back of his head with the end of his gun. "Thought we were having a freakin' earthquake the way the castle was shaking."

Rad's stomach jiggled against mine, a laugh starting low and spreading to both of us. It felt good to laugh amidst all the shit coming down. Good to just lay there in his arms.

He trailed his fingers across one of my cheeks, the defiance gone from his eyes. His nostrils flared, and his pupils dilated. I knew what was coming before he said it. I could see the craving in the golden orbs, feel the hunger building inside him. "I can smell your blood."

What was it like to be consumed with such a ravenous appetite? To know your life depended on the blood of another? I tried to imagine it, but it went against every cell in my body. After breaking free from Maria's hold on me at seventeen, I vowed never to let anyone, supernatural or human, have that kind of influence over me again. "No feeding."

Rad lowered his hand, grabbed my wrist, and brought it to his lips. He kissed the healing cut from the previous night's feeding, where I'd slashed my wrist for him. Kissed the older scars that were nothing but silvery lines on my skin. A shiver ran down my spine.

"What's this about you dying?" he murmured against my wrist. His lips pressed their way to the palm of my hand. "Is that why your blood smells different?"

So he noticed, too. "Cole said my iron is low, and that's what's causing me to smell off. Dru thinks it's some type of withdrawal from Nudra's blood. I've gone nearly six weeks since Nudra injected me, and my body's having a weird reaction. We don't really know what's going on, only that it's screwing up my system."

"Screwing it up enough to kill you?"

"That's one of the theories."

Rad frowned, shifted off me, and helped me stand. My legs shook, but I still felt light and satisfied. He walked me upstairs to my bathroom without a word and drew me into the shower.

We stood together under the rainfall shower head, sharing the soap and enjoying a few minutes of tenderness. A rarity in our relationship. Rad asked questions about my blood disorder. I answered as best I could.

Once done with the shower, the boneless feeling from earlier clung to my limbs and I closed my eyes as Rad skillfully dried me with a soft, fluffy blue towel. He turned the towel on himself, buffing his skin with it. "What does Cole think of Dru's offer?"

Rad and Cole were usually at each other's throats but nonetheless seemed to respect each other. "That he's only making it to force me into having sex with him."

"Hunh."

"That's it? *Hunh?* The idea of me being a vamp's sex slave doesn't bother you?"

He dried his hair with the towel, tossed it on the floor. "It would bother me if I thought you'd accept the offer."

"I may have to in order to save you and Arman."

His hair stuck out in disarray. He headed for my walk-in closet. I followed, admiring his fit body, but my attention kept landing on the Noctifector tattoo between his shoulder blades. The peace filling my chest for the past hour dissolved in a rush as if the elaborate knife embedded in Rad's skin had come to life and cut it out of me. "Becoming Dru's blood slave won't save any of us."

Did he know something about demon and vampire blood the rest of us didn't? "Why is that?"

He dug through a black nylon duffel bag on the floor and drew out a pair of wrecked designer jeans, tugging them over his legs. Zipping the fly, he looked at me from under his bangs. "The minute he touches you, I'll kill him." He set his hands on his waist. "And then we're back to square one, needing a new blood donor."

Alrighty, then. I sauntered over, stood on my toes, and wrapped my arms around his neck. "Jealousy is a sin."

Rad grabbed me by the waist and jerked me closer. My breasts smashed into his chest, my toes skimming the floor. "If I were Dru, I'd make the same offer and do whatever it took to make you mine. This reeks of a trap, Kali. I'd lay my life on the line to keep you from dying, but I won't share you with a vampire. There has to be another way."

I teased his lips with mine. "Damon taught me years ago that there's always more than one solution to any problem. I just have to figure out an alternative."

"When you have those stomach pains, is it only when Dru's around?"

"Yes." Come to think of it, that was weird, too. "There were vamps at the club last night before Dru got there and I didn't react to them or Maddy when I was with her after we left the club."

"There you go. Maybe it's not a vampire thing as much as a Dru thing. He's trying to manipulate you."

The thought left me queasy. I disentangled from Rad, paced away. "But why? Why go to all this trouble to force me into being his blood slave. He can have any female he wants, supe or human. What's the big deal about me?"

Rad's gaze slowly perused my body, mouth quirking to one side. "You're unique. The Nocts know it. Damon knows it. Dru knows it. Hell, even Queen Maria knew it all those years ago."

Maria. I'd almost succeeded in putting her out of my mind. "She's back. I think."

The smirk disappeared. "Back? How? You killed her."

"I did." Locating a bra and underwear, I put them on, then dressed in black jeans and a black long-sleeved T-shirt while Rad gave me a perplexed stare. "She's back as a ghost. At first, I wasn't sure if it was well and truly her. I mean, I killed her in the old way, marking her body before destroying it, making sure her spirit was locked away and there was no one in the vicinity for it to escape into. It doesn't make sense." I shook my head. "But after this morning, there's no doubt in my mind she's back."

He located a T-shirt in his duffel and jerked it on. "What happened this morning?"

We walked out of the closet and into my bedroom. "Cole and I were in the parking lot at the Institute. Dru was there with his bodyguard and we were talking. Suddenly, the air got thick, and this ghost appeared in front of me. She spoke my name and brought my demon to life. It was Maria, Rad. The only thing that makes me doubt my sureness about that fact is that she sparkled."

He lifted both brows under his bangs.

"I know. Weird. Glowed is maybe a better term for it. I've only seen that type of glow once: when we went to see Lucifer."

"Angel light?"

I nodded. "Remember that soft light his body emanated?"

Rad suddenly avoided my eyes, brushing past me to look out the clear floor-to-ceiling window. The snow from that morning had stopped, and the freshly fallen snow in the cemetery below had already taken on a gray cast. "Kali, I need to tell you something."

My stomach did a hop and a skip. "Conversations that start with those words never end well for me."

My attempt at humor fell flat. He hooked his thumbs in his pockets and stared with unseeing eyes at the gray and white world below. "When we, you know, screw around? You glow when you..." He glanced across the room at me. "When you...you know."

"Yeah, right," I scoffed, but his face was serious.

Too serious.

The floor seemed to fall out from under my feet. I sat down

hard on the pile of blankets, crumpling papers with my ass. "Are you sure?"

He strolled over and dropped onto his knees in front of me. Took my hands in his. "You glow, Kali. When you climax. Even when we were kids back in Maria's court, the first time we did it, you lit up. Scared the shit out of me, but it was more beautiful than anything I'd ever seen. I've never seen anything like it since."

"Except with Lucifer."

His hands were warm and firm, holding me steady. "Remember what Lucifer said? About you and your origin?"

A crossbreed of good and evil. How could I forget?

Rad squeezed my hands. "In Nudra's coffin. Remember the light show?"

"But that would mean..."

Rad waited for me to finish. I couldn't. He did it for me. "You and Maria are both original vices."

FIFTEEN

I scrambled out of the room, went downstairs, and ran into Cole. He said something to me, but I didn't hear the words. My mind swam in muck, and fight mode had descended. I needed to hit something to work out the frustration and good old-fashioned rage eating away at me.

My home gym was equipped with lots of steel and mirrors. I hardly ever used it, preferring my workouts to include a fighting partner and finding one always available at the Institute.

Now, I needed that same kind of workout, but my options for partners were two men who'd do nothing but question me rather than go fisticuffs.

I didn't even take time to wrap my hands, I just busted loose on Bob, my life-like punching bag bolted to the basement floor. He was made of a heavy polystyrene substance that felt like a muscled human when punching him, and no matter how much abuse I gave him, he kept on smiling.

In Nudra's coffin, the first time Rad had tasted my blood after

I'd been infected, we'd created a light show that made the coffin glow. The first few times after that, when we fucked, sparks flew. I thought it was all part of our connection because of the blood.

I was wrong.

During our first light show in the coffin, I'd thought I glimpsed heaven. Crazy, right? Heaven is a pipe dream for demons and one I wouldn't waste time on anyway. If you're not sinning, you're not having fun. In fact, being evil at my core, the one place that would truly be hell for me is a place with nothing but goodness in it.

But oh, the seduction of that light. The seduction of heaven still existed, whether I admitted it or not. And if there was one thing I would never let Maria take from me, it was Rad and that connection.

I fired off punches, kicks, and full-body slams. Sweat poured down my back and made my hair hang in strands in front of my eyes. I yelled and grunted and pounded until my body begged, *non più*.

I ignored the begging and continued to attack Bob. Poor guy. My knuckles left bloody prints on his chin, my kicks busted off chunks of his body and sent his stuffing flying. The demon inside me roared her pleasure and grabbed his head, ripping it off.

It was at that point when two sets of strong hands grabbed me from behind, hauled me across the room, and pinned me against the padded wall. I fought, but Cole and Rad together created a formidable demon wall. Once or twice, I broke free from their grasps and got a punch in, but my strength left as fast as it had come. After one last bout of yelling, I yielded to their restraints and sank to the floor.

"Feel better?" Cole glanced over his shoulder at Bob, or rather, at what was left of my life-size punching bag, and hooked a thumb in his direction. "How come he gets to have all the fun?"

"Because you're too much of a wimp."

He smiled, gave Rad a wink. "You hungry?"

"Starved." And I was. My stomach was as empty as my now spent body.

Cole patted my cheek and motioned for Rad to help him lift me up. "That's my sweet demon."

Though exhausted, I had enough adrenaline flowing in my system to shove away their attempts to assist me upstairs. I made it just fine on my own. The last thing I heard before I climbed the stairs to my loft was Cole calling Outback Steakhouse with an order.

I showered again, going through the motions. Same with getting dressed. I bandaged my knuckles, then tore off the tape. Pain was good. Kept me angry.

I sunk into the blankets on my bedroom floor. The pillow smelled like Rad. I buried my nose in it and went to sleep.

Sometime later, I woke to Cole nudging me. The room was shadowed, and I could smell grilled steak and greasy fries. My stomach growled.

He handed me my cell phone. "It's Maddy."

"Yeah," I said into the phone. "What's up?"

Her voice was almost normal. A little snarky, but no more than usual. "*What's up? That's my line. You bailed on me and Arman last night, so what's up for tonight? Are we sniffing out the witch or what?*"

She knew I hadn't purposely bailed on her, that I'd been out of commission. I flexed my left hand, saw the knuckles had healed. My body felt stronger after the nap, but my attitude was still a bit prickly. I wanted to say, *Gee, Madison. A simple, 'Hello, Kali. How are you feeling?' would be nice since I was cold-cocked last night, discovered I'm dying from a sick twist on blood poisoning, and realized the entity who turned me into a walking torture machine at your age has come back for round two. And oh, by the way? She's also one of the seven deadly sins just like me!*

What I said instead was, "I'll meet you at the occult shop at seven."

I was too pissy to wait for her reply and hung up. For once, I wanted a friend to talk to. A girlfriend whose shoulder I could cry on.

Wimp. Facing down demons and evil supernatural creatures went with the territory of being the Bridge Council's enforcer and a vengeance demon for hire. I'd been doing it for years. Thick skin? Mine was refined steel. Rarely did anything in my line of work get to me.

But tonight, I was blown out. Tired of tackling one shitty situation after another.

Cole watched me with his intense warrior stare. Reached out and helped me up. "She freaked when I told her something at the psycho hospital got the jump on you last night. Shook her up but good."

"Yeah, I could tell she was worried about me."

"She puts on a decent tough girl act." He grinned. "Like someone else I know."

I brushed imaginary dust off my pants. "It's not an act. Not for me. It's real."

"Maddy knew if she asked how you were, you'd say fine. That's what you always say."

It still stung she hadn't asked. I wondered when I'd turned into such an emotionally needy demon. "I'm going to tackle Dalinda first, then Vicky and Toel."

"What about the blood problem?"

"What about it?"

"And Maria?"

I had another snarky comeback on the end of my tongue. Instead, I told the truth. "I need to tackle a couple of things I can control right now, Cole. Then I'll figure out what I'm doing about my blood and about Maria."

Cole understood my need to control something. He also understood what I was facing with Dalinda and Toel. "You can take the succubus, but you're too weak to face Toel on your own."

"That's why I have you," I said, walking out of the room and ignoring the mess inside my head. "Where's my steak? You didn't eat it, did you?"

In the kitchen, he reheated a plate full of steak and fries for me. Standing at the sink, I stared out the kitchen window at the cemetery, cut the rare steak into pieces, and inhaled them. Plenty of ghosts out there in the graveyard. Usually, they hid from me, not wanting me to send their spirit asses to some other plane.

I didn't bother them and they didn't bother me, but now I wondered if they could help with Maria. The internet was loaded with information about ghosts, but all of it was from humans. I needed real information from a direct source.

The French fries were limp and greasy. I ate them anyway. About halfway through the pile, Rad wandered in and snatched a fry from my plate. "Got you something."

He held out a long, skinny package, wrapped in fancy silver and blue paper with an enormous bow on top.

Another early Christmas present. Oh, joy. "What is it?"

"Open it."

Wiping my greasy fingers on a towel, I accepted the package with a sigh. It was surprisingly heavy and weighted on one end. As I tore off the paper and opened the box underneath, I caught sight of black metal. A flashlight?

My annoyance at receiving a Christmas present lifted. At least it was something functional.

"No way," I said as I slid the sleek tube out of its packaging. "Is this what I think it is?"

When Nudra had me kidnapped, his Mercenary demons had used a stun baton on me that packed enough electrified silver current to take out every supernatural in downtown Chicago. After I'd staked Nudra and become the owner of all his assets and estate, I'd searched high and low for one of those batons. Nudra had amassed enough weapons to fill the Department of Defense, from antique swords to modern-day surface-to-air missiles, but nowhere in his immense collection did he have a baton like that.

Rad nodded, smiling from ear to ear. "Merry Christmas."

I played with the on/off switch, tuned into the low-pitched buzz of the baton warming up, and grinned. "Where did you get this?"

One shoulder rose and fell. "A buddy of mine hooked me up with a supplier. There's only a dozen or so of these in circulation, but he tracked this one down. Got me a deal."

I looked at Rad, then at Cole, stroking the smooth, cool metal. "Who wants to go first?"

They both jumped back, hands in the air. I made a pouty face. "Come on, I gotta try it out on someone."

They exchanged a look, and while neither was going to let me zap them, they were both relieved at my return to normalness. Cole shook his head and motioned for me to follow him. "Come on, vengeance demon. Let's go find you a target."

I kissed Rad on the way out and practically skipped to the front door, snatching up my cape and putting it on. Such a simple thing could make a girl's rotten day turn positively delightful. Like finding a twenty dollar bill you'd forgotten you'd tucked into your purse or uncovering your favorite candy bar behind a cereal box in the pantry.

He followed me to the door, grabbed my hand, and pulled me around for another kiss. "What about Maria?" he said when we parted.

Fear for me filled his eyes. I touched the side of his face. If Maria was back, she'd love nothing better than to get her hands on him. She'd had a thing for Rad, and because he'd been in love with me, he'd blown her off repeatedly. She hated him as much as she hated me. "Whether it's her or not, we need to act like it is and take precautions. Lay low and watch your back. Anything strange happens, call me or Damon."

Strained impatience lined his face. He scrubbed a hand over his features. "Strange? I'm living three lives, every one of them strange. I'm losing my mind trying to keep all of them straight. One minute, I'm performing on stage for thousands of people; the next, I'm helping the Slayers wipe out a nest of Erinyes crones, and after that..." He ran his fingers over my cheek, down my neck. "I'm watching you glow like the Madonna underneath me."

Was it the blood withdrawal talking, or had Maria already infected him with her sins? Maybe he was just well and truly tired of being a rock god, Noctifector, *and* my secret lover. "I know it's hard to balance all three but we have to keep our relationship a secret, just like you have to keep your human fame and fortune separate from your Noctifector life."

"It's like Maria's court all over again. Us hiding. Keeping secrets from those closest to us. Looking over our shoulders twenty-four-seven. Jumping at every shadow. I hate it. I want the world to know you're mine. I want to protect you and show you off at the same time. Wipe out Maria and tell the Noctifectors to go to hell."

I squeezed his arm. Hugged him. "When the time is right,

maybe we can make that all happen. But not now, not tonight. For tonight, you stay here, work on your music, and dream of me, okay?"

He blew out a heavy sigh. "The band and I are heading to New York tonight for the weekend. We've got some promo gigs —a Christmas concert at the Garden and an appearance on one of those god-awful morning shows. We'll be back Monday night."

The thought of him so far away made my stomach tight. Now I wondered when I'd become so clingy. "Can you go that long without feeding?"

"I've got a bottle of your blood stashed at my suite at the Blackstone. I'll pace my drinking and do the best I can."

"By Monday night, I'll have this all figured out. Promise."

His eyes darkened, and he clutched my arm hard. "Don't take Dru's offer because of me. We'll ride this blood thing out together, and worst case? You go down, I go with you. We face this together. Got it?"

The sentiment was generous, but I couldn't condemn Rad or Arman to a death sentence because of my stubbornness. "I can handle Dru whether or not I take his blood."

Rad searched my gaze. His eyes reflected thirst, hunger, but he was fighting it with sheer willpower. "How?"

Flicking on the stun gun, I aimed the buzzing, arching end at a nearby floor lamp and hit the button. A bright zigzag of silvery light danced across the open floor. The metal pole exploded in a display of blue fireworks, and I laughed low in my throat. "Oh, I'll think of something."

SIXTEEN

Dalinda was first on my list of jobs. Thinking about the coming confrontation cleared my head and gave me a sense of purpose.

Leave it to Damon to spoil my fun. "Under the circumstances, do you think it wise to spend the entire day at your home rather than the Institute?" he said on the car's speaker phone as Cole drove me to Dalinda's house in north Evanston.

"I had a warrior demon, a Noctifector, and a psychic one-man wrecking crew protecting me. Plus all the high-tech security I put in last month. I was entirely safe. So yes, I thought it was wise."

"And yet it did not solve either of the pressing issues you face at the moment."

"Tarrying at the Institute while Kirill performed a physical exam on me was unlikely to solve those issues either."

Cole glanced at me, a half-smile on his face at my professional-sounding tone and Damon-worthy choice of words.

"Alexandru believes you have less than forty-eight hours

before the withdrawal impedes your ability to control your demon."

"And he knows this how? He's basing his statements on a couple of ancient legends about demon-vampire hybrids and, I'm guessing, his own interests. Manipulating a vengeance demon to get her under his thumb is a vampire's wet dream. You can't take what he says as gospel, Damon. Surely you know that."

Damon's voice rose ever so slightly. "The Undead's cooperation with the Institute has been a huge success so far. Why would Alexandru jeopardize that?"

Huge success was stretching it. And it was because of me and my sacrifice to lower my standards to accept the role as vamp queen that produced the *coaptation*. What the hell kind of word was that, anyway? "Since when does an archdemon believe a vamp Master over his own kind?"

Silence met our ears. Cole shot me another look, this one saying I'd stepped in a pile as big as the Sears Tower. I rolled my eyes. "I want to believe Dru has my best interests at heart, boss, but I don't. You, of all people, know me and how I handle things. If I have forty-eight hours, then I'll be putting every one of them to good purpose to figure out what my options are. Meantime, I have a job to do. Several of them, in fact. I will check in with you later."

I disconnected and slouched back in the leather seat. Outside, a new snowstorm threatened, turning the dark sky above the city's lights into a roiling mass of clouds.

Cole chuckled. "He's so going to have my ass for not bringing you in."

"What's new?"

"One of these days, he'll assign you a new bodyguard—one who isn't a pushover like me. Then what will you do?"

I hadn't thought of that. "Resign, probably."

Dalinda's house was a couple of miles from Northwestern University. The neighborhoods morphed from college housing to private residences, all blanketed with the slick, wet snow falling from the clouds. Soft, welcoming lights beckoned from inside the houses on Dalinda's block, but her house was dark.

On her front porch, I took off one glove and laid my hand on the house's wooden shakes. A slight buzzing rose from the ground and sifted through the framing and insulation to answer my demon's magic. No one was home, but the place was warded with a spell.

A security system also sent off silent warnings to my hand. The smell of the plastic sensor panel inside the door gave me the impression the system was brand-spanking new.

"Ever known a succubus to have a mundane security system?" I asked Cole, who stood behind me watching the street and the neighboring houses.

His gun hung by his leg on the off chance he might need it. "Must be expecting human criminals."

A succubus could handle any human with a simple touch. "She's not here, and if she was, she's a better security system than a mundane one. She must be using it to guard something else while she's not here."

"Something a human might steal?"

I shrugged even though he wasn't looking at me. Whatever Dalinda was hiding wasn't my problem.

Since I'm not a witch, disabling the magic wards was a touch trickier than dismantling the mundane security system, but I found the tail end of the spell after a minute of feeling my way around the house's structure, gave it a zap, and basically blew its fuse. Once that was taken care of, I sent another wave of magic through the outside wall where the mundane system's panel existed on the interior and overrode that electrical system as well.

On the street, the snow continued to fall with wild abandon, the neighbors tucked securely in their houses. I opened the front door after picking the deadbolt with my magic and let us inside.

The second we stepped over the threshold, I was hit with the human scent of sweat and sex. Dalinda's smell—sickly sweet and reminding me of fruit-flavored cough syrup—also assailed my nose. Cole made a low, nauseated sound in the back of his throat, and I had to breathe through my cape's collar to keep from choking.

The outside street lights threw filmy illumination on a living room with high ceilings and a brick fireplace. Eschewing the lights, I used my demon vision to see more clearly. I couldn't tell for sure, but the room appeared to be a cacophony of raspberry-colored everything. Curtains, couches, throw pillows, and even the large area rug appeared to be pinkish red. Between the smells and the endless color, it was claustrophobic.

The human smell got stronger as I weaved a path through the kitchen (also decorated in pinks and reds) and into a back bedroom. Layers of raspberry-colored furniture and accessories? Check. Satin sheets on a king-size bed? Check.

Human chained to the posts? Check.

Dalinda was hiding something all right. Her latest succubus treat was lying in the center of the bed, a blanket thrown over his splayed-out body—and thank Satan for that. He slept with his head turned toward the single window in the room, the cheek I could see gaunt and sunken.

For a moment, I felt sad. I'd succumbed to a succubi's magic once, and I was a demon. Sure, I'd been an impressionable young female at the time, but at least I'd had the ability to overcome her magic eventually. A human couldn't, no matter how strong they were or how determined.

Don't take this personally, I reminded myself. *Don't get emotional.*

A vengeance demon's creed.

Jeremy Stewart's features matched the picture in the file at Sweet Investigations—the one his wife had given me when she hired me to take this job. In the picture, though, Mr. Stewart was the healthy all-American high school quarterback turned financial advisor. Now, his body was wasting away from Dalinda feeding on him. His human life was a shambles. And according to Di, his wife had fallen under Dalinda's spell as well.

But where was Mrs. Stewart? Where was Dalinda?

I called the Institute and requested a transfer for the man on the bed, all the while running various revenge scenarios through my mind. He'd be taken to a medical facility that would help him regain his health, if not his mind. Again, I felt sadness and regret. If I'd gotten to Dalinda the previous night, it probably wouldn't have made any difference, but anger at Maria for getting the jump on me mixed with anger at myself for letting her keep me from my job.

After assuring ourselves Sara Stewart was not chained anywhere on the premises, Cole and I ventured back into the living room to wait for Dalinda. After an hour, I grew impatient, both for her return and for the Institute's transporter. Impatience and anger don't make me fidget, though. If anything, I became calm—a charged calm, filled with the quiet intensity of a cat waiting for its prey.

When I heard the distinctive sound of a garage door opening, I smiled.

The succubus was home.

My prey was within striking distance.

Dalinda blew in the door connecting the garage to the kitchen and flipped on the overhead light. I stood by the living

room fireplace and saw her set down a handful of plastic shop-
ping bags on the counter before she came into the room, unbut-
toning her long, wool coat. The color? A bright pink raspberry.

Cole sat half-hidden in a lounge chair in the far dark
corner, gun lying on one thigh. I made no attempt to hide, but
Dalinda was in her own world, brushing snow from her hair as
she crossed the living room to reset the security alarm. She was
reaching for the keypad when she finally noticed the light
was out.

"Shit," she whispered under her breath and slowly turned
around to face me.

Dalinda was no small female. She was taller than me by a
good six inches and plump all over. I was feeling pretty pissy at
this point and couldn't have cared less about Damon's insistence I always stay professional whether I was working for the
Bridge Institute or Sweet Investigations. Bringing my fingers
and thumbs together, I raised my protective magic and put my
gloves back on. Then I took three steps forward, grabbed her
around the neck, and slammed her against the wall, right next
to a cheap reproduction of Klimt's Lovers done in a mauve-
tinged wash. "Dalinda Kroning, vengeance is mine."

She clutched my extended arm and reached for my neck as
I held her against her will and exerted pressure on her throat.
This wasn't the vengeance I had planned, but blowing off a
little steam and roughing her up would make a point before I
even got started. Even as she fought to free herself, she tried to
turn her succubus charms on me. I batted her hand away from
my neck, then my face. If she touched my skin, she could
enchant me.

Or so she thought.

It was laughable for an ordinary succubus to assume she
could beguile me. My demon jeered. Volante, belted around
my waist, pulsed, begging to be turned loose. I held Dalinda a

moment longer, letting my demon stare her down, and witnessed the change in her demeanor. Her eyes widened, and her body drew back from mine as if she could compress all that plumpness into a smaller package—one that might be less noticeable.

I gave her a little shake and unleashed Volante with my free hand. "The Stewarts are no longer your playthings. Your love-fest with them is over, and if I catch you accosting either of them again, I will cut your hands off."

"You...don't...understand..." she gasped.

I released her neck, and she slumped to the floor. Uncoiling Volante in an intimidating, if harmless, crack of the whip, I stepped back to let her stand. The gloved hand that had held her against the wall sizzled with her enthralling magic. Without the glove, it would have penetrated my skin and gave me a warm, fuzzy feeling. As it was, my palm itched, and my fingers tingled as if they were asleep. "I understand quite well. You succubi are all alike. Only this time, you messed with the wrong human male and seduced his wife when she made trouble for you. But this ends here, tonight."

Her hands splayed on the floor as she pushed herself into a sitting position. Her brows drew down in confusion. "You damaged the ward. How did you do that? The witch said it was impassable."

Up until a few months ago, I didn't care much about witches. Witches use magic and bend it to their will, but they're human, not supernatural, and they rarely gave me trouble. Until Victoria, my witchy, bitchy blood slave, who raised Lilith from hell.

I cut Vicky's tie to me by allowing Maddy to turn her into a vampire. That also cut Vicky's magical tie to Lilith since it killed the human in her. Not my finest day for saving human life, but sacrificing Vicky allowed me to exorcise Lilith back to

hell. A lot more humans would have died—all of them, in fact—
if I hadn't pulled that trigger.

Cole walked up beside me. "What witch?"

Dalinda's plump body shook like Jell-O as she stared at me.
"She said you'd tamper with it, but you wouldn't be able to
break it. And as soon as you touched it, she would know."

"Trap," Cole murmured. He grabbed my elbow and started
dragging me toward the back entrance. "Time for us to go."

Yanking my arm from his strong grasp, I planted my feet.
"What does the witch look like? Crazy, kinky hair or sparkly?"

"Sparkly?" Cole harrumphed. "Seriously?"

The succubus got a faraway look in her eye. "Long red
hair..." She shivered, and her Jell-O shakes looked like a tiny
earthquake. "Cold. She was so cold."

The Undead were ungodly cold. I couldn't understand
humans' fixation with them. They felt like dead fish to me.

Ghosts were cold, too. The body Maria was ghost riding
was a witch with long red hair. Was it too much to ask for a
simple, straightforward answer? "Why did the witch want to
trap me?"

Dalinda raised a hand and pointed toward the bedroom.
"She made me do that to Jeremy. When you didn't come right
away, she forced me to seduce his wife as well. Said you'd have
to come as enforcer of the Bridge Council." Her eyes were wide
and pleading. "I didn't want to, I swear. It was her. Please don't
cut off my hands."

"Did this witch have a name?" Cole again.

As the succubus shook her head, she seemed to draw
further into herself. "She had the Mark of the Beast. Right
here." She touched her forehead with one hand. "I couldn't see
it until I touched her, and even then, her glamour was strong. I
felt it more than saw it."

Mark of the Beast? Hadn't seen one of those since...

"Oh, hell, no." I closed my eyes in frustration. Opened them again to Cole's curious stare. "Did she mark you?" I said to Dalinda. "Anywhere?"

"No." If anything, the succubus scrunched up even more, moving her body parts as far away from me as possible.

Which only made me suspect the opposite of her denial. "Prove it."

"I don't know what you're talking about."

Cole stepped to the side of a nearby window and covertly glanced out at the falling snow and lawn. "I don't care if she's marked by every entity in heaven and hell both, we need to get the fuck out of here."

True, that. But I couldn't leave Dalinda behind if Maria had marked her in any way, shape, or form. Letting my demon out for a stroll, I reached forward and laid my hand on her fore-head. Sure as shit, an electrical charge jumped from her skin to my gloved hand. The soft leather did nothing to stop the white-hot heat from searing my hand and racing up my arm. My demon arched her back and rode the current.

I snapped my eyes shut, and on the inside of my eyelids, dozens of occult symbols and runes danced in a black and gray rainbow over images of hellish faces. Demons I had known, some I didn't recognize. Their true faces, rarely shown on Earth, bled into skulls and other monstrosities.

Maria hadn't cursed Dalinda with *the* Mark...she didn't have that type of power. That was my domain—or had been when I'd lived at her court. Instead, Maria had simply put her own twisted demon mark on the succubus. A little succubus-on-succubus violence.

Some humans believe hell exists only in people's minds. Demons know the mind is the most powerful tool on earth or any plane. All of our minds are subconsciously linked because humans and supernaturals come from the same origin. That origin—God, the Universe, whatever you prefer to call it—has an aberrant sense of humor.

Good thing I have an aberrant logic to match. Jerking my demon's leash, I reeled her in from her pain/pleasure orgy with Maria's mark and tugged Dalinda up from the floor. "You're coming with us."

Dalinda fought me. "Not my hands! Don't take my hands!"

I snapped the whip again and Volante's handle trembled in my hand. Dalinda trembled in the other. "Don't make me repeat myself, D. You're coming with us."

Cole shook his head in exasperation. "We don't have room for her in the TT."

"She can sit on your lap."

Both War demon and Succubus looked horrified. I pushed her ahead of me toward the kitchen. Volante floated off the ground as if I were walking a ghost dog. As we reached the door to the garage, she went rigid.

Merde.

I held up a hand to signal Cole. He gave me a chin-up acknowledgment. Motioning Dalinda into a corner, I flipped off the kitchen light and sniffed the air.

Nothing unusual. No trace of witch, demon, or supernatural, just the scents of Dalinda's house, the slowly receding fumes of her car, and the almost odorless, clean smell of snow.

My gut didn't care what my nose said. Something was off.

A sharp pain, like claws digging into my intestines, cut through my abdomen. I held back the scream jammed in my throat and clutched my stomach. Forced my chest to breathe through the agony as I motioned Cole to look out the window.

Moving like an oversized cat, he snugged up to the small, square kitchen window and peered out. His face went totally blank, and I knew we were in trouble.

Big trouble.

Without pause, I hauled out my phone, sent a text to Damon and Dru with nothing but Dalinda's address. They knew my shorthand. Knew to send backup. Whether that backup would arrive in time remained to be seen.

The burning sensation in my stomach didn't subside, and my demon, still sensitive from her encounter with Maria's mark, raged inside at the pain. Not that she didn't enjoy it. Like all demons, pain brought pleasure as well as torment.

"Is it Dru?" I ground out softly. Cole wouldn't have had that kind of reaction if it was. Sure, he hated vampires—who didn't he hate?—but I'd been around him long enough to know his tells. The blank face was one of those.

He didn't answer. At least not verbally. Without taking his attention from the window, he waved his gun at me in a *get over here* motion.

I crossed the linoleum, staying out of the faint moonlight filtering through the glass to slip up beside him. The sight that greeted me in the backyard made my face go slack as well.

Dozens of Undead, all dressed in long, black trench coats, faced the house in rows of five. None of them moved, and every one had a white film over their eyes.

Toel's minions. Half-vampire, half-zombie, they creeped me the hell out. Vicky had no doubt reanimated their human corpses and Toel had then turned them.

Ick.

The wind gusted and blew through the sparse line of trees, driving snow into their faces. No one blinked. They stared straight ahead, watching the house like white-eyed zombie watchdogs.

Cole left the kitchen, came back with news I didn't like. "Out front too. At least another dozen of them, doing nothing but standing guard."

"You ever see *I, Robot*?" I asked.

"Course I saw it. Will Smith kicks ass. I always substitute the robots for vampires in my mind when I watch it."

"Me, too." There *was* a strange similarity. "You know that scene where Smith's character is in the warehouse looking at a thousand VS5's?"

"A thousand and one," Cole corrected.

The one being Sonny, the robot Smith's character was hunting. "Yeah, that one. That's what they remind me of. They're like drones, waiting for the command to move. They are tied to Toel. He must be ecstatic."

"So, are they zombies or vampires?"

"Depends on what Vicky and Toel did to create them, but my gut says both. Vicky is good at raising things. Who knows? Maybe they're a new kind of demon spawn."

Cole grunted in disbelief. Another cramp racked my intestines, and I flinched. He shot me a concerned look. "These vamps causing you pain too?"

"Not them," I said as I thought about Vicky's trap. I had no trouble identifying the Undead population in general from the tug of their blood calling to mine, but this was like Dru's presence. Dru, a Master vamp born from Vlad the Impaler. "Shit," I said.

"What?"

"Toel Chase, Vampire King of the Western United States. He's here."

SEVENTEEN

Human politics are a mess, but the politics of the Undead are a quagmire of backstabbing, closed-door deals, coup d'états, and blackmail. Their canons of rules, regulations, and ceremonies make the Catholic Church look like child's play.

Being queen of the Central U.S. Undead population and having sworn allegiance to Vlad when he was still alive did not spare me from Toel's desire to depose me. Likewise, being a demon did not spare me from the politics. Rather, I'd spent a good deal of time since my coronation sidestepping vampire politics, thanks to Dru's help, and another good deal of time hunting Toel. The night of my coronation, he'd disappeared when a group of Noctifectors, led by my Rad, stormed the place and disrupted our fight. I'd regretted letting him get away every second since then.

As the cat inside my stomach used my intestines as a scratching post, it was the memory of that night that flashed across my mind. I'd allowed Toel to bait my demon into making an appearance because he'd pushed me to my limits. I wanted to tear him limb from limb, and I wanted to cause him as much pain as possible. We had been inside Carpathia House, no humans nearby, and my demon had been itching for a fight.

She got her chance, but because of Rad and the Noctifectors, she didn't get to finish the job. Thing was, she did leave her mark on Toel, and that was suddenly in the forefront of my mind.

I gasped and bent over as fresh agony ripped through me. In the dim room, my knees buckled and hit the tiled floor. A checkerboard of dots danced along my peripheral vision. Even my demon struggled to get away. The sensation was unnerving, like I was splitting in two.

Cole's voice came from far away. He grabbed my arm and lifted me to a standing position. He was talking, but to my ears, it sounded muffled and didn't make sense. All I wanted to do was lie down on the cool floor tiles and curl into a ball.

When Dru was near, my stomach rebelled and hurt enough to get my attention, but this was taking it up three notches. My head swam, my legs shook, and dizziness made the sink in front of me appear to rise and fall as if it rode a wave. I grabbed onto the countertop with both hands and spit blood from my mouth.

Blood. The night of the coronation. There'd been a lot of blood that night. Vampires had died. I'd bitten a chunk out of Toel's neck...

"Oh, no. No, no, no, no." I clung to the counter and blinked back the dots. A soft noise echoed in my ears, sounding like fine-grit sandpaper rubbing over my eardrums. *Shish-shish. Shish-shish. Shish-shish.*

The sound of my heartbeat.

The feel of magic. The taste of blood on my tongue.

Shish-shish, shish-shish. My heartbeat, my blood, responding to the call of a sire vamp to his underling.

"Kali." Cole half-dragged, half-carried me to the tiny table and sat me in a chair. He kneeled in front of me. "What the hell is going on?"

"It's Toel," I whispered, my teeth chattering like I was outside in the winter storm without clothes. In actuality, my body was burning up. Sweat broke out along my hairline and ran down the back of my neck. Waves of heat, invisible to the naked eye, but readily apparent to my demon, flowed off my skin. I was suffocating, and the cold, wet snow outside held definite appeal. If I could just throw myself in it and stop this awful burning...

"You said that already." Cole shook me this time, interrupting my dream of bathing in the snow. "I know Toel's out there. How can I help you?"

I couldn't make my mouth form all the words flooding my brain, the most prevalent still being *no*. I'm not one to live in denial, but this was one instance where denial was the pick *del giorno*. "Not Nudra." I pointed to my stomach and hoped my shorthand would make sense. "Toel."

Cole squinted and tilted his head in confusion. Then, as if my crazy brain flashed a picture over the top of his head, his body stilled. The expressionless poker face returned. "That's not possible." He felt my forehead with his hand as if I were a child running a fever. "You're delusional from the pain."

The splitting sensation tore through me again, my demon trying to extricate herself through the magical bars of her prison. In the past twenty-four hours, I'd come to believe anything was possible, and at the moment, I knew Dru had spoken the truth to Damon about my withdrawal. I was losing control of my demon.

If she got loose, there was no putting the genie back in the bottle. Right and wrong did not exist for her, only desire. She had no moral quandaries, no soul. She was the essence of the seven deadly sins and the top predator on the earthly supernatural food chain. Chicago would be one big sandbox of human toys for her if she succeeded. "Need...silver...knife."

Cole's jaw clenched. "Bullshit. I'm here to save your life, not take it." He shook me again, hard enough to rattle my teeth. "You will keep that demoness under control, Kali. You hear me? Do not let her out. You're the strongest vengeance demon in the western hemisphere, so quit overthinking this and just kick some ass."

Without waiting for any response, he released me, grabbed Dalinda, and shoved her at my feet. She whimpered, her fearful eyes glaring up at Cole even as she tried to slide away from me. He grabbed her by the hair and put his face nose-to-nose with her. "Put your Satan-loving succubus hands on her and relieve her pain. Now!"

Her gaze ping-ponged between us. "But, I..."

Cole held his gun to her temple. His eyes were hard and flat. "The only reason I don't kill you right now is because you can help her. Your choice. Put your hands on her or die."

Dalinda bit her bottom lip and surveyed my body, looking for a prime spot to touch me. She started to remove my gloves in order to take my hands, but I reached for hers and jammed them under my cloak and against my stomach.

She opened her magic a crack, unwilling to go full bore. I couldn't blame her, but I was running out of time. Using my hands to continue pressing hers against my stomach, I accessed my magic and let it flow over her, strong, possessive, and demanding. I truly didn't think this would work, but if we were going to try it, we were going all in.

She gasped and tried to jerk away when my earth magic hit her. My hold was too strong, though, and within seconds, she succumbed to the exquisite thrill of exchanging our magics. My pain flooded into her, but so did the power high of my magic—a high no succubus never came close to when feeding off humans.

At the same time, her seductive magic lured my demon back. The invisible but captivating succubus venom transferring from her hands to my stomach flooded me with desire, releasing endorphins in my brain with the speed and efficiency akin to Rad's ardent love-making. The pain subsided, or rather, it dulled. It was still there but masked by her efforts.

It wouldn't be enough. "Restraints," I muttered to Cole. "In the bedroom."

He read my shorthand again with the ease of a long-time companion. "Keep your hands on her," he told Dalinda as he maneuvered me out of the kitchen chair and into his arms.

In the bedroom, he laid me beside Jeremy Stewart, removed my cape, and switched the restraints from the human's wrists and ankles to mine. Mr. Stewart didn't wake up.

I hated the feeling of the leather cuffs, the heavy clinking sound of the chains, and the loss of control confinement instilled in me. A rush of memories from Maria's torture chamber rose in my mind, ghosts coming back to haunt me. The evil inside me clawed her way closer to the top.

"Get...out," I said through clenched teeth to Cole. "Take the human...the succubus...clear the block."

Cole withdrew the stun baton from my cape and stuck one of my cherry wood stakes inside his jacket. Dalinda's hands were still on me, but I could tell she was losing the war against my pain. Her hands trembled on my stomach; her face was pale and drawn above me. Her scent had morphed from sugary sweet to briny—my true demon nature scared her.

Smart female.

My demon smiled and clawed harder, wanting to turn the tables on the succubus and suck the life out of her.

"I'm not leaving you," Cole said. "End of discussion."

"You have to." He wasn't looking at me, and if I'd had a free hand, I would have smacked him to get his attention. A burning sting zipped down my spine, making my back arch off the bed. "Cole...I can't hold her back...any...longer."

The tone of my voice made him look. He frowned, finally losing the unemotional front. A war waged behind his eyes. He'd sworn to stay with me and protect me, but how could he protect me from the one thing that made me who I was?

My body bucked on the bed, my teeth shearing off enamel and my hands and feet straining against the restraints. "Get out! Now!"

Cole motioned Dalinda away and she jumped from the bed, looking like an actress in a horror film. Eyes huge, fear clearly written on her face. She rubbed her hands as if they itched or burned and stumbled backward until she hit the wall.

Tears pushed against my eyeballs, the pressure too great. Magic burst through me into the room, a crack of loud thunder echoing over the house so loudly that the bedroom mirror broke and shattered into dozens of tiny missiles. They drove jagged points into Dalinda and Cole, bringing a scream from Dalinda and colorful swearing from my bodyguard.

The last time I'd let my inner demon free with no restraints was when I'd confronted Maria and taken revenge on her. I took revenge for my family, for Rad, for all the innocents...and when I was finished, there was nothing left of her. Almost nothing left of me. For months along the southern coast of Italy, earthquakes and tsunamis erupted from the force of our fight and her eventual annihilation.

Before I'd attacked Maria, I hadn't realized my full potential. During the years in her court, I'd nourished my demon and fine-tuned her abilities, but it was easy when my prey was given to me on a daily basis. When there was nothing personal about the pain I inflicted. It was a job, one I performed well and took pride in. But with Maria, it went beyond personal. The rage, the hate I had ignored for so long, became profoundly intimate. I'd spent those years in her court guarding my private thoughts, ignoring the inner conflict she caused inside me. So when all that was stripped away, and I had nothing left to lose, the predator in me became a ferocious nightmare.

Cole had never seen my true nature. What he'd witnessed of my demon during some of our more intense workouts was a tenth of what she could do. Since her last period of freedom, I'd kept her on a sturdy leash.

Now she was breaking that leash. So close...

The house shook. Dishes in the kitchen fell and crashed on the floor. The pictures decorating Dalinda's bedroom walls jumped from their nails and sailed through the room, Frisbee-style. The succubus fled. Cole looked defeated. My demon howled her delight.

Taking the stake out of his jacket, Cole slapped it into one of my hands. His fingers brushed across my skin. Being a demon, he burned hotter than humans, just like I did, but his skin was cooler than mine. So much so, in fact, his touch felt like a soothing splash of water. "Then you use her, Kali, and kill every last one of them hell-damned vampires."

Vampires. God, I hated them as much as Cole did. And the one I hated the most had some kind of power over me. I'd underestimated him too many times before, ending up here, in this situation.

Mai più. Never again.

My hand tightened on the stake, and I shivered. The feel of it in my hand, the determination in Cole's eyes, the touch of his fingers against the pulse beating wildly at the base of my wrist... a renewed sense of purpose rose, fighting the inner demon for control. She was full-on evil, but I'd had two hundred and eighty-some years of training. Of holding her back just like the restraints now wrapped around my wrists and ankles. Of building my resistance to her dangerous nature and tenacious attempts to set herself free.

I had one motto when it came to my demon: *Mai arrendersi.*

Never back down.

"Free me," I said to Cole, my voice hoarse but louder than it had been.

He hesitated for half a heartbeat, then released the wrist blade from its sheath on his left arm. The knife sang as it shot out, and in one fluid motion, he cut through the leather straps binding me, nicking my skin and drawing blood. Next went the ankle straps.

My demon purred her approval at Cole. The restraints wouldn't have held her down for long anyway.

But now I definitely had to pull out all the stops to trick her back into her cage.

The moment Dalinda had removed her hands, the wicked pain had returned, but because my demon had invaded so much of me again, she was absorbing it to spur on her power. I needed her to keep soaking it up. At the same time, I had to keep her from growing stronger.

Or at least redirect her end game.

Like all demons, she craved human blood. Craved taking over human bodies and bending them to her will. In some ways, all demons were ghost riders like Maria, using others to draw more power, more energy to themselves. We fed off their wills, their very essence, because they were made in the image of God...nothing more powerful on any plane...and we were created from the earth. Where they were filled with souls, we were filled with sin. Undesirable, harmful, and destructive, we lived to ruin them, and, in doing so, fulfill their insatiable desires, at least temporarily, by absorbing their life force.

In other words, we were the worst kind of druggies, needing endless hits to feel even a tenth of the high we constantly craved.

We also enjoyed destroying humans. Reducing them to dust. Demons considered themselves the indigenous population. Humans were the invaders, the ones trying to take over our world even though they didn't believe that was true. They considered Earth to be their domain and hell to be ours. Thus, the Noctifectors, the Catholic Church, and others, were always trying to send us "back" to hell. Demons considered Earth an extension of hell, not a separate existence.

Damnat quod non intelligunt. They condemn what they do not understand. For us, that meant a constant fight to stay topside.

Lucky for us, humans were easy to infect with sin. Easy to manipulate. Easy to kill. And yet, they continued to survive.

Not just survive, *thrive.*

Unlike my fellow demons, I admired that tenacity, but the evil monster inside me wanted human blood, human sacrifice. I had to redirect that hunger to Toel and his minions.

They were banging on the doors now. Clawing at the windows. "Get the human and succubus down below," I growled at Cole, holding my breath against the smell of Jeremy Stewart nearby. Fortunately, Dalinda had left little of his human essence intact. To my demon, he resembled a piece of dry leather rather than a juicy raw steak.

Cole picked up Mr. Stewart and flung him over his shoulder. "Dalinda's a lost cause. I'll put him downstairs and come back."

There was no guarantee I wouldn't lose control again and

kill everyone inside that house, vampire, demon, or human. "Stay down there with him or risk your life."

My bodyguard grinned. "And miss you bringing it all over their punk asses?"

He disappeared, and I heard the pounding of his booted feet on a set of wooden stairs. My senses were going crazy. The smell of old blood and grave dirt assaulted me as the doors and windows gave out under the minions' attacks. My stomach roiled, cramping hard, but I rode the pain, accepting it instead of fighting it.

Raising one of my bleeding wrists to my nose, I inhaled the scent of my blood. I closed my eyes and concentrated, drawing out the individual elemental traces of the minerals and the blended magics. I hadn't noticed it before, but with Toel close by, I could now detect the hint of his stench inside me as well as outside the house. The dead seaweed tang of his magic, the ancient odor of his blood.

What I'd assumed before was the smell of Nudra's blood mixed with mine, I now recognized was the heady tang of Toel's bloodline. He and Dru had different mothers but shared Vlad's Undead DNA. Like an expensive vampire perfume, the top notes were diverse, but the base and middle notes matched.

I sicced my demon on that smell. I promised her she could have her fill of humans after she wiped out the enemies wanting to hurt her.

A lie, of course, but one that worked.

Toel's minions burst through the house in a flurry of snow, leather, and fangs, and I slid the cherry wood stake under a pillow. Their nostrils flared as they smelled my blood. In my ears, the *shishing* sound of my heartbeat grew louder. Toel was close.

I sat on the bed and bowed my head, Volante humming

around my waist and my demon waiting with edgy anticipation. We were all ready for a fight.

Toel knew my fighting style, so I needed the element of surprise. When his minions swarmed the bedroom, I stayed on the bed, hands up and head bowed in subjugation. My version of waving a white flag as they closed ranks on me, making sure I didn't escape.

I sensed Vicky before Toel, her magic confident but uneven as she entered the bedroom, her long cloak making a sweeping noise as it brushed the wooden floor. "It worked! My protection spell nailed your demon ass. I bet you thought it was for Dalinda, didn't you?" Her flippant laughter grated on my nerves. "You thought you'd seen the last of me after the party, but guess what?"

She stopped in front of me and had the *cajones* to reach out and grab my chin with her cold, Undead fingers. Jerking my head up, she forced me to look her in the eye. Her fangs were bared, and her eyes glittered with manic light. "Witch or vampire, doesn't matter. I'm more powerful than you'll ever be, and I'm taking over as queen of Chicago's vampires."

The fact she would touch me pissed me off. The idea she thought she could usurp my position made me laugh. A part of me would have gladly handed off my duties as queen, but not to her.

Blood pulsed in my head, and her admission to being the one to set the alarm confused me. How did Maria fit in the picture?

My chest rose and fell with rage. Tamping down the urge to snap Vicky's neck, I held my body motionless. My dislike of her was entirely personal. My response would be, too, when the time was right. First, I needed information. "Did you raise Maria's ghost?"

The question caught her off guard. She wasn't the brightest

vamp in the nest, but once she switched gears, her lips curved in a knowing smile. "I want you to suffer like you've made me suffer. You took Lilith away from me, so I brought Maria back to haunt you. Brilliant if I do say so myself."

I had to give her credit. She wasn't smart, but she was devious and wired like a demon. I assumed when she'd raised Lilith, she had demon blood somewhere in her family. Her magical abilities were a throwback. Mix in the blood she'd drank from me and now her vampire skills, and she was more than a dangerous weapon.

She was Toel's dangerous weapon.

But she was still a vampire.

And one who'd been marked by Maria. That's how she'd passed on Maria's violent signature to Dalinda.

Lightning fast, I grabbed the wrist of the hand holding my chin. "I can't thank you enough."

She flinched, but still clinging to the idea she had the upper hand, she narrowed her eyes and gave me a challenging look. "For what? Making your life miserable?"

I stabbed my thumb and forefinger into the spots between her wrist bones, smiled as she cried out, and fell to her knees in front of me. Her face morphed into fear, and the vamp minions shifted forward as if to stop me. "For giving me an excuse to kill you once and for all."

Before the Undead soldiers could move, I seized her by the neck with my free hand. At that moment, Toel walked in, flooding the room with his power-hungry magic. I held Vicky suspended, let him take a good look at her, and then I released her neck and her wrist. She toppled to the floor at his flip-flop-encased feet.

Wet snow flattened his blond hair. His eyes were hard, but his grin was full of surfer boy charm. "*Kal-i*-for-ni-a. I've missed you."

My hand automatically started to form a rude gesture, but I caught myself. I'd gone head-to-head with Toel before, but this time, a new trick was in order.

Going down on my knees, I shoved a choking Victoria out of the way and bowed my head. "My liege. How can I be of service?"

EIGHTEEN

His surprise was as genuine as Vicky's had been a minute before. My surprise at sounding sincere was genuine, too. I was amazed I could bring myself to bow at his feet rather than stake him in the heart. In my opinion, the whole *my liege* stuff was Emmy-worthy.

In his opinion, I was a touch too close. He retreated a step, changed his mind—because, let's face it, showing fear over a submissive demon was ridiculous—and advanced again. But he must have motioned at the minions to pull me back a few steps since that's exactly what they did.

I played possum, letting their cold hands jerk me a suitable distance away and then hold onto me. Toel was playing things safe.

Or so he thought.

"Why the change of heart, dude?" He planted his feet wide and crossed his arms. As usual, his speech was loaded with surfing slang. "Last time I saw you, you tried to murk me. Totally pulling a kali." He snickered and winked. "Get it? Pulling a kali?"

Pulling a kali is surfer slang for doing something stupid. If he thought trying to kill him was stupid, wait until he saw what I had in mind for him now. "You're right, I was stupid." The words burned my tongue. "Once I ingested your blood at the party, I realized that."

Much like Vicky, Toel wasn't the smartest vamp around. He was shrewd and calculating—weren't they all—but far from intelligent. So it took several seconds for understanding to dawn. When it did, his lips curved in a mock smile. His eyes glittered with sly canniness. "No way. You're my slave."

"What?" Vicky's voice was hoarse, but her disbelief still came through loud and clear. She'd gained her feet and was rubbing her throat. "That can't be."

"It's true," I said, giving Toel a seductive look. "I'm all yours, King Toel. I need your blood."

His body relaxed a notch, and a wave of pure lust mixed with the magic in the air, raced over my skin as his gaze dropped from my face to my breasts and lower to my legs. His fangs descended, and he nodded at the minions holding my arms. "Put her on the bed."

"No!" Vicky screamed. "You can't. She's a demon."

As the vamps lifted me none too gently and tossed me onto the bed, Toel snarled at Victoria. "Get out if you don't want to watch."

She dropped her hand from her throat, eyes livid with rage. "She tried to kill you."

Toel stepped up to her and shoved her toward the door. "And now she's my slave. The blood link won't allow her to kill me."

In most cases, that was true. A blood slave was beholden to his or her creator and couldn't turn against him. The link could only be broken if the vampire sire or blood slave died.

But I'd killed Nudra shortly after he poisoned me with his blood. A fact Toel seemed to have forgotten.

Maybe Nudra's blood hadn't had enough time to tame my demon DNA before I'd staked him. Or maybe a demon's base nature couldn't be wholly subjugated by vamp blood. There were no medical tests or field tests to support either theory, and although supernatural genetics weren't difficult to understand, outliers existed. Mutations and crossbreeding created a variety of abnormal creatures, and abnormal creatures did abnormal things.

But who was I to bring up that little issue? "Master, please," I moaned and writhed on the bed, drawing Toel's and Vicky's attention.

His eyes flashed red—it had been a while since he'd eaten—all the better for my plan. Vicky, on the other hand, glared at me with intense black eyes. Her fangs descended farther, but out of pure hatred rather than lust.

Around my waist, Volante pulsed. Inside my chest, my demon itched with her personal brand of lust. She wanted to blind Vicky for daring to look at me like that and tear out her throat so her voice would quit grating on my nerves.

Mentally, I stroked my demon and Volante. *Soon, my pets. Soon.*

"Remove yourself," Toel said to Vicky in a voice that sounded like the king vamp he was. The minions in the room shuddered at the commanding tone and she wobbled, fighting against his magical will. In their hierarchy, no one in that room could disobey him. They were all under his power and unable to disconnect from his authority. Resistance was useless.

That didn't mean Vicky didn't try. Stubborn, that one.

Fighting the connection Toel held over her, she reached out and hit him, screeching her displeasure. In turn, he defended himself, and a second later, they were in an all-out catfight.

Annoyed and running out of patience with this game, I reached under the pillow, brought out the stake, and nailed both minions in the chest before the two on either side of the bed realized what I was doing. They went poof and turned into two separate piles of ash.

Toel and Vicky didn't notice, but the other two minions did, jumping forward and lunging for me. Vampires are fast, but demons are faster. The smaller of the two got within an inch of my face with his claws but froze when I shoved the bloody stake under his ribcage and buried it in his heart. Before he dissolved, the bigger one charged forward, grabbed my ankles, and yanked me off the bed.

My back hit the floor with a hard *whack* that rattled my teeth and knocked the breath out of me. My demon laughed. She liked pain with her entertainment.

As the big guy brought a fist down straight at my heart, I kicked up and smashed his face with my steel-toed boot. His eyes rolled up into his head, and he fell on top of me. I hugged him tight as I rolled over, then I sat up, raised the stake above my head, and sunk it hard and deep into his heart.

My ass hit the floor a second later when he went poof like the rest of them.

In my peripheral vision, Toel wrestled with Vicky in the doorway, their bodies shifting in and out of the room. Like me, she was an outlier. Witch, vamp, demon...whatever the hell was in her DNA, she had some serious supernatural mojo. She craved power and could use magic to do almost anything she wanted, including rebelling against the son of Vlad the Impaler and King of the West Coast vamps.

"You just want to fuck her," she screamed, slapping Toel upside his head. "That's all you've ever wanted. What about everything we've worked for? You'd throw it all away for her?"

A loud growl rose from Toel's throat, feral and pissed. Oh, yeah, he was in full vampire mode. This was going to be fun.

I snuck over to the dresser and put my back against the wall, allowing me to listen to their fight but stay out of sight in case one or both of them noticed I'd offed the robot squad. Outside, the storm continued to rage, the street lights reflecting off the snow. The whole neighborhood looked like a winter wonderland in the blizzard, and I stared at the beauty of it.

And then, out of nowhere, lightning flashed. It was there and gone so fast, I blinked a couple of times, wondering if I was seeing things, but even when I closed my eyes, I saw the fractured light on the back of my eyelids.

Chicago sometimes has thundersnow, as it's referred to. Snowstorms and blizzards often produce it, and Satan knows, we have plenty of those most winters. This lightning was different, magical I was betting, and I wondered what convergence of elements had come together to create it.

I didn't have time to contemplate it further. Vicky flew through the air, across the room, and hit the far wall hard enough to make the house shudder. Toel stepped through the door, saw the leftovers of his minions on the floor, and me standing less than a foot away with a stake in my hand. His magic morphed from aggressive to smug, and his face mirrored it. To say he looked hostile was an understatement. In surf slang, he was amped.

A pugnacious smile lifted the corners of his mouth, his elongated teeth growing by the second. "Gnarlacious, dude." He bent his knees like a boxer, held up a hand, and made a bring-it-*on* gesture. "Let's dance. And just so you know? When we're done, I'm going to bodyboard you all the way to hell."

"Good luck with that." I switched the stake to my left hand and released Volante with my right. "Because the only one going to hell tonight is you."

And then I pulled a kali and went for his heart.

NINETEEN

I n my three hundred years, I've rarely faced an opponent twice.

As enforcer for the Bridge Council and the most highly skilled vengeance demon on earth, if you and I tangle, odds are you'll lose.

I'm not bragging, it's just fact. If I weren't at the top of my game, I'd be dead.

But here I was, facing Toel a second time. Our first fight back in November had been interrupted by Rad and his Slayer friends. The fight lasted long enough, however, to tell me what I needed to know about my enemy.

You can be street savvy, well-trained and a smart fighter and still end up dead if you don't understand your opponent's weakness. You can be inexperienced and a lousy fighter and still bring down the biggest, badest Goliath out there if you do.

Sun Tzu advises in *The Art of War* to know your enemy. I say, know your enemy's biggest weakness. Find his Achilles' heel.

Consider Toel Chase. Direct descendent of Vlad the Impaler.

Arrogant? Check.

King of the West Coast Undead.

Pretentious? Check.

Killed his father in order to take over as leader of the Undead Nation.

Power-hungry? Check.

Impersonates a surfer.

Cuckoo for Cocoa Puffs? Check.

Of course, simply being a vampire meant his basic nature embraced all of these attributes, but the ultra-rank of his vampness intensified each of them to a level I could use against him.

He believed he was better than me. Smarter, faster, more dominant. His cockiness was obvious. From the confident look on his face to his casual fighting stance, he screamed overconfidence and attitude. Two sure chinks in his armor I was happy to take advantage of.

Toel always shoots for dominance. Because of his standing in the Undead community, he rarely encounters resistance. When he does, this causes rage. Another weakness.

From our previous encounters, I'd witnessed how his emotions fueled his fighting. The more enraged he became, the more violent he became. But violence fosters stupidity. A fighter who gives into rage also gives into weakness. Especially in the supernatural world where our magic and emotions are tied together.

Sun Tzu devotes a chapter in *The Art of War* to discussing the opportunities that arise when you understand your opponent's weaknesses. I've found through the years that this chapter and this philosophy are more important than the rest of Tzu's advice. One of the reasons an enemy has a weakness is because they don't recognize it—a detail Damon has often drilled into my head. If they don't identify their weakness and take steps to protect it, they leave themselves open to you.

As Toel and I circled each other in the small bedroom, I knew what I had to do. What my demon had to do.

Don't get emotional.

Don't take it personally.

Show no fear.

Act like an equal.

I feinted with the stake over Toel's heart, and as he went for the block, I stepped toward him, hooked my leg behind his, and swept his leg out from under him using his off-balanced weight and my upper body to propel him backward. The flip-flops he always wore were an obvious weak spot—I'd noticed that the last time we fought—so I used that to my advantage.

He swore, grabbed the stake, and tried to push me away. My nose picked up the scent of metal, and I knew Cole was somewhere behind me. He knew better than to jump in, and, knowing my bodyguard, was probably enjoying the show.

Toel's preternatural strength was up there with the big boys, but mine was still superior, and I hadn't even broken a sweat. It was sort of like Spiderman meeting the Hulk, only my skin wasn't green, and I was a whole lot prettier.

Once you have an opponent pinned on the ground, you don't let up. This fighting stance is up close and as personal as it gets, but the moment you hesitate, you lose momentum. In turn, you lose the advantage. So I straddled Toel's hips, securing him to the floor and grinding my pelvis down on his. Immediately, I felt his response. Once a vamp, always a vamp. They just can't control their blood lust or sex lust, and distraction has always been one of my favorite weapons. If my wrist hadn't already healed, I would have waved the wound in front of his nose.

The last time I'd fought Toel, I'd toyed with him. Let him

have the upper hand and get in a few good hits in order to rile up my demon. This time, she was on the frontline, ready to go to work. No need to be coy or play cat and vamp games. I'd had enough of Toel, and although I'd promised Dru and his brothers I wouldn't kill *il bastardo*, anything less would come back to bite me in *l'asino*. Not just me, all of us.

But I had to have one last minute of fun. After all the crap Toel had put me and the Chicago vamps through, and because he'd killed his own father without any remorse, I had to make him regret the fact he'd ever crossed me. So for a few seconds, I let him try to wrestle the stake from my fingers. Let him believe if he just exerted a little more effort, he could throw me off and gain the upper hand.

I let his arrogance and overconfidence undo him.

My free hand held his arm down, the other held the stake. His free hand also grappled with the stake, forcing it high and off to the side. Inch by inch, I surpassed his strength and brought the smooth cherry wood point directly over his heart.

No longer swearing, he tried to buck me off. I clenched my bent legs tighter along his sides, and my demon laughed. Nothing like a good bronco ride.

When that didn't work, he raised his head and spit in my face.

Don't take it personally. If I was looking into the face of my killer, I'd do the same, and I wasn't about to show any weakness. Emotions would not trip me up. I was a machine, and this is what I did. Took revenge. Secured justice.

"Vengeance is mine," I whispered in his face.

Before I sunk the stake into his worthless heart, I smelled the heavy scent of wood smoke, and Cole yelled, "Kali!"

A wall of magic hit me with the force of a freight train, lifting me off Toel's body and slamming me against the ceiling.

TWENTY

The stake fell from my grasp, dropping worthlessly on the floor beside Toel. He stared up at me in full shock mode, a certain archdemon next to him.

"Let me down," I growled, fighting the magic pinning me to the ceiling. It did no good. The only thing I could move was my mouth.

So I let fly a string of curses at Damon when he refused to drop his outstretched hand and release the powerful restraining magic holding me. "Toel will be dealt with properly by his brothers and the Undead Nation."

My demon was furious. Furious that she'd been interrupted and furious that Damon could best her. I'd always known he was far more formidable than he'd ever revealed at the Institute, but it still stunned me that his magic could so completely over-whelm mine. On one level, it was pretty cool. On another, it was alarming.

Archdemons. My new enemy.

A warm trickling sensation invaded my mind, sending a shiver down my spine. The trickle became a strong pressure, pushing against my frontal lobe. *I'm not your enemy, Kali. You lost control. I'm taking it back.*

Merde. *Get out of my head!*

Not until you have your demon tamed again.

Never, my demon screamed, but I mentally shoved her down.

I have her under control.

He cocked his head. *Your actions say otherwise.*

You don't understand...

Now I sounded like Dalinda and a hundred other supernaturals I'd confronted over the years. Maybe Damon was right. I thought I had the upper hand with my demon, but did I?

Had I ever?

She chuckled, low and deep. Ran a caressing hand up and down my spine, making it tingle and setting my jaw on edge.

Damon wasn't my enemy. The demon inside was.

She wasn't going back in her cage without a fight. As soon as I grabbed for her with an internal fist, her claws came at me. My vision blurred, and my body seized. Not even Damon's magic could stop the bucking and arching as seizure after seizure racked me from head to toe.

I was aware of everything and nothing. Cole called my name and demanded that Damon release me. Toel backed up to make his escape, and Dru emerged from the shadows, his brothers a solid wall of King and Master vamps behind him, blocking Toel's way.

On the flip side, the internal war between my two selves raged on. Black, evil magic warred with the shackles and chains I tried to bind it with. *Why?* my demon shouted inside my head. Why did I fight my nature when it felt so good to give in? Why did I believe I could ever imprison her for long? I was evil. No matter what I did to balance it—no matter how many humans I saved or how much justice I served—I was going to hell. In the end, none of the humans would know or care what I'd done to keep them safe and the supernaturals I'd taken revenge on would enjoy exacting their own revenge when the world ended and I fell into the pit with them...if I wasn't already there.

Her words flooded my brain, and she was smart. She used my own fighting acumen on me. She stopped the violent assault and, instead, beckoned me to join her. Her magic turned feather soft, cradling my battered senses and exhausted psyche. Under my closed eyelids, light danced and formed interesting runes...ones I hadn't seen since my mother was alive. A memory from the distant past encircled me. I was a small girl sitting in Mama's lap. She rocked me and soothed my cries. *Everything will be okay, Calina. Big girls do not shed tears for all to see.*

My demon, like my mother, wrapped her arms around me, and a new mental and emotional wall went up. A protective wall. I could rest now. I could let her take care of...

The magic pinning me to the ceiling disappeared, and I fell through the air like a sinking rock, landing flat on my face and interrupting the dream. I sputtered and opened my eyes.

Damon's Italian loafers came into view, and suddenly, I was flipped onto my back. "Don't you dare give in to her." He slapped my face, shook me hard. "Fight, dammit. You're more than your sinful nature, Kali. More than just a demon. Don't let her win."

And then the pressure of his mind assaulted mine. *Non arrenderti mai!*

Never give up. Easy to say when you're not fighting the monster inside who's suddenly turned into your mother. I opened my mouth to tell him I was okay, that I was me again, but nothing would come out. I was mute.

His eyes narrowed, and he shook me again, which pissed

me off. Like I hadn't been manhandled enough in the past few minutes. Raising a hand, I punched him in the stomach.

Bad move.

Thinking I was still controlled by my demon, he grabbed my throat with one hand and placed the other on my forehead.

Exquisite supernatural power raced from my forehead to my toes, once again making my body seize. Unlike my demon's magic, this was astonishing in its magnitude, magnetic in its dominance. A rolling darkness pervaded my senses, one that smelled like dusky wood smoke and rich-scented sovereign earth. The blood in my veins sighed with a weird kind of relief, my cells welcomed it. The darkness offered release. An end to the fighting.

Death? I asked Damon as the weight of what he was doing brought burning tears to my eyes.

Not death. Sleep. Surrender. Everything will be okay.

Everything will be okay? It was a lie, of course. Just like it had been with my mother. Like it had been with my demon. Nothing was *ever* okay.

For half a second, I fought the darkness, fear pumping hard in my veins, my heart beating against my chest like a timpani. But Damon's hands were warm and firm, his voice cajoling and his magic, undeniable. Fighting was a moot point. In the end, he was taking me under.

I fought anyway. This felt like more than sleep and self-preservation is a strong motivator.

But my fight didn't last long. His magic was too strong. His supremacy, too formidable. He reached under my skin, through my walls, shields and safeguards. He touched me where I could no longer defend myself...a place I didn't know existed.

A falling sensation...a flash of light...and then everything went black.

TWENTY-ONE

I woke in darkness. Complete darkness and an odd feeling permeated me inside and out as if my center of balance had shifted. Along with that, my highly perceptive senses seemed to be heightened even more.

I wasn't sure I was truly awake. Maybe I was still wandering around in my dreams—nightmares, really. Maria, Toel, Rad. Dru and his brothers. Noctifectors in their red uniforms, gutting me with silver daggers. Vampires forcing me to drink their blood. One nightmare faded into another with no reprieve. I was staked, crucified, tortured. Struck with lightning over and over. Dying, only to be resurrected so I could suffer and die again.

But this cold, hard place I woke in was less mystical, more solid.

The floor where I lay was metallic, the icy feel of it cutting through my clothes and raising gooseflesh on my skin. It sunk into my bones and made my normally hot blood congeal. My heart beat a slower pace but seemed efficient at moving the thicker blood through my system.

I sniffed and smelled well-refined steel reinforced with restrictive magic hexes. Old hexes. Older than me and directly linked to the earth.

Sitting up, I reached out to touch the wall, running my fingers over its smooth surface. My eyes fought to find even a trace of light, but there was none.

I breathed deep, searching for smells that would clue me to my location. A faint scent of smoke drifted in the stale air. Very faint. Damon had been here, but not recently, and that was the only scent I could find.

I switched my focus to listening, straining my ears to catch even the slightest sound. The only thing I detected was the racing beat of my heart and the pump of blood in my veins. A touch of claustrophobia hit, and the unbalanced sensation intensified. My pulse jumped, and a band of anxiety tightened around my chest.

No light...check. No fresh air...check. Total isolation from the outside world...check.

No doors, windows, or furniture...check, check, and check.

I was in prison. Not just any prison. Damon's solitary confinement cell in the basement of the Institute.

How inconvenient.

How annoying.

My boss assumed I'd gone off the demon reservation and had locked me up tight. Couldn't blame him, but I was irritated. And claustrophobic.

Breathe. This is all a misunderstanding.

After a minute of concentration, the worst of the anxiety passed. My pulse continued beating at a healthy clip and I had to keep one hand on the nearest wall so I didn't fall over from vertigo, but the tightness around my chest eased. On a whim, I tried using my magic to find an exit point. My demon slept deeply, probably because Damon had put a *lethargus* curse on her, sending her into a magical coma of sorts, and my magic core felt sensitive and raw. Nevertheless, I touched my fingers and thumbs together to see what would happen.

Energy sparked—I did a mental fist pump—and then it promptly fizzled out.

Okay, then. Next idea?

I had no weapons, no magic, no way to communicate with anyone.

Wait. I did too.

Damon, I mentally called to him. *Are you there?*

No response.

Come on, Damon. Let me out.

He was silent.

Bastardo. Solitary confinement? Really? Don't you think that's a little extreme?

While it was possible the magic and steel interfered with our psychic link, I had nothing better to do than to keep calling to him. *Look, I know it looked bad at Dalinda's, but I was in control the whole time. And I'm fine. My demon's back in her cage.*

Nothing.

I know you're listening.

Nada.

I continued ranting for a few more minutes, but he didn't respond. Frustrated, I considered my opponent. What made him tick? What was his biggest weakness?

The archdemon and I had worked together since I was hired by Damon's wife back in Spain in the late 1700s to take revenge on him. She'd been my first client after I'd left Maria's court behind. Believing Damon was cheating on her, she'd hired me to settle the score. Turned out, Big D was an archdemon setting up Europe's first Bridge Institute. He wasn't cheating on his wife with another woman, he was cheating on her with his job.

Figuring out what made Damon tick had been an ongoing hobby of mine. I still hadn't nailed it down. Figuring out his biggest weakness wasn't any easier. One thing I did know was he liked me. He wanted more from me than I was willing to give, personally and professionally.

Damon? Talk to me. Please. I'm going crazy here by myself. I know you think I overstepped my limits with Toel, but if you'd just listen to my side of things.

Ah, yes. Bargaining. Not an approach I liked using in my line of work. I heard a lot of it, but I never used it myself. I found it demeaning.

But apparently, it worked.

Sharp pressure filled my head and I pressed the tips of my fingers to my temples as Damon's voice rapped against my temporal lobes. *I'll be down shortly.*

Score. Time to get out of this hellhole and back to work.

Standing up, I fought the unbalanced feeling still worming its way around my brain stem. The absence of light and fresh air intensified the claustrophobia, so I paced, keeping one set of fingers on the walls to guide me so I didn't walk into them. I was wearing some kind of cotton tunic that hung to my knees. It had been washed a lot, but when I lifted it to my nose, I caught a whiff of Damon. His scent and his magic were embedded in the cloth. This was his shirt.

Weird.

Weirder still was when a wave of magic hit the steel off to my right and a previously invisible door opened.

My visitor was backlit, and since I'd been in complete darkness for a long time, my pupils wigged out on me over the sudden light. I slammed my eyes shut. "Damon?"

The smell that hit my nose wasn't of wood smoke. It reeked

instead of unrefined wool, holy water, and wax candles. The trappings of the Catholic Church.

Dio cano. It was the Templar Knight priest.

Run.

Blinking to regain my vision, I backed against the wall, anxiously touching my ring fingers and thumbs together. Stupid, right? My magic was dead in the water, but self-preservation is a hard instinct to overcome with mere logic.

Run.

Logic also told me I was overreacting to the presence of the priest. Didn't matter. Maybe the dreams I'd had while I was out were still playing games with my mind, or the fact I had no weapons and no magic and every priest I'd ever encountered wanted me dead.

Time to go on the offensive. "I don't want to hurt you," I said, wondering what weapons his hands hid inside his bell sleeves. "But I will if necessary."

He didn't answer. His face, in fact, didn't change. Only his eyes offered a response. They slid from my hair to my face to the shirt hanging off my frame. Did he think it preposterous that I could hurt him or was he silently laughing at how I looked?

Didn't matter. I was offended either way. "Just so we're clear, human, I've taken down bigger fish than you with less."

His left eye twitched. He stepped forward.

For all my big talk, self-preservation was still paramount. I edged a step away. "What are you doing here? What do you want?"

"*Spiritu sancto.*" One of his hands appeared, and he made the sign of the cross. "I've come for you, *vitium.*"

TWENTY-TWO

There was that damn word again. Vitium. Vice. "Well, *Spiritu sancto*, you can't have me."

I squeezed closer to the wall, slid sideways, and eyeballed the opening. If I could just get past him and out that door...

Another figure stepped from the light into the doorway, his shoulders nearly touching the sides. While his features were shadowed thanks to the priest, the fine cut of his suit and the expensive loafers were a dead giveaway. "Relax, Kali." Damon entered the room, raised a hand, and magical light illuminated the cell. "The priest is here to help you."

I eyed my boss with serious confusion. "You feeling all right, Damon?"

"Yes." He frowned. "Why?"

"Priests don't *help* us. They send us to hell, in case you've forgotten."

"Salmad is not here to harm you."

Whoa. More confusion. "Salmad, the mad priest? But he lived in Rome when I did. That's three hundred years ago. Humans don't live that long."

"My given name is Belphagor." The priest lowered his hood and glared at me. His head was shaved down to a quarter-inch of peach fuzz that glowed white under the overhead light. His eyes were a sharp blue, one that reminded me of the rare blue beach glass Neve sometimes found along the lake. "It is true. I lived as Salmad, the mad priest, and was left for dead in Rome."

There was something in the way he glowered at me—something more than a priest hating a demon. It was rare, but I'd seen that look a few times in others' gazes, especially in the Italian Court. "Have we met before?"

"You don't remember." It was a statement, not a question. His voice was low and controlled, and every time he spoke, icy fingers of caution tickled my spine.

Scanning his features, I flipped through my memory vault. Salmad—my father had talked about him on many occasions when I was a girl. Not in my presence, but I would hear him in his and my mother's bedroom, directly above mine, pacing the floor at night and telling my mother about the priest's latest miracle. The mad priest healed the sick, provided relief to those who suffered odd maladies. He exorcised demons and brought still-born babies back to life.

A miracle worker, some said. Like Jesus. Others claimed Salmad was possessed by Lucifer and was a son of perdition. A false prophet.

My attention returned to his eyes. Humans claimed the eyes were windows to the soul. His tugged at me, demanding recognition. I searched my memories harder. "I know your name and have heard the stories about your miracles, but I don't remember ever meeting you."

The priest unbuttoned the upper half of the robe and opened it to reveal his chest. The dangling crosses on the end of his metal belt swayed from his motions. "Do you remember this?"

A large, circular scar covered his body from throat to stomach. Inside the circle were runes, both words and magical symbols, dissected into seven sections. The runic words, derived from Old Latin, flowed around the circle. The sacrificial symbols were grouped in threes.

He needed to gain a few pounds, the skin covering his muscles stretched taut over his lean frame. I didn't need to read the words on his chest. I knew them by heart. I'd carved the same curse on many a human's body while working in Maria's torture chambers.

I, master of vengeance, conceal here runes of evil, power and damnation. Incessantly plague this human with maleficence. Doom him to insidious death. I am the way of his destruction. Vengeance is mine.

Looking away, I swallowed the sudden tightness in my throat, tamped down the nausea twisting in my stomach. My past was determined to come back and haunt me one way or another. And the fact was, I deserved it. "How is it you still live, Salmad?"

From the corner of my eye, I saw him close the robe. "Because I am one of you."

I met his intense gaze once more. "You're not a demon."

"I am a vice, like you and Maria. Cast out of Mary Magdalena by Christ."

My demon jerked even though she was still asleep. I shot a questioning look at Damon. His body language was always reserved, but now it was downright frosty. Combined with the distance he'd put between us, I had no doubt he was planning something I wasn't going to like. "I don't know what you're talking about."

One thing the priest excelled at was conveying emotion

without so much as breathing. It was the eyes, I decided. The way he transmitted disgust, irritation, admonishment...it was all there in those blue orbs.

Damon was probably jealous the priest had such control and could communicate so effectively without the slightest change in demeanor. The archdemon always held his cards close to his chest and could command most of us with a simple brow lift or jaw clench. The priest's total lack of facial affect, while still suggesting exactly what he was thinking and feeling, was off the charts. A form of mental language I'd only seen in one other entity.

Me.

How do you do that with your eyes? Maddy constantly asked me. I pretended I didn't understand what she meant, but I did. When anyone looked into the window of my nonexistent soul, they saw my demon staring back.

"Damon tells me you consider your demon separate from yourself." The priest's gaze once more scanned my attire and dropped to my bare feet. "That you are two entities in one body."

I will not squirm under that gaze. I crossed my arms to hide my shaking hands. "It's important I keep my base nature suppressed." I motioned at his chest with my chin. "For obvious reasons."

"And why do you think it's possible to accomplish such a task?"

Sheer determination had my vote. "I don't hurt humans anymore. That was Maria's influence. Don't get me wrong, I take responsibility for my actions, and I was a horrible creature then, but I don't torture people anymore. I protect humans now."

"To make up for the atrocities you committed under Maria's rule?"

Nothing could make up for that. "I'm a different demon than I was then. And I'm sorry for what I did to you."

His face softened. It was the weirdest thing. One minute, it was hard as stone. The next, the tension drained away, and his gaunt cheekbones appeared more regal and less haggard. "You are the same creature, Kali, but your virtue has been reignited."

Virtue? Somebody was smoking the magical bong. "Next, you'll tell me I have a soul, priest."

"When Christ cast us out of Mary Magdalena, we became both vice and virtue. I am the vice *acedia*. Sloth. I am also the virtue *industria*. You are *superbia*. Pride. *Superbia* and *humilitis*. It is your virtue that tames the vice." He tapped his chest with a balled fist. "You could not kill me, as you could not kill Maria. Harm us, yes. Obliterate us? It is not in your power or the powers of anything on earth." He lowered his fist, drew a deep breath. "God giveth and God taketh away."

A weird buzzing noise set up shop in my ears. My legs gave out, and I slid to the floor, my ass hitting the cold steel with an undignified *thud*.

Neither Damon nor Salmad moved to help me up, so I sat there, legs sprawled and head spinning. The temperature in the cell seemed to drop as I digested the priest's information, turning it over and over in my foggy brain to see if any of it rang true.

Truth, I decided, was highly overrated. I shivered uncontrollably, my lips unable to form all the questions racing through my mind.

Salmad broke the silence. "You're name is on the Noctifector's list, as is all of ours who walk the earth. They want to round us up, and since they can't kill us, not permanently anyway, they plan to incarcerate us. But now that Maria is back…"

I found my voice. "You're sure she's one of us? You're sure *I'm* one of you?"

Just as the priest opened his mouth, a brilliant white light burst to life directly behind him. In the next second, his head snapped forward, and he dropped to his knees, his shocked blue eyes locking with mine.

Until Maria's ghost hit him again, and he did a face-plant in my lap.

TWENTY-THREE

Shit, shit, shit.

The priest was down. Maria was floating in front of me. I couldn't see past her to Damon. My fingers involuntarily tapped my thumbs, but again, I had no magic, no weapons.

Damn it all to hell.

Maria's sparkling ghost noticed my movements and laughed. A soft tinkling sound that raised the hair on the back of my neck. "You cannot protect yourself from me, Calina. I am the strongest of the seven sins."

Conceited bitch. Truth was in her claim, though. Sin was the root of all evil, but lust was the root of most sin. Humans and supernaturals alike wanted what they couldn't have, craved what they didn't need. Sex, money, power...they always wanted more, no matter how much they already possessed.

She might be the strongest of the sins, but she wasn't the strongest entity in that cell.

I shoved Salmad off my legs and reached under him, fingers searching for his cross belt even as I stayed away from the sparkling light. I started to mentally reach out to Damon but hesitated. Could a ghost eavesdrop on a psychic link? Neve said anything was possible with ghosts. No way would I give her the upper hand. Damon would have to follow my lead or get the hell out of the way. "What took you so long to come back? It's been nearly three hundred years. Lose some of your mojo when I kicked your ass?"

The snarky Italian in me couldn't resist taunting her. Plus, distraction was my best weapon until Damon either stepped up or I ripped the belt off the priest. I'd never talked back to Maria at Court. Never said one word to her when I hijacked her later on and put her in the ground. Would be interesting to see how she responded to it now. How she would react.

Her brow furrowed, her mouth turned down. "You dare to provoke me?"

My fingers touched cold metal, and the belt shocked me.

Of course, Salmad had blessed it, but he must have also soaked it in holy water or placed some sort of holy spell on it. That was both good and bad. Good because Maria's evil would be affected by it. Bad because mine would, too.

I gave the belt a hard jerk, and it came loose. Running the chain between the fingers of both hands, I ignored the stinging sensation on my skin and stood. The silver crosses spun on each end. I would have preferred iron since I was dealing with a ghost, but at least I had something.

"Provoke you? That would be foolish." I stepped over Salmad's body and circled to the right. "I've seen what you can do. In fact, that blow to my head at the psych hospital was quite impressive. Put me down for the count. But then, you got the jump on me, didn't you? Instead of facing me like an adult, you snuck up behind me like a child. Why?"

Damon was edging toward the open door. Was he leaving me? When he caught my eye, he made a *no magic* sign and hooked a thumb over his shoulder. The steel of the cell was interfering with his magic too.

"You were always full of questions, Calina." Maria sighed and shifted closer to me, paying no attention to the archdemon. In her world, he was meaningless. She raised a ghostly hand to touch my face. "Why should I think you altered now? But you know what questions get you, right, my sweet? What happens to the cat who is always curious?"

I stood my ground, refusing to let the chill of her hand affect me in any way. Questions in Maria's court were not tolerated, especially when it came to her actions. By the time I was ten, I knew better than to ask her anything for fear she would embarrass me in front of her entire entourage. A prideful demon does not want to be embarrassed.

But I wasn't a child demon anymore, nor was I worried about my pride. All I wanted to do was trap Maria's ghost inside that cell. Would steel work as well as raw iron when it came to ensnaring a spirit? I had no idea.

Damon now stood outside the doorway motioning for me to get out as well. We shared the same idea—trap Maria inside the cell. There was only one problem. Salmad was lying unconscious on the floor. He would be trapped with her. There was only one thing I could do.

Going down on one knee, I bowed my head to Maria and shot a quick look from Damon to the priest. "I protect the innocent now, not harm them," I said in Italian, hoping Damon understood the double meaning. Salmad wasn't human but damned if I'd leave him behind with her. "I am of no use to you anymore."

Maria chuckled and answered me in Italian. "First, you challenge me. Then you play the humble servant while pretending you have changed. The games we play, no?"

Damon shot magic into the cell, trying to lift Salmad's

body. The moment the magic crossed the threshold, it dissipated into dozens of tiny sparks that fizzled and fell to the floor behind Maria.

Damn. So much for that idea.

It was going to take more than a simple distraction to keep Maria occupied in order for Damon to remove the priest's body. Or I was going to have to sacrifice Salmad for the greater good of keeping Maria locked away from the world.

Decisions, decisions...

Using the silver belt like I would have used Volante, I swung it around Maria's feet which hovered a few inches above the floor. The greater good was going to get screwed this time. I had harmed the priest enough.

And I'd taken Maria down before. I could and would do it again.

The blessed silver cut through her ankles, and she cried out, toppling backward. Not the direction I wanted her to go but I was still pleased at the effect the belt had on her. I jumped up, raised one end of the belt above my head and spun the cross in the air. My heart pumped hard and fast, that previously slow-moving blood now swimming through my veins with ease. And while my demon continued to sleep, my body moved with effortless grace and enhanced abilities.

I whipped the cross at her heart and it connected, slicing through her ethereal chest. Not deep enough for my liking, but keeping her off balance. I snatched the cross back and went after her again, driving her away from the priest and backing her against the far wall.

She screamed at me in Italian and raised her hand to throw magic at me. Just like Damon's attempt, her magic fell flat.

Behind me, I heard the sound of Damon's loafers shuffling across the steel floor as he grabbed Salmad and dragged him to safety. I was within two feet of Maria and wondering what would happen if I jumped on her when she flew off the wall and went right through me.

The abruptness of her actions startled me. The sudden chill of her spectral body mingling with mine shocked my organs, and I went rigid. My already amplified senses screamed in overload. My heart threatened to explode.

And then she exited through to the other side.

My body still in shock, I turned a second too slowly and saw her touch Damon's head. The sparkling light around her hand changed to red, the color of passion and lust. Apparently, her succubus skills worked even inside the cell. Salmad's body was mostly out the door as I tackled Maria from behind. Once more, our two forms intertwined, and mine rebelled at the awful sensation.

My attack, however, shoved Damon through the opening, taking the priest with him. As I fell out the other side of Maria's ghost, my senses reeling, I rolled left and threw the cross belt at her head.

If it connected, I didn't see. The instant I rolled toward the door, Damon grabbed me by the shirt with one hand and hauled me out of the cell. With his other hand, he closed the opening and magically sealed it.

TWENTY-FOUR

"We did it!" I was breathing hard, pinned against Damon's chest. "Do you think that cell will hold her?"

He didn't answer, just stared at my face. Correction, he stared at my lips. The next thing I knew, my back was against the wall, and Damon's hard archdemon body pressed against me. His large hand brushed back my bangs and then stroked the side of my neck. His smoke scent inundated my nose, and his mind ambushed mine.

I have to have you. Now.

Oh, boy. Not good. Maria's touch had lessened his inhibitions. Not just lessened them but infused them with raging lust. This should be fun, telling my boss no. Wouldn't be the first time, of course, but previously he hadn't been unstable and consumed with uncontrollable desire.

His other hand found the hem of my shirt and slipped underneath it, feeling up my thigh. A thrill of return desire made my knees weak. What was up with that? Damon was handsome and I liked him when he wasn't nagging at me, but he was my boss. We rubbed each other the wrong way so often and so extremely these days, I couldn't be in the same room with him without going on the defensive.

"That's Maria's influence," I told him, checking his hand and removing it from my thigh. My voice was breathy and as sensuous as if I were in the throes of lust myself. My pulse throbbed in my ears loud enough that I was sure he could hear it. So much for not leading him on. "She touched you. Even as a ghost, she can infect you with her sin."

His lips sought my neck and nibbled my earlobe. I shivered. "I've always wanted you. Since the first day I saw you."

That was a lie. Damon loved his wife, and when I met him, he treated me like a younger sister. He was protective, helpful, and willing to forgive most of my faults while he trained me to work for the Bridge Council.

But his wife was human and had died in childbirth a few years after she hired me to take revenge on him. Once I'd convinced her he was not cheating, but loved her deeply, she and I became friends. The two of them showed me the value of preserving human life, helped me get over Rad's abandonment, and grieve properly for my dead family. Damon and the European Bridge Council gave me purpose.

As I learned a new way of life as enforcer, my confidence in the field protecting humans grew, and Damon and I disagreed more often than not. Long years after his wife's death, I would occasionally see a flicker of longing in his eyes when we talked and especially when we argued. He was lonely and craved companionship. He was an archdemon filled with needs. The attraction between us was there, born of a long-standing friendship and a shared determination to protect humanity...but this confession? It stroked my ego, but it wasn't true.

I squirmed to get away from him. "Stop it. That's Maria's lust talking, not you."

Maria's influence or not, he refused to let me go. Magic swirled around us, his scent growing sharper and tangier as he continued to curtail my escape. Like someone had thrown apple wood on a fire when they'd previously been burning oak. "Her sin only highlights what is already there," he countered.

If that was true, and Damon's actions were any indication, I was in big trouble. His hands roamed my body, and in return, my body arched into him. Heat built low in my stomach and my inner thighs tightened.

What the hell? Was this a side effect of my collisions with Maria?

That's when I felt a familiar sensation deep inside my chest. My demon was purring.

Awake now, she wanted Damon. Nothing new there. She wanted everyone, demon, human, and anything in between. Once I'd exited the magic-suppressing cell, she'd been released from her coma.

Damon kissed me, demanding and powerful as always, and my demon rushed to the surface to meet him. I closed my eyes and fought the emotions crashing through my system. I had to get a handle on my demon and on Damon before we brought down the Institute and decimated Chicago.

I pressed my ring fingers and thumbs together, but before I could raise my protective shield, Damon grabbed my hands and pinned them over my head. Without my magic, and with my body rebelling against logic, I was at his mercy.

The thing is, I've never been submissive. In Maria's court, I obeyed her because I believed her propaganda about demons and what our duties were on earth. Maria was the ultimate coercer. She used physical and emotional blackmail to make me and other supernaturals in her court do anything she wanted. She used her sin and her skills to make obeying her pleasurable and disobeying her terrifying.

Coercion. A useful tool at times.

"Let's take this upstairs," I whispered against Damon's lips. "To your apartment. I've waited a long time for this. I want it to be special."

He slowly pulled back, his eyelids lowered with lust. "I don't want to wait. I'll have you here and then again upstairs." He nuzzled my neck. "I want to bury myself inside you. I want to hear you scream my name."

I was going to scream all right. And so was he once the effect of Maria's touch wore off and he remembered this conversation. Too bad I couldn't run with Damon's plan for a few earth-shattering minutes just to piss off Yasmin, but we'd already gone too far with this escapade.

"I don't do sex against a cold, stone wall, Damon." I let my demon peek through my eyes so he knew I was serious. I was lying, of course, but still serious. Rad and I had done it against every surface around, but up against a wall wasn't my preference. Gravity tended to be a bitch. "We've waited this long, we can wait another two minutes until we're in the privacy of your apartment."

I sounded like an ad for abstinence. Damon growled low in his throat, and the hair on my neck rose to attention. Something inside made me want to bare my teeth and growl back...and it wasn't my demon.

Miracle of miracles, my words sank in and he released my hands, giving me another deep kiss as he did so.

That was all the opening I needed. The second he broke it, I raised my protective magic and punched him hard in the stomach.

He was in the throes of lust and distracted by thoughts of what he was going to do to me once he got me upstairs. That was probably the only reason the sucker punch worked. He doubled over, and when he did, I used one of Cole's favorite leg kicks and sent Damon sprawling to the floor.

He spun sideways on the way down and knocked his head hard against a metal pipe. It didn't knock him out right away and he rolled over and tried to lift himself up. The damage was enough, though, to send him back down, unconscious.

Run, my demon told me, and this time, I listened. I jumped over Salmad's limp body—when Damon came to, he'd take care of him—and took off for home.

TWENTY-FIVE

Home was over three miles away. I didn't have weapons, didn't even have my cell. Trekking through the South Side of Chicago in my current state of dress without weapons and no way to contact anyone in the middle of December seemed, as Damon would put it, imprudent.

I stopped before I got out the basement door. If I could sneak upstairs to my apartment, I could get out of Damon's old shirt, change into my own clothes, secure my weapons, and grab my phone. But I ran the high risk of encountering Yasmin or Kirill.

Explaining how I'd escaped the cell after being imprisoned for letting my demon loose and why Damon and Salmad were both unconscious would take a lot of time and energy. I strongly doubted the other archdemons would be receptive to my story. Yasmin especially wanted to think bad of me and put me in hot water. I figured it was better to let Damon handle them and explain the situation once he was awake.

Cole was an option. If I could locate him, I could hide out in the locker room next to his gym, and he could retrieve my things. The gym was also in the basement, and Yasmin and Kirill rarely ventured any lower in the Institute than the first-floor kitchen.

Making my way cautiously from the dank prison wing to the warmer, well-lit gym, I prayed Cole was working out or giving lessons to Dru's vampire warriors, and I could catch his attention while staying covert.

He was indeed giving a certain vampire a lesson when I peeked into the gym from the locker room door. Brianna was pinned to the floor underneath my bodyguard. They were both laughing, and the sound rang through the otherwise empty gym and bounced off the high ceiling.

When was the last time I had heard Cole laugh? I couldn't remember. He was having fun, and it was about damn time.

I backed away from the door and pressed my hands against the concrete wall, a tiny bit of sadness and jealousy pinching my heart. Cole was one of my closest friends. I trusted him with my life. But in the past month, all I had managed to do was stress him out and exhaust him. He deserved a few minutes of relief, of happiness, and laughter. I just wished I was able to make him laugh like that.

Maria was in Damon's prison cell. Toel was no doubt in something similar at Carpathia House. No way was I inter-rupting Cole's time with Brianna. I was on my own, but I had my magic and I wanted to go home. Alone. So imprudent or not, I snuck out of the Institute in my bare feet and started running.

By the position of the moon in the night sky, I assumed it was between ten and midnight. The snow was knee-deep, the air bitter cold. The usual gray Chicago sky was instead a blue-black color, and for once I could see stars twinkling and creating their heavenly patterns.

Even though it had been dark for hours, I had to keep off

the streets and out of sight as I ran through the snow, jumping snow banks and avoiding streetlights. There were sections of trees, ravines, and empty lots between the Institute and my place that were easy to cross, but more often than not, I ran into row houses, fenced yards, and an endless grid of streets. Lots of barking dogs. Neither the lateness of the hour nor the cold winter air deterred good South Siders from gathering on front porches, snow-packed sidewalks, and under basketball hoops in the sparsely laid out parks. Hip-hop music, cars without mufflers, and random voices punctuated the crisp air as I stayed in the shadows.

A distance that normally took fifteen to thirty minutes in my car, depending on traffic, took over an hour. By the time I arrived at the church I lovingly called home, I had frostbite from my toes to my knees, my hands were frozen into fists, and my face felt like it would shatter into a hundred tiny pieces if I smiled.

Good thing I was a demon. I would heal and heal fast.

Since I'd taken the back way to get there, I came upon the church from the side with the old graveyard. The last snow-storm had dumped several inches, and here in the cemetery, the snow was undisturbed. Moonlight filtered through the thick canopy of overgrown trees and vines to touch the snow and partially visible headstones in random patterns. They reminded me of crooked teeth. Where the moonlight landed on the snow, the snow sparkled.

To most, the cemetery appeared creepy, but to me, it was peaceful, and even in my frozen state, I wanted to simply sit down under one of the giant oak trees and catch my breath.

But I'd already pushed my luck enough that night. I needed to warm up, eat, and sort out what I'd learned about Maria and myself.

At the back door, I placed my frostbitten fingers against the large stones of the church. The earth magic wards I had on the building responded, tickling my palms. No one was inside, not even Rad.

What day was it? Was he still in New York? I had no idea how long I had been in lockdown. It could have been days or weeks. I was too tired to care. I released the back door lock with the touch of my hand and entered.

Five minutes later, I had drawn a hot bath and made myself a *giganto* mug of steaming French roast. I'd also gathered several weapons from the stash hidden in a safe under my closet floor. I felt naked without Volante wrapped around my arm, and I was pissed that I had lost the stun baton, but having a premium wooden stake and a silver dagger at my fingertips eased my nerves. I added a few drops of lavender-scented bath oil to the hot water and sank my chilled body into the tub.

Once I was situated and the scented water relaxed my muscles, I sipped my coffee and dialed Di's home number from a cheap, pay-as-you-go cellphone that had also been stored in the safe. She didn't answer, so I left a message letting her know I was fine and asking her to call me when she got my message. During the week, she worked nights with me at Sweet Investigations and slept during the day. On the off chance she might be at the office, I called there too. No one answered, and I was transferred to voicemail. I hung up without leaving a message.

After half an hour, my skin turned prune-like, so I forced myself out of the tub and dried off before slipping into my favorite pair of Hello Kitty pajamas. In my bedroom, Rad's makeshift bed looked as inviting as my queen-size bed at the Institute. I brushed a couple of sheets of music off the blankets, crawled under them, and fell asleep with the stake from my stash in one hand and the dagger in the other.

Sometime later, I jerked awake. There was a body next to mine and unfamiliar voices in the room. Before I opened my eyes, I grabbed the person next to me, pinned him to the floor, and rolled on top of him, raising the stake over my head. The scent of jasmine tea filled the air.

"Kali! It's me."

Maddy's voice penetrated the sleepy fog in my head. I looked down at her face, released my grip on her shirt, and lowered the stake. "What the hell are you doing here?"

She pointed to the flatscreen on the wall. "Watching movies and keeping you company. Cole wasn't here. Rad wasn't here. You looked like you needed sleep. I figured I'd keep an eye on things while you did."

I climbed off her, crawled back under the blanket, and laid my arm over my eyes to block the light. "You smell like vanilla and sugar."

She shifted and I heard the clang of cheap metal. "Di and I baked cookies. Want one?"

I glanced at the red tin filled with iced cutout cookies, all in Christmas shapes and colors. "Where are the demons and balls of fire?" I joked. "You don't really expect me to eat an angel, do you?"

Handing me a reindeer with red sprinkles on his nose, she rolled her eyes. "Just try one."

The cookie was soft, just the way I liked them, and the frosting tasted like real butter and vanilla flavoring. I sighed, content to eat the sugar cookie while the TV flashed and flickered over the walls and floor. On-screen, a single mother fought to keep her three kids from being taken away from her on Christmas Eve. "Why do you watch these shows? They're depressing as hell."

"No, they're not. If you would actually watch one from beginning to end, you'd see they always have a happy ending."

"Real life isn't a fairytale."

"God, Kali. They're movies, not real life. I know the difference, and if I want to watch movies with happy endings, I'm entitled."

So she was. I sat up, nudging my shoulder next to hers as we both leaned against the wall for support. "You have two choices, you know. Either you go see your parents and tell them you're a vampire, or you mourn the loss of your family and move on."

She sat silently watching the TV, but I could see her mentally stewing over my Damon-esque advice. "My mother always baked hundreds of cookies at Christmas time. Every night after dinner we would make a batch of whatever new recipe she found in her magazines. I'd wake up every morning to the smell of cookies. Then she'd put together half a dozen different kinds in tins like this one, and on the weekends, we'd deliver them to people at church, the nursing home, and our neighbors. She would even stuff the mailbox with a Ziploc bag for the mailman."

Maddy wasn't one to cry, but her voice wobbled. "My mother loved baking those cookies. It was our thing. We always did it together. I wonder if she's baking any this year."

I put an arm around her shoulders and gave her a squeeze. "I'll go with you if you want to tell them what happened."

She tilted her head, leaning it against mine. "They'll never accept who I am now."

Real life. Always a bitch. "I'm told miracles can happen."

"That would be one big-ass miracle."

Was it any surprise I liked this kid? "I think we make our own miracles. We just don't realize at the time that we're doing it."

She straightened, grabbed the tin of cookies, and set it between us. "And what miracle are you currently working on?"

"Staying out of solitary confinement."

"Is that why you're here alone? Did you run from Cole?"

I snagged a snowman and bit his head off. "Damon. What's the status on Toel?"

"Dru scheduled a trial for the end of the week. Why are you running from Damon?"

"Misunderstanding." I finished the cookie. "Why a trial? They know Toel killed Vlad."

Maddy shrugged. "Vampire politics. How's your blood thing? Are you still having withdrawal?"

My stomach rumbled, but it wanted another cookie, not vamp blood. This time, I chose an angel. She was decked out in pink and yellow frosting and sported tiny silver balls on her wings. A definite Di creation. "Actually, I feel better than I have in weeks."

"Maybe Dru's idea worked."

I stopped the cookie halfway to my mouth. "What idea?"

"The one with his blood."

"I didn't take him up on that. No way I'm becoming his blood slave on top of being queen."

"But Cole said..." She frowned, then shrugged. "Whatever."

Not whatever. "What did Cole say?"

She played with an ornament cookie. "I was worried about you after I heard what happened with Toel, so I went to the Institute. No one would let me see you. You must have been in solitary confinement already. When I asked Cole what was going on, he said it was for your own good. Like an intervention. You were going to die without Dru's blood."

My stomach soured. I tossed the angel back into the cookie tin. "Was Dru at the Institute?"

Her nod was tentative. "But if it worked, it's a good thing, right? You don't want to die."

I bent my knees, set my elbows on them and scrubbed my face with my hands. This couldn't be happening, but it made sense. My dreams, the way I felt when I woke up in the cell. Even when I was running home, I felt stronger, faster, like I was one with the shadows.

Combining Undead blood with demon blood was a dangerous science experiment. If the vamp blood was from a direct descendent of Vlad and the demon blood was as old as mine—never mind that I might be one of the seven original vices cast out by Jesus—and the science experiment morphed into Frankenstein's monster on a super colossal scale of *holy shit, we're all fucked now.*

"Why would Damon do that?" I was talking to myself more than Maddy. I hung my head between my hands, the implications beating against my brain like a jackhammer. "*Porca miseria.* How dare he do this to me?"

Maddy scrambled up and headed toward the door. "How about I make you a nice cup of tea? Di always says tea relaxes the nerves."

"I'm Italian, Maddy. Coffee, no tea."

"Strong coffee, coming right up."

She scrambled out of the room. I sat back, mindlessly watching the TV for several long minutes. To say I was in shock was putting it mildly.

But after the shock wore off, I was pissed. Retrieving the cheap phone from the bathroom, I dialed Dru's number. He picked up on the first ring, but since I wasn't calling from my normal phone, he didn't recognize the number. "Hello?"

"I'll give you a one-hour head start." My hand gripped the plastic phone so hard, I heard the case crack. "And then I'm coming after you."

I disconnected before he could respond and threw the

phone as hard as I could. It hit the wall above the TV and shattered into a dozen pieces.

It would give me great satisfaction to do the same to Dru's head.

TWENTY-SIX

I ventured downstairs to the kitchen, refilled my mug with Maddy's coffee and stared out at the cemetery. Maria's ghost was contained in Damon's cell but what were we going to do with her? Could we keep her there forever?

Once again, I wondered if I could get the cemetery ghosts to talk to me, give me some information. While they weren't at the supernatural level Maria was, they'd still seen and experienced dark magic here. A war of some sort. And the cemetery held a portal between worlds. I'd warded it to keep the portal closed, and to keep the ghosts inside the graveyard and humans out of it, but I'd also used it to send Lilith back to hell. That portal might be a better magical prison cell for Maria's ghost than Damon's solitary confinement.

Maddy poured herself a cup of coffee and canted one hip against the sink. "What did you break upstairs?"

"Cellphone. How many days has it been since I attacked Toel?"

"Five or six, why?"

Wow, guess I was really out, thanks to Damon's magic. "How many since Dru fed me his blood?"

"Um, three, I guess. You're like super-supernatural now, huh?"

The landline on the wall rang. I knew without looking at the Caller ID it was Dru. I set down the mug. "I'm not sure what I am."

"Want me to answer that?"

I walked across the floor and snatched up the phone. "Do you know what you've done?"

Dru's voice rang with concern and a touch of irritation. "I saved your life."

"I didn't ask for your help, and by the way, what you and Damon did was sentence me to death. A demon with Vlad's blood in her is a nuclear bomb with a hair trigger."

There was a long pause, and I swear, in my mind, I saw him sitting at his enormous walnut desk in the office at Carpathia, staring at me with his intense eyes. "You can handle my blood. You can control its effects on your system. Neither Damon nor I would have followed through if we thought you'd detonate."

"You had no right to force it on me."

Again, I could see him in my mind sitting forward and banging a fist on his desk. "We saved your life, Kali. If you hadn't taken my blood, you'd be dead right now."

"How do you know that? Damon had me in a coma."

"We woke you three times. Every time, you were so weak, your demon didn't stir when prodded."

For once, I had no comeback. Maddy was staring at me. What did it matter? Like Maddy, I was a victim of a vamp, but there was nothing to do but move forward. "So what now?" I asked, keeping my voice unemotional.

"Are you going to kill me?"

"Depends. You try any Undead mojo on me and I will."

"Fair enough. If I promise not to seduce you, will you come by so we can discuss Toel's trial?"

Like he could seduce me. "And my fee. You owe me for bringing him in."

"Technically, you brought him down and nearly killed him, which was against my wishes."

"A capture is a capture. You got what you wanted. You got Vicky, too. My fee should include a bonus."

He chuckled, and the sound made me smile for some stupid reason. After all the shit, it was a nice feeling. "Your fee will be direct deposited as soon as the bank opens in the morning. With a bonus."

Charming *and* smart. No wonder we were friends. At least when he wasn't double-crossing me and turning me into his blood slave against my will. "I'm taking tonight off." I glanced at the clock over the sink and saw Maddy making a face at me and not so subtly nodding at the doorway. I turned and saw Rad, in all his rock god glory, standing there watching me. "What's left of it, anyway. I'll see you tomorrow night."

We said our goodbyes and hung up. Rad removed a knit cap from his head. "You're okay."

Relatively speaking. "I am."

He looked so damn handsome, especially when he smiled. "Good. Get your coat."

Maddy perked up. "Where are we going?"

He held up a pair of fancy leather ice skates, the laces wrapped around two of his fingers. He wore gloves, but the ends of the fingers were cut off. "Out for a little winter exercise."

I'd had enough winter exercise that night to last a lifetime. "I'm going back to bed."

As I passed by Rad, he grabbed my hand, raised my arm over my head, and twirled me around. A wave of happiness washed through me. His? Mine? I laughed and lost my footing, although I didn't feel unbalanced like I had in the cell.

I stumbled into his chest. He tossed the skates to Maddy and hugged me tight. "I missed you while I was gone. Just one turn around the pond. That's all I'm asking for."

"It's four in the morning. You can't get into any rinks right now. Besides, we can't be seen together in public, remember?"

"Exactly why we're going to a private spot while everyone else is sleeping. No one will see us." He grinned down into my face, his gold eyes dancing. "Come on. Live dangerously."

Live dangerously. He had no idea.

I couldn't resist his enthusiasm. And I'd missed him too. I felt a little adrift after everything that had happened, and I didn't do *adrift*.

You're just restless, I told myself. *It's either this or you go pick a fight with a certain War demon and get your butt kicked.*

"Did you bring cocoa?" Maddy asked.

"Of course." Rad dug into a pocket and withdrew a miniature plastic-wrapped candy cane. "And for you, candy canes to stir it with."

She squealed, snatched the red and white cane from his hand, and clutched the skates to her chest. "Can we go, Kali? Please? I haven't been ice skating in years."

The look on her face was as hard to resist as Rad's. This was *such* a bad idea, but since when had that ever stopped me? I sighed, heavy with Maddy-like drama, just to be sure they understood I was only doing this for them. "I'll go change."

Another whoop from Maddy and a kiss from Rad sealed the deal. Then he turned me loose, and I went upstairs to dig out my insulated underwear and my parka, ignoring the lightness in my step and the sudden fullness in my heart.

TWENTY-SEVEN

The Chaos Demons are a band made up of exactly what the name implies: Chaos demons. In the demon world, there are multiple levels of Chaos, with lower-level demons and higher-level ones.

Even though Rad was half-human, the Chaos magic inside him was upper-level. He possessed elemental magic—the ability to manipulate air, earth, water and fire (although fire was his weakest element)—and he could mess with a human's mind and emotions, creating simple confusion all the way to total madness. Put both skill sets together and his magic was strong enough to create anarchy or start a war.

The other members of his band were lesser demons. The drummer, Bottrill, could whip up a strong wind and cause clouds to come and go. Shine, the keyboardist, could get into the minds of animals and control them. Some shifters as well. The bassist and guitar players, Que and Ozzie, were weak demons who majored in troublemaking.

How Rad managed to hold the band together was beyond me, but he did. Somehow out of all that chaos and bedlam, he managed them into a unique type of order. Unique and very talented.

Rad seemed better than the last time I'd seen him, before New York and my incapacitation. There were still circles under his eyes, and he needed a shave, but the emotional angst and inner bedlam seemed eased. Had Damon extracted my vampire-infused blood and fed it to my slaves while I was unconscious? Seemed like a good bet.

We took Rad's brand new Lamborghini Urus, a prototype SUV that wasn't yet for sale in the U.S. Rad claimed to know one of the company's owners who'd shipped the Urus to New York for him. Another reason he'd made the trip. The SUV was luxurious and sporty and completely over the top in the gadget department...a bigger version of the standard Lamborghini. It was even red.

The sound system was exceptional, and Rad let me control the music. I dialed up my favorite pirate radio station on the satellite, and we rocked out to Stone Sour and Breaking Benjamin as we left the burbs and entered farm country. Lake Michigan was on my right, the dark, choppy water absorbing the moon's light. I scanned the horizon for any signs of storms or errant lightning and saw none.

The private ice skating rink wasn't just some pond in the backwoods of Illinois. Less than an hour after we'd left my place, we were slightly northwest of Lake Forest and smack dab in the middle of an estate, hidden from the main road by a curving, tree-lined drive.

The elaborate gated fence swung open the moment Rad drove up. Fifty yards in front of us was a beautiful Italian-style mansion surrounded by statuary, snow-covered lawns, and white Christmas lights decked out top to bottom.

Maddy leaned forward from the backseat as we drove up to

the front door, eyes wide and mouth hanging open. "Holy pretentious, Batman."

To me, it wasn't pretentious at all. In fact, it reminded me of home. As in Rome.

Arched windows, iron-railed balconies. Stepping out of the car, I could almost smell baking *filone*, wet cobblestone streets and sputtering tallow candles. "I thought we were going ice skating."

"We are." Rad opened the SUV's back door and hauled out three pairs of skates. "Come on."

We skirted the house, taking a shoveled sidewalk around to the back. Inside, lights were on and rock music thumped. Several vehicles were parked out front, so I wasn't surprised there were people there. The owners appeared to be throwing a party.

"Our publicist lives here," Rad explained as we passed an in-ground swimming pool covered for the season. "He's out of town for the holidays, so he's letting the band use it."

The band. Hmm. I hadn't officially met any of them and didn't really want to. I'd seen them plenty of times on various tabloids, in the news and on my computer at work when Maddy'd been surfing the web. "I thought you and I were keeping our relationship a secret."

Rad took my hand, led me to a gazebo draped in more Christmas lights near a man-made pond. A thick layer of ice covered the surface, the water underneath appearing black. High stone banks held back the blowing snow and a set of Victorian lamps built into the stones illuminated the landscape around it. Swags of evergreens lined the gazebo's walls and wrapped around the light poles.

"Everyone saw you at the Halloween party, Kali." Rad made me sit on a white bench inside the gazebo. "The guys know who you are. But they're cool with it. Nobody's going to out us."

Looking back at the house, I saw several curious faces in a downstairs bay window. Female faces. "Uh, huh. And what about their human girlfriends?"

He bent in front of me and tugged off one of my boots. "I told them you were a CIA agent, and they couldn't take pictures or post anything on Facebook about you because it could blow your cover."

Maddy dropped down beside me, her normally pale Undead cheeks showing a hint of pink from the brisk temp and even brisker wind. "A secret agent? That so rocks. Can I be a spy too?"

Rad secured a skate on my foot. "Tonight, you can be anything you want, Mads."

A few minutes later, she and I were flailing our arms, spinning in unruly circles and randomly grabbing each other's coats to keep from falling on our asses. Skating seemed to come easy to Rad, and he took turns guiding Maddy and me around the pond and showing us tricks to turn and stop without breaking anything.

After twenty minutes or so, I found my sea legs and started to get the hang of it. My breath came in white plumes, and my thighs felt strong as I raced Maddy from one end of the pond to the other. It ended in a draw, both of us slamming into the stone wall and laughing ourselves silly. Then, being the fierce competitors we were, we turned around and raced back.

Rad caught me on that end, and Maddy lost her balance and tumbled to an ungraceful stop at my feet. "I won," I called out, and she flipped me the bird.

Rad spun me away and took me on a slow skate around the circle. The sky was lightening in the East, sunrise approaching. Out here, away from the city lights, the stars seemed brighter, closer. The woods around the estate were still dark and ominous, but peaceful. Maddy dragged herself to the gazebo for hot cocoa, and the only sound I heard was the swishing of the skate blades on the ice.

Rad's emotions were balanced. One of his hands held mine, the other wrapped around my waist as he skated alongside me, our feet moving in a synchronized motion. The people inside the house had either passed out or gone to bed. Most of the lights had been shut off and there was no longer any music coming from the first floor. I drew in a deep breath and relaxed into the flow of our movements. For a few seconds, my world seemed complete. Normal.

I didn't want the night to end, but it did. We packed up the Lamborghini and headed back to Chicago, stopping once at a fast-food place to grab some breakfast for the road. We were halfway home when Maddy fell asleep in the backseat, and Rad turned off the radio. He seemed like he wanted to say something, but he kept glancing out his side window and drumming on the gear shift.

"So, how are you?" Maybe if I initiated the conversation, he'd relax and tell me what was bothering him. "How was New York?"

"Fine. We did our guest appearances, signed a contract for *Bullet Blues* to be used on the next Call of Duty soundtrack, and finalized two more stops on next year's world tour."

Busy weekend. "Was it all work, or did you have time to do fun stuff?"

It was a weird thing for me to ask, and Rad side-eye said that. The winter sunrise was a washed-out color behind his profile. "I picked up my new baby," —he patted the steering wheel— "So, yeah, I guess so."

I waited for him to pick up the conversation, but he didn't. After the last couple of hours of lighthearted fun, I wanted to close my eyes, lean back in the seat, and remember the feel of him spinning me around. The freedom of not worrying about Toel or Maria's ghost or Damon or Dru.

We sat in silence for several more miles. Maybe nothing was bothering him, and maybe it was all in my imagination.

I'd just started to relax when he said, "And what did you do over the weekend while I was gone?"

It wasn't the words so much as the tone. An obvious accusation was present. The truth about my run-in with Dalinda, Toel, and Vicky wouldn't shock him, but the story was so convoluted, especially when added together with my solitary confinement, Salmad's appearance, and the fact I now carried Dru's blood, I hesitated. For the first time since I'd met Rad, the two of us had acted normal. No psycho queen trying to tear us apart, no job responsibilities conflicting with our relationship, no enemies ambushing us and no addictive blood disorders driving us mad. In fact, if I'd been more like Maddy and Di, I would have called the past few hours a miracle.

My hesitation seemed to confirm his suspicions. "You smell different again. You look...healthy."

My smell. *Merde.* I no doubt smelled like Dru now. "It's a long story."

His hand tightened on the wheel. "Tell me you didn't."

Crap. This conversation was not going to go well. "Not by choice."

He shot me another hard glance. "What the hell does that mean? He forced you? I'll fucking kill him."

Long version or short version? Bad news sucked either way, and I was never one to beat around the bush. "I had a run-in with Toel, Damon thought I lost control of my demon, and he put me into a coma. Apparently, while I was out, it appeared I was going to die, so he called in Dru, and they pumped me full of his blood."

He swore in French and the crushed paper bags from the fast food joint rose from the floor and flew into a whirlwind spin, smacking Maddy in the face. She sputtered, jerked upright, and batted them away. "What the hell?"

"So now you're his fucking blood slave?" Rad shook his head, his eyes glued to the road and his jaw tight. "Is Damon out of his goddamn mind?"

The Lamborghini's radio flipped on without warning, the digital dial spinning through station after station, not settling on any. My cushy leather seat's built-in seat warmer jumped several degrees.

So much for Rad having his emotions in check. Wait until I told him he'd already drunk Dru's blood as well if he'd had a fresh bottle in the past week. "I would never let a bloodsucker control or manipulate me." I glanced at Maddy. "No offense."

She waved me off. "None taken."

Rad wasn't appeased, but his face had gone blank. Like Cole's did when he faced an opponent. "You can't control the blood's pull on you, Kali, no matter how strong you are. No matter how strong your demon is." He took a breath, let it out slowly. "You'll give in. In the end, you'll succumb."

Didn't anyone have faith in me? "I won't succumb. I've already set the ground rules with Dru, and he's in total agreement. This is an inconvenience, nothing more, and if it keeps us all alive and functioning, so be it."

Now Rad glared at me. "So be it? You become an Undead Master's slave, and that's all you can say? So be it?"

During the conversation, the car's speed had reached a hundred miles an hour. I needed to calm him down, but really, there was no way to do that, and I was growing annoyed at his attitude. "Don't you think I hate this? That I'm pissed as hell that Damon took my free will away and turned me into Dru's bitch? I was out, Rad. Totally gone. They thought I was dying, and I probably was. I don't remember anything but awful dreams where I *was* dying, over and over again. But there's nothing I can do about it. What's done is done. I can't extract Dru's blood from my system. If I could, I'd open a vein right now and bleed all over your brand-new car."

That shut him up. He returned his attention to the road, but he didn't slow down. Traffic grew heavier as we neared downtown and early morning commuters headed out. Rad passed car after car as we flew toward my house.

Finally, he had no choice but to decrease speed due to the traffic, and I breathed a quiet sigh of relief. Twenty minutes later, he drove into the church's parking lot. He, Maddy, and I stared at the line of cars parked there.

A big-ass black Land Rover—Bridge Institute-issued—a shiny black BMW, a flashy red Porsche Carrera, and a rusting Chevy hatchback filled the lot. Damon, Dru, Aphrodite, and JR.

My fighting instincts kicked in, my hands closing into fists, although I wasn't sure why. My heightened Undead awareness, thanks to Dru's blood, was sending clear warning signals. "This can't be good."

"We can leave," Rad said, his hand shifting the SUV into reverse. Funny how fast his attitude changed when he sensed I was in danger. Or maybe his awareness was heightened as well.

I bit the inside of my lower lip, mentally chewing over my options. Running away accomplished nothing. I preferred meeting trouble head-on anyway. "Take Maddy home for me?"

"No way." She shot forward, sticking her head between our seats. "Whatever's up, I'm staying with you."

There was no sense fighting with her. I touched Rad's hand. "Thank you for this morning. I had a good time. I'll call you."

I slid out of the car, Maddy on my heels, and walked to the

front door. Di—the traitor—had a key to the place and must have let in Damon and Dru. Why JR was here, I had no idea.

Behind me, the Lamborghini's engine shut off, a door slammed.

My heart skipped a beat when I looked over my shoulder and saw all that Chaos demon stalking toward me. "What are you doing?"

Rad sidled up to me, grabbed one of my hands, and gave it a squeeze. "I told you, we ride this blood thing out together. You go down, I'm going with you."

A rush of renewed confidence hit me as I stared into his eyes, his sweet salty ocean scent reassuring me.

But behind his golden gaze, I saw another emotion. One I knew all too well. Revenge.

"You're sure that's the only reason you're going in with me?"

He gave me a half-hearted grin. "If I get the chance to kill a certain vampire, I'm going to rip his fucking Undead head off."

*Al*righty then. I opened the door.

Someone—most likely Di—had straightened up Rad's mess, and my living room looked respectable once again.

Respectable, except for the multiple supernaturals glaring at me. Cole and Brianna had joined the group.

"This better not be another one of your crappy interventions," I said, unzipping my coat and ignoring the sudden heat coursing through my body as Dru looked me over. He licked his lips ever so slightly, and the spot between my thighs got happy.

I withdrew the dagger hidden in a shoulder holster and flashed it to get their attention. "Because I've got news for all of you. The first one of you that lays a hand on me is going to bleed silver."

TWENTY-EIGHT

"Where have you been?" Di shoved the dagger aside and hugged me tight. "We've been so worried. You just disappeared with no word. Are you all right?"

"I was with Rad and Maddy. I'm fine."

She looked me over, keeping one arm around my shoulders. Turning to face Rad and Maddy, she shook a motherly finger at them. "Shame on you for kidnapping her at a time like this. You all could have been killed."

I glanced at Damon and Dru, my intuition running amok. Magic zigzagged in the air, its energy spiking and falling with their emotions. "At a time like *this*? What *this*? Did something happen?"

Dumb question. Obviously, the get together wasn't a simple welcome home party or the intervention I'd suspected.

Dru leaned against the fireplace mantel, his eyes tired and resigned. "Toel escaped Carpathia."

Che cavolo. "How the hell did that happen?" I held up a hand before he answered. "Wait. Don't tell me. I don't want to hear it."

I started toward my stairs. Damon's voice stopped me as I reached the bottom tread. "Maria has escaped as well. We believe she's the one who released Toel from his cell."

Hand on the newel, I hung my head. Damon was emitting a weird vibe, and I knew why. He couldn't quite look me in the eye, remembering his earlier behavior. "Your quarantine cell doesn't work on ghosts, I take it?"

"I believed it would, but I have never had the opportunity to experiment with a ghost of Maria's caliber."

I almost laughed. Not because it was funny. Funny was the last thing I'd say about this goatfuck. No, I almost laughed because I was so stupid. Stupid to believe I could defeat Maria so easily. Stupid to have not sunk my cherry wood stake deep in Toel's heart.

Stupid to have bought into the dream Rad and Maddy gave me a peek at that morning. The one suggesting I could ever live a normal life. A happy life.

"Is Salmad all right?"

"After some healing, the priest is fine." Damon finally looked me in the eye. "We discussed what Maria did to both of you. We believe, in both instances, she was trying to take over your bodies."

Again, I held back a frustrated laugh. The seven deadly sins had once coexisted nicely inside a human before Jesus ripped us out and separated us, placing his Son-of-God magic spell on us and casting us as entities with flesh and blood into the world. Maria seemed to be planning to bring us back together as one. How insane and weirdly cool.

Dru caught my eye. "Intel suggests Toel is once again raising his army and plans to attack soon."

"That's swell. Good luck with that."

I took a couple of steps, feeling every one of my three hundred years.

"Kali," Dru's voice sounded the way I felt. "Humans will die by the hundreds, if not thousands, if you don't help us stop him."

Whirling around, I set my death glare on him. Dark energy sparked between us. Dark and sexual. Damn. "Don't you dare put this at my feet. If you'd allowed me to do my job and take out Toel to begin with, instead of tying my hands with your petty Undead politics, you wouldn't be in this mess."

He stepped forward, all heat and anger and lust. "Petty? He killed my father. My liege. The creator of the entire Undead Nation. Toel must be made an example of what happens to a vampire, any vampire, royal or not, who stages such a coup. Who breaks our laws and flaunts our traditions. There will be complete anarchy if we don't."

I stomped down the steps and got in his face. "Anarchy? That's what you're afraid of? A bunch of vampires killing each other? Well, guess what? That's exactly what Toel's going to do now. Create anarchy. And while he's killing you and your brothers, he's also going to wipe out Chicago's human population. How's that for anarchy?"

The energy between us swirled, and my lower parts tingled. My nipples went tight.

Damn it! I do not want Dru, I told myself in no uncertain terms.

Too bad my lower parts, as well as those much higher, weren't listening. His blood—the blood he'd shared with me—was heating up.

He raised a roguish brow and challenged me. "As queen of the Central United States, you will assist me in stopping this war."

He was calling up his royal dick and showing me how big it was. Pushing it in my face. As his slave, the blood in my veins responded, wanting me to kowtow to him, but I held my ground physically, mentally and magically. It was time he learned that if he shoved his royal self in my face, I might bite something off. "As Queen of the Central United States, I'll be changing a few of your fucking rules and traditions. *If* you survive the coming holocaust. Quite honestly, at this point, I'm thinking Toel's the smartest, most powerful vamp on this planet, and I'd be smart to switch sides."

That did it. Dru's magic hit me full force. I was ready for it and threw mine at him as well. The air crackled as if lightning danced between us. My stupid parts throbbed, nearly in pain from the swell of desire sweeping through me, and I sucked in a breath. His pupils were huge, and he was breathing hard. The smell of sex met my nose, and I flinched. We weren't even touching each other, and yet, here we were, magically locked in a tug of war that somehow mimicked sex.

Too weird.

"You overstep your boundaries, demon," Dru snarled. His fangs descended.

Unable to restrain myself, I pointed a finger at his chest and gave a shove. "I haven't even begun to overstep my boundaries with you, you blood-sucking piece of..."

Suddenly, I was lifted off the ground and swung around to face the stairs again. Briny ocean scent replaced Dru's sex smell as Rad kept an arm around my waist. "Back off, Dru."

"Or what?" he challenged.

The muscles in Rad's body tightened, and he stepped toward the vamp Master. The table lamps vibrated on their bases. A stack of his music swirled into the air. I struggled against him, but he held tight, keeping my feet off the ground. "Or I'll hang you up by your toes and cut your cold, dead heart out."

There was scuffling, and Cole intervened. "All right, children. Enough."

Rad backed up, me still in tow. The stuff in the room settled down, even though his emotions continued to be erratic and chaotic. It was cute that he was standing up for me, but I could handle Dru, tingly parts notwithstanding. "Put me down."

He did reluctantly, but I was in control again. I stayed several feet back from Dru and locked eyes with him. "No more contracts, no more of you calling the shots with regards to Toel. If I go after him, I do it to save humans, and I answer to no one."

I switched my focus to Damon. "Not even the Bridge Council. If you two hadn't stopped me from killing the *testa de cazzo* in the first place, none of this would be happening. And if any humans get hurt because of Toel Chase? The blame lies with both of you."

Damon's lips thinned. "May I have a word with you in private?"

I knew what he wanted...to discuss his earlier actions, although I doubted I'd ever hear an apology from his mouth. I didn't need one, and I was too emotionally strung out to get into it with him. We didn't have time, nor did I have the inclination, to analyze what had happened. "No, you may not. What happened between us was because of Maria's magic, nothing more. So drop the guilt and don't buy into the idea that there was more to it than that."

Curious stares assaulted us. Damon's jaw tightened, released. "You are impertinent, demon."

"I work at it. Guess I'm just a cross you have to bear, boss." I turned to JR, who'd spent the entire time playing a game on a new tablet computer I was sure I'd paid for. "What are you doing here?"

Flustered out of his gaming stupor, he stood abruptly, glanced at my chin and then around the room. "I'm tracking Toel."

"Tracking him how?"

He touched a couple of places on the tablet's screen and held it up. A map of the Chicago area appeared with a blipping red dot.

Brianna stepped forward. "I inserted a tracking device on Toel while he was in custody. Under the skin on the back of his neck. He was unconscious when I did it. JR's been able to keep tabs on him since."

Well, what do you know? Apparently, Cole's training lessons were actually working. "Nice job. Why haven't you picked him up?"

Dru circled us, keeping his distance from me while looking at the tablet and the blipping dot. His face was full of loathing and the energy rolling off of him was tight with anger. "We tried twice, and both times, he disappeared like smoke."

"Like a ghost," Cole amended. "We think Maria's putting up some kind of smoke screen around him."

In my mind, she was the real threat. I needed to take care of her before I could corner Toel and stake his sorry Undead ass.

Staring at the dot, which appeared parked on a side street west of Lake Forest's downtown area, I ran various scenarios through my head. *Know your enemy. Know his weakness.* "He's not moving. He's ditched the tracking device."

"He's sleeping," Dru said, nodding toward the tall windows across the room, through which weak sunlight filtered through. Daylight finds most of us asleep, and his time in captivity was, shall we say, strenuous. He needs to recoup his strength before he can attack."

"How soon will his army be ready?"

JR messed with the touchscreen and the view of Lake Forest zoomed out to include the entire Chicago metro area. "Intel suggests he has three groups of vampires stationed here,

here and here." He pointed to three random places with a stubby finger.

Except they weren't random. I mentally watched as Chicago became a 3D game board with Toel's minions lined up like Battleship pieces in the three distinct zones JR had pointed out.

It was startling—like I was seeing inside Toel's mind. "Do you see that?" I asked Dru.

He glanced at the map again. "What?"

So he didn't see the Battleship scenario. Interesting. "Last night, when you and I spoke on the phone, I could literally see you in my mind. I thought I was imagining it, but now I'm not so sure." I pointed at the tablet. "When I look at this, I see Toel's strategy. Or at least his initial strategy."

Everyone stared at me like I'd suddenly turned into a Klingon. Maybe I had. The energy in the room spiked again, but this time it was full of more than simple curiosity. Surprise, yes, but it was laced with fear.

"I'm picking up...vibes, I guess, is the best way to describe it." The realization that I could now detect what Vlad's sons were thinking and doing sent my stomach to my knees. Mix a high-powered demon, who might be one of the original sins, with royal vamp blood, and you get...

Me.

A freak of colossal proportions.

"I need a moment," I said, grabbing the tablet and heading toward my home office. The link to Toel was extremely weak, but maybe if I could get away from everyone's judgmental energy and rollercoaster magic, I could coax it into a full-blown psychic connection. Talk about knowing your enemy.

Rad followed me and I didn't try to stop him. There was no judgment in his energy, no fear. Only concern.

But as I walked into my office, I heard him say, "She wants to be alone."

Damon's commanding voice responded. "Get out of the way, Chaos demon."

Rad was blocking the door. I expected him to tell Damon off. Respond with some kind of snarky comment. Instead, he lowered his voice, said something cajoling, and pulled the door closed, leaving me alone.

Drawing a deep breath and letting it out slowly, I rubbed my temples and sat down. Concentrating on Toel, I stared at the blipping light. Even though Brianna was sure he hadn't known about the tracking chip, I had my doubts. He'd outsmarted me on more than one occasion, and I was gun-shy about taking anything for granted.

Staring unblinkingly at the red dot, my vision fuzzed out, and I opened all my preternatural senses. My physical body melted away, and I felt like I was flying. This was new.

I didn't fight it, whatever it was. Astral projection, maybe? The sensation of being ungrounded induced a small amount of anxiety, but I squelched it and opened myself up further. After a couple of seconds, the last of my inhibitions disappeared, and I found myself riding a different plane of consciousness.

I'd like to say it was all wowie new age fun. You know, wind in my hair, a taste of heaven or whatever. For me, it was none of those things. It was scary as hell. Like riding the world's most intense roller coaster. Heart-stopping plunges, cobra rolls that made me want to vomit, spinning unceremoniously around in the air with no metal bar to hang on to.

My demon freaked. I freaked. For several moments, I thought I might be plunging to purgatory, but then, what do you know, I leveled out. Took control again. My heart was still in my throat, but I sensed Toel's magic, guiding me in like a beacon. Or maybe it was his blood. Either way, I locked onto it and let it pull me in.

The second my magic rubbed up against Toel's, it recoiled, my hate for him running deep. But my magic also shifted slightly in a new direction. I had royal vamp blood in my system, the same blood running in his veins. My magic, my body and my mind all identified with that, and just like the way Dru had appeared in my mind when we spoke on the phone, I sensed Toel's physical presence. Saw him in my mind's eye.

Dru had been right. The vamp king was sleeping.

My sight was limited, but it appeared he was sleeping on the floor of an abandoned warehouse. It was dark and grimy and Toel's dead seaweed scent drifted past my nose, the faint whiff of old motor oil and decaying wood mixed with it.

If only I could make like a ghost and transport myself to his location with a stake in my hand.

There was nothing directly drawn on the floor where he slept, but I saw the traces of magic all around him. Golden lines floated above the floor but were connected to it as well. They formed an inverted hexagon around his body. Various protection runes, a few squiggles I didn't understand but recognized as very old, very dark magic, added punch to the spell.

Maria. She was protecting him as Cole and Dru hypothesized. Or was it Vicky? I compared what I saw around Toel with the alarm spell I'd encountered at Dalinda's house. There were similarities, but the magical prints were different. Like human fingerprints, magic was unique to each supernatural.

I spent a few minutes trying to infiltrate Toel's mind, but it didn't work. Because he was sleeping? Or because I didn't have that kind of power yet? Maybe it was simply Maria's spell. The only thing I could get from him was the 3-D game board image I'd seen earlier with the initial plan of attack.

A new level of exhaustion crept into my system. The sensation resembled holding back a dam of water and made my mind and my magic tremble. I shifted my focus to returning to my body inside my office and rode another roller coaster, albeit weaker, home.

The red dot was still flashing rhythmically on the tablet's screen. I blinked several times, my heartbeat jumping around like I'd just run a marathon.

Rad sat across the desk watching me with a concerned look on his face. His hair was mussed to perfection, but his eyes were too tired, the skin over his cheekbones, too drawn. He'd been hiding his blood lust well earlier. Now, it was taking a toll. "Must have been some trip. What exactly were you doing?"

My brain felt as weak as the dim light outside. My limbs were lifeless. I knew Rad needed to eat, but I couldn't feed him. Not yet. "Is everyone still here?"

"Yeah. Why?"

I didn't answer, rising from the chair and heading for the living room. It was time to prepare for war.

TWENTY-NINE

In times of war, correct positioning of troops is crucial military strategy, whether those troops are human or supernatural. The problem with positioning is that once the battle begins, troops must respond to changing plans, initiatives, and counterstrikes. The environment shifts, the enemy goes in a different direction, and a system or plan fails.

I was no War demon, and the strategy stewing in my brain was outside my comfort zone, but as a vengeance demon, I understood how to use an enemy's Achilles' heel against him.

Or her, in this case.

The various entities in my house were gathered into groups: Dru and Damon, Cole and Brianna, JR, Maddy and Di. I motioned them all into the sunken living room and gave them the info I'd obtained from the 3-D model Toel had provided. "Toel and Maria are definitely working together. They have three main initial strikes planned." I zoomed out on the tablet to show the group the map of Chicago proper and pointed to the corresponding positions. "Carpathia is one. Obviously, Toel wants this because it's the center of power for this region. Control Carpathia, control the Central U.S. and power is Toel's greatest desire. Next, is the Bridge Institute." At this, Damon and Cole both straightened. "Destroy the Bridge Council, anarchy will erupt between the supernatural population and humans. Maria wants this, and so does Toel."

The last position was in between the other two. "Lastly, Toel needs Chloe's blood bank, and that's where he'll strike first tonight. Then he'll go after the other two targets tomorrow night."

"Why the blood bank?" Dru's lust and magic were more contained now, although his body language and cold gaze suggested he was still pissed at me. "His minions will need more blood than Chloe has, so won't he be looking for a large human event? Like a Bulls game or a concert to sic them on?"

"Yes, he will, and Damon will send scouts to the various public events taking place tonight who can be on the lookout for any unusual activity." I looked at Damon for confirmation, and he gave me a reluctant nod. "But remember, this is Toel. It's all about him and his power. Chloe has between fifteen hundred and two thousand bottles of high-quality supernatural blood at any time. Blood from many different species. He wants that blood for himself. Once he's secured what he wants, he'll worry about his minions."

Cole's arms were crossed over his massive chest, a calculating look on his face. "Why does he want all that blood?"

"He doesn't want *all* the blood, just the right combination. Mixing other supernatural blood types with his royal Undead blood could make him the ultimate vampire. He'll then be able to step into Vlad's footsteps without anyone interfering, now that his father is out of the way."

The freaky staring continued. I set down the tablet and pointed a thumb at my chest. "Supernatural Frankensteins are possible, case in point: me. He knows this. Maria's probably filled his already oversized head with all kinds of possibilities. He'll want the rarest blood and the most powerful blood, and he'll find it at Chloe's."

From the looks I got from my audience, they were convinced I was batshit crazy.

Shadow Hill Asylum, here I come.

"Toel is greedy and power hungry, but this?" Dru shook his head. "Mixing blood from different species could kill him."

We could only hope. But then I'd miss out on staking him, and I wanted to gleefully cross that item off my bucket list. "It didn't kill me, and now I have a few extra handy skills, like I can get a read on him since we're related by blood now." I sent a death glare at Dru. "I sort of astral projected myself to where Toel was a few minutes ago. You're right. He's being guarded by powerful dark magic. Maria's magic."

Damon, always thinking on his feet, arched a dark brow. "And does this connection between the two of you run both ways?"

I wondered that myself. If so, I had to be ultra careful about my thoughts once the sun went down, and I'd better watch my back around Damon. It was one thing for the Institute to train vamps to fight Noctifectors. Another to have an Undead king like Toel reading the enforcer's mind and knowing everything there was to know about the Bridge Council. "No idea, but I guarantee, when he wakes up, he and a small contingent of his minions are heading to Chloe's. Once he goes super vamp, there'll be no stopping him."

Cole stroked his jawline. The simple movement sent Brianna's lust zipping around him. She had it bad. If I tuned into it, like I had the magical spell around Toel, I could almost see the bright edges of her energy reaching out and touching Cole in various spots. He seemed oblivious, but he wasn't. His own lust greeted hers and held it close as he locked eyes with me. "And the others? They'll be at Carpathia and the Institute?"

"By tomorrow night, if Toel can find the right combo of blood to increase his powers. The Carpathia vamps that turned traitor at my coronation are leading the House's overthrow. They know the security system and how Dru thinks."

"Bastards." Dru paced away from the collective group, and his blood called to me. He was angry and a little nervous. After losing his father to Toel, the idea of losing Carpathia also sent his magic spiraling in tight, angry circles that flared and surged. His blood pulsed in a furious rhythm, and mine throbbed with it.

A fine line of sweat broke out around my hairline. My lungs seemed too tight. My legs wanted to cross the room on their own accord. My arms wanted to hug him.

Gah, vampires.

And what I was about to say would probably put my throat in danger from his schiavona sword. "If it comes down to it, we're going to give Carpathia to him." I glanced at Damon. "And the Institute."

"What?" The question came from almost every mouth in the room.

I raised a hand before they broke free from their shocked stupor. "Toel has fooled us at every turn so far. The plan I see may be a decoy, and if so, this time, we fool him. We'll be ready for him and his minions, no matter what occurs. Just in case he decides to attack Carpathia and the Institute tonight before he figures out his perfect blood formula, we're going to pretend to put up a fight, but we'll let his minions win. Either way, we go for the kill at Chloe's."

Maddy stood on tiptoes to look over Rad's shoulder. "And how do we do that?"

I smiled, my demon showing through. "I have a plan."

"Christ on a pony," Cole said.

More like Toel on a pony, but a minor detail.

For the next several minutes, I discussed aspects of my plan. Vicky was still in captivity at Carpathia. She and I were going to keep Maria busy with a summoning spell, so Dru agreed to send her to my house under guard just after sunset.

The Master Vamp had already called on Juliana and Rafael, regional managers in the south and east. Troops from both regions were on the way and the first wave would arrive by midnight. Another wave by sunrise. If things went as planned, we wouldn't need them.

Things never go as planned.

Dru knew this as well as I did, and both of us felt better knowing we had backup. "My brothers and I will lie in wait for Toel at Chloe's."

"Won't work. He'll sense you're there." I motioned between us with my finger. "It's the royal blood thing. Whether you recognize it or not, your blood does."

"Who then?" Di asked. There was a gleam in her eye.

"Not you."

The gleam turned bitchy. "I'm a goddess. I do possess a few magical powers."

Powers in the department of love and attraction. "You're not a killer, Di, but you and Chloe working together will make a nice distraction." As a Tempter demon, Chloe was also highly skilled in the art of seduction. "The thing is, Toel won't be easily distracted, and anyone who gets in his way will be eliminated. I don't want you and Chloe to engage him in any other way than to be submissive and helpful. Suggest various blood types to him, keep him entertained and focused on his potential super vamp status until the cavalry arrives."

Cole's gaze bored into me with obvious challenge. "And who is the cavalry?"

Forcing myself not to glance at Rad and give away that part of my plan, I met Cole's challenging stare. "A special group I'm going to put together. As soon as I have everything in place, I'll give you the 411."

Damon looked incensed. Cole glared daggers at me for bullshitting him. I was losing patience. "Look," I told them both. "I'm not keeping you in the dark for grins and giggles. I need you to trust I know what I'm doing. Each of us has a role to play in this takedown. This is mine."

Grumbling and arguing ensued. I held firm. If I'd been in their shoes, I'd have been pissed, too, and demanding more information. But there wasn't much they could do to force me to give them details I hadn't yet acquired.

I sent Dru back to Carpathia with his bodyguard in tow and a set of instructions to prepare for Toel's onslaught the next night, just in case he escaped us at Chloe's or changed his strategy. Neither Dru nor Brianna were happy about my plan, nor was Bri happy about leaving Cole, but Dru agreed to talk to his brothers and convince them to bait my trap. They had to be close to Chloe's that night, ready to take out Toel, but they couldn't attack before he was inside and distracted.

Cole was unhappy as well. He needed to go to the Bridge Institute and guard the archdemons while fighting Toel's minions in a half-assed manner if necessary. Plus, his girlfriend was in the line of fire and I was throwing out battle plans like a seasoned pro without consulting him.

A little professional jealousy and a lot of worry clouded his face and turned him into Mr. Gruff again, but I understood his concerns, so I didn't bristle. Much. He wouldn't agree to allow Damon, Yasmin, and Kirill to stay inside the Institute if the Undead were going to take over and that sort of screwed up my trap. The Institute wasn't the prize if the archdemons who ran it weren't in attendance.

We argued, Damon not taking either side, mostly because he thought my entire plan sucked. Occasionally, he tried to access my mind and speak to me mentally, but I blocked his attempts for the first time ever. That, of course, pissed him off but pleased me to no end. I'd never been able to block him before.

Score one for Frankenstein.

"JR and Maddy, you guys call Arman and help him organize a shifter battalion. I want you to position yourselves in three groups about a mile outside the Institute's perimeter and lay low. Really low. I don't want the minions to smell you or sense there are so many of you in the area. If we snag Toel at Chloe's before he gives the word to attack, we won't need your battalion, but if the plan his mind has handed me is bogus, you'll have to invade the Institute and kick minion butt if I give you the signal."

Maddy nodded vigorously. JR stared at my chin. "What's the signal?" Maddy asked.

Good question. Maddy lived on her phone, but if a cell tower signal went missing, so did my message. Cole would be there, so I motioned at him. "Whatever our War demon, here, decides it will be. He'll give you the signal, you'll surround the Institute and cut down any Undead who get in your way."

"Cool," she said.

JR looked green.

"And what about Maria?" Damon may have been quiet up to that point, but he wasn't backing off. "She's the unknown in this strategic plan of yours. How will you capture Toel if she's protecting him?"

Ye of little faith. "I'll take care of Maria. The succubus and I have a score to settle, and Vicky's going down with her."

"You'll need Salmad." A statement, and not one to argue

with by the powerful magic he was shedding like water. "I'll send for him."

"Not until tonight." I didn't need a priest hanging around all day, even one I had freaky ties to. "You and the council members should go to Nudra's house in Oak Park. It's totally fortified with a sick security system and Toel won't suspect you're there. You can drop Salmad off on your way."

A tense silence descended. Maddy and JR left with Di in tow. Damon insisted Cole should stay with me since I was still on so many hit lists, but I refused on the basis that no one could protect me from Maria, Toel was sleeping the day off, and I had Rad for protection against the Noctifectors. Since Damon preferred to argue with facts and logic on his side, he begrudgingly admitted I was right and he and Cole left a few minutes later. On the way out, Cole gave me a knowing look. Rad or no Rad, Cole would be back before the day was over to watch my six if he could.

Once everyone had left, my home seemed more empty than usual. Rad and I stared at each other across the sectional sofa in silence. His lips were pale and pinched, and shadows darkened his eyes.

"As much as I hate to admit it," he said, lowering his head and looking at me from under his thick lashes, "I need to feed."

Absentmindedly, I licked my lower lip, sensing the pulse at the base of his throat and the blood pumping in the veins of his neck. I had no desire to drink his blood, but the throbbing between my legs from Dru's presence hadn't subsided.

I leaped over the sofa and tackled him. "So do I," I said, taking him to the floor.

THIRTY

I fed Rad and he fed me. Sex was always intense between us, but that day, it was an intense marathon. He drank my blood as if this were his last meal. He worshipped my body and took me on a feast of emotions and sensations I'd never before experienced. From the tips of my toes to the top of my head, every inch of me was given due diligence...more than once...by Rad's lips, tongue, and talented fingers.

Kama sutra, demon style.

I gave as much as I took. Except in the blood department. His delicious scent—an ocean storm rising and falling—completely filled my senses, heightened by the royal Undead blood now cruising inside both of us. The smells of hot sun, warm sand, and salty water were so intense, I felt like I was on a tropical island during a rainstorm. Hot, sweaty, freefalling off a giant cliff into the cool, welcoming water below. I could hardly catch my breath. Even my demon was in ecstasy.

His emotions were on overload as well, as his senses amplified in a similar way to mine, thanks to the blood. I still didn't like vamps, but this royal blood thing kicked ass.

At one point, I was on top of Rad, riding him for all he was worth, when I heard the crash of thunder and saw a flash under my eyelashes that could only be from lightning. In the throes of passion, I managed to crack an eyelid open, and sure enough, another flash outside the tall living room windows lit the interior, throwing odd shadows over our naked bodies.

The moment wasn't right for discussion, so I let it go. Later, body intertwined with Rad's on the sectional—the fabric would need a professional cleaning, thanks to the blood we'd smeared everywhere—I nuzzled his chest. "What's with all the thunderstorms we've been having? Doesn't Mother Nature know it's December?"

He lazily stroked my back with his fingers and said in a groggy, satiated voice. "Have there been a lot?"

"Three or four since last week, haven't you noticed?"

"Not really." He pointed at the storm raging outside. "Looks magical."

"That's what I thought too, but what kind of magic and why?"

"Is Damon concerned?"

"He hasn't mentioned them."

"Then I wouldn't worry."

I tried not to, snuggling closer to his warmth. His heart thudded solidly under my head, the rhythm lolling me into a dreamy stupor. One of his hands rubbed comforting circles on my back. I had enough to worry about without obsessing about the storms, but the magical component nagged at me. Was Maria causing them? Was I?

If Maddy had heard my internal thoughts, she would have rolled her eyes and yammered at me about being conceited and self-absorbed. One of Rad's long, callused fingers touched my temple. "You're thinking too much like always."

"A serious fault that's saved a few people over the course of my lifetime, but thanks for pointing that out."

He laughed at my snarky tone. "When are you going to tell me your plan?"

"As soon as I have you in an uncompromising position where you can't say no."

"You've already had me in at least three of those. What gives?"

I wanted to sleep. Forget about Toel and Maria for a few hours. Enjoy my time with Rad in case this *was* our last meal. My senses were on overload, my body exhausted. "I'm still working on the details. After I have a nap, I'll give you full disclosure."

He drew a deep breath and let it out slowly, reminding me of Damon. Rad had more patience than the archdemon. And more skill at manipulating me without seeming like it. "It involves the Noctifectors, doesn't it?"

He sounded disappointed. "As skilled as you are...and believe me, you have mad skills...sending you in by yourself against Toel would be reckless."

"You don't think I can take him?" Less disappointed, more playful.

"He's a wild card. I'm always two steps behind him." I rubbed a hand over Rad's bare chest. "This trap has to be fail-proof or a lot of humans will end up dinner for his Undead army."

"The Nocts won't go near Chloe's though. They stay away from that strip of downtown. Too many supernaturals. Too much danger."

"That's where you come in." I pushed up onto my elbow. "You have to convince them to do this. Toel can't sense them the way he can his brothers and me because they're human. I'll set it up with Chloe to keep out the worst of her supernatural customers so the Slayers can lie in wait for Toel. Once they have him surrounded and contained, either I'll step in and dispose of him, or Dru and his brothers will."

"I thought you were going to be distracting Maria."

"I am. If my plan goes right, I'll trap her here. Then I can head to Chloe's and clean house with Toel."

"The Nocts won't agree to turn him over to you and certainly not to his vamp brothers. They'll want to finish him off."

Of course they would. And if that's what it took to get them there, I'd lie and pretend I was all for it. "Be my guest."

Rad studied my face, knowing I would never give up the chance to take out Toel myself. "The Noctifectors are pretty effective at their job."

"Which is why I'm putting this part of the plan in your hands. No one's more capable of pulling this off than you."

A trace of a grin touched his mouth. "You are such a brown noser."

"Oh, I'm more than that, Noct Boy." Slithering down his naked body, I kissed a particularly nice part of it, smiling to myself when he hardened instantly. "I'm Kali Sweet, and I know exactly how to wrap you Slayers around my little finger."

"And thank the devil for that," he said as I kissed him again and showed him my mad skills in the sin department.

HOURS LATER, he shook me awake, forced me into a sitting position, and tugged his shirt over my head. "Kali, wake up. I want you to see something."

I shoved his hand away, dug deeper into the soft sofa. Waking a demon who hasn't had her fill of sleep is a suicide wish, but Rad always loves a challenge. He scooped me up, lifting me with the ease he would a child, and jogged up the steps of the sunken living room. I protested and started to throw a hex at him, but he kissed me, and...

Protest aborted.

He carried me through the church, upstairs to the second floor and past my bedroom loft to the back stairwell. A set of metal stairs led to the roof. There, my coat and boots were waiting and he threw some jeans on me while I staggered from sleep deprivation and held onto his shoulder. Then he led me upstairs and out onto the roof.

The storm had moved on, leaving behind a pale gray sky with peach-colored ribbons. The sun was setting.

Usually, I sat on the roof to watch the sunrise, a stamp on my life that asserted I'd lived through another night of being the Bridge enforcer and a vengeance demon. In all the years I'd lived in the church, I'd never watched the sun go down.

Rad had shoveled the snow from my favorite spot and set two old recliners side-by-side. How he got them up the metal stairs was a mystery, but magic was a good guess. A small fire burned in a metal fire pit, and blankets were draped over each chair.

In the distance, cars swished by on the interstate, and limbs cracked as snow fell from them in the wooded area behind the cemetery. Here and there, the low drone of snow plows broke through the air, and birds in the distance called their good-nights to each other.

It was serene and peaceful. I guided Rad to a chair and pushed him into it, crawling onto his lap and draping a blanket over us. We sat like that, listening to the city's chorus and watching the sunset for long minutes. He told me he'd talked to the head of the Chicago Noctifectors, and while they were reluctant to go to Chloe's, he'd pleaded the case for humankind and won their confidence. He'd already alerted Chloe as well.

She was pissed he was bringing Slayers to her business, but they were the lesser of two evils. Literally.

"I brought you something," he said, shifting me so he could pull a small blue box from his coat pocket. "From New York."

The last of the light was fading in the west, the peach streaks turning a dark purple. Fire danced low in the fire pit, throwing shadows around the rooftop. The bright blue box seemed completely out of place and made my insides freeze up, even though my body was physically warm and content.

Light blue box. New York. Ugh.

What to say, what to say... "Tiffany's, huh? Wow, um, you shouldn't have."

On top of it being a Tiffany's box, it was ring size. Double ugh.

There were so many things going through my head at that point, it felt like my brain was doing eighty on Lake Shore Drive.

Rad tapped an index finger against my temple. "You're thinking too much again."

Right. Taking the box with shaking fingers, I untied the white ribbon and held my breath as I eased the lid off.

Nestled inside was a tricked-out Hello Kitty pendant. She was sporting a Santa hat and red bow and holding a wrapped present. My heart melted a little. "I love it."

I love you.

I couldn't say those words, but the ones I did speak out loud were true. I did love the pendant and the fact he'd thought of me while he was in New York. Even with the obvious Christmas overtones, the pendant was gorgeous. She sparkled and had that sly look in her eyes that always made me laugh. I even loved the little blue box she came in.

Merde. I was turning into a complete mush. Sliding an arm

around Rad's neck, I kissed him as the sun lost its fight with the night and disappeared.

We made out like a couple of high schoolers for a few minutes, then I heard a car door slam in the parking lot. Shit, I'd forgotten about Salmad and Vicky being delivered to my doorstep.

We gathered up the blankets, and Rad snapped his fingers to douse the fire. On the way downstairs, I avoided eye contact. This was it. He would be heading off to join the Noctifectors at Chloe's. I'd be totally winging a plan to trap Maria so she couldn't hide Toel or harm the others. If things worked, we'd be back here tomorrow. If they didn't...

In my bedroom, I left Rad's shirt on, grabbed my fully-stocked cape of weapons that Cole had returned to me from the Institute, and strung the Hello Kitty pendant on a platinum chain. She slipped under Rad's shirt and warmed instantly against my skin. Last but not least, I stroked Volante and allowed her to snake around my waist. She tightened briefly in a small hug.

Downstairs, Vicky waited at the front door, four Undead bodyguards surrounding her. I let them in and had the bodyguards escort her to my basement where a special room like Damon's at the Institute awaited her. A panic room of sorts in case I ever needed it, but I'd never stocked it, so it was more of a prison cell than anything, embedded with magic to protect what was inside. A touch of my hand, and it switched directions, stopping what was inside from leaving.

Victoria's red hair stuck out from her head and she looked gaunt. Her pupils were red. Dru had starved her and I hoped that didn't deaden her magical abilities too much. Otherwise, she'd be useless to me when the time came.

"Make yourself at home," I told her, reinforcing the cell's

door as it closed. She sneered and tried to spit on me, but the cell's magic blocked it.

The head bodyguard extended a hand gloved in leather and we shook. "Asmund."

"Kali."

He gave me a nod, but it was full of challenge. Dru had apparently warned him I was a renegade. "We stay here by orders of Master Alexandru."

"Of course. I wouldn't have it any other way. Do you have a cellphone? I'll text you when I'm ready for her."

We exchanged numbers and I left the Undead crew to go back upstairs. Salmad paced in front of the fireplace while Rad lounged on the single spot of the sectional free of bloodstains. I wasn't sure if Salmad was pacing because of the intense glare Rad was giving him or because of the blood. Probably both.

"How's the head?" I asked the priest, wondering if he knew Rad was actually a Noctifector and not as badass as he was pretending.

Salmad stopped pacing and touched the fine short hairs at the back of his skull. "The archdemon relieved my pain. He has remarkable abilities."

"That he does." Especially in the piss-off-Kali-department. "Did he explain the plan for tonight?"

"Yes, although I'm unsure of my part in this plan."

"How much do you know about ghosts?"

Salmad's beautiful blue eyes locked with mine. "Enough."

"Good."

Time to set my plan into motion. I gave Rad a *be careful out there* nod, and he returned the same. Yeah, we both sucked at saying goodbye, and neither of us wanted to admit, even to ourselves, that this might really be goodbye.

I motioned for the priest to follow me. "Let's get Toel and Maria on the road to hell."

THIRTY-ONE

Salmad followed me out the backdoor. The day had warmed enough to melt some of the snow, forming a crusty top layer. A sliver of moon peeked out from behind heavy clouds as our boots crunched the ground.

"How is it you're a priest?" I asked, leading us to the cemetery's ancient iron gate.

He looked surprised at the question, his angular cheeks more pronounced in the moonlight.

I stopped to explain. "Sacred ground, holy water, vows to serve God. Not exactly happy hour at the demon bar. I mean, how can you even walk inside a church?"

He motioned at my home, "The same way you can. I have great good and evil inside me—almost like a human."

"There's only one area of that church that's consecrated, the inner sanctum, and I stay the hell out of there."

"Have you ever tried entering it?"

"No, and I don't intend to push my luck."

"Your fear is what traps you, not your vice."

Easy for him to say. My fingers still tingled when I remembered how his holy belt had burned them at the Institute. I may have had good and evil inside me, but there was definitely more evil.

His gaze moved over the cemetery, analyzing. "What happened here?"

"A war between good and evil." We continued walking. The gate creaked as I opened it, and the magical barriers I'd erected around the acre of land shivered at my touch. "Evil won."

A small *hmm* escaped his lips, his breath turning white. He touched the gate, stroked one of the iron bars, and drew back his hand. "And were you present during this war?"

"I came afterward. Dark earth magic resides here. Human souls were sacrificed on a massive scale, possibly to Death himself. Be prepared when you enter."

I stepped across the threshold, felt the rush of magic. My demon woke and welcomed the skittering evil as it danced over my skin, infiltrated my body. The sensation was like coming home to my demon and she reveled in it.

Invisible fingers of magic probed me from head to foot, poking and teasing. Around my waist, Volante shivered with delight. Even though the war and sacrifice had been centuries ago, she sensed the blood that had been spilled there like a cat sensing catnip. She wanted to play.

Salmad's face was shadowed by the low-hanging trees surrounding the area, but his eyes caught a shaft of moonlight and flashed silver. He regarded the threshold with unease. "Why do you have this place so heavily spelled?"

The spells I'd placed on the area were thick as fog. Inside the perimeter, I couldn't hear the normal night sounds outside. "The cemetery contains a portal. One I used not long ago to send Lilith back to hell. There's no telling what might come out of it if I don't keep it under spell and key."

His Adam's apple bobbed. "*Pseudothyrum infernum?*"

A secret door to hell. "Pretty much. Thanks to Buffy, we refer to it in America as a hellmouth."

"This Buffy, is she the keeper of the door?"

Only in JR's world. "For now, I'm the keeper of the door."

He still hadn't crossed the threshold. "You cannot send Maria into the *pseudothryrum*."

"Why not? I exorcised Lilith here. I'll do the same to Maria."

A female voice, full of irritation, called from behind Salmad. The soft crunch of snow filtered across the cemetery's threshold. "Because she's not in a physical body."

Neve. I shoved Salmad out of the way to see my friend fighting her wheelchair to move it across the snow. The fat tires on the wheels and the layer of frozen snow on top kept her from sinking too far in, but she still had to wrestle against the uneven path and the magic meant to repel humans. "What are you doing here?"

The wheelchair's motor revved. So did Neve's emotions. "Di told me you were trying to stop Maria. I came to help."

"For the love of the devil, humans are not allowed in the cemetery. And what do you mean she has to be in a physical body? Why can't I exorcise her spirit? You force spirits to cross over all the time."

Neve's coated chest heaved with exertion. Normally, I would have helped her out—against her protests since she hated for anyone to help her—but this was no place for a human. "This is why you need me. You don't know jack about ghosts. I don't *force* them. The spirits choose to move on after my counseling."

"You cannot come in here."

She kept rolling, her finger steady on the forward control and aiming the wheelchair at my legs. "Get out of the way."

Great. I was going to have to manhandle a woman in a wheelchair. "Neve, don't be stupid. There is nasty dark magic swirling around in here. Even the priest doesn't want to come in."

She pulled up next to Salmad and gave him a nod. "Neve Vaselli. Ghost whisperer."

"Salmad de Roca. Priest."

"JR said you were a Templar Knight."

Salmad glanced at me, back to Neve. "Once."

"Were all you supernaturals?"

"Only a few."

"This is all fascinating," I interrupted, "but Sal and I have business to get to, and no, you are not helping us."

Neve's eyes shot silver stakes at my heart. "Excuse me, but who's being stupid here? You need a professional ghost whisperer, and you have one. I'm perfectly capable of handling whatever ghosts and dark magic are inside there."

God. Damn.

Satan be damned too. Behind me, the fingers of magic reached forward, wanting to grab Neve and drag her inside. Touching my fingers to the gate, I let go of a zap of vengeful energy that sent the dark magic reeling. Then I leaned forward and set my hands on the arms of her chair. "I love you, Neve, from the bottom of my worthless heart, and I mean this with all due respect, but you either leave on your own, or I will carry your skinny, human, wheel-chaired ass back to that church and lock you inside."

"Picking on a poor disabled woman, are you? What would your mother say?"

She only went for the disabled label when she knew she was losing an argument. Topping it off by mentioning my mother in order to push my buttons meant she was desperate to get in on the action.

I wished I could let her. "Don't turn this into a lecture on political correctness. I'm *not* an equal opportunity demon, and you're about as disabled as I am. But this cemetery? It will eat you alive and spit out what's left, which won't be much, and then those leftovers will get a one-way ticket to some other plane of existence. One you won't like." I straightened and planted my feet. "You're not crossing this threshold, my dear, so back the hell off."

"I can't believe you." Petulant. "You are such a bitch."

Humans. Say no and you've thrown down a challenge. Problem is, determination alone won't save their skin against evil. "I'm also your friend and I care what happens to you, so deal."

"Fine. I'll coach from the sidelines."

It wasn't a bad idea, except that Neve had no intention of sitting on the bench. I could see the truth in her eyes and smell it in the wind. "I appreciate the offer, but the only safe place for you is inside my house or back home in yours."

Her brain was working overtime. "Why can't you put a protection spell on me?"

If only it were that easy to protect the ones I loved. "Because I'm not a witch. My magic protects me and me only. I'm a demon. We're selfish that way."

"You protect the church." She nodded her chin at the ground behind me. "And the cemetery."

"Different types of spells, and both are still for my safety as much as anyone else's."

She stewed some more, and I resisted the urge to tap my foot. Sunset was long over, and I needed to get started on trapping Maria. Otherwise, the others would fail to capture Toel and stop the vampire war he was bringing.

I sent a quick text to Asmund and motioned for Salmad to cross the threshold. He hesitated but drew a deep breath and took the plunge. He didn't explode, which relieved his mind, and he exhaled loudly.

Leaning over, I hugged Neve. "Sorry to argue and run, but I really need to get on with this. A lot of people's lives, both human and supernatural, depend on me."

Neve huffed out a sigh and hugged me back. "I'm worried about you. This ghost is stronger than any I've encountered, and you don't know what you're doing."

Aha. All that bluster was because she was worried about me getting my ass kicked. My heart warmed. "I know Maria better than anyone else, no matter what form she's in. She's an enemy whom I'm well acquainted with. Salmad knows her too. Don't worry. Everything will be fine."

Platitudes suck, I know, but toss a worried human in front of me and there you go.

Asmund and crew appeared on the path behind Neve, Vicky's wild hair the only thing visible about her as the over-sized bodyguards stuck close. The path was barely wide enough for Neve's wheelchair, much less four hulking vampires and their prisoner. They moved as one, and in the shadowed yard, it was an ominous sight. The Undead magic rolling off them made all of my instincts scream *fight*.

As they neared, Asmund looked to me for guidance: was he supposed to go around Neve or move her out of the way?

He and his posse were so big, there was no way they would fit around her and still maintain their positions. "Neve," I said, motioning my head at the group. "Go back to the house and stay warm. Asmund will IM you with any questions I have, and you can help me from there. Deal?"

An air of renewed confidence straightened her spine. Her

teeth flashed in the darkness. "Do you have any ginger green tea in the pantry?"

She knew I did. I kept a tin of the pricey imported stuff just for her. "If you didn't drink it all the last time you were here."

Waving a finger at me, she turned her wheelchair in the snow, parted the bodyguards, and nearly ran into Vicky.

The red-haired bitch snarled at her. "Watch where you're going, cripple."

Without missing a beat or a turn of her wheels, Neve pulled out a stake I'd given her eons ago and cracked Vicky across the front of her knees. The stake was rosewood. Hard, dense, and heavy. I preferred my stakes a little lighter since I carried them in specially made pockets inside my cape, but other vamp hunters liked the weightiness of rosewood. I'd given the stake to Neve when I decided to switch to cherry wood and she used it as a truncheon.

A crunching sound resonated in the winter night as Vicky screamed and dropped to the snow. Her hands were bound behind her, but before she pitched forward, Asmund grabbed her by the jacket and lifted her from the ground.

See what I mean about Neve being about as disabled as I am? Her motto was roll softly and carry a big stick.

Dangling in the air, Vicky screamed obscenities at Neve, who sat there and smiled. As always, Vicky's simple presence pissed me off, so adding the fact she'd insulted my friend and was now screaming at her made my vengeance demon roar with anger. I caught Asmund's eye and gave him the sign to bring Vicky to the threshold.

Asmund held Vicky in front of me, and I slapped her face. "Shut up, or I'll stake you right here."

Her knees weren't working too well after the clubbing, but she still kicked out at me, adding a few choice descriptions to her verbal tirade. I started to grab my own stake out of my cape when Asmund turned Vicky by her scruff and brought his face even with hers, stopping her kicks with his massive legs. "You do not talk to the queen of the Central Region like that. You do not raise your voice to her."

Vicky loved powerful men, dead or Undead, and the one holding her in the air radiated power in all directions. "I pledge no allegiance to your queen." Even in the dim light, her eyes flashed with an inviting dare. "And there's nothing you can do about it."

She was wrong on that count. Asmund used his other hand to grab her hair and yank her head back, exposing her neck to his now descended fangs. In one swift movement, he lunged, sinking his fangs into the pale skin waiting for him.

But he didn't drink. Her body arched and then went stiff as a mannequin. A frozen ballerina.

Neve's eyes went wide. Salmad's did as well. "Don't kill her," I yelled.

He ripped a hole in her neck, not bothering to retract his fangs before releasing his hold there. Then he set her on her feet in front of me, where she wobbled, body still rigid in the cold night air.

"Bow," he commanded.

A single word, but growled with so much emphasis, I swear the ground under my boots vibrated.

Vicky stared at me with unseeing eyes. Her neck bled black in the darkness. When she didn't kneel as instructed, the body-guard kneed her from behind, and another faint cracking noise echoed in the air. She went down, knees kissing the snow.

Asmund was my kind of guy. Less talk, more action. And action was what we needed.

I signaled Neve to get to the house. She stuck her tongue out at me, but fired up the wheelchair and left. Grabbing Vicky by the collar, I hauled her up and propelled her across the threshold and into the cemetery. "Thanks, As. Appreciate the backup."

"My queen," he said with a nod. He licked his lips. "Master Alexandru insists I accompany the prisoner wherever she goes."

That could be a problem. I didn't want anyone in the cemetery but Vicky, me, and Salmad. "For your own safety, it would be better if you remained outside the graveyard's perimeter."

"My safety is not the issue. Yours is. I will take my chances to serve and protect you as instructed by my Master."

Well, hello, new bodyguard. Dru might be pissed at me, but he was worried about Maria kicking my ass, just like Neve. Either that or this was a simple political move any House Master would make for his queen.

I stepped closer and lowered my voice so Vicky wouldn't hear me. "Just so we're clear, I'm summoning a spirit. On the off chance she possesses your body, I'll be forced to stake you."

"Understood, my queen."

Cool. I could use Asmund as more than a bodyguard inside the graveyard. He was now my new anchor to this world. Once that portal opened, any demon inside the boundaries was at high risk of heading to the pit of hell. Vamps, however, had some kind of innate immunity. Hell didn't want them any more than I did. "The rest of your men will stay here. One of them should be able to contact Neve if necessary. Your phone won't work inside these borders."

"Agreed." He and his second-in-command traded phones.

I looked over my shoulder at Vicky. She was still zoned out, leaning against a tall grave marker and staring at nothing. "What did you do to her?"

"My skill set includes the ability to temporarily paralyze my prey. I shared a small dose of toxin with her."

Nice. There were demons and shifters who could do the

same, but they were rare. Very rare. I needed this guy on my payroll. "It won't hamper her abilities to summon the ghost will it?"

At this, he tilted his head, considering. "Should wear off in about thirty seconds. Her normal faculties will be dulled, but not inoperative."

Perfect. I waved him in, shut the gate, and started walking the perimeter, running my fingers over various gravestones and trees—the touchstones of my magical barrier. The snow was deep, forcing me to raise my knees high, and the brambles and overgrowth impeded my progress.

My demon was happy, cavorting and frolicking with the cemetery's dark magic. But as I reversed the spells I'd placed on the area and walked the inverted pentagon created by the tombstones, I noticed she was a little off. The earth magic swirling in the graveyard buoyed her, but she wasn't as hyper and obsessed as she usually was. Her energy was dulled in direct contrast to my senses which were so heightened, I could smell the decaying bones and moldy soil buried under several feet of frozen ground and snow.

Salmad joined me halfway through my spell reversal. I had to lower the barriers inside the place in order for us to get Maria in. "How will you summon Maria's ghost?"

"The vamp over there. She was a witch and is still practicing the dark arts. She summoned Lilith from hell. Maria should be a snap."

"And then you'll exorcise her?"

"*You'll* exorcise her. To a different plane of existence."

"Me?"

"You're Salmad, the mad priest, aren't you? I thought that was one of your special skills. Exorcising demons."

His robe made shuffling noises against the snow. He seemed to wrestle with a response. "I have only performed a few successful exorcisms, and as your friend pointed out, if Maria does not inhabit a physical body, it will be most difficult to exorcise her."

Details, details. "And if I get her in a physical body? Will that help?"

Vicky was coming out of her stupor. Her eyes narrowed as Salmad and I emerged from behind a mausoleum. "Hey, wait. I know this place. Why have you brought me here? Going to send me to hell like you did my savior?"

Only a fucked up witch would think Lilith was her savior. "That's one option." And a pretty good one. "But first, I want to thank you for resurrecting Maria. That's some powerful magic you've got."

Asmund stood off to her side, his gaze shifting between watching her and watching the area. Vicky was suspicious of the compliment, but proud enough her ego puffed up. Her chin rose a bit.

I hefted my butt up onto a marble tombstone with a wide, flat top, and swung my legs as if I had all night to sit there and chat. "Was it your idea or Toel's to bring back her ghost?"

Again the chin lift. This time in defiance. Guess that answered that question.

"To help Toel with his quest for world domination or for revenge on me?"

The fog in her brain was completely gone now. She was warming to the task of schooling me. "Maria is not just your everyday spirit. She's a *revenant* and I can control her because she's Undead like a vampire. Her power will manifest with mine and secure the future of the Undead. And her desire for revenge on you matches mine. She'll wreak havoc on you and yours while I sit back and watch."

Revenants were more like vamps or zombies than ghosts, but they didn't come back from the grave in their own bodies.

They jumped into one that was already walking and talking. "Then why not summon Maria and let her possess your body rather than that other witch?"

Her face twitched. "What other witch?"

Just as I suspected. She really had no idea what she was dealing with. "You didn't know? She's been inhabiting the body of a sexy witch who hangs out at club Fright Night. If you have the power to summon her from the ghostly plane, then why not use Maria yourself? The powers you have now...she could increase them tenfold. Maybe more. Combine that with your vamp blood and your skills as a witch, and you'd be more powerful than Toel."

Salmad shifted from foot to foot. Cold or nervous. Maybe both.

"What do you care?" A strand of red hair blew across her face. "Either way, you'll be dead."

"Exactly. And I'm not ready to die, so I want to make a deal."

A shot of renewed energy made the ends of her hair lift. She hated me to her core, but she couldn't resist hearing me out. "Toel doesn't make deals."

"I'm not asking Toel for a damn thing. I'm talking to you. Nothing would please me more than to see you get what's rightfully yours. You're already more powerful than Toel, and we both know it. I mean, you raised Lilith from hell. You summoned Maria. He couldn't do that on a bet."

The defiance was gone, and in its place, measured contemplation. I had her full attention. The gears in her head were turning. "Why would I make a deal with you?"

"Because Toel's plan to take over Carpathia and the Bridge Institute won't succeed. I've already made sure they're both secured against his attacks. And I know about his plan for the blood at Chloe's. I've taken steps to thwart all three."

"But...how?"

I waved her question away. "The how doesn't matter. The *why* is what's important. I'm sick of being a puppet for the Bridge Institute, and I'm now a blood slave to Alexandru. Do you know how much I hate him right now?"

In the background, Asmund stiffened, but he made no move to strike me down. Dru had probably warned him I'd do and say some things that went against vamp politics.

In front of me, Vicky's contemplation turned calculating and I continued. "So here's what I'm thinking. I know the Bridge Institute like the back of my hand, and I have an easy in with the sons of Vlad the Impaler. I can sense everything they're thinking. Everything they're feeling. You and I team up, and we could run the world, Vicky. Without Toel. Without Dru. And no Bridge Council to stand in our way."

Her body leaned forward the slightest bit. The fish eyeing the hook.

I gave her what she wanted. "All you have to do is summon Maria to this place and let her enter your body instead of that other witch who's so weak and worthless. You're the most formidable witch in this area, maybe the whole continent. It's time you took your proper place and quit relying on Toel to get what you want. Maria is the key."

Her mouth worked but she didn't say anything. She worried the inside of her bottom lip. "You're saying this to trick me."

"Trick you how?" I slid off the tombstone and spread my hands wide. Time was ticking by. I'd known this wouldn't be an easy sell, but dealing with Vicky always made me impatient. "I'm offering to help you instead of kill you. Where's the trick in that?"

"The last time you brought me here, I ended up a vampire."

There was that. "And stronger and more powerful than you were as a witch, correct?"

She eyeballed me, still looking for the trick.

Come on, come on.

Her body stiffened, her gaze went blank.

What the hell? I shot a look at Asmund, but he remained still and silent. Had I done that to her?

Take the deal, Vicky. I pushed at her mind with mine. *You know you want to.*

Her body jerked like I'd startled her. Her features went as flat and unemotional as the headstones dotting the landscape around us. "I'll summon Maria."

Hot damn. Another new skill to add to my burgeoning set. I clapped my hands together. "Let's do it. And when she gets here, bind her to you to make sure you have control over her."

She responded with a single downward nod. "I must draw a triangle on the ground to contain her."

"Of course. Salmad will make one with his holy chain."

Asmund regarded me with cold, hard eyes, but seemed to understand this was all some wacky demon plan. Salmad looked like he wanted to give me a high-five...and then strangle me.

At my suggestion, he hurriedly undid the chain from his waist. I drew him and Vicky to a spot in the center of the cemetery and instructed him to form the triangle there. My demon recognized the portal under our feet and started throwing herself against the magic imprisoning her inside my chest. She wanted out of there. Fast.

When Salmad finished, we both looked at the witch-turned-vamp. "Will that work?" I asked.

She stepped forward and raised her shackled hands toward me. "Cut me. I must bleed inside the triangle."

Her neck wound had already stopped, so a quick slice of

my dagger across her palm opened up a new blood source. She dripped it around the inside of the triangle, chanting a spell under her breath. When she finished, she looked up at me. "I have your word, demon, that you will assist me in my endeavors."

"Whatever you need," I lied.

Demons, you can't trust 'em.

THIRTY-TWO

Vicky went into a trance-like state, muttering a spell in another language. I glanced at Salmad and he shrugged. Neither of us was familiar with it. It sounded like a combo of ancient Hebrew and Martian.

The temp dropped ten degrees, raising gooseflesh all over my skin. I motioned Sal and Asmund off to the side, and we huddled together against the cold air. "Things are about to get messy, so I need you to both be ready to act," I told them. "Salmad, perform the exorcism as quickly as possible and don't sweat the details. The opening is directly under that triangle, and once I open it, it will suck Vicky, Maria, and probably us in."

"Us?" His face was all hard lines and shadowed determination. "I prefer not to travel through that portal."

"Me, neither. That's where Asmund is going to help us out." As the wind picked up, lifting the edges of my cape and blowing snow over my boot tops, I explained how the Undead bodyguard would be an earthly anchor to me and Salmad, so the exorcism didn't toast us as well as Maria.

Asmund puffed up his chest and looked down his long nose at me. "I will keep you safe, Queen Kali."

"Salmad, too," I reminded him. The priest may be susceptible to the exorcism, so do whatever it takes to keep him topside. Got it?"

Above us, clouds roiled and darkened. Whatever Vicky was doing was certainly having an effect.

"I have performed a few exorcisms in the past on the battlefield. I was never susceptible to them," Salmad said over the rising noise of the magical storm.

"But you weren't standing over a *pseudothryrum infernum*. You may have more *vitium* than vice inside you, priest, but the vice is still there. Don't ever forget that."

His jaw tightened in displeasure, but he gave me a confirmation nod.

A bolt of lightning flashed, striking a nearby tree and splitting it down the center. We all jumped. "She's here," I said.

We broke our huddle and turned to face Vicky inside the triangle.

Pale lips continued to move, although no words came out of her mouth. Her wild, kinky hair rose from her head, flying in all directions as if she were plugged directly into an electrical outlet. Her irises were white, the pupils black as the clouds overhead. And around the vamp's body, the air sparkled and surged with white sparks.

On the previous 4th of July, Di had dragged me to a fireworks display at Navy Pier. I preferred my fireworks to take place over U.S. Cellular Field after a White Sox game, but I enjoyed the show at the Pier even though I complained through the whole thing to Di. I didn't want her to think I'd gone soft.

The triangle of space surrounding Vicky was minute in comparison to Navy Pier, and yet, as we watched the vamp try to bind Maria's spirit to her, the show was no less incredible.

"Why have you summoned me?" a disembodied voice said as Vicky's lips moved. "What do you want from me?"

"That's not Maria," Salmad said at the same time I said, "Oh, shit."

Asmund grabbed my arm and started to step in front of me, my own personal Undead shield. I stopped him and stepped toward the triangle. "We didn't mean to call you," I told the spirit, wondering why it sparkled like Maria but was obviously of demon origins. I would have opened the portal and sent Vicky and the unwanted spirit on their way, but Vicky was my conduit to Maria. "Our apologies for bothering you. You may go."

From behind the three of us, I heard a laugh. A female laugh full of seduction, lust, and gluttony. "Did you really think you could fool me, Calina?"

Double shit. I touched my fingers and thumbs together to raise my protective magic, but before I could turn and confront Maria, lightning struck once more...

And I was the target.

Intense, burning pain seized me, a giant hand lifting me from the ground before dropping me just as fast at Maria's feet. Talk about a stun baton of epic proportions. My blood boiled inside my veins for a split second. My heartbeat flickered, went out, came back on with a stuttering *ka-thump, ka-thump*.

My brain stuttered as well, then rebooted. This wasn't exactly what I'd planned, but there *was* a silver lining. Maria was here. Which meant she wasn't protecting Toel.

I sunk my hands into the snow, pushed myself into a sitting position, and coughed against the snow swirling in my face. The lobes of my brain did a cha-cha dance with each other inside my cranium, and my magic mimicked the snow, whirling in frantic circles.

But my senses were overachieving in the sensation department. Wet snow soaked through my pants, freezing my ass. Maria's magic sucked at my skin, luring my demon into a stupor. The night smelled of white-cold electricity, frigid winter air, and the rotting scent of dark magic running through the ground's veins.

Salmad ran to my side, dropped to his knees, and gripped my upper arms, supporting me as he glared up at Maria's ghost. "I adjure thee that thou torment us not, evil spirit, *Per Dominum nostrum Jesum Christum*. Be gone."

The storm went wild, a great wind bending the bare branches of trees, lightning cracking in jagged bunches at the directional four corners. Raising my gaze, I met Maria's, keeping my hands buried in the snow and digging furtively to reach the soil beneath. "No. Don't leave. Stay with me. I need you."

I didn't need to see Salmad's and Asmund's faces to register their shock. Salmad made the sign of the cross and folded his hands in prayer. I was a bit shocked myself, but I had to do something to keep Maria engaged. She never could resist being needed.

The ghost of my tormentor regarded me with suspicious pleasure. "Change of heart, Calina?"

You don't fight evil with prayer any more than you fight vampires with Q-tips. I bowed my head in acquiescence, my stiff fingers striking gold and touching the frozen ground. Bingo. At that same time, I let the demon inside rise to power, the direct connection to earth magic fueling her vigor. "My queen, I live to serve only you."

Complete folly, this, but Maria saw what she liked in my eyes. "There you are, *daemon*. Time to come out and play."

She reached forward and stroked her slender ghost fingers down the side of my face. I shivered. Succubus energy flowed from her fingertips, an eerie, potent touch, causing me to lean into her hand, a dog seeking his master's caress. Maria was smart, but like all good demons, she had her weaknesses. I licked my lips, calling her attention to them. Then I shifted my head and kissed the palm of her ethereal hand.

"Rise, *daemon.*"

Tendrils of earth magic continued to shoot up my arms, and the graveyard's noncorporeal citizens huddled around me. I couldn't see their ghostly bodies, only sense their sinister energy. Whether they were attaching themselves to me out of fear of Maria or because I'd linked into the earthly magic below, I couldn't be sure. Either way, I accepted the union of their energies with mine, and as Maria stroked my face and sent her paralyzing venom into my cells, I sucked it up with relish. It was time Maria was treated to a dose of her own medicine.

But I had to get her into a physical body.

Using Salmad or Asmund was out of the question, and Vicky was still carrying her ghost rider—I could sense his struggle to get out of the trap going on behind us. Which only left one entity in the graveyard with a physical body...

Me.

THIRTY-THREE

A normal demon would never allow a fellow evil spirit to possess their earthly meat suit. It just isn't done. We're all selfish enough to want complete control over our bodies, minds, and magic at all times.

I'm no ordinary demon.

Giving Maria free access was as dangerous as setting my demon loose. Like I didn't have enough entities inside my consciousness. Damon always chattering in my head, Rad filling me with his emotions. My demon angling to break free from her prison bars.

Hell, what was one more crazy psyche invading my space?

Step into my parlor, said the spider to the fly...

Lifting my hands from the earth, I raised them in supplication. "Use me, my queen, to make yourself corporeal once more. Together we will reestablish your kingdom in this world."

A gasp went up behind me. Salmad was still murmuring prayers and Asmund didn't strike me as the gasping type. That left Vicky.

"No! Use me." She'd managed to get free from the

unwanted ghost and kicked away Salmad's chain belt. Shoving me aside, she supplanted herself at Maria's feet. "*I* summoned you. I'm the one who should get to be your vessel."

And they say demons are covetous.

Maria was more than amused. She was practically giddy. The demon she'd trained to bring pain down on humankind, and a vampire with incredible necromancy skills, were both vying for her favor. The queen was back in business.

I was happy to turn the floor over to Vicky, but in order to convince Maria of my sincerity, I couldn't throw in the towel too easily. Plus, I never back down from a good fight, especially if it involves an annoying Undead bitch.

"Why you..." I jerked a stake from inside my cape and jumped Vicky. She let out a startled cry, but her vamp reflexes kicked in, her stance changing to predatory, her fists coming up.

I tossed out a combination of punches that were parried. I lunged with the stake high overhead, which she easily avoided. The stake caught the thin material of her long cloak, renting the fabric and causing a gaping hole in the clothes underneath though.

That was fun.

As if she couldn't believe I'd scored the first hit, she bounced her wild gaze to my face, down to the torn clothing, and back to my face. The she bared her fangs and hissed.

My demon laughed.

I curled my fingers, egging her on. Around my waist, Volante jumped and bucked, wanting her turn at the Undead. But there was no time to grab her. The vamp charged.

Spinning to the right, I knocked the flat end of the stake into Vicky's bread basket. She let out an *umph*, grabbed her stomach, and tried not to pitch forward. Once again, her vampire reflexes kept her upright, but she hadn't been in Cole's training center learning how to hone those reflexes. I brought an elbow down on her shoulder, driving her farther off balance and her forehead smacked a tall, pointed tombstone, the crack reverberating in the cold air of the cemetery.

Inside, I felt nothing. No fear, no anger, nothing. But *merde*, I didn't want to knock her out so soon. What fun would that be? And how would I get Maria in her body if Vicky was unconscious?

On second thought, maybe that would be easier. I wished I had time to ask Neve. Wasn't going to happen, though, because Maria made the choice for me.

She waved a hand and a crack of lightning exploded over my head. My vision fuzzed out in a white, sparkling flash and something hit me with the force of a snowplow's blade. I knew that sensation. Maria's ghost had jumped my body.

My brain scrambled, my heart played a rabid tune.

The fly was in my parlor. A tasty, juicy prey.

My demon wrapped her arms around Maria's spirit and squeezed tight.

THIRTY-FOUR

I was passing out entirely too much these days, so when the next crack of lightning hit, lifting the hair on my body, I gritted my teeth and rode it out even though my brain disengaged and my legs buckled.

I heard a sizzling sound and smelled burning hair. Locking my knees and looking around, I saw a smoking black circle burned into the ground surrounding me, steam rising from the melting snow. Outside the circle, Vicky lay semiconscious on the ground, Salmad was backed against a tree trunk, and Asmund had drawn a sword, prepared to fight.

Some form of communication passed between the two men. Asmund wanted to rush the circle, Salmad knew it would be pointless. Inside my head, I sorted through the whirly-gig of thoughts, emotions, and magic, ciphering between mine, my demon's, and...Maria's.

Her spirit had succeeded in jumping my body. She was now a ghost rider, pushing her way into my physical being and controlling my movements. Funny thing was, I could touch her magic and feel the lust and greed at her core, but I could not read her mind.

Control. I needed to make sure I was still in control.

I wasn't. When Asmund rushed me with his sword drawn, my left hand rose and flicked him away as if he were no more than a pesky bug. The magic from my fingertips hit his chest so hard, it drove him back, feet in the air. He hit a mausoleum and dropped to the ground.

My feet started walking without any effort on my part, leaving the circle behind and heading for the iron gate. I commanded them to turn around and head back toward the portal, but nothing happened to stop my forward trajectory.

If I let Maria take my body outside the cemetery, how would I get her into that portal?

I wouldn't. She would walk the earth in my body, causing pain and destruction wherever she went.

Sinking mental fingers into my demon to get her attention, I mentally, physically, and magically put on the brakes. My demon screeched, and in turn, I did the same. The world tilted in front of my eyes, and I stumbled. That didn't, however, stop Maria.

An internal magical hand grabbed my throat, choking off my air and forcing me forward. The iron gate loomed ahead. Three more steps and my hand was on the iron, lifting the clasp.

Using my body, Maria threw open the gate's doors, shoveling away a new accumulation of snow. While I fought with all my might to gain control of my footsteps, she crossed the threshold with ease.

She was free. Trapping her in my body kept her from interfering with Toel's capture, but at what price?

My queen, I mentally projected at her, reaching for any way to make her turn around, *it is not safe for you out here.*

If she could read my mind, she ignored my warning. On the path leading to the church, she raised her arms to the dark sky and drew a deep breath. My voice sounded peculiar as she spoke through me. "This world belongs to us now, Calina, and oh, the things we will do here."

She sounded like a Dr. Seuss rhyme. If only she were that harmless.

"This world does not belong to you, Maria." Damon stepped from the shadows onto the path, blocking it. Flanking him were Yasmin and Kirill. "Remove yourself from my enforcer."

His enforcer? Even in my current state, being claimed as property annoyed me, but underneath it all, I was happy as hell to see him. I wasn't facing this situation alone.

Maria chuckled from my mouth and spoke again in that weird-sounding voice. "She gave herself to me, and I owned her long before you came along, archdemon. You are no competition to me."

A few steps behind Damon and crew, Cole stood with his hands crossed nonchalantly in front of him. I didn't buy the casual stance, especially with his gaze boring into mine telling me he was trying to figure out how to kill Maria without killing me. Didn't appear that he had any ideas. Great.

Maria stepped forward, putting me face-to-face with Damon. My hand rose and stroked the side of his face. He didn't flinch or back away. "You are a fine specimen. Perhaps there is room in my new court for one such as yourself."

I had always been on the receiving end of Maria's magic, the warm, sensuous desire seeping through my skin and sensitizing my nerve endings. Now, as she touched Damon with her succubus magic, I sensed what she felt. The top layer of Damon's emotions was a smooth impassive plane. But Maria's magic was like water running downhill and finding a crack to drip through. Damon grabbed my wrist and jerked my hand from his face, but not before Maria's magic touched his turbulent emotions underneath that plane.

There was love and hate and fear all tangled in a ball of passion. A new wave of lust washed through me. Damon's or Maria's?

Damon's dark eyes glared at me with a yearning as intense as the one I had seen in Rad's eyes. My free hand, acting on Maria's accord, grabbed him by the back of the neck, and I kissed him.

Ack, my brain screamed. *No kissing the boss!*

Maria, however, did not appear to be listening. Either that or she just didn't care.

Kali?

Damon? You can hear me?

His lips moved against mine, warm and inviting. Maria's lust raised a notch. *Of course, I can hear you.*

So Maria hadn't broken our funky ESP connection. But could she hear our brains having this convo? *What the hell are you doing here?*

Saving your impertinent ass.

My lips parted, and my tongue, thanks to Maria, took a spin around Damon's mouth. *My ass doesn't need saving.*

Damon's tongue groped mine back. *Appearances are deceiving then because it looks to me like your ass is in deep trouble.*

As Maria raped Damon's mouth, I had to admit, he was a damn fine kisser. His lips took command of mine, which wasn't easy to do since Maria was a control freak, and I had to stop myself from sighing into this mouth. I also had to stop myself from feeling relieved he was there to save my extremely troubled ass. *This is all part of my plan.*

His mind made some kind of noise that sounded a lot like a laugh. I nearly kneed him in the balls. *Well, now that you have her, how will you get rid of her?*

Good question. *I'm still working on that part.*

I see. Are you sure you don't require assistance?

What's your idea?

Before he could answer, Maria broke away. My chest heaved from her panting. She patted the side of Damon's face and reveled in the way his eyelids hung at half-mast, and his dark Basque eyes beckoned her to do more than kiss him. "You are a demon of worth," she said. "I may have use for you later."

With that, she shoved him aside. Kirill and Cole both started to move toward her. Yasmin, the wimp, shuffled out of the way. Yasmin's idea was the better one since Maria waved one of my hands and sent a bolt of magic at the three demons. Damon, being the closest, was hit the hardest, the magic knocking full force into his chest and driving him into Kirill and Cole. All three of them ended up on the ground.

About that idea of yours, I mind-texted Damon. *Now would be a good time to share.*

Fight her, Kali, and take back control.

He was lying there on his ass, looking shell-shocked. If an archdemon of Damon's power couldn't fight off Maria's magic, how the hell was I supposed to? *Thanks for the backseat driving, boss. I'll get right on that.*

My feet started walking on their own accord again, heading toward the castle. Heading...I raised my head and sniffed the air...toward the nearest human.

Neve.

Nonononono. Once again, I put the mental brakes on and fought like crazy to turn my body around against Maria's wishes. Just like before, it didn't do a damn thing. I glided over the top of the snow, barely leaving imprints from my boots, hurrying to the one thing that Maria desired even more than me, or an archdemon-induced orgasm.

Human flesh.

Use your magic, Damon's insisted said in my head.

I am!

Your demon's magic.

Don't be ridiculous. My demon loves Maria.

Control her. Like you did with Toel.

I was at the back door of the castle. My hand on the door-knob, turning, turning…

Could I do it? Did I have a choice?

Damon, can't you use some of your extra-juicy archdemon magic to stop her?

A heavy mental sigh answered me. *That was my plan until you let her possess you. Now I cannot harm her without harming you as well.*

Maria shoved the door open, and we stepped across the threshold. The scent of warm human invaded my nose, drawing us toward the living room.

So harm me. Whatever it takes to stop her.

I will not, Damon answered. He and the others were staying a careful distance behind me. *You are the one who must stop her now.*

Gritting my internal teeth, I reached deep and tickled my demon. She hissed, baring her teeth back at me.

Come on, bitch. Step up to the plate. Time to play with your queen. Isn't that what you want?

She snapped at me, but her interest was piqued. She was already embracing Maria's emotions and drooling at the thought of her mentor being so close. If I lowered the prison bars keeping her from freedom, she could literally tap into Maria's magic. Or so I thought.

But if I couldn't keep her on a leash, it was lights out. She would overtake my system...and this time, there were a whole lot more resources for her to use. The vamp blood, Maria's magic...

Neve would be dead meat.

But my friend didn't stand a chance against Maria alone, so in the end, the point was moot.

Through the kitchen and into the living area we went, dropping plops of snow all over my hardwood floors. I tried not to think about the mess we were leaving behind, but it pissed me off even more. With every step, I loosened the leash around my demon, coaxing her to surface but trying to keep her focused on Maria rather than Neve.

Which was hard to do, since Maria's total attention—and therefore mine—was focused on Neve's slight body in the wheelchair. A fire burned in the fireplace and she sipped from a cup, watching the fire burn. A blanket covered her lap.

She heard us enter and turned her head to look at me. "Kali? Did it work? Did you send the bitch back to hell?"

I felt Maria's shock, then heard her laughter bubbling up from my throat. "The bitch is well in hand, my dear." She walked in front of Neve and leaned down to put my hands on Neve's wheelchair arms, almost exactly the same way I'd done earlier. "Don't you worry about her."

Neve reared back, sensing something was amiss. Steam rose from her cup, wafting up with the smell of her tea. "Kali?"

Her pretty brown eyes searched mine with concern, and when I thought of the damage Maria would wreak on her soft skin, vomit rose in my throat. And that was nothing compared to the destruction Maria would do to Neve's incredibly generous human soul.

Rage gripped me. My demon roared full-throttle from the center of my chest, scaring the hell out of Neve and shocking me as well. Not that my inner monster gave a demon's ass about Neve, she was simply responding to my rage.

Neve saw it in my eyes. Saw my demon take over, the inhuman roar only adding to the effect. She threw the hot tea in my face, but I didn't feel it. There was a strange clawing sensation inside my frontal lobe...Maria fighting with my demon and losing traction?

The world tilted sideways, and I hung onto the wheelchair to keep from falling.

Stop Maria, I ordered my demon. *Take her powers for yourself.* My shifting weight upset the chair, and Neve and I spun to the right, then left as my feet fumbled to find stable ground. From a distance, I heard Damon and the others enter the room. He said something, and Neve hit me with the cup, striking my left temple. Can't say that helped my dizziness, although it seemed to loosen Maria's hold a little more. I definitely felt a weird cleaving sensation inside my chest, as if my heart was being ripped into two pieces.

My demon roared again, confused at the sensation. The clawing in my brain intensified, my chest was being shredded by invisible talons. *Attack,* I told her. *Maria is doing this. Stop her.*

Attack she did. Demonic magic ripped through me, striking out at the invader inside my skin. Aggressive, defensive, and violent, it was all about self-preservation. It was one thing to share the body with Maria, another to let her destroy it. My demon was suddenly ready to wipe her out of my system, right down to my very cells.

The monster inside wasn't the only one who went on the attack. Neve, not entirely understanding what was going on but filled with human self-preservation as well, drew a weapon from under the blanket. The iron fire poker from my set.

Iron. Ghosts. "Wait," I said through gritted teeth.

"No," Damon yelled.

"I'm sorry." Neve's soft brown eyes were sad. "It's the only way to get rid of her."

With one swift movement, she speared me, running the poker straight through my stomach.

THIRTY-FIVE

A sharp, burning pain exploded in my guts. I fell to my knees at Neve's feet, the poker iron embedded in my stomach.

The world got fuzzy around the edges, and a loud ringing set up shop in my ears. My head throbbed, my chest felt like my heart had been ripped out, and my stomach and back...well, they felt like I'd been run through with an iron poker. Go figure.

I'm a demon kabob, I thought, laughing like a drunk human before I tipped sideways and landed on the floor.

There was a lot of shouting. Neve yelled for Damon, Damon yelled for Kirill. Neve was crying my name. Cole's hands were the first to touch me, but he didn't really know what to do. He couldn't flip me onto my back, couldn't pull out the poker. It had a tiny hook at the end. If he yanked it back out, he'd take muscle, intestines and maybe an organ or two. Being a demon, and a supercharged one at that, I could recover from a lot of injuries on my own. But losing an organ? Not so much.

The poker wasn't like a fishhook or an arrow where you had a straight end or could break the barbed end off to form a straight end. Iron, even for a demon with the strength of the Hulk, is difficult to break. Bend, yes. Break, no.

Add to that, I was starting to bleed out. A warm stickiness pooled underneath me. Cole went into triage mode on my front, yanking the blanket off Neve's lap and pressing it hard around the poker's entry point. Someone—probably Kirill—did a similar thing to my back. There was a lot of discussion about how and when to remove the poker. Should they take me to the Institute or perform the surgery here? But once the initial agony passed, a deep numbness infiltrated my body. My vision grew shadowed and I closed my eyes.

The smell of wood smoke, more heady and intense than the one created by the fire behind me, teased my nose. A warm hand gently tapped my cheek. "Kali, is she gone?" Damon's voice seemed to float through my brain. "Is Maria gone?"

I ran a mental probe around inside my skull and found nothing that didn't belong there. My faculties were weak, but I was pretty sure she'd disappeared. Cracking my eyes open, I gave my boss a feeble nod.

That was good, right? Or was that bad? I suddenly couldn't remember, but I thought it was both.

His hand cupped my cheek, and he gave me an enervated smile. "Try to stay awake. We'll get you to the Institute and fix you up."

They were the last words I heard for a while. Cole picked me up, poker and all, and carried me toward the door. I fell asleep in his arms.

When I woke sometime later, I was in a sterile room, white everywhere. White walls, white blinds, white bed linens. I was tucked under a blanket. Heart monitor leads were stuck to my chest, and an IV needle was wedged into the skin of my left wrist.

I flexed my fingers and toes and noticed my stomach hurt like a son-of-a-bitch, but for the life of me, I couldn't remember what had happened to put me in the Institute's recovery room. My brain seemed to be wrapped in cobwebs, the last memory I could call up had Rad in it. We were on the roof of my castle. The sun was setting.

The Hello Kitty pendant.

Absently, I raised my hand and touched the spot where the pendant had lain. It wasn't there, but I remembered how it had warmed against my skin. Where had it gone, and what had I done?

I rose up on my elbows, and a sharp pain hit me in the gut. Along with that, it felt like I had a wide seatbelt around my stomach. Lying back down, I raised the blanket. A broad white bandage wrapped around my torso. In the center, there was a bloom of red blood.

Another recent memory caught in my hippocampus. Neve's sad eyes.

A slow trickle of images cleared away some of the cobwebs. The cemetery, the storm, the portal. I'd lowered the protective magics around the portal, but shit, I couldn't remember raising them again. Actually, I couldn't remember why I'd lowered them in the first place. I had to get back there. All manner of uglies could get through otherwise.

"You're awake." Kirill strolled into the room as I threw off the covers. His gaze did a quick scan of my naked body, zeroing in on the bloody bandage. "Going somewhere?"

Now upright, everything ached. I white-knuckled the handrail. "Where are my clothes?"

"I'll ask Yasmin to bring a fresh set from your suite." He used the room's call system and ordered up some clothes.

Then he ripped the heart monitor patches off my chest and started working on removing the IV needle. "How do you feel?"

It was said off-handedly like any good doctor would ask a patient, but there was a note of something else in his tone that raised my suspicions. "Like hell. What happened to me?"

"You don't remember?"

"No."

"Hmm."

"That's not an answer." I pointed at the bloody circle. "Was I staked?"

I knew that didn't make sense. I'd been staked before in various body parts, and it hurt, but it healed almost immediately.

"Sort of."

Wow, he was just full of information. "Explain 'sort of'."

At that moment, Damon arrived. I reached down and grabbed the blanket, covering my upper body as he took one look at me sitting up and gave Kirill a frown. "How's our patient?"

"She appears to be normal, with the exception of some short-term memory loss."

"Hmm." Damon did a visual inventory of my face, concentrating mostly on my eyes. What was he looking for? "Trauma to the brain?"

Kirill shrugged. "I could do some tests."

"I don't need tests." Damon's unwavering stare made me increasingly uncomfortable. I tugged the blanket closer, internally checking on my demon. Had she gone ballistic again? Had she hurt someone? Was that why he was studying me so intently? "Just tell me what the fuck happened."

"What is the last thing you remember?" Damon asked.

For crying out loud. I drew a shaky breath, winced at the

discomfort in my stomach. "Neve. I remember Neve. Please tell me my demon didn't hurt her."

"Neve is fine. She's safe at home and wishes me to convey her heartfelt apologies." Damon crossed his arms and continued his cross-examination. "What else do you remember?"

"Apologies for what?"

He let the question hang in the air. I touched my stomach as something clicked. "She did this to me?"

A nod. "With an iron poker from your fireplace set. The tip did some internal damage to your intestines but missed vital organs. You're lucky. Organ damage would have been more severe and more painful."

Iron. That's why I wasn't healing as quickly as normal.

Iron wasn't deadly like silver. In fact, since I was a demon and made from the darkest recesses of the earth, my body could absorb iron under certain circumstances. It still made a hell of a weapon. "Why?"

His brows dipped. "Maria's ghost. Neve knew it would drive her spirit from your body."

Maria. *Merde.* How could I have forgotten about her? Seemed like there were others I should be asking about as well, but every time my brain tried to pull up their faces, I lost the thread of conversation. "Wait. Maria was in my body? Is that why I planned to open the portal? Was I going to jump in?"

Again the brow dip. He continued to look at me as he spoke to Kirill. "I believe testing is in order to understand the extensiveness of her brain trauma."

"I don't have time for tests." I wanted to stand up and shoo them out of the room so I could get dressed—there had to be a gown or robe in here I could wear until Yasmin showed—but instead, I shifted the blanket to cover my legs. Why did I feel so weird with Damon all of a sudden? So exposed? "For whatever reason, I lowered the portal's protective magic. It could be open right now. I need to get back to the cemetery and close it."

"Salmad has already taken care of it."

"Salmad? He couldn't even perform an exorcism." I wasn't sure how I'd remembered that, only that it was true.

Yasmin appeared, Maddy followed, and Cole brought up the rear.

"You're up." Maddy embraced me, plopped down on the bed, and ran her fingers through my hair on that side. "You look like shit."

"Thanks."

Cole did a Damon-like scan of my face, saw what he wanted, and gave me a relieved nod. Yasmin, who was focused on Damon as usual, tossed a pile of folded clothes on the bed without even glancing my way.

There's nothing like being naked under a blanket with a roomful of your bosses and a couple of your friends. Similar to a nightmare, only you're fully awake. "I need to get dressed."

No one took the hint. They all stayed exactly where they were. Damon spoke. "The portal is secure. Your human friend is safe. Maria is no longer possessing you, although we're not sure where she disappeared to." The last sentence held some reserve, and he scanned my eyes as he said it. Looking for my demon? Or Maria? "Even your plan to capture Toel has been a success."

"More or less," Kirill added.

Toel. Another memory dropped into place. "The Nocts killed him, right? Or did Dru and his brothers nab him?"

Damon shook his head. "He was captured by the Noctifectors. No word yet on his execution. An ingenious plan, I must admit. How did you get the Slayers to Chloe's?"

Rad. His face swam across my mental vision. My heart felt

heavy, our uncomfortable goodbye surfacing. "I don't remember. Where's my necklace?"

Maddy dug in a pocket, held out a sparkly Hello Kitty in Christmas drag to me. "She's cute, but I thought you hated Christmas."

"I do."

She rolled her eyes and strung the necklace around my neck. Instantly, the pendant warmed against my skin and I took a satisfying breath. Stupid thing made me feel better.

"What did you mean 'more or less' about Toel's capture?" I asked Kirill.

He glanced at Damon as if seeking permission, and Damon nodded. "Alexandru and his brothers arrived shortly after the Slayers, and a fight ensued. Alexandru was injured."

Vamps, like demons, had incredible healing abilities, but the tone of Kirill's voice made it sound serious. "How bad?"

Another of those looks passed between him and Damon. A look that said I wasn't going to like this. "A stake nicked his heart. He's dying. Slowly, but the wound is fatal."

My stomach dived. A stake to the heart killed instantly. But nicking the heart? The area hit died first, then like a fast-acting gangrene, it spread, eventually killing the rest. "No."

"I'm afraid so," Damon said. "There's nothing that can be done."

I clutched the rail again. My voice rasped as I challenged Damon. "There has to be something. You healed me and Salmad after Maria's attacks. Can't you work some of that magic on him?"

The room was silent, and Yasmin let out an exasperated sigh. "Twenty-four hours ago, you wanted to kill the vamp. Now you're crying because he's going to die?"

Crying? Sure enough, my lashes were wet with unshed tears. I brushed them away with the back of my hands. "Fuck you," I bit out, wanting to grind her face into the wall. "Dru is my friend." *And a more loyal one than you.*

Maddy put her arm around my shoulders. "He was asking to see you."

I swallowed the tightness in my throat, slid off the bed, and met everyone's eyes. "Get out and let me dress."

Damon uncrossed his arms. "It is ill-advised for you to go to Carpathia. There's nothing you can do for him."

I pointed a shaky finger at the door. "Get. Out."

Cole opened the room's door. "You heard the demon. Everybody out."

My three bosses gave Cole a round of raised brows, arguments, and self-righteous irritation. They were used to my insolence, not so much his.

Cole can be persuasive without opening his mouth, and as he and I both stood firm on the request, the archdemons filed past Cole and huddled together to figure out a way to stop me.

In their absence, Cole winked at me. "I'll drive you as soon as you're ready."

I gave him a tremulous smile and grabbed Maddy's hand to keep her there with me. I needed some of her smart mouth and skill with a brush. "Give me five minutes."

THIRTY-SIX

Carpathia rose in all its ostentatious glory as we drove through the gate and up the curved drive to the front door in one of the Institute's official SUVs. The stars were out in abundance, seeming to cluster overhead. Landscape lights spotlighted the sidewalk and front porch. I'd called ahead and told Stephan, Dru's French brother, we were coming. He had been noncommittal, but when we arrived, one of the House's servants, Oliver, appeared on the front porch and immediately came down the steps to escort me inside.

Maddy came with me, Cole a few steps behind. Outside of Dru's bedroom door, Cole gave me a nod and sauntered off. Probably to find Brianna.

I didn't know what I'd find on the other side of the door. Didn't know how I would handle this. Death in my world was usually fast and violent. This type of slow, but ultimately fatal death wasn't my thing. On the drive to the House, I'd tried to figure out what I should say, mentally rehearsing platitudes I knew Dru would hate hearing. Now that I was looking at the massive double doors leading to his chambers, the words "no" and "this can't be happening" seemed to be the only ones my brain would produce.

I raised my hand to knock, lowered it. Swallowed the bile suddenly tightening my throat. Oliver, waiting patiently beside me, was a husk of a man. Thin, frail, white hair. His eyes were kind though as he said, "My queen, allow me."

He knocked, and when Dru answered, he opened the double doors and announced me.

"I'll just wait out here," Maddy said.

It took everything I had to step across the threshold.

"Ah, my double rainbow of demon." Dru was propped up in the middle of an enormous bed at the far end of the suite, his voice echoing through the room, and yet, the sound was a fourth of what it had been just days ago. The room was divided into two living areas, his bedroom at one end, a sofa, and a fireplace at the other. The furniture was modern, just like in his office, and no surprise, he had a full wall of electronics and a massive flat screen over the fireplace. "I was afraid you wouldn't come."

The first time we'd met, at my coronation ceremony, he'd made the rainbow demon comment in a snarky manner. Since then, he'd used the nickname a few times as a joke. The once healthy vampire looked as frail as the servant who'd just ushered me in, and at least to my ears, the joke fell flat. His breath rattled in his chest, and he coughed. I searched my brain for something to say as I crossed the room, took his hand, and sat on the bed. "You're a conceited vamp, always trying to get attention, but really, this is taking things a bit too far, don't you think?"

His eyes lit up, appreciation for my flippant teasing evident. He didn't want to hear platitudes any more than I wanted to give them. He didn't want our last meeting to be full of sadness and drama. He smiled, his pale lips still full and inviting. "I do have a flare for drama, don't I?"

I returned his smile. "You're a *master* at it."

He acknowledged the pun and waggled his eyebrows at me. "I have one last dying wish."

"I'm not sleeping with you."

His laughter shook the bed, and he splayed his fingers between mine, giving my hand a squeeze. The rattling in his chest kicked up a notch, and he coughed harder. "You would deny a dying man his last wish?"

That rattle made me nervous. "You're a dying *vamp*, not a man, but even if you *were* human, if your wish had anything to do with getting me naked, I'd still say no."

"You love him, don't you? The Chaos demon?"

Yes, my heart said, and then it said, *no*. Loving someone left you vulnerable. That annoying Achilles' heel thing stared me in the face as sure as Dru's impending death. Feeling anything other than anger hurt too much. Especially when the person you felt it for up and died on you. "I'm a vengeance demon. I don't do love."

Dru's eyes reflected my lying face back to me. He squeezed my hand, seeming to understand my secret and the front I was putting up. "I have another last wish."

"I'll take care of Carpathia the best I can. I assume your brothers will want me to step down so they can appoint a new queen or king for the Central Division, but until then, I'll do my best to keep things the way you have them. I'll take care of the House and your Undead family."

"Thank you." He raised my hand and kissed my palm. A shudder ran through me. His blood was in me, and even in his dying state, a spark of lust flared between us. "The favor I wish to ask, however, is not about the House. It's a personal favor just between us."

I'd already said no to sex, so what else 'personal' could he want? My blood? "It's a terrible idea, but the only one I can think of to keep you alive."

His brows scrunched together. "There is nothing that will keep me alive."

I shifted on the bed and brought out the dagger I carried in a thigh holster. "My demon blood might."

Our gazes locked, and there it was again, that spark of lust. Dru's eyes darkened, and his magic rose, stealing over my skin and raising the hair on my arms. "That would go against every rule and law in both of our communities. The Bridge Council wouldn't just fire you, Kali. They'd shoot you for treason."

Damon didn't use guns. He'd draw and quarter me the old-fashioned way. Roast my intestines and grind my organs into mush. "You shared your blood with me and saved my life. I'm returning the favor."

I started to slice my wrist when his hand locked around it. He may have looked weak, but his grip was a vice. "I will not drink your blood."

"I'm sure it'll taste like gasoline, but you've got to try."

"And if it succeeded? What kind of monster would I be?"

A scary-ass one. And that would make two of us. "So we'll go to Frankensteins Anonymous when you're healed. I'm already in the club. It's no biggie."

He shook his head. "It will not work. My body will reject demon blood."

"How do you know? Toel was going to mess with different blood types to create a supervamp. Maybe he was onto something."

Dru released my wrist, seeming to struggle with taking a deep breath. "There have been other Undeads who've experienced this situation. Nothing could save them. It's all been tried, even demon blood."

Frustrated, I stood and paced. "Look, I'm more than your average demon, and you're dying anyway. It can't hurt."

A curious glint lit his eyes. "Of course, you're more than average—you've lived nearly as long as I have—but even if you were Jesus Christ himself, you couldn't stop this."

I returned to sit beside him, both of us silent and staring at each other. My sinuses filled with pressure. My stomach knotted.

"Kiss me," he said, his chest heaving as he tried to breathe. "Just one kiss. Nothing more."

Bad, bad idea. But in the end, how could I deny him such a simple request? I wasn't cheating on Rad, wasn't breaking any Bridge laws. All I was doing was setting my lips against his for a quick moment. "One kiss."

I leaned forward, shifting closer, and shuddered at the look in his eyes. His gaze locked on mine, drawing me in, but he wasn't messing with my mental abilities or putting me in throe to him. The blood bond we shared drew us together like a magnet to steel.

Definitely bad. If it hadn't been for the gravity of the situation, I would have been out of there in a flash.

It helped he didn't move, didn't try to take control of the kiss. I brushed my lips against his and felt the spike of magic between us. His breathing sped up, and he parted his lips. To breathe better or to invite me to do more? I gave him my breath and my lips, kissing him self-consciously and half-ass wishing this was one of Di's crazy fairytales where my kiss would break the curse and he would be healed.

This was real life, not a children's story, and so my kiss had no effect on his ailing body other than raising his blood pressure. I broke away, leaned my forehead against his. "How long do you have?"

"The doctor gives me twenty-four hours or less. I prefer less. This waiting is a bitch."

I held out my wrist. "Please. Take my blood."

His long fingers reached out, stroked my skin where the pulse beat. It sped up under the pressure from his stroking thumb and a warm flush washed over my body. "I want you to do me a favor."

"Anything you want if you'll just take a sip."

A sad laughter came from his chest. The rattle grew worse. "I want you to stake me. Properly."

Shit no. Hell no. Absolutely no way on God's green earth. My lips moved—nothing came out.

Noting my obvious blank stare and fish-sucking-air antics, he patted my hand. "I'll call my brothers as witnesses, so there will be no backlash on you. You owe me this, as queen of Carpathia. It's a duty in service to your Master and your liege."

"*Che cavolo.* You've got to be kidding."

"The Canon expressly states that the king or queen of a House must perform duties required by the Master. Plus, I'm sorry, but I'm pulling the liege card. You are my blood slave. You must obey me."

"I know what the fucking Canon says." That was a lie. I'd read maybe three pages of one volume, and there were something along the lines of a hundred volumes of the Undead Canon. "And you can blackmail me all you want, but you can't ask me to stake you."

"As Master, I'm afraid I can."

"I'm not talking about Master to Queen. Or liege to blood slave. I'm talking about friend to friend." A hard pressure filled my tear ducts. My jaw tightened. "I can't do it, Dru. I won't."

He released a tired sigh. "It is only because we *are* friends that I'm asking you for this distressing favor. You're a professional when it comes to these things. I trust you far more than most of the vampires in my life. You aren't motivated by politics or love. You will perform the job skillfully and with competence."

I withdrew my hand from his, stood, and gathered my cape. How could he put me in this position? Tears overflowed my eyes, and I brushed them away, searching for the willpower I needed not to punch him for asking me for such an outrageous favor. "I'm sorry. I can't."

Feeling like I couldn't breathe, I hurried across the room, heading for the door. Nice, right? Bailing on him when he was dying. I hated myself, but I couldn't stop my feet from running away.

"Kali?" he called, another cough racking his body.

I faced him, hoping he was going to take it back. Ask me to stay and watch TV or listen to music or that he was going to relent and agree to take my blood.

"Think about it. Please. It's the only thing I've ever asked you for."

Swallowing hard, I took one last look at him. "You think about *my* offer. It still stands. Call me if you change your mind."

I blew out the door, scrubbing the tears off my cheeks and hurrying down the corridor. Maddy was slumped on the floor next to the door, texting or playing a game on her phone. "Hey. Wait up."

She asked several questions and gave up when I refused to answer. Cole was outside on the steps talking to Brianna.

As soon as the fresh night air hit my face, I bent at the waist and gulped lungfuls of it. Maddy rubbed my back, and Cole grabbed my arm and steered me toward the car. None of us said anything as we drove away.

Hitting a speed dial button on my phone, I called JR. "Do you know anything about the vampire Canon?"

"Uh, a little, but it's not my specialty."

"Is there anything that states the Master of a House has to agree to do what the queen of a region demands?"

He thought for a minute. "Maybe if it has to serve the greater good of the Undead in that region."

"Good. Find it. A rule, a law, hell, I'll take a fucking footnote. Just find me something that forces Alexandru to do what I want him to."

"It'll take a while."

"You've got until noon tomorrow. Hurry."

I reached over and turned on the radio, cranking up a song by Theory of a Deadman, which seemed ridiculously appropriate. Then I laid my aching head against the cold window.

A few miles outside of Lake Forest, Maddy cleared her throat from the backseat loud enough for me to hear over the music and tapped my shoulder. "I need a favor."

Crap. Apparently, it was my night for them.

Shutting off the radio, I put my head in my hand. "I'm not staking you."

Cole gave me a funny look. Maddy said, "O-kay. I'm sure I don't want to know what that's about, but thank you. I guess."

"What is it, Maddy?"

She blew out a heavy sigh. "I want to go see my parents. Tonight. And I need you to go with me."

THIRTY-SEVEN

Since the death of my parents and sister, and Rad's abandonment when I was seventeen, there have been many days, weeks, years even, when I felt alone. Empty. Destined to live a life of sleeping away my days and working away my nights.

Yes, I've had friends in my lifetime. Not many, but a few. They cared about me and helped fill the void left by the absence of my family and Rad. But each of us walks this world alone—or at least I do, which I guess confirms Di's theory that I believe I'm an island. There are times for me when the next hour seems like it will last an eternity. When my job as enforcer is a burden rather than a blessing. When even Sweet Investigations and the work I do in this world to save humans from supernaturals like myself seems absolutely pointless.

My heart was raw after my meeting with Dru, but I couldn't say no to Maddy. So I put my rattled emotions in lockdown and asked her for directions to her parents' house.

Cole shot Maddy an irritated look in the rearview mirror. "Maybe this isn't the best time."

"I know." She chewed at a fingernail. "But after seeing Dru...you know...I just..."

I did know. Vampires feared death just like the rest of us, and that fear drove a lot of emotions. Maddy needed to see her family and find some kind of peace. "Tonight's fine. Let's go."

Maddy's home was a small bungalow in Elmhurst squeezed between several larger houses that looked to have been built in the past five years. Where the modern houses on either side filled out their yards to the max, her parents' house sat back from the street with a quaint sidewalk and two large oak trees out front.

By the time we arrived, all her nails were bitten to the quick. "What do I say?" She gripped my seat with both hands. How do I tell them?"

There was no script for this. Some humans accepted there were supernaturals in the real world. Others thought they were fiction. "You knew this was going to be a tough encounter," I reminded her. "But whatever happens, I'm here for you."

She got out of the car and stood staring at the house. A Christmas tree stood proudly in the bay window, lit up with white lights. Behind it, the glow of a lamp was the only other light on in the house. No other outside decorations, as if Maddy's folks had only had enough energy to put up the tree.

The moon reflected on the snow in the yard, giving the scene a bluish tinge. "Keep the car running," I told Cole. We won't be long."

He nodded and switched the radio to a Top 40 station, started humming along.

Cole was humming. Maybe miracles really did happen. Obviously, his time with Brianna was mellowing him out.

I climbed out of the car, my heart heavy. Over Dru, over what Maddy was about to encounter. I had no doubts this was going to get ugly, and what kid, Undead or not, needs to be kicked in the ass by her own flesh and blood?

Starting up the sidewalk, which was free of snow, I hesitated when she didn't join me. She'd shoved her hands in her pockets and stared hard at the Christmas tree in the window. I walked back and put my arm around her. "You don't have to do this," I said.

"Yeah, I kinda do. I'm just...scared."

I gave her shoulders a squeeze. "Come on. Big girl panties."

She drew a breath that had to come from the bottom of her feet. "Right. I can do this."

"I'm right here beside you all the way."

On the porch, her hands stayed in her pockets so I pressed the doorbell. Chimes resonated inside. A moment later, the porch lights came on and a face appeared in the sidelight. A woman.

It was too late for carolers, and a crease appeared on her forehead when she saw me in my red cape, leather pants, and motorcycle boots. But then Maddy stepped out from behind me, and the woman's expression switched to total shock.

"Roger!" We heard her yell. The *thunk* of a deadbolt sliding open.

She threw the door open, and a man rushed up behind her. The two of them, completely bewildered, stared openly at the skinny girl standing next to me. "Madison?"

"Mom. Dad. Merry Christmas."

Maddy's mom looked like an older version of her, which she was, with about forty extra pounds on her frame. Maddy's dad was tall and thin compared to his wife, and his hair was prematurely gray. The woman flew out the door, grabbed Maddy in a bear hug, and started crying.

Unfortunately, it went downhill after that. We were motioned inside, the hugging and crying continued from Mom.

Dad drilled us with questions. Who was I, how did I find Maddy, blah, blah, blah. Maddy introduced me, explained that she'd been sort of living with me, and it came out sounding weird even to my ears. Dad accused her of running away while Mom sat us down in the kitchen and made us cocoa.

Maddy started to explain what had happened to her at Nudra's hands, but her father overrode the explanation and accused her of getting mixed up with drugs and proceeded to allege she'd been prostituting herself.

That was a mistake.

The house had been built during the middle of the twentieth century and the interior boasted a traditional look with lots of religious paraphernalia and pictures of Jesus on the wall. Maddy's mother wore a gold cross around her neck, and as the interrogation continued, she narrowed her eyes at me and started asking pointed questions about what I'd been doing with her daughter and if I was the reason she'd been led astray. As Maddy ripped into both of them, I stayed quiet and pretended to be intently interested in the décor and my cocoa.

"I'm a vampire," Maddy announced in a loud voice. Silence fell for the first time since we'd entered the house. "I went to that concert with Jordon and Avery back in the summer and ended up a freakin' vampire."

"Language," her mother chastised. "And blasphemy. Really Madison. There are no such things. You've always had such a vivid imagination."

"She's always made bad choices." Her father waved a rather large hand in front of her face. "Are you delusional? Are you on drugs right now? How dare you upset your mother all these months, letting her believe you'd been kidnapped by some serial killer, some heathen animal, when all this time, you've been doing drugs and acting like this?"

Maddy came out of her chair. Her anger bounced around

the room, but tears flooded her eyes. Her voice came out low and strained. "I'm not on drugs. I never did drugs. You know that. If you'd shut up and listen for a minute, I can prove I'm a vampire."

He pointed a finger in her face. "Don't you tell me to shut up, young lady. You weren't supposed to be at a concert that night, but as usual, you broke our rules and did what you wanted. Now you want us, after all this time, to take you back when you're obviously doing drugs and God knows what else?" His fingers made air quotes. "'I'm a vampire.' That's your excuse?"

My heart ached for the kid as she searched her brain for a response. Thing was, she wasn't thinking with her head, she was thinking with her heart.

My parents had been killed, effectively severing our physical bond, and there had been nothing I could do about it. Maddy's parents were here, and yet their family bond was ripping at the seams. "Vampires are very real, Mr. and Mrs. Weber. I know it's a lot for you to take in, but..."

Maddy's dad walked over to the kitchen phone, picked up the handset and shot some righteous scorn my way. "Miss Sweet, I'm calling the police to tell them you've been aiding and abetting a runaway and providing her with drugs."

Looked like it was time to go. Sucked that we had to end things here, but the energy coming from Roger and his wife told me we could argue this point for days and never change their mind. Keeping Maddy safe was my foremost goal, and if the cops got involved, I couldn't do that.

I rose from my chair and pushed it in. Meantime, Maddy showed off her Undead speed, crossing the kitchen floor in the blink of an eye and ripping the phone from her father's hand. "Don't you dare," she seethed. Her fangs were out, and her eyes were flat and predatory. "Kali's been the only person I could count on since Nudra changed me. You can blame me and curse me and reject me as your daughter, but don't you dare threaten her."

Daddy-o scrambled backward, speechless, and ran smack dab into the counter. "What have you done to yourself?"

A small cry came from Mom, and she heaved herself up from the table and made her way to Roger's side. "Are those implants? Tell me you didn't ruin your beautiful smile with those awful things, baby."

Maddy deflated like a popped balloon. She tossed the handset on the island counter and turned to me. "Let's go. This is getting me nowhere."

As she vacated the kitchen and headed for the door, I nodded at her parents. "Thanks for the cocoa."

She was in the living room, giving the Christmas tree one last look. When I came up behind her, she yanked a small handmade ornament with her name in an off-kilter child's handwriting from a branch and stomped out the door. Her mom and dad stood several feet away, still shell-shocked.

I shrugged. "Kids these days."

And then I followed my friend into the moonlit night, got in the waiting car, and took her home with me.

THIRTY-EIGHT

"Why don't they understand?" Maddie paced my kitchen. "They never listen to me."

I made supportive noises as she continued to rant about her parents and the unfairness of her life while I restocked my pantry with groceries we'd stopped for on the way home. She was right on most counts, although overdramatizing others, but she needed to blow off steam. No harm in that.

"You always have a home with me, Mouse."

She hugged me and continued her rant. My mind wandered, her complaining just background noise as I put the groceries away on autopilot. All I could see was Dru's face, the rattle of his breathing continuing to echo in my ears. Forcing myself to put it aside, I purposely focused on Maddy's situation. She was really torn up, and rightfully so, and deserved my full attention.

Withdrawing a couple of the teen magazines she loved to read from a bag, I handed them to her along with a container of Ben and Jerry's Cherry Garcia. "I'm sorry, Maddy. How about we watch one of those happy Christmas movies you like so much?"

Taking my offerings, she sighed deeply. Her lashes were damp with unshed tears. "I'm not much in the mood for happy."

That made two of us. "There's still a couple of hours of darkness left. We could go beat up a few supernaturals who need their asses kicked."

She sniffed, thought about it for a moment, and looked me in the eye. "Can I bring the ice cream?"

I tossed the bag onto the counter. "Of course. Bring two spoons."

"Make that three." Cole walked in carrying two more bags of groceries and set them on the table. He slipped a bottle of his favorite whiskey from the bag and pocketed it. "If you're going out, I'm going with you. Damon's orders."

"The Noctifectors are busy with Toel, and you can't protect me against Maria."

"Orders are orders."

"I call shotgun," Maddy said, heading for the door.

I took off after her. "Hey, that's my seat."

"We are not listening to that awful music again. I'm sitting in front with Cole and we get to pick the music."

Glad to have her back, I still gave her grief all the way to the car. When she tried to make good on her promise, I hauled her skinny butt out of the front passenger seat and deposited it in the back. She cussed me out, and Cole and I shared a smile over the roof of the car before we got in.

Three hours later, we had served Bridge papers to a couple of out-of-town demon visitors who were recruiting humans for dark magic spells and wiped out a small but vicious renegade vampire nest on the South Side whose members were kidnapping human kids and draining them of blood. We also wrapped up a couple of Sweet Investigation cases before Cole forced me to return to the Institute. Damon wanted to talk.

I didn't. He wanted an update on Dru and I wasn't ready to discuss it. The fieldwork had cleared my head. My emotions were back under control. If Damon wanted an update, he could call the House for it. I wasn't his messenger demon. And he sure as hell didn't need to know the details of my visit.

The early morning workout staking vamps and clearing cases off my desk left me feeling lighter. Once I was inside the Institute's walls, that feeling evaporated. Cole headed for the training center, Maddy for the media room, magazines in hand. There was no reason for me to be there. I wanted to be home to watch the sunrise. I needed to hunt down Maria.

As I trudged up the stairs to the second floor, I considered jumping in my car and leaving. Avoiding Damon. Pretending Dru wasn't dying or already dead. Forgetting about the fact that Toel was still alive. But I felt wrung out and I smelled like the Undead. My feet carried me up the stairs and into my room where I shed my clothes and took a long, hot shower, hoping to wash off the dread leaching its way back into my bones.

I'm not one to avoid anything. I don't pretend, and I never, ever forget.

After the shower, I dressed in my standard black everything. Downstairs in the kitchen, I grabbed a ham and egg sandwich from Lainie, our resident cook and house mother, and took it with me to the roof where I could watch the sunrise.

The day dawned cloudy. Big surprise. Winter in Chicago is one long cloudfest. This morning, it was particularly dark, the clouds roiling and fighting with each other, and totally blocking out the sun. I endured the cold wind coming off the lake as I scarfed down my breakfast and went through my mental list of shit once more.

Taking my emotions out of the picture made things simpler.

Simple is good, especially when it leads you to do the right thing.

"Thought I might find you up here," a familiar voice said, startling me out of my revelry.

Rad. So much for keeping my emotions at bay. "What are you doing here?"

Looking over my shoulder, I answered my own question. He looked pained, his gold eyes too pale and his cheeks sunken. Trying to hide his need to feed, he glanced up at the sky and flashed a smile. "Not much of a sunrise, is it?"

I shifted my focus to the lake. The edges were icy. The center teemed with white caps. "Seems appropriate, considering everything that's going on."

His footsteps drew close, his tall frame casting a shadow over me. "If Dru dies, we're back in the same boat with the blood, aren't we? You'll go into withdrawal and possibly die."

"Yep." But I wasn't going to let Dru die. *Please JR. Come through.* "I'm working on it."

"I can't honestly say I'm sorry to see him wiped off the planet."

A fissure of anger cracked my emotional shield. "Don't go there."

Rad folded his legs and sat down beside me. Our nylon parkas *swished* against each other as his shoulder touched mine. "You know you couldn't have denied him anything."

Logic said as much. I didn't give a damn about logic. "The blood slave to liege bond is strong." I released a tendril of my magic to call my blood that was inside Rad's veins, seeking to prove a point. We locked eyes and his magic responded, lust coiling tight between us. "But that doesn't mean it's unbeatable."

The cold wind blew stronger, whipping hair across my face. I leaned forward and kissed the corner of Rad's mouth.

Switched sides and kissed the other corner. "Say, for instance, I could command you to help me save Dru. Would you submit or resist?"

His mind resisted, but his body strained to yield to me. He caught my bottom lip with his teeth, released it. "You can't save him."

So everyone kept telling me. I drew back, scanned the horizon, and toyed with the Hello Kitty necklace at the base of my throat. "Can't save a loyal friend. Can't stop an evil spirit. Can't make anybody happy. Failure is my middle name today."

Rad rested his arms on his bent knees. The wind lessened. "You can't fail at being yourself, Kali."

My mind turned that over and let it take root. "I think that's the problem. I'm not being myself."

"What do you mean?"

I looked at my Achilles' heel. His face was perfect and beautiful to me, even with the strain in it. "I'm letting my emotions get in the way of my job, my friendships, everything."

"You're breaking up with me."

"I should, but I just can't seem to do it."

"And how exactly am I causing you problems with your job and friendships?"

How to explain? "I opened my heart to you."

He studied my face. "And you think that's a weakness?"

Shifting my gaze back to the sky, I ignored the pinch in my heart confirming his suspicion. "Dru asked me to stake him. To put him out of his misery. I refused."

Rad was silent; his comforting ocean scent enveloping me.

I kicked snow off the roof. "If the situation was reversed, I'd ask the same from a friend. But some friend I turned out to be. I ran away when he needed me most."

"Nah, that's crap. Friends don't stake each other, Undead or not."

Maybe not in Rad's world. They did in mine. I stood up and brushed snow off my butt. "Sounds like a line from one of your songs."

He chuckled and stood, sinking his hands into his coat pockets. "The Noctifectors are not going to kill Toel," he said.

"What the hell are they going to do with him then?"

"They're taking him to Rome."

"For what?"

"I don't know."

But he knew something, I could see it in the way he avoided my eyes. "Have they left already?"

Concern creased his forehead under his dark bangs. "Stopping them would be a mistake."

Letting them take Toel out of the country would be a bigger one. "They'll never make it to Rome. He'll kill them all."

Rad looked like he wished he hadn't told me. The Achilles' heel problem went both ways. He handed me a folded paper from his pocket. "I'm just a foot soldier. They don't tell me anything. But there's a private flight leaving O'Hare before noon. The plane belongs to the Church."

I snatched the paper from his hand, looked at the flight manifest. "Then we'd better go stop it."

He glanced down at his shoes and shifted his weight. "We can't be seen together in public, remember?"

"Right." Damn, this was getting old. It wasn't just being seen together in public that was the issue. The Nocts would string him up if they found out their half-demon foot soldier was a double agent. And his fans would probably mob him wherever he went. "I'll take care of this on my own. But first, we better feed you."

Grabbing him by the hand, I snuck him downstairs, past Damon's apartment and to the door to my room. On the threshold, I touched the antique copper knob with my fingers, using my magic to unlock it. Before I could drag him into my room, he swept me into his arms and kissed me deeply. Lust and dark magic flowed, making my head swim. "You're like a drug I've never had before," he murmured against my lips. "One I can't live without."

Breathing hard, I ripped open his coat and grabbed the lapels of his shirt, ready to rip that open as well. The sound of a door across the hall opening and my boss clearing his throat stopped me in mid-tear. "I'm afraid your little unauthorized rendezvous is going to have to wait," Damon said. "We have a problem."

By my calculations, the problem was standing three feet away wearing Armani and looking like he was going to kill me. I released Rad's shirt and tried to reason with Damon. "I already took care of that renegade nest of vamps."

"That's not the problem."

Merde. "Is it Dru?"

"I have not been notified of his passing, no."

Phew. "Then whatever it is, it can wait ten minutes."

"Fifteen," Rad interjected.

Damon gave us an admonishing glare. "My scouts have notified me that Toel's army is en route to O'Hare airport to retrieve him."

"It's daytime. What can they do?"

"It appears we're about to find out." He checked his watch. "The first wave is due to arrive within the hour."

THIRTY-NINE

On our way downstairs, we ran into Maddy. She was carrying one of her teen mags, and when she saw Rad behind me, she hid it behind her back and gave him a narrow-eyed look. "I need to talk to you," she said under her breath while trying to pull me aside.

"Not now."

"It's important."

"Not as important as an Undead army invading O'Hare." When her eyes went wide, I nodded. "Call Arman and see if his shifter battalion is up for another run at Toel's minions. We've got to stop them before they hurt any humans or rescue Toel."

"In the middle of the day?"

Technically it was early morning, but Maddy was a vamp. Sunrise, sunset. Everything in between was either night or day. "Have you seen how dark it is outside for seven a.m.? It's like night..."

As a thought struck, I stepped back and closed my mouth. Rad touched my arm. "What is it?"

"Maria. The storms, the lightning. Now this. How the hell is she manipulating Mother Nature? She's a ghost."

"A *revenant*." Salmad appeared at the bottom of the steps and held up a ginormous leather-bound book that looked like one from Damon's personal collection. "Much more powerful than your everyday spirit, which is no doubt why you were unable to control yourself once she possessed your body."

I touched my stomach, which had healed but still felt odd. "Don't remind me."

Revenant. My memories of the cemetery and what had happened afterward inside my house had slowly trickled back, but out of order and disjointed. "What did Vicky say about her? That she was able to control Maria?" I glanced at Damon. "Tell me you didn't let Vicky escape."

He clasped his hands behind his back and looked abashed. "She's disappeared."

"What? You let her walk off into the sunset?"

"Give him a break," Cole said, coming down the hall and stopping next to Salmad. "Saving you was more important than keeping eyes on Vicky."

I pinched the bridge of my nose. "Asmund. What happened to him? Why didn't he keep her from running?"

"Asmund died, Kali." This from Damon. "We assumed you knew."

I thunked my head a couple of times into my hand. "My memories are still a mess. I'm not sure what's what."

Blowing out a painful breath, I put the lock on my emotions again but stated the truth. "He was a good soldier." Asmund also added another mark to the tally of entities who had been hurt or killed because of me. "Vicky's the key. If Maria is controlling the weather and Vicky can control Maria, even a little, I have to find Vicky."

My boss shook his head. "We don't have time for that. I'm

sending all Institute employees to the airport post haste to intercept Toel's minions. You will assist with the plan of attack,
should one be necessary."

"Has Stephan called up the troops from the other regions?
We'll need them."

"Neither Stephan nor his brothers will be of much
assistance with this dilemma, I'm afraid."

Guess I wasn't surprised. Outside of Dru, none of Vlad's
descendants seemed all that upset about their father's demise.
"What exactly happened at Chloe's when Dru was staked?"

Damon glanced at Rad, back at me. "We're not sure."

Just as I suspected. Was it a Noct who had staked Dru or
someone else eager to get rid of him? Theorizing wouldn't
accomplish anything, and we had an army of Undead to take
care of. "Time to go kick minion ass. We'll meet you at
O'Hare."

Grabbing Maddy's arm, I gave her a shove to get her
moving down the staircase and shot Cole a *get us out of here*
look. Rad followed behind me, and once we were outside the
Institute's doors, I placed a hand on his arm and lowered my
voice. "Tell your friends they need to kill Toel and end this
before his minions cause a fight."

He touched my face. "I'll do what I can."

"There's a bottle of blood at my place if you need it."

A tiny, sad smile touched his lips. "I need you."

I squeezed his arm. "Be careful."

"You too."

"Kali?" Salmad appeared behind Rad. "A word, please?"

"Not now, priest."

I jumped into the car with Cole and Maddy, blowing off
Salmad and leaving Rad in the parking lot looking pale and
haunted and more like a fallen angel than a deeply damaged
demon.

"You're not going to like this," Maddy said, tossing her magazine in my lap. "Lover boy's a douche."

Folded back to show a bunch of chopped-up photographs and colorful text, the magazine sported a headline that read *Rock God Radison Beaumont Engaged!* As I scanned the pictures, my throat closed up. There, amongst the publicity photos and meaningless words, was a shot of Rad coming out of Tiffany's in New York City with a blonde Barbie doll hanging on his arm.

"That's Parker Burkett." Maddy pointed at the woman. She was holding her left hand out to the cameras, and sure enough, on her ring finger was a diamond the size of one of my throwing stars. "Her daddy's the CEO of Burkett record label. He's a millionaire and has produced all kinds of hit bands and singers. Parker's living large off her dad's money and apparently his pull with rock stars."

My teenage friend sounded almost jealous. "There was a video on TMZ and all social sites, too," she continued. "I thought maybe the pictures in the magazine had been Photo-shopped, but you can't argue with TMZ."

I didn't know or care what TMZ was. I lowered the car window as we hit the street and tossed the magazine out into the dirty snow.

FORTY

I gnoring the way my stomach clenched after seeing Rad with a hot human chick in his arms, I called Stephan, Dru's brother. "How's the Master doing?"

"Not well." His tone was cold, even for a vamp. "We don't expect he'll live through the day."

Not that you're unhappy about that. "Tell him to hang in there. I'm working on something."

"I'm sure he'll be delighted."

Zing. Someone else was going to be *delighted* when I rammed a stake up his ass. "Toel's at O'Hare with the Noctifectors getting ready to leave the U.S. for Rome. Problem is, his minions are in route to stop that plane."

A slight pause and a yawn. I'd woken up the poor vamp. "And?"

"Get your army together. All the Carpathia vampires and the ones the other regional managers sent to us. We're forming a perimeter around Terminal 5 to intercept them." I rattled off the details about the plane and the flight. "We need to be as unobtrusive as possible and secure the safety of all humans in the area."

"*Il nous est impossible de laisser Alexandru seuls.*"

"I'm not asking you to leave him alone." As if he really cared about Dru. "Leave a set of guards with him. The rest of you gather our vamps and meet me at Terminal 5."

"You do not issue orders to me, Mademoiselle Sweet."

"As queen of the Central Division and the enforcer for the United States Bridge Council, I'm asking for your help."

"I'll discuss it with my brothers and speak to you again."

The picture in my mind was clear. He had no intention of talking to anyone. "If you fail in this, Stephan, I will hold you accountable."

I disconnected and heard Maddy talking to Arman. She shifted the phone away from her mouth. "The shifters are on their way. The alphas want to know if they can start killing vamps before you get there."

I love shifters. Low maintenance, non-political. They keep to themselves and rarely bother humans. Oh, and they hate vamps as much as I do. "Only if they do it covertly. No messes, no human witnesses."

Not that I was happy about them starting before I saw the game board, but shifters have one fault: an inability to stay focused. The monster inside caused all kinds of attention deficit problems. Better to keep them entertained until I arrived than to make them sit on their hands until their impulse control overloaded. We'd have a far bigger mess on our hands.

"How is Arman?" I asked Maddy once she'd disconnected. "Any weirdness?"

"Arman's always weird."

"I mean, like obsessive or radical or violent?"

"No. Why?"

"Just checking."

My cell buzzed, JR's avatar of Yoda popping onto the screen. I hit the connect button. "What do you have for me? It better be good."

"I contacted a buddy of mine in Germany who's an expert on Undead Canon. There's a footnote in one of his books that might help you out."

A footnote, I knew it. The important stuff was always found there. "Cool. What is it?"

"The volume is an older European version that isn't used in America, but since Master vamps are different than regional kings and queens in both places, you could try it. A Master is focused on protecting the House and its occupants, right? And the king or queen is a political pawn. They handle rules and elections and..."

"JR. I don't need a lesson in Undead politics."

"Right. Well, if I'm translating this correctly, it means the king or queen may take jurisdiction of a House from a House Master if he's unable to perform his duties, but only until a suitable replacement is found and only if the House is under extreme stress. Natural disaster, human persecution, war. That sort of thing."

Hunh. "That'll work. Do you have a hard copy of that footnote?"

"I can print one."

"I also need you to make up a decree from the Bridge Council stating that the House is in violation of XYZ code, and as enforcer, I have the right to temporarily seize the house in the name of the Bridge Institute and the occupants must carry out my commands."

"You want me to forge a document and make up a false Bridge code?"

"You got a problem with that?"

There was a noise like he'd knocked over his Han Solo

bobblehead. "Uh, no. I'll get right on it."

"Good. I'll be at the office in..." Checking my watch, I did the math in my head. "Eight minutes."

"Eight minutes?" He hung up, I assumed in order to get to work.

"Hit the office first," I said to Cole. "Then we're going to Carpathia."

"I thought we were going to the airport."

"We are, but we have to make a couple of pit stops first."

Maddy sat forward, set her chin on the back of my seat. "What are you going to do about Rad?"

Damn. I'd almost forgotten about him and his fiancé. "No time to worry about that right now."

"I can't believe he did that to you."

Touching the Hello Kitty pendant, I clenched my jaw and stared out the window. "Neither can I."

As I'd predicted, we arrived at Sweet Investigations eight point six minutes later. JR was fanning an official-looking document hot off the printer in his office. A bunch of the boxes he'd piled in the corners were open, the contents gone, and packing materials everywhere. "What did you buy?" I asked him. "And how much did it cost me?"

He kept his eyes on the floor as he handed me the fake Bridge injunction. "It's a surprise."

"I don't like surprises."

"It's a Christmas present, all right?" Handing me another piece of paper, he knocked a couple of boxes out of the way to get back to his desk. "Just don't go in your office."

The first Kali law of physics: don't tell me not to do something.

Folding the papers and sticking them in a cape pocket, I brushed past Maddy, who'd followed me in, and beelined for my office. The room was dark, and as I stepped across the threshold, I reached for the light switch. Didn't need to. The moment my foot breached the threshold, the lights came on.

A woman's modulated voice came from unseen speakers. "Welcome, boss. How may I assist you?"

The entire west side of my office had been turned into NASA command control. High-tech flat screens nearly covered it from floor to ceiling. On the sides, a series of clocks showed different time zones from all around the world. Each of the TV screens sprang to life, showing me views of the Bridge Institute, my house, the parking lot outside Sweet Investigations, and more. There was one dedicated to Carpathia, another showed the front entrance to Di's place. A third, Neve's. I could keep eyes on everyone and everything I cared about.

CNN ran on a lower screen in the corner. Opposite that, one of the Underworld movies was playing.

"Oh, my God," Maddy said.

"Not God," the female voice over our heads countered. "Sophia, keeper of the knowledge of all that is righteous and just."

JR scrambled in behind me. "I know you don't do Christmas, so Happy Holidays, boss."

Holy hell. For once, I was speechless.

My techie guru headed for the desk. The piles of files and paperwork had been cleaned off, probably by Di, and the old, outdated PC had been replaced by...nothing. The only thing on the desk was a metal cube the size of a cigarette lighter.

"I named her Sophia, after the goddess in Michelangelo's painting. You know the one?"

Sophia is considered by some practitioners of Gnostic and Judeo-Christian ideologies to be the Mother of All. The Mother of Creation. Wisdom in its purest female form. "The Sistine Chapel. Yes, I know."

"Sophia," JR said.

"Yes, master." His solemn eyes jumped to my face, back down. "That, uh, master thing? I was just testing her out. I'll switch it so she calls you master instead."

"Boss is fine." I was still somewhat dumbstruck.

"Sophia, keyboard."

"Yes, master." A small light on the cube came on, and a red laser keyboard appeared under JR's fingertips.

Did I mention, holy hell?

He tapped the virtual keys, and one of the wall screens, the one of the Bridge Institute, switched to a scene at O'Hare. Terminal 5. "This is just like an ordinary keyboard, but I've installed a few shortcuts. You can use voice commands for the normal views, but for specific places like the airport, you'll have to type in the location. Everything you see on screen is also being recorded, so you can go back and look at particular places at precise times. Not only will it help with security protocol, but maybe with cases too. You can type in a subject's address and Sophia will put eyes on them for however long you want. If you know places they hang out or want to capture evidence about who's coming to see them, she'll be able to run surveillance twenty-four-seven if there's any camera in the area or I'll install one that she can tap into. There are so many municipal and private security systems and cameras anymore..." He shrugged. "I probably won't have to rig up many of our own."

I scanned the screens once more, noticed one I'd missed. "Is that the Vatican?"

Another shrug. This one smug.

"I think it's official, JR."

"What?"

"You're getting a raise."

Was that a smile? It was over so fast, I wasn't sure. "You better wait on that until you see the credit card bill."

"Sophia?" I asked.

"Yes, boss."

"Give JR a raise."

"I have given JR a five percent raise, starting with his next paycheck."

"Make it eight."

"I have given JR an eight percent raise, starting with his next paycheck."

Maddy was grinning from ear to ear, pacing around the screens. "Sophia? Can you get SoapNet on one of these screens?"

Sophia answered in the affirmative, and the main screen flipped to two people in a heavy embrace. I snagged Maddy by the arm. "Come on, Mouse. We've got some staking to do."

We said our goodbyes to JR—and Sophia—and returned to the car.

FORTY-ONE

"That took long enough," the gruff War demon said when we climbed in.

Maddy slammed her door shut. "Best. Christmas. Present. Ever."

Cole gave me an inquisitive eyebrow lift as he shifted into drive, and we left the parking lot. "Airport?"

"Chloe's," I said.

A set of arms snaked around my neck from the backseat. Maddy's head leaned into mine as she gave me a hug. "Do I get a raise?"

"You're not on the payroll."

"Remind me again why that is?"

"You're my friend, not an employee."

"Being your friend is o-rated. I want to work for you."

"I don't hire vampires. Too undependable."

She smacked the back of my head. " do stuff for you all the time."

"True. And you're fairly dependable. Which is why I feed you, clothe you, and let you crash with me on a daily basis."

She slumped back into her seat. "Merry Christmas to me."

"What's at Chloe's?" Cole said. "Thought we were heading to Carpathia and then hunting down that asshat Toel."

"We are." I dug out my phone, dialed the Tempter demon. "One more pit stop before Carpathia."

Chloe was not happy when she finally answered her phone. "This better be an emergency of hell-size proportions, Kali Sweet, for you to wake me at this ungodly hour."

While it looked like it was closer to midnight outside, it was actually eight o'clock in the morning. Like most of us, Chloe worked nights and slept days. "It is, Chloe, otherwise, I would never have bothered you. I need three or four large bore syringes, and I'm on my way to pick them up right now."

Her light southern accent grew deeper. "Whatever in Satan's name do you need large bore syringes for? Heart surgery?"

"Close. You do have some, don't you?"

"Why, of course, I do." She sighed as if I were a pesky child begging for a piece of candy. "I'll have them ready when you get here."

"Love you, Chloe."

"Um, hmm." She hung up.

"I'm going to have Sophia put me on the payroll," Maddy announced from the backseat. "And I'm clocking my hours as of today."

"Who the hell is Sophia?" Cole asked.

"My Christmas gift from JR." I pocketed my phone. "Then you better get ready to work, Mads. I only hire the best, and I don't put up with lazy vampires."

She slung her arms around my neck again. "I'll help you take out the bottom feeders, but my real job is going to be taking care of you."

I exchanged a look with Cole. "If you haven't noticed, I have a bodyguard."

She huffed. "Am I not the one who uncovered Rad's two-timing ass?"

Cole smirked. I unhitched her arms from around my neck, ignoring the sudden pressure in my diaphragm. There was nothing to say to that. The old wound had scabbed over but never healed. Seeing Radison Beaumont, the only male I'd ever loved, in that magazine with Parker Burkett made my stomach twist in a familiar and unwelcome manner.

But I wasn't that seventeen-year-old demon anymore. I'd lived through his betrayal in the past, and I'd do it again if necessary.

FORTY-TWO

Chloe didn't just have the syringes ready for me; she met us on the sidewalk in front of her place and climbed into the car with an old-timey black doctor's bag. "I assume this has to do with that dying Master vampire that I've heard so much about?"

The sky was dark enough, streetlamps were on. The only streetlamp on Chloe's block that hadn't been shot out illuminated her smooth black skin through the car window. "It does, but I doubt there's anything you can do for him. Carpathia's resident doctor couldn't."

She waved at Cole to drive. "What is it you think you're going to do for him?"

"Yeah," Maddy piped in. "What *are* you going to do to Dru?"

I hadn't planned on sharing my idea with anyone outside of the vamp himself. All they would do was try to talk me out of it or tell me I was insane. "A hail Mary attempt to save his life. The Central Region needs him." *I need him.* "If he dies, chaos will erupt in the Undead world. That's all you need to know."

Skeptical looks abounded. They wouldn't be the only ones I'd see that day.

At Carpathia's gate, we were momentarily stopped since I hadn't called ahead. The guards on duty knew me, knew I was queen, but someone—Stephan?—had ordered I not be allowed on the grounds. Hmm. Seemed like a certain vampire needed schooling.

I flashed my Bridge badge and a stake at the guard leaning in my window. "Open the gate or die."

Simple. Works every time. Or at least once in a while.

The large gates crept open. The moment the Land Rover would fit through, Cole accelerated. We drove the circular driveway and stopped at the bottom of the front stairs. The mansion was locked down for the day, windows shuttered. I expected to have to ring the doorbell more than once, but as I jogged up the stairs, my retinue of friends behind me, Oliver opened the door. He hesitated only slightly at seeing me, then bowed low. "Queen Kali. We were not expecting you."

I didn't want to hassle the old blood slave and I figured he'd gotten the *don't let Kali Sweet through the doors* memo, but no one was going to stop me from seeing Dru. If he was still alive. "I'm here to see Master Alexandru."

"I'm afraid that's not possible."

"Is he...did he..."

Oliver took pity on my stumbling inability to say the word die. "Master Alexandru is still with us. His brothers, however, request he not be disturbed in his final hours."

I figured as much. Removing the faked Bridge document, I held it in front of his face. "I'm here on official business."

Silence descended as Oliver looked the paper over thoroughly. I wasn't worried about JR's handiwork. It would pass inspection, even by Damon. I was, however, out of patience. "Move out of the way, Oliver, or I'll move you out of the way."

The slave swept backward and bowed us through.

Taking the steps to the next floor two at a time, I wound Volante around my wrist and loaded one hand with a cherry wood stake. The house was quiet, most of its occupants in their coffins or beds, and that was good. I preferred not to stake anyone if I didn't have to.

The minute I hit the second floor and rounded the corner, that intention went to hell. Heading to Dru's room at the far end of the hallway, an extra layer of magic hit me—a strong layer laced with royal blood, although not full of it like Stephan's. Brianna, standing guard at the Master vamp's bedroom door, shifted the moment she saw me. Every atom in her system went on defense.

Then she saw Cole and her body softened, her fight instinct deflating by a generous amount. Her spicy magic flared with desire. Inside my veins, Dru's blood called to her, and in turn, hers responded. The back and forth see-sawing motion, combined with my dislike of the vampire bodyguard and my slight jealousy of her relationship to Cole, woke my demon. If I'd had fangs, I would have bared them.

She immediately sensed my threat as if it were an accusation, a challenge. It was both of those things and more. No one was going to stop me from seeing Dru, and I was as protective of my bodyguard as he was of me, regardless if it was any of my business or not who he fucked.

Going on the attack once more, Bri crouched and met my gaze full-on. "You are not welcome here, Kali Sweet."

I kept walking straight for those doors. "I'm your queen, Brianna. Move, or I'll stake you for insubordination."

She stood her ground, bared her teeth. *Ding, ding, ding.* The vamp wanted to do things the hard way. My favorite.

Vamp speed is nothing to sneeze at. Vamp strength, either. If I hadn't already gone a couple of rounds with Brianna at the training center, I might not have expected her to be exceptional in both areas, even for a vampire. She led with a roundhouse kick to my face, which I anticipated. It was her go-to move any time she initiated a fight. Blocking it and grabbing onto her leg, I spun her around and slammed her against the wall. The crack of her nose breaking made my demon smile. Then I yanked her by the hair and threw her down the hallway, where she hit the banister, pinwheeled around, and took out several spindles.

She wasn't down for more than a minute, jumping to her feet and running at me. This time, though, Cole stepped in front of her and shut her down. He body-locked her with his arms, her momentum swinging them around, but it was enough. I left him to deal with his girlfriend, opened the door to Dru's room, and led Maddy and Chloe inside.

The room was dark, lit only by the prolific digital equipment on the far end, the shades and heavy drapes drawn against a nonexistent sun. In the center of the bed was a mound of blankets.

I expected Dru's brothers to be keeping vigil. At the very least, the House physician monitoring his deterioration. There was no one, and where the rest of the house had been eerily silent, his room was filled with the sound of rap music, but even at the fairly high-decibel it played at, it did nothing to mask the sounds of his distressed breathing and the death rattle of his lungs.

In the semi-darkness, Chloe and I shared a depressed look, then went to work. We flanked the bed, and I turned on the lamp in the corner so we could find Dru under the covers.

His face was so pale, I would have sworn he was already dead. Maddy snatched up the remote to his equipment and lowered the volume of the music. Chloe opened her doctor's bag and removed a long stretch of rubber, several syringes and a needle, the size of which made me a little queasy.

Hey, even demons hate needles.

Removing my cape and rolling up my sleeve, I gave her my arm as I sat on the bed next to the vamp. Volante was pulsing against my wrist, so I waved off the rubber tourniquet and let my whip do the job instead. Chloe seemed to know what I was going to do without me explaining anything, so she went to work attaching a glass vial to the syringe.

Averting my attention from that awful needle, I stroked Dru's face. "Hang in there, Master. I'm going to help you out."

His eyes moved under the lids, but he was too far gone to respond or even open them. I wasn't sure he'd even heard me. I found his hand under the covers and pulled it out, clasping it tight and trying to will my determination into him. I let my magic rise and blanket him, then reached out with my mind and pushed at his. *Stay with me.*

Chloe didn't warn me she was about to stab my arm, so I jumped a little when the needle hit. My demon hissed as blood poured from my vein and collected in the glass vial. I held my breath and watched Dru's face.

A second vial filled with my blood. The blood loss was small and wasn't bothering me. Or so I thought until the door opened behind us, and I whirled my head around to see Cole being pushed through by two of Dru's hulking brothers. Stephan brought up the rear, smirking.

That smirk tipped slightly to one side, along with the rest of the vamp, as dizziness struck. I leveraged my body against the bed, but I moved so jerkily that Chloe had to hold onto my arm to keep the needle in place.

"You are not allowed in this room, in this house, demon," Stephan said. Get out, or I will have you removed from the premises."

Maddy grabbed my cape and tossed the Bridge document at him. "Official biz, Steve-o."

"Get the other document out, too." I nodded at my cape. "As queen of the Central United States Undead, I hereby relieve the Master of Carpathia of his duties according to Canon Law MXIII, footnote 2A. In his place, I take charge of the operations of this House and act as Master until a new suitable Master is secured."

My demon and I smiled at Stephan as he took the proffered papers and read them through. If there's one thing that will stop a vampire, besides a good staking, it's politics.

Chloe was almost done filling the third vial. I released my hold on Dru's hand, removed Volante from my bicep. She curled over Dru's body as if protecting him. "I hereby, as queen, and as acting Master of Carpathia, *and* as enforcer of the Bridge Institute, order all of you out of this room. If you refuse to obey my orders, I'll have you physically removed from this room, from this house," I mimicked Stephan. "And just for grins and giggles, from this city."

He stood his ground, his brothers a silent but formidable wall behind him. "Give it your best shot, Ms. Sweet."

I knew he was going to say that. Chloe must have too. She withdrew the needle in one swift movement at the same time as I rose, Volante in hand, and snapped the whip over her head at the vamp I most wanted to take a little revenge on. Not for me —because, of course, I can't take revenge for myself—but for Dru.

Cole, used to working in tandem with me, shoved Stephan forward, right into Volante's path. She nicked his face, toying with him before she recoiled and struck again.

Stephan, for all his French bluster, cried like a girl and went down. Absentmindedly, I noted Chloe slapping a bandage on the inside of my elbow while I sent Volante speeding toward Stephan's brothers. Cole helped me out again, tackling one and kicking the other on his way down.

Brianna and two guards showed up at the door. Her nose was back in place, her eyes full of anger. Snaking Volante back to me, I prepared to deliver another round of whippings, but Brianna held up a hand as a peace sign. "My queen, we will take care of this."

Hunh. Guess the female vamp had a change of heart after Cole was done with her. Whatever. I was a smidge disappointed I didn't get to sick Volante on her ass, but if she was pledging allegiance to me over the others, I didn't have any cause to.

Fighting resumed, with Maddy throwing various heavy objects from Dru's collections at the brothers' heads even after Cole and Brianna had subdued them. Stephan yelled profanities at me and made various threats. There was going to be fallout from this, but his revenge was the least of my worries.

Once the room was cleared, Chloe handed me the first vial with a clean needle attached. "Hit him in the heart."

Allowing Volante to snake around my wrist again, I swallowed hard and took the syringe of blood. "His heart's been deteriorating. How do I find what's still there?"

She took my empty hand, guided it to Dru's chest. "Blood is as elemental as the air, the earth, fire, and water. His blood is in you, from what I hear. Use it to locate the living tissue that's keeping him alive."

Cole and Maddy stood inside the closed doors. Theirs and Chloe's gazes heated my skin. "The fallout from this will be on my head, and my head only. I'll take full responsibility for this. Understand?"

Cole rolled his eyes, Maddy nodded. Chloe gave me a tolerant smile, once again reminding me of a mother being patient with a child.

Closing my eyes, I willed my blood to call to Dru's. Willed his blood and his magic to lock onto mine. Under my hand, I felt nothing but his cold skin. I pressed harder, searching for the smallest evidence of life. The rise and fall of his chest was negligent. The rattle had died down to a wheeze.

Come on, come on. I was running out of time. *Grab onto me, Dru. Fight for your life.*

No response. Not under my hand, not in my blood, not with my magic.

Kneading his skin with my fingers, I found a spot between the bones of his ribcage and stuck the needle in, his muscled pectoral resisting the stainless steel. I shoved harder...and hit nothing. "Damn it."

Moving the needle to another spot, I repeated the procedure of finding an opening in his ribcage and sliding the needle into it. This time, I found something, and a spurt of hope soared through me. I depressed the needle end and drained the blood into what I hoped was his heart.

His eyelids flickered, but he didn't wake. The wheeze became a soft whistle. An uncomfortable minute ticked by on the bedside clock and he seemed to get worse in that minute. Had I finished him off rather than reversing the effects?

I shot a look at Chloe, and she handed me the second syringe. "Try another dose."

My fingers shook as I searched again for his heart with the tip of the needle. I felt the same resistance but wondered if it was his heart or my imagination. Sweat broke out along my hairline. *Please, Dru. Help me.*

He drew a breath, stopped, drew another. I bit the inside of my inner lip, stuck the needle as far in as I could on his next inhale, and released the blood.

Nothing changed over the next thirty seconds. His chest rose and fell intermittently, and what seemed to me with more time in between hitches. Tears dampened my eyelashes, but I refused to cry.

And then he stopped struggling to breathe the air he didn't need. His body sagged. He lay still. Seconds ticked off, and a sudden surge of anger rose inside me. I climbed up on the bed and straddled him, snatching the third and final vial from Chloe's hands. "Don't you dare die on me, you bloodsucking son-of-a-bitch."

Lifting the syringe high over my head, I rammed it home, not caring if I hit a bone, and smacked the plunger down, shooting the last of my blood into his heart.

His body jumped under mine from the force, but in the aftermath, it remained still, cold...lifeless.

FORTY-THREE

Crying for Dru wouldn't bring him back.

Tears threatened, anyway. I ground my teeth and blinked them away. Never in a million years would I have believed I would cry over a vampire, but lately, it seemed as though the tough shield I had kept around me for so long had become filled with holes. Holes created by friendship. Holes created by love.

I had turned into a sucky emotional pincushion, and I was pretty sure it was because I was *not* the island Di believed me to be.

I didn't want to feel this pain. Didn't want to think about how hard it was to lose Dru after knowing him for such a short time. How it would feel to lose any of the other people I cared so much about.

Pressing my hand against Dru's unmoving chest, I fought back the anguish, stuffing it in a deep crevice inside my heart.

It wasn't just the loss of my friend that overwhelmed me. I could feel the emotions of the others in the room. Maddy laid her hand on my back and spoke consoling words. There was so much turmoil in my brain that I couldn't understand her, but the tone of her voice was soothing, and I knew she was doing her teenage best to comfort me.

She felt the loss, too, only her emotions drew from the loss of her family as well as the death of the House Master. The loss of her childhood, her friends, and the future she had envisioned as a human.

Cole's warrior magic reached out to mine, attempting to fortify my defenses. Underneath it, though, he was hurting along with me. He was hurting *because* of me. He'd never seen me break down and it troubled him. Along with that, he was distressed over Brianna. Underneath his tough exterior, he was one tormented demon.

And Chloe? Her emotions were the hardest for me to take. She was sad I was upset, but she didn't understand it. Vampires, in her world, were disposable. Some of them helped keep her in business, and she never had any quarrel with Alexandru. My reaction to his death, however, disturbed her because she suspected I had become weak. She pitied me for letting a vampire reduce me to a quivering ball of emotion, and she wondered how a demon with so much potential could constantly screw up her life.

Anger bit me in the ass. She was right. I dashed the wetness off my cheeks, sat back, and took a deep breath. I wrapped Volante around my arm, combed my hair back from my face with my fingers, and blinked away the last of the tears. "What happened in this room today stays between the four of us."

There were murmurs of agreement, although I knew Chloe would tell everyone what had happened. I looked down at Dru's face. The dark eyebrows, the sharp cheekbones, those soft, pale lips that would never smirk at me again. "*Faccia di culo.*"

Something smacked me in the ass where I sat on his lower

stomach. I looked around and found the sheet tented above his pelvis. The site, and what it meant, was almost funny. Even in death, the vamp had a hard-on for me.

Then out of nowhere, the hand I had held just minutes before rose up and locked around my wrist.

I gasped, as did Chloe and Maddy. Chloe backed off that bed, nearly falling in her haste. The eyes I never thought I'd see again flipped open, black pupils nearly filling the irises and a red-tinged ring outlining them.

"Dru?" I said.

It was him...but it wasn't. His gaze was harder, flatter. The eyes looking back at me were half-vampire and...

I knew that look. Had seen it in the mirror a time or two. Windows of the soul. Had my blood turned Dru into a half-demon?

Whatever he was, he was hungry.

In the next second, I was thrown down on the bed, my head slamming into the pillow, my body covered by Dru's as he reversed our positions. I saw a flash of fangs, and then he struck my throat hard and fast. His teeth drove deep into my carotid artery, a fiery pain igniting in their path, and a powerful scent sheeting off his body. The Undead usually smelled of old blood and grave dirt, but at that moment, a dark, rich aroma, like grilled meat and expensive cabernet, invaded my senses. My body responded by arching into him, even as my hands fought to push him off.

For a dead guy, he was damn strong.

He was also starved for blood. Mine was apparently on the menu.

Taking great drags from my vein, he seized what he needed to heal his damaged heart and survive.

There was shouting and a blur of faces above me, but it was if I was seeing and hearing them from a distance. As both pain and pleasure rocked me to the core, all I could focus on was Dru.

Thank Satan there was a sheet between us because my hips parted as he moved against me, allowing him access to the sweet spot throbbing between my legs.

Someone tried to tug him off—Cole, no doubt—but Dru was locked on tight, continuing his feast. The room spun for a second, black shadows dancing on the edges of my vision. I had the sensation of lifting out of my body, like the astral projection I'd experienced seeking out Toel. While the odd feeling disoriented me on one level, it cleared my head on an entirely different one.

If Dru drained me, I would die.

My demon flashed to life. A growl came from low in my throat, grabbing Dru's attention. His drinking slowed, and without losing his hold on my neck, he lifted his face enough to look me in the eye. Lots of eye-to-eye contact, my demon and his vampire playing tag with each other. The red ring around his irises had dulled, nearly to the point of blending in with their dark depths.

Recognition awakened deep inside him. He retracted his teeth reluctantly and licked his blood-covered lips. The action, combined with the scent he was giving off, triggered an instinctive desire in my bones. I shuddered underneath him.

But with the direct connection broken, my body sagged into the sheets, limbs trembling. The pain, the unexpected pleasure, the implications of what had just happened. The ginormous loss of blood...I blinked several times, trying to clear the dots from my peripheral vision and clear the damning thoughts swirling like a blender in my head.

Didn't work.

"You're alive," I whispered, touching the hair at the side of his head.

A stake appeared at Dru's throat, the point digging deep into his skin. Cole, standing over us, pressed the point even deeper, a trickle of blood escaping and dripping onto my chest. "Get. Off. Her. Now."

Dru released my wrist, shifted to my left, and raised his hand in a conceding gesture, but something lit his dark eyes. They were still wild with blood lust, but less so. There was a controlled message in them. Commanding. Demanding.

Strike. Protect.

You're mine.

In one swift movement, I knocked the stake from Cole's hand—no easy feat, considering his strength and warrior reflexes. He didn't expect me to attack, though, so I jumped from the bed and tackled him. We both went down on the floor, me grabbing the stake and using it as leverage across his windpipe.

Dru was my master. Master of my Undead House, yes, but also my *master.*

"Never attack him again," I threatened Cole. "Or I'll destroy you."

Cole's eyes widened. I was pretty shocked myself. What was I doing? I was no one's slave, blood or otherwise.

The sudden burst of activity exhausted me. Dazed, I slid off Cole and threw the stake across the room. "I'm sorry," I murmured. I don't know what just came over me."

"I do." Cole stood and helped me to my feet. His face was drawn tight. "You are one fucking messed up demon."

Rubbing my temple, I agreed with him. Chloe's early assessment of me was spot on. I screwed up everything.

Damn.

"We need to get to the airport. I've already wasted too much time."

"What about him?" Maddy asked, pointing at Dru.

He stared at me with half-lidded eyes. "You did it, demon. You gave me life again. I won't forget that."

The words sounded like a thank you. They also sounded like a threat. I had little strength to figure it out. Nearly falling against Cole, I murmured, "Get me out of here."

Cole made a chin motion at Chloe and Maddy, and they scurried to grab the doctor's bag of supplies and my cape and follow us as he held me tight against him and headed for the door.

Dru's voice rang out behind us. "Send in Brianna on your way out."

Jealousy, hot and fierce, clawed at my heart. He wanted Brianna because he wasn't done feeding. First Cole and now Dru. Who was next? Damon? Rad? I stumbled out the door, images of her locked in Dru's embrace making me sick to my stomach.

But then my demon kicked me in the ass. Who was acting like a pubescent teenager now? Not Maddy. I slammed my emotions down and let my demon rise. She was happy to oblige, as confused as I was about my succumbing to the vampire. In the doorway, I broke away from Cole's grasp and stood proud. "I'm going to bring Toel's head on a stake to you, and then we're done."

The insolent grin I'd wanted to see again crossed his lips, red from my blood. But there was no evil in it, only a friendly teasing. "We'll never be done, Kali. You're in my blood, literally, and I like it that way."

My knees wobbled. Just a little. I locked them and flipped Dru the bird before turning on my heel and stomping out.

Brianna was standing guard again outside in the hallway, her sharp gaze snapping to Cole's as he followed me out. Questions poured from her mouth. "Are you all right? What happened? Is he..."

"He's alive," Cole told her. His voice was flat, his movements tight. The images flickering in my brain starring Dru and Bri were alive and well in his too.

"I did what you asked," she said, and Cole nodded. I wondered what that was, figured it had to do with keeping Dru's brothers out of our hair.

Cole didn't tell her Dru wanted to see her. We just kept walking until we were out of the House and in the car. I sank into the backseat and blocked out any further thoughts of what would go on inside Carpathia while I was gone. What might happen inside the House once I returned.

I'm no one's slave. I'm no one's slave, I repeated over and over.

Only time would tell if I was lying to myself.

FORTY-FOUR

As we left Carpathia, a dozen large, black SUVs joined us. "Friend or foe?" I asked Cole.

He eyed them in the rearview. "Your vamp army."

Stephan and his brothers hadn't sent anyone to O'Hare. "Brianna rallied the troops, I take it."

"Yep."

Annoying, but I had to give her credit for stepping up and casting her lot with us rather than the kings of the Undead. Gutsy move, all considered. That move would probably get her a nice stay in the dungeons under the House, or worse, unless Dru intervened.

I was sure he would intervene. "Thank you for...you know."

"Yep."

"Here," Maddy said, handing me her scarf and pointing at my neck. "You're bleeding a little."

The wintery day was as dark and foreboding as earlier. As we tore down the road and I wrapped my neck, I wished I had a wall to beat my head against. "I screwed up. Again."

I expected another monosyllabic response from Cole. Got nothing. That was almost worse. A damning confirmation.

But Cole was a straight shooter. He didn't believe in platitudes any more than I did. Needing to drown out the nasty voices in my head, I reached for the radio button.

His hand stopped me, encasing mine with his rough, warrior fingers and holding it. "I would've done the same thing. If the situation was different. If you were dying and I could save you."

I held his gaze for a long moment before he looked back to the road. "Regardless of the consequences?"

"Worrying about consequences is a pussy move."

Maybe so, but I was worried anyway. The car ate up the road, making me dizzy. He released my hand, and I closed my eyes, sinking low in the seat. In seconds, the loss of blood and my exhaustion put me to sleep.

I woke as we left the Kennedy Expressway headed for International Parking Lot D. O'Hare airport is a world unto itself, and the international terminal is like a separate island next to that world. The entire airport dominates the northwestern corner of Chicago and claims to be one of the busiest airports in the world. I happen to think it's also one of the nicest, even though my flights are most often delayed in and out of there.

Terminal 5 was located on Concourse M, and going through that section of the airport, even though it was separate from the main airport, would have been futile. Cole and our band of merry Undead rolled into the terminal's parking lot and spread out on foot.

We'd already dropped off Chloe at a friend's house. She'd get a ride to her place from there. I insisted Maddy stay in the car, but she refused, and I didn't have the energy to argue.

Which bothered me. I didn't have much energy, period,

even after my nap. I'd hoped it would restore my strength, and at least the little black dots were gone, but I still felt drained. Maybe I should have taken a bite out of Dru before I left.

For some reason, that thought hit me as inexplicably funny.

It wasn't, of course. Something was definitely wrong with me. I had to get control and prepare myself to not only kill Toel but take on the Noctifectors if they were still here.

Apparently, they were. If Rad had contacted them and told them what was going down, they'd ignored his advice to kill Toel and get out of Dodge. Cole was in communication with Damon, who relayed details and instructions to us, as well as the head of the vamp brigade and the shifter battalions. So far, no one had seen any action, although several shifter trackers had located a dozen of Toel's minions inside the airport, staking out the entrance to Terminal 5. The shifters reported the minions were wearing sunglasses in order to hide their weird eyes, but the shifters could smell them.

Speaking of smells. I sniffed the chilly air and picked up plenty of scents. A lot of them were out of place. Grave dirt in December? Not normal. But were those smells coming from Toel's Undead or mine?

Snagging an earpiece, I listened in to the strategy conversations, but after the sixth different approach offered and shot down, I'd had enough. My ear buzzed from all the strange voices and arguments.

I tossed the earpiece at Cole. "I'm going in. Cover me."

"What?" He tapped his earbud to shut off the mic. Grabbed my arm and spun me around. "One fuckup today isn't enough? Now you're going to throw the whole battle into jeopardy because you can't think through a simple operation?"

"You call this simple?" I jerked my arm out of his grasp. "Simple is me walking up to that plane and kicking Noctifector ass."

"And bringing hundreds of vampires down on the human population inside?"

"Not if I kill Toel before they have a chance to attack. They're wired to save him. Once he's dead, their tie to him goes poof."

Cole set his hands on his waist and shook his head. "Look, I get it. You're mad as hell at the Chaos demon because he pissed in your beer. But being reckless as well as stupid is not the way to get back at him."

"This has nothing to do with Rad," I said through gritted teeth.

"You sure about that?"

Yes. No. "Do you have my six or not?"

He took a moment, tried to stare me down. "On one condition."

"Conditions are for pussies."

That got a grin out of him. "They are, aren't they? Well, tough shit. There's a condition if you want me to join you on this stupid, reckless mission."

Heading in to take on the Nocts and Toel all by my lonesome wasn't the cheeriest thought, so I played his game. "What?"

"You follow *my* lead this time."

My bodyguard had something up his sleeve. All counts considered, though, he was a War demon. Whatever was up his sleeve would probably work as well, if not better than, my simple but extremely rash plan. "As long as I get to kill Toel, I'm in."

He held out a hand, and we shook. "Whatever happens, you stay focused on Toel. Nothing else. Not me, not the Nocts, not Guitar Boy. Agreed?"

"Agreed."

Glancing up at the sky, he frowned. "Is Maria here?"

I followed his gaze. "Not that I can tell, but there's a high probability."

"Why does she give a fuck about Toel?"

"She doesn't, but Vicky does. It's Vicky who's controlling her in an effort to keep Toel safe. The only problem, as we've already seen, is that Maria can loosen Vicky's hold on her when she wants. That's how she uses the other witch's body, and how she appears as a ghost to me."

"How do we defeat her?"

"Get her back to my place and send her to hell. It's the only way I know."

"Toel first." Cole reached for his gun and checked the barrels of holy water bullets. Satisfied, he pulled out a second gun. This one was loaded with regular, human-killing bullets. "After that, you hunt the bitch down and get rid of her."

For the second time that day, we agreed.

FORTY-FIVE

Cole and I snuck our way past security cameras, human guards, and fences to land on the edge of the concourse's northwest area. It didn't take more than five minutes for Cole to slip inside an Employees Only door and secure two navy blue coveralls and badges to match. Giving up my cape wasn't my favorite, but I shuffled some of my weapons into the deep pockets of the coveralls and slid Volante around my waist. In close quarters, she wasn't the best weapon, but she gave me more satisfaction.

A passenger jet with the official Catholic Church symbol nestled among bigger international planes at Gate 17. Hoses ran over the ground, and several luggage carts sat empty nearby. While maintenance workers walked, ran, and drove around the other planes, no one appeared to be doing anything with the Noct plane.

"Maybe they got word about Toel's plan of attack and left," I murmured to Cole.

He scanned the plane, headed for the set of stairs leading to the open door. "One way to find out."

His guns were out before I caught up to him. The scent of dead seaweed filtered through the air. "You're not going to just walk up there, are you?"

"Yep." He hit the first stair. "Stay here. Stay focused."

"There's only one way in, one way out. What's your exit strategy?"

He grinned. "You're my exit strategy."

"Wait," I called just above a whisper, but it was too late. He hit the top step and disappeared inside.

And *I* was reckless?

Touching fingers to thumbs, I raised my protective magic. A soft but strong bubble surrounded me, and I felt stronger. Maybe my nap *had* done some good. I strained my ears to listen for any sounds of fighting, but all was strangely, eerily quiet. My nerves were on hyper-alert, and I chanted Cole's directions. *Stay here, stay focused.*

Rocking back and forth on the balls of my feet, I stroked a stake in the pocket of the too-big overalls, my hand itching to use it on someone. *Any*one. Just thinking about it gave me an extra rush of adrenaline.

"Hey," some big guy on the tarmac next to me yelled. He was also wearing ugly blue coveralls and a badge. "What are you doing? Get to work."

Fuck this staying put shit. I gave him a mock salute and took the metal steps two at a time.

What greeted me inside the plane was one scary-ass sight.

Toel sat in a plush leather plane seat, a wooden table in front of him with a glass of blood on it. On the floor lay a human Noctifector, his head twisted at an angle and blood running from a large gash on his neck. A gash made by very sharp teeth.

Toel raised his glass. "*Kal-i-*for-ni-a. I've been expecting you. Come in. Have a seat. We need to talk."

In the back of the plane, Vicky held Cole's gun to his head. He was on his knees and his arms were pinned behind him. A giant vamp flanked him along with Vicky.

Toel's voice lowered a notch, became more dangerous. "Sit, or the War demon dies."

Toel had no intention of sparing Cole, but I sat across from him anyway, stepping over a second Noct body to get to the chair. I counted at least five more in various death poses throughout the cabin. Stupid humans. "What is there to talk about?"

"You. What you did for my brother."

Word travels fast in the vamp world, but this was impressive even for them. "Which one?"

"Playing dumb doesn't suit you." He sipped his drink, set down the glass, and laced his fingers over his stomach. He was wearing his usual surfer dude clothes, complete with flip-flops. Thankfully, the surfer dude expressions were absent. It was the first time I'd seen him serious and clueless. "How exactly did you do it? Save him?"

Negotiation. Not my strongest skill, but worth a shot. "Let the War demon go, and I'll not only tell you how I did it, I'll show you."

His interest peaked, and so did his power. He crossed his legs casually, but the energy pouring off his body was anything but. How long before he knew it was my blood that had saved Dru? How long before he came at me with those powerful fangs?

My hand started to reach for my stake. He pointed a finger at Vicky. "Keep your hands where I can see them, or my friend there might lose control of her trigger finger."

"If you want the secret to Dru's salvation, you have to let Cole go."

His Undead eyes stared at me unblinking. Vicky called from the back, "You can't actually be considering making a deal with that bitch."

Her magic was chock-full of jealousy. Her voice was tremulous with unrequited love. If she hadn't been such a bitch herself, I might have felt sorry for her. As it stood, I wanted to stake her. Repeatedly. Anything to shut her up.

But she might be my key to controlling Maria, so for now, the best I could do was use her Achilles' heel against her. I leaned forward and gave Toel a charming smile. "I meant what I said at Dalinda's. I'm ready to serve you if you'll just give me the chance."

"As I recall, you raised a stake to me."

"I lost control of my demon. She stakes everyone. Don't take it personally."

"And do you lose control of her often?"

I licked my lips. "Not if I have enough royal blood to quench my thirst."

"You..." he looked even more perplexed. "You drank from Dru?"

I gave him an evil smile. "And the others. But *your* blood is the best. I want more of it. More of you. I'll do whatever you want, master. Just let the War demon go."

Zingo, bingo, bam. That sealed the deal. He nodded at Vicky and motioned for the vampire behind her to release Cole. The vamp grabbed Cole under the armpit and propelled him forward. Cole shot me a look that said there was no way in hell he was leaving me alone with Toel, but when he got even with me, I kicked him in the ass and gave him a hard push toward the door. He went flying but so did the Undead guard hanging onto him, throwing them both off balance.

In one motion, I yanked Volante from my waist and

snapped her toward Toel's neck. He ducked but she nailed him in the ear and wrapped around his head, blinding him as her well-worn leather covered his eyes.

He cried out, being the wuss he was, and I snapped Volante back and cracked her at the guard, who was back on his feet. He charged me at the same time her weighted tip gouged a bright red stripe across his cheek and knocked him sideways.

As he fell, he hit the table in front of Toel, pitching the wine glass of blood onto his master's Hawaiian shirt and cutoffs. Toel had stood, but being smacked across the eyeballs with a whip left him partially blind and he didn't see his guard falling until it was too late. The guard tried to catch himself on the small table and ended up sending it directly into Toel's upper thigh.

Toel lost his balance, too, falling sideways into his chair, but only catching the outer edge. The bucket seat swiveled and dumped him, the table, and the bodyguard over the body of a fallen Noct, and into another chair behind him.

The comedy of errors was laugh-out-loud funny, especially since Vicky was yelling at the top of her lungs for Toel to do something. She still had Cole's gun and shot it at my head, but the bullet missed me by inches.

I sent Volante sailing her way, and the whip swept the gun from Vicky's hand. The guard shoved off Toel and tried to help him to his feet. On the way back around, I let Volante wrap her leather around the guy's waist and sent him flying down the aisle and into Vicky.

Cole had shucked his cuffs and was headed for Toel, who bared his fangs at me as he prepared to lunge. I stopped Cole with a hand. "I got this."

A crack of Volante, and she caught him around the neck like I'd planned to begin with. Once, twice, three times, she wound herself in circles, cutting through his skin. His eyes bulged, and his fingers dug at her restraints, but it did no good. Once she was locked on, she didn't let go until I gave her the command.

"Kill," I whispered, sending a shot of magic into the whip's handle.

She cranked down harder, cutting through tendons, muscles, and finally, bone. The guard and Vicky had picked themselves up off the floor and stopped dead in their tracks at the sight and sounds of me decapitating Toel. I gave one last good jerk, and Toel's spinal cord popped, releasing his head.

Lotta blood as both his head and body dropped to the floor. Vicky screamed; the guard charged, so I withdrew the stake from my pocket and sent it sailing directly into Toel's heart. His body jerked and turned to ash.

The guard almost hit me, but Cole jumped over me and the Noct at my feet and collided with the guy in midair. Cole flung out one of his massive arms on the way down, grabbed the stake from the ash pile, and the guard went poof alongside his master.

By this time, Vicky was in a frenzy. She rushed Cole, dived over a seat when he reached out to stop her. Her foot caught on the seat, and she fell forward, grabbing for me. I smacked her face and reinforced my protective bubble. I would have killed her right there, but damn it, I needed her to stop Maria, and to the contrary, I was rarely stupid or reckless when push came to shove.

The force of my slap knocked her into a window. Good thing it was reinforced for flight. The glass still cracked, but didn't break, and the blow KO'd Vicky.

Toel's bulging eyes looked up at me, unseeing, as I went to stand over him. Cole flopped down in one of the empty chairs, scraped a hand through his hair. "Shit, that was fun."

A small laugh escaped my throat. "Yeah, it was."

He was slightly out of breath. "We should do it again."

"I have to admit, your exit strategy was a good one."

"She was," he agreed, and like in the car when he held my hand, something passed between us.

"I'm sorry for beating up your girlfriend."

"Not a deal. I'm going to beat up your boyfriend. We'll be even."

"My boyfriend?"

"Guitar Boy." He got up, lifted Vicky, and threw her into a fireman's hold over his shoulder. "And I'm going to enjoy digging his heart out with a dull spoon to make him pay up for hurting you."

I didn't deserve them, but it sure was nice to have friends. I glanced down at the dead Nocts, and a small part of me, even though I was still mad at Rad, was grateful he wasn't among the fallen. "A lifetime of slavery might be more satisfying. He's good at bringing us coffee."

Cole shifted Vicky's weight, seemed to consider it. "Okay, but only if I get to beat the shit out of him at least once."

I picked up Toel's head by the hair, grabbed my stake, and impaled him on it. From somewhere far away, I heard the low blaring of an alarm. "Deal."

Cole led the way to the door, and I used a blanket from an overhead bin to cover my gruesome trophy. Volante was once again around my waist and purring contentedly. I wiped some sweat from my forehead and noticed Cole had stopped, blocking the doorway. "What it is?"

"We might want to rethink our exit strategy."

He shifted Vicky's dead weight to the side so I could peer around him. Here by the door, the blaring alarm was louder, and red flashing lights from the building jetted over the ground. But the sight that held my attention made my stomach sink. "Holy minion army," I said under my breath.

Spread out across the concourse, runway, and field were

hundreds, maybe even a thousand, of Toel's vampires, lined up and still as death just like they had been outside of Dalinda's house.

"I thought their link to Toel would break once you killed him," Cole said.

"Apparently, they didn't get the message. Maybe I better make it clear to them."

I didn't see any humans in the near vicinity, but there were probably enough watching the minion zombie fest parade, snapping pictures with their cellphones and not having enough common sense to vacate the premises even with that annoying alarm blaring away. But this was going bad in a hurry and I didn't see many options. We couldn't ignore them so the only option left was to try and reason with them. If that failed, there was Plan B: fight.

Lifting the blanket off Toel's head, I raised the stake high and stepped out on the stair landing. The sky was a deep blue satin color, the snow surrounding the concourse and runway reflecting a lighter blue. "Toel is dead," I yelled over the alarm, projecting my voice as far as I could. Even yelling wouldn't reach past the first few rows of vamps. "I'm your new master. Return to where you came from, and you're free to go. Stay and cause trouble, and you'll meet the end of my stake, too."

All their blue-white minion eyes looked up at the display in my hand, but none of them moved so much as a muscle. Then in unison, they bared their fangs and hissed.

Definitely a thousand of them. The hiss was so loud, it sounded like I was facing a python the size of Godzilla.

"Looks like we're doing this the hard way," I said over my shoulder, draping the blanket over my prize once more and setting it on a nearby seat inside the plane. I released Volante from my waist, and instantly, she vibrated with anticipation in my hand. I chucked the overalls and grabbed my stake.

Vicky fell to the floor with a thump. Cole withdrew the gun he'd recovered from the floor and pulled the second one—the one with human bullets—from an ankle holster. "I always did prefer the hard way."

We fist-bumped and implemented Plan B.

FORTY-SIX

Together we flew down the airplane stairs, and as we did so, shifters invaded the runway from the south and east. The vamp soldiers who'd accompanied us came from the west, and Bridge soldiers rained down from the north, skirting buildings and jumping fences with the ease of ninjas.

"This is SPARTA!" Cole yelled, launching himself into the madness, and I laughed while raising my protective magic.

Sparta, indeed. The clang of weapons echoed over the open air as the invading armies came up against the minions. Shouts, yells, and death cries rose and fell. All around me, blood spurted, limbs dropped, heads rolled.

I cleared paths with Volante in one hand, turned my fair share of minions to dust with the stake in my other. I lost sight of Cole, and ended up surrounded by a dozen or so of Toel's army, all hunched and ready to attack. None of them spoke. They just circled me, their blue-white eyes locked on my face and not paying much attention to my weapons.

Twelve to one. By most standards, I was in trouble. But I'm Kali Sweet. Odds were in *my* favor.

I took out four with one swipe of Volante. Another two with my stake. I kicked out at one of the bigger one's knees, but as he fell, he clamped a beefy hand around my ankle, ignoring the small spikes of my boot slicing through his skin and the electrifying effect of my protective magic against his skin, and throwing me off balance.

A second minion tackled me from the back, ramming his head into my spine. A sharp pain ran up the back of my neck, but I twisted around and slammed the side of the stake against his temple. He fell, came up on a knee. The other minion jerked hard on my leg and nearly dislocated it. A third jumped into the fray, and by that time, my demon had had enough.

"Vengeance is mine," she roared through my mouth. A sudden silence descended in the area around us, all eyes on me.

With supernatural strength, I kicked the minion holding my ankle in the face, caving in his features. Then I tossed the minion riding my back at the one still on one knee in front of me. The two of them pencil-rolled to a stop a few feet away as I staked the one with the caved-in face first.

Jumping over to the minion sandwich, I raised my blood-soaked stake above my head. "Oh, look. A two-for-one special." Bringing the stake down, I jammed it straight through one and into the second, feeling the familiar rush of accomplishment when their bodies exploded into ash anthills.

Then I was being lifted through the air by no visible force. There was a tight vise around my chest, crushing my lungs and cutting off my ability to yell. A bright light burned my eyes, pressure burst inside my head and the sights and the sounds of the battle now going on below me faded into nothing. Volante and my stake fell from my hands and I watched, helpless, as they dropped out of sight.

Blind and fighting an invisible enemy, I heard crunching

noises and felt the snap of my ribs. I kicked out and tried to grab onto whatever was holding me. My demon roared, and instinctively, I reached over my shoulder and clawed at the entity behind me.

My hand found purchase. Hair. Thick, kinky hair.

Vicky? Shit, I knew I should have tied her up.

Or was it Maria?

The hair in my fist felt pretty real for a ghost.

In my ear, a voice said, "You must not die on the battlefield, *bambina*. I have plans for you."

The hair might have been Vicky's. The accent, not so much.

"Let me go, Maria."

"Never, my pet."

Her magic fell like a heavy, sickly sweet blanket over me, eating away at my protective bubble like acid. Lust and greed scraped against my skin, my hand lost its grip. I struggled to fight it, fight her, but the earlier exhaustion came back in a suffocating wave.

I gasped for air and willed my legs to keep kicking and my fists to find something to hit, but my movements were weak, and she only laughed.

And then, out of nowhere, a thread of magic that wasn't mine nor hers tickled me. A warm finger of sensation sliding under my skin entwined itself with my magic and fortified it. But it wasn't coming from outside me; it was coming from the pendant lying on my collar bone. "Rad?" I said softly.

The magic strengthened, the wind rose. Lightning flashed and thunder rolled as the wind gusted so hard, Maria and I spun in a circle.

"No," she cried out, tightening her grip on me. "She's mine!"

The struggle between all of the magics sent us tumbling and spiraling in a chaotic rotation of hands and arms, legs and hair. I reached out mentally and magically to draw more of Rad's energy into my demon. If I gave her enough juice, she'd take care of Maria.

Sure enough, the monster inside me threw up a wall of magic a nuclear bomb couldn't have penetrated. I'd never felt anything so fierce and unmovable come out of my demon except the last time she'd faced Maria. The instant it snapped into place, the force holding me let go.

The sensation of falling stole my breath as effectively as the crush of Maria's arms. I spun and tried to orient myself, but all around me was a white fog. I couldn't tell the sky from the ground, up from down. I closed my eyes and forced my body to relax—not an easy thing to do when you're skydiving without a parachute.

Just before I made contact with the ground, the white fog cleared, the storm stopped, and my body punched into the top of a large Swiss International jumbo jet. The shock left me paralyzed for a few seconds, and I stared at the sky. The dark clouds were moving out, and a ray of sunshine peeked through.

My body had hit hard enough to dent the plane's exterior and make a bed for me. I considered laying there for a long time but was afraid the plane might take off with me embedded in its roof. I like to fly, but not like that.

Literally peeling myself off the metal, I groaned at the searing pain in my body. For once, I didn't particularly like the hard way.

Getting down off the roof was my next problem, but I was already so banged up, I figured what the hell and just slid over the side. I landed on my feet but totally off balance, catapulting demon ass over sinfilled cart. I ended up rolling across the tarmac until I came to an awkward stop at Damon's feet.

"I assume you can explain this," he said.

"Of course," I lied, breathing hard and trying to make his three faces swimming in front of my vision merge into one. "Just give me a minute."

FORTY-SEVEN

In the aftermath, killing Toel and stopping the minions was somewhat anti-climactic. Maria was still running around, and I had no choice but to skip thinking about my awesome takedown of the asshat and move on. In reality, I wouldn't have spent much time thinking about Toel anyway. While he'd colored way outside the lines, I'd brought him down like I had hundreds of other vampires and supernaturals.

What I did end up stewing about were the bite marks on my neck.

Maddy retrieved my cape for me, snapped a picture of Toel's head, and sent it out over the Undead airwaves. The few minion stragglers faded away as Cole helped me limp off the concourse, but it was important the vamp grapevine had the details immediately.

Arman caught up with us at the Land Rover. The shifters wanted to throw a party and had sent Arman to invite me to be their guest of honor. Shifters throw parties for hangnails, so it wasn't like they were bent on having me there. Sure, they loved that I'd killed off the big, bad vamp, but they were probably more excited they'd got to bag a few vamps themselves. I begged off, telling Arman I needed sleep and medical attention before I went hunting for Maria. He hugged me before taking off, promising to stop by Chloe's for a bottle of my blood before he went out partying. All I needed was for my one reliable and fairly docile blood slave to get himself into trouble.

Damon opened the door to his big, black SUV and motioned me to get inside. "Let's get you back to the Institute and check out your wounds."

In Damon-speak, that translated to, *I want a full briefing by the time we hit the interstate.*

"We'll follow you," I said, but he shook his head.

"You'll ride with me. Cole will drive your SUV to head-quarters."

Cole had a dislocated shoulder and a swelling lump on the side of his head. "Damon, I swear, I won't run off. Cole needs a doctor worse than I do. I think I should drive."

I was still seeing three of Damon every time I moved my head too fast, but I dreaded getting into the car with him. If the vampires all knew about my Jesus trick resurrecting Dru, Damon no doubt knew it too. I was in for an ass-chewing.

And maybe getting fired.

"I'm fine," Cole said, ramming his shoulder against the SUV to snap it back into its socket. With his other hand, he tossed the car keys to Maddy. "Maddy can drive us to your place, where I'll drop her off. Then I'll head for the Institute."

The traitor. Maddy gave me a big smile and a little squeal before running for the driver's side door.

Too exhausted and achy to fight, I blew out a breath that lifted my bangs. "But someone needs to retrieve Vicky from the plane."

Damon barked orders at two Institute soldiers nearby, and they jogged away. He motioned me into the car again, but I held onto the door for a minute until I saw the soldiers carrying Vicky out. "Just wanted to be sure she was still there," I told my boss. "I want her placed in your solitary confinement cell."

"Agreed."

"And I need to take my trophy to Carpathia. Now. Before you put me under house arrest at the Institute."

He opened his mouth to argue—and it was an argument I would have lost because I was in no shape to actually make good on rash threats—but seemed to change his mind, giving me a short, irritated nod.

As I lifted a leg to climb into the backseat, I winced, and he put a hand on my elbow to help me up. For once, I accepted his kindness.

But the minute he climbed in on the other side and the doors shut, I felt claustrophobic. My vision was so blurry, I couldn't make out the digital numbers on the car's dashboard clock and when the driver put the car in gear and drove out of the parking lot, I had to grab the door handle to keep from falling over onto Damon's lap.

A mob was spilling out of the hanger onto the curb of the terminal. "What's going on over there?" I asked.

One of Damon's hands came up to support my wobbly head. "Radison Beaumont helped divert attention away from what was happening outside with his presence. The crowd recognized him immediately and, as Maddy is fond of saying, went wild."

I knew it. I knew I'd felt him tapping into my magic and helping me with Maria. My fingers played with the pendant around my neck. "What about the rest of the humans? The staff and passengers who *did* see what happened on the tarmac?"

His hand was warm and comforting at the base of my skull, his skillful fingers massaging my tense muscles. "I've already persuaded the staff and local news organizations that it was a scene for an indie movie. One featuring monsters, of course. That it was all fake. There were a few dead bodies, but they'll be cleaned up in a matter of minutes."

Damon could persuade a mother to sell him her firstborn son. "Quick thinking."

He smiled, bracing me as the car swerved around a corner and merged with oncoming traffic. Several traffic jams had occurred on the streets heading in and out of the airport, but the police directing traffic waved us through. Damon magic at work again. Archdemons, can't live with 'em and can't fight a mob of minion vampires without 'em.

I expected the interrogation to begin at any moment, but he remained silent, so I did the same. His fingers gently massaged my neck, and soon my eyes drifted shut. Next thing I knew, my head was in his lap and we had arrived at Carpathia House.

Damon had called ahead while I napped, so the gates swung open and we were waved through by the guard. I managed to climb out of Damon's lap and wipe drool from the corners of my mouth—that would teach him to put me to sleep with his magic hands.

Nearing the front porch, I righted my cape and blinked my blurry eyes into submission. If I blinked enough times, my vision cleared. Good enough.

The front door of the House opened, but instead of Oliver, Brianna stepped out to greet me as I carried Toel's kabobed head up the steps. Damon had offered to accompany me in, but I didn't want him anywhere near the vamp brothers or my new master. Even though Bri was as stunning as ever, her face was tight, her movements weary. Her ponytail had slipped a notch. Her lips were naked instead of glossed. She hadn't slept, and it looked like it was taking its toll. Or maybe Dru drained more of her blood than normal.

I mentally smacked that image right out of my head. So not going there.

Hoisting the stake a little higher, I started to limp past her into the foyer. "I brought Dru a present."

"He's not here." She followed on my heels. Dozens of vampires milled around, most of them ones who'd been on the tarmac with me. They were drinking and laughing and telling stories about taking out minions. "I thought he was with you."

"With me? I didn't see him at the airport." Didn't feel him, either, and I would have. He would never be near me again without me knowing it.

"At your home. A woman came and spoke to him. She wanted him to go to your house with her and he agreed. He refused to let me or any of the bodyguards go with him."

My insides went still. "What did this woman look like?"

"I've seen her before, but I can't place her. Red hair, green eyes. She had on enough sparkly eye shadow to blind me."

Miss Sparkles. Maria had taken over the witch's body again. "Did she touch him?"

A hard light appeared in Brianna's eyes. "She stroked his face and ran her hand down his neck and chest. He responded like nothing I've ever seen before. For a minute, I thought she might be a succubus, but Dru—I mean, Master Alexandru—is immune to them. She practically threw herself on him and fucked him right here on the foyer floor. I about gagged."

My gag reflex sympathized. "She's a witch who's carrying a *revenant*, which is a form of an exceptionally strong ghost. That ghost happens to have been one of the most powerful succubi I've ever encountered. I know this is asking a lot after what you've already done for me today, but would you come to my house with me? I'll explain what's going on in the car."

"I did it for Cole," she said. "Not you. And if Master

Alexandru is in danger from this revenant succubus, I'll do whatever it takes to secure his safety."

Okay, then. Glad we had that straight about her loyalty to the War demon versus her loyalty to her queen. "Where are Stephan and the others? Sleeping?"

"Actually, they're having a secret meeting in the library."

"A secret meeting you know about."

"I know everything that goes on in this House."

"Will you escort me to the library? I have to return a book."

She lowered her gaze in a show of acquiescence. "My pleasure, Queen Kali."

Her tone was mocking but not overly rude. In truth, I understood her dislike of me. I could feel it in the air between us. But there was grudging respect as well.

Making our way through the milling vamps, I received many bowed heads and verbal acknowledgments of a job well done. A few of the resident Undead stood in the background watching me carry Toel's head up the main stairs and not lowering the gazes when I looked at them. A direct challenge, but I didn't have time to reprimand them, and I was about to resign as their queen anyway. Vampires. Too much goddamn work.

Brianna seemed to relish busting through the library's locked doors and announcing my presence. "Queen of the Central United States, Kali Sweet."

I limped to the Undead kings sitting around the long table. At the sight of me and Toel's last remains, their faces went from annoyance to surprise. Stephan, who sat at the head of the table, rose abruptly to his feet. "How dare you..."

"How dare I what? Take out your psychotic brother? Interrupt your secret meeting?" I laid Toel's head on my end of the table and gave the stake a shove so the trophy slid across the polished surface like a shot glass to the other end. The brothers reared back as the gruesome souvenir slid past them, and one of the nagging ideas I'd had surfaced once more.

I'd intended to hand over my resignation, but as the idea seemed increasingly logical, I decided to pursue it. "Who exactly nailed Dru with a stake at Chloe's? Was it really a Noctifector, or was it one of you?"

Stephan blubbered, and his brothers' gazes turned to him.

My suspicions somewhat confirmed, I set my fists on the table and let my demon peek out at him. "I'm calling for a complete investigation into Dru's staking, and once I prove that you intentionally tried to kill your brother so you could take over North America for yourself while he was dutifully fighting Toel and protecting this House, I'm going to take revenge for him and see that justice is done."

I turned to walk out and saw Brianna smiling at me from her post in the doorway. "If I were you, Stephan," I said over my shoulder. "I'd pack my bags and go back to France. And take your brothers with you."

Bri and I jogged back down the stairs, my ribs crying out in protest. My body was healing at a decent rate, but because of the earlier blood loss and the chronic exhaustion I'd been fighting all day, the healing process was slower and more painful than normal. Even with the naps, it wasn't enough.

My stomach growled. Brianna, at my side as if she were ready to catch me if I fell, looked at me from the corner of her eye. "You're really pale. When was the last time you fed?"

It seemed like a week. "I can't remember. A while."

We made our way back to the foyer and through the crowd. She grabbed her coat, took my elbow as we descended the outside stairs. Damon waited at the car, the door open. When he saw Bri, he gave her a welcome smile and a small bow. "Brianna, so nice to see you again."

Gag.

"Archdemon Damon." She returned his smile. "We need to get Queen Kali food, and then we must stop at her house."

The Undead bodyguard was giving commands to my boss. How...interesting. My respect for her climbed a notch.

Damon helped both of us into the car and took the front passenger seat for himself. "Why do we need to stop at your house, Kali?"

"Maria has kidnapped Dru. We believe she's taken him to my castle."

"For what purpose?"

The question of the hour. "It's me she wants, so I'm not sure."

Damon's dark eyes met mine over the seat. "She wants to bend you to her will, like she did before, yes?"

"Yes."

"What better way to do that than blackmail?"

My stomach twisted. "Threatening the people I care about is damn good blackmail."

"Then, most likely, Dru is not the only one she has kidnapped."

Images of Neve, Di, Maddy, and Rad flashed in mental movies across my brain.

I'm going to kill that bitch once and for all.

Worry creased Damon's forehead. "Torturing your friends is also the best revenge she could take on you, Kali."

I leaned forward, hugged my stomach. "Forget the food. Get me to the church."

FORTY-EIGHT

I didn't wait for the car to come to a full stop in my parking lot before I bolted for the church. On the way, I'd dialed Dru, Maddy, Di and Rad on my cell...and none of them had answered.

Bri jumped out at the same time and ran with me. It seemed I had a new bodyguard, even if she hated my guts.

Damon yelled at me as he exited a second later. "It is unwise to rush in before we know the extent of..."

I cut him off in mid-sentence. "Shut up and get out here."

Dark clouds boiled overhead. The one streetlamp had come on, the heavy cloud cover mimicking night. Laying a hand on the stone near the entrance, I opened up my magical senses. The protection spell inside the walls zinged around like a ball in a pinball machine. It connected with my magic with a great flood of relief and tried to reestablish itself. Every time it poked its barbs into the stone and earth, though, it was zapped by another source.

The sensation reminded me of the ward that had been on Dalinda's house. It was witch magic combined with something darker. Something cloying and teasing me. "She's here, all right," I murmured to the others.

As I let my magic expand, a flash of light went off behind my eyelids. The same kind of white light flash that had happened at Shadow Hill. Pain, fear, and a soul-sucking vacuum grabbed on and jerked my magic into the stones. My body hit the outside stones as well, my face smacking nose-first into the rough surface. A new agony exploded behind my eyes. The bitch's ward had broken my nose.

This time, though, I was better prepared. On the drive over, I'd explained the situation and my theories on what Maria was doing with her blackmail attempt to Bri and Damon. I'd warned them this, or something similar, could happen. My physical energy was low, and my wounds were still healing, but my magic was strong, thanks to a combination of my Frankenstein blood and my absolute rage.

Don't piss off a vengeance demon unless you're ready to pay the price.

As soon as I face-planted into the outside of the house, Damon and Brianna raised their own magics and connected them with mine, grabbing my arms and peeling me off the church. Blood gushed from my nose and mental images of what was happening inside played across my mind. Di was there and so was Neve. Dru and JR. Maddy. All of them nailed to crosses, all pouring blood from various orifices and wounds. Another teaser by Maria to make sure I came inside. A teaser that sent me vomiting into the nearby bushes.

There was nothing in my stomach, so I dry heaved and spit out blood that ran into my mouth from my broken nose. After the worst was over, I set my hands on my knees and took several deep breaths, trying to clear my head.

Rage is an interesting emotion. At least for me. It emboldens me and jacks me up, but it also has a calming effect.

On the inside, my demon yearns to draw blood, and yet, she gets Zen-like once she hits a certain stage. This is what she knows best. What makes her tick. Payback will be swift and merciless and she has absolute confidence in what she can and will do to her enemy.

When I rose and turned back to my boss and vamp body-guard, my demon was in full force. Not out of control like she'd been with Toel back at Dalinda's, but *in* control. I didn't need to worry about the leash I usually kept on her. She had one target, and one target only.

Bri, seeing the change in me, took a step back. Damon, sucking in a breath, actually stepped forward, unafraid of me but still cautious. "Where is the most effective entry point?"

"No point in pussying around," I said, walking back to the door. "It's my house. I'm going through the front door."

I felt him before I saw him. The priest emerged from the shadows off to our left, the silver crosses on his belt catching and reflecting the streetlamp's feeble light. He gave me a nod. The simple gesture spoke volumes. He was there to help. "You should know," he said quietly, "that if Maria succeeds in possessing a body, any body, we are all in great danger."

No shit. "I'll take care of her."

"She hasn't been able to stay permanently in the witch's body. The human isn't strong enough to hold her magic. That's why she's been trying to possess you as well."

"Tell her the rest," Damon said.

"The rest of what?"

Salmad nodded to Damon and said to me, "The seven sins have never been on earth all at the same time since Jesus exorcised them from Mary Magdalena. That is why you don't remember anything between the time you left Mary's body until you were born to earthly parents three hundred years ago."

While that explained one of my questions, I was antsy to get inside, and the priest's slow, seemingly meaningless story grated on my nerves. "And?"

"There are currently six of us on earth at this moment. Maria, if she can take human form again, would make the set complete."

"That's bad, as in super bad, right?"

"All seven sins on the earth at the same time will bring about the Apocalypse. It will open the door to the Beast and The Four Horsemen. The earth and its human occupants will be destroyed."

As I turned that little morsel of information around in my head, my stomach threatened another revolt. "Why didn't you tell me this sooner?"

"I tried."

Damon quirked a damning brow. "As always, you efficiently avoided those of us who can help you the most with your job and personal problems."

"Really? You have the balls to lecture me right now?"

He held his stance and the quirky eyebrow. "I have the balls, as you say, to help you out of this difficult situation. But only if you'll accept the fact that you don't have to confront Maria alone."

"I ended her ass the last time on my own. I don't need your help."

"The stakes are higher this round. Both personally and professionally."

Damn. I hate it when he's right.

But he was right. This round, I couldn't take Maria by surprise or trap her like I had the last time. She had my friends nailed to crosses, and she was dead set on possessing a physical body and starting the flippin' Apocalypse. The stakes were definitely higher than anything I'd previously faced.

You may be an island, Kali Sweet...

"We're wasting time." I motioned for the three of them to follow me in. "Let's do this."

"Together?" Damon had to drive the point home.

"Yeah, yeah, together and all that mushy Hallmark stuff. Just don't get yourself killed. And don't get in my fucking way, or *I'll* kill you."

In the back of my mind, the intro to Hells Bells from AC/DC started playing as I touched the doorknob, and it responded to my mental command to open. The bells of hell were ringing for Maria, and if I had to personally escort her there myself, I would.

FORTY-NINE

My friends had been crucified in the sanctuary of the church.

Maria had used various materials to pin them on the crosses: wooden splinters and a few actual nails, all magically driven into their hands, their feet bound with ropes. I could sense her magic, sense her thrill at their pain.

On the way through my living room, I grabbed the iron poker Neve had stabbed me with. When we reached the doors leading to the one spot I never entered, I broached the first roadblock to getting to Maria aloud. "You're sure I can walk on consecrated ground without burning to a crisp?" I asked Salmad.

He studied the wooden doors as if the answer were carved into them. "You said there are two vampires inside that have not burned?"

I was sure the ground in the center of the church was holy. Every time I got close, my demon froze. Even now, she was fighting her natural flight mechanism. "If my vision was accurate, that's true, and I'm ninety-nine percent sure the vision is spot on. So what do you think? Consecrated or not consecrated? My demon is laying high odds that it is."

"Mine is unhappy, too." He touched a door with one hand, and his body twitched. "There is a central core of purified ground, but it is the heavenly bodies watching over the sanctuary that imbue the space with God's blessed magic."

"Heavenly bodies?"

"Angels."

"There are angels in my sanctuary?"

He gave me a look that said, *of course, why wouldn't there be?* Then returned his attention to the door and narrowed his eyes. "Guardians."

"Of what?"

"The core."

A mental light bulb went off in my head. "Is it a portal?"

"Possibly. An antithesis of the cemetery's portal. A balance to the evil."

Hot damn. "And how do I access it? Where does it go?"

He frowned. "If the cemetery's portal leads to hell, I imagine this one, its counterpart, leads to..."

"Heaven," I said, cutting him off.

"Yes." He closed his eyes, sinking deeper into his connection with the room. "The angels only need to be called on for assistance in opening it, but you realize, Maria cannot be sent to heaven."

"Why not? What could be a worse hell for her than being surrounded by good?"

Lowering his hand, he opened his eyes and cocked his head at me. One corner of his lips sliced up. "I've never considered such an idea, but it has truth in it."

"What do I say to the guardians to get them to open the portal?"

"Let me handle that. You'll have enough to take care of with Maria."

"What do you want me to do?" Brianna asked.

"As soon as I distract Maria, you get Dru and the others off those horrible crosses."

I glanced at Damon. "Tap into my mind, like you usually do, so I can communicate with you mentally. If I need to attack, which is sort of a gimme, I may need you to back me up."

"It will be my pleasure."

I drew in a deep breath, raised my protective magic, for all the good it would do, and opened the doors.

The room glowed with candlelight and an iridescent glimmer from the portal. During all my remodels, I'd never installed electricity here, but Maria wouldn't have known how to use it even if I had.

"Bambina," she cooed from the witch's body, as she faced me and licked blood from a silver knife. She was standing in front of Maddy, and a fresh cut was open across my friend's stomach. How had Maria gotten hold of Maddy? She'd been with Cole last I'd seen her. "Finally. I thought you would never arrive."

The room was filled with scattered pews, old hymnals, silver cups, crosses, and other holy ornamentation. It looked as though Rad had turned his demon loose inside those walls. Even the towering stained glass windows, with their scenes of martyred saints and the Crucifixion, added to the overall chaotic scene.

Chaos. Rad.

My skin crawled as I walked in, an eerie sensation flooding my senses as I scanned the crosses for him. I couldn't look at my friends' agonized faces, or I'd lose my focus on Maria, but as my gaze tumbled across the communion table, my heart stopped. Rad was on his back, his shirt torn open and his eyes closed.

Blood ran over his skin from the runes Maria had carved in his chest.

My feet tripped over themselves, and my demon gnashed her teeth. My pulse pounded in my ears. I heard Di yelling at me to get out, Neve was chanting some kind of Wiccan blessing, and Maddy was crying softly from her wounds. The scent of their mixed types of blood permeated my nose and nearly choked me. The emotions swirling in the room clogged my other senses.

Rad seemed to be passed out or under some spell. Dru was quiet, as was JR. I wasn't sure of the extent of their wounds, but Dru's blood inside my veins warmed and I felt his magic massage through me, giving me a needed burst of physical healing.

"One more is all we need, Calina." Maria waved a hand in front of her lineup of potential targets, then she glided over to Rad and trailed her fingers through his blood. "One more tortured victim at your hands to make six-hundred-and-sixty-six sufferers." She lowered her voice to a conspiratory whisper. "I thought Radison Beaumont should be the one since he betrayed us both. Mark him so The Beast will rise, and we will run the world."

"Running the world is o-rated," I replied, using Maddy's term. "And I'm not interested in a world where you exist."

Wooden benches lay in random crisscross patterns around the outside edge of the portal. I skirted them and erected a shield that kept the itchy, intense energy coming from the portal at bay. As I walked with purposeful strides to meet Maria at the communion table, I grabbed Volante's handle and released her from my waist.

The glass sconces on the walls vibrated as I passed them, the lit candles sending their flames high into the air in response to my raging anger. Maria felt the tremor as well, and before I could send my whip in her direction, she raised a hand and flicked her wrist. A bolt of magic shot out of the witch's fingertips, and a clap of thunder shook the building. I whirled to one side, the white, hot bolt of magic penetrating my protective shield, skating by my head and zapping the end of my ponytail. I heard a sizzle and smelled the distinct scent of burning hair.

The bitch had fried the ends of my hair. Like I didn't have enough bad hair days.

My demon kicked in full throttle, and I went back on the attack, but this time, I stayed put and sent Volante to confront her. If I could get her away from my friends, I could move her closer to the portal.

She raised her hand again, but a bench skated across the floor, courtesy of Damon's magic, and smacked into her, throwing her off balance and sending her magic shooting off to the side. At the same time, Volante made contact, missing her upper body, but wrapping around the witch's throat.

I could have snapped her head off like I'd done to Toel, but I didn't really want to kill the witch if I could spare her, and since Maria was already a ghost, killing the witch wouldn't dispose of the spirit. The iron poker was in my left hand, so I reeled Maria and her witch in toward me and went Neve on her, driving the poker through the witch's stomach.

The woman's green eyes, complete with way too much glittery eye shadow, went wide. She screamed, but it was Maria's voice that came out. Behind us, Neve sent up a cheer, weak but happy.

Salmad's voice echoed through the sanctuary, rising past the glowering stained-glass windows of saints and bouncing off the towering ceiling to flow over those of us below. "Heaven's angels in this place, spread your wings and keep us safe. Release your hold on heaven's door and accept this sacrifice evermore."

The rhyme was right up Neve's alley. She took up the chant, her voice rising with Salmad's for another chorus.

Maria wasn't going down without more of a fight, of course. As the witch's body slumped to the floor, bleeding profusely from the stomach wound, Maria's spirit detached itself and went flying. She circled back around, her ghost eyes black as night, candlelight reflecting in the bottomless orbs. As she flew at me, I reinforced my protective bubble and prepared for her attack.

Send me some juice, I told Damon. *Like you did the bench.*

A sudden wave of archdemon magic hit me with such force that I might as well have been on a bench. It knocked me off my feet and sent me flying to meet Maria in midair, all Matrix style.

Unfortunately, the intensity of the magic sent me flailing around like a helicopter blade that had come unattached from its rotor. I cartwheeled across the space, hitting Maria's ghost with a roundhouse kick without even trying.

My feet and legs passed through her noncorporeal matter, a chill sweeping over my skin and seeping right through my boots and pants. The good thing was, her transparent being allowed me to follow up with a smack of the poker and then my fist that still held the handle of my whip.

While all my limbs passed through her, they managed to still do some damage, especially when the poker cut through her from head to toe. She flinched and cried out, but refused to be deterred and wrapped her arms and her magic around me in that vice-like grip I'd experienced at the airport. Her succubus skills were the strongest I'd ever known, and without warning, she drove magic into every orifice on my body. As if she had transformed herself into a ghostly octopus, her magic filled my ears, my eyes, my nostrils with suffocating penetration. I couldn't breathe, couldn't see, couldn't hear.

And she didn't stop there. My lower openings were also raped by her magic, the driving force of her desire and determination stretching me until I thought I'd rip open at the seams.

My ribs were healed but her grip crushed them again as we tumbled together to the floor, either due to my magic or Damon's latching onto our swirling mass and grounding us.

Maria could fight better in her spirit form in the air, but I had the advantage on the ground. I returned the crushing grip by feel only and wrapped my arms around her barely visible form, driving the poker into her lower back and jumping toward the portal.

The iron or my magic kept her from slipping through my grasp and also caused her to withdraw her succubus tentacles. I could breathe again. I could see. A sweet sensation, to be sure.

Even as my demon fought and arched back from the iridescent light at the center of the church, I felt a sudden magnetic pull toward the portal. Lowering the shield I'd erected, I felt a cool breeze brush across my face. Feathers.

Maria tried to dig in her heels and latch onto my demon, which continued to fight against the draw of the portal. When I'd sent Lilith to hell, I'd called on the powers of heaven to help me. This time, I called on my boss.

Push me, I ordered Damon. *Push me hard, now!*

There was a moment's hesitation, and then he did.

Thunder boomed again, this time loud enough that the foundation of the church shook violently. A new flash-bang of light went off, obscuring my vision and sending a jolt of electricity down my spine. My nerve endings burned. Severe pressure exploded inside my skull. In my ears, though, I heard the others all taking up Salmad's chant. The sensation of flying took hold, tugging me skyward.

I looked up through the white light and saw the ceiling was open. Lightning flashed like fireworks in the sky. A burning sensation invaded my collarbone, heat streaking to my heart, and I let go of Maria's spirit, more because I was totally dazed than because I was afraid that if I didn't, I'd go to heaven with her.

Because, let's face it, there's no way God would hang out with me.

My ascent stopped as I cleared the open roof, one giant lightning bolt jetting out of the ether and striking me full force.

This round, there was no sense of pain, no jolt of electrical shock. In fact, I felt nothing at all. The entire thing was absorbed by the Hello Kitty pendant lying at the base of my neck.

I fell through the sky in a repeat performance of para-chuting *sans* parachute. I hit the sanctuary floor flat on my back, arms and legs splayed as if I'd been crucified along with my friends. But again, there was no pain. Just the opposite, actually. As I stared up at the white light above me, I felt at peace. My demon was at peace.

Shouts and voices echoed around me, but they seemed distant and inconsequential. Maria's invasion of magic had probably damaged my hearing. The portal's magic enveloped me, soothing my body, mind and spirit. I felt the brush of wings on my face, the tug of something in my chest wanting to let go and float into the light. There were no regrets, no guilt, no struggle. Only tranquility.

A few seconds of that shit and I'd had enough. I told what-ever it was inside my chest trying to break free to buckle itself back in. I wasn't going anywhere.

"Kali?" A strong, deep voice that had rocked my world since the first time I'd heard it, brought me back to the church and reality.

Blinking away the heavenly blinders, I stared up at Rad's

face. His head was backlit with the iridescent light of the portal. *An angel*, I thought.

I laughed, an edge of hysteria making it sound harsh even to my damaged ears. My throat was raw, the sound emerging from its depths, guttural.

And very, very angry.

The sconces that had tremored earlier at the energy pouring off my body, exploded, sending glass shards flying. I pushed my aching body into a sitting position and looked the Chaos demon in the eyes. Maria's spell had been broken, and the wounds on his chest were already healing.

He grinned at me. "Nice job, babe."

Babe? I raised my hand and smacked him square across his angelic double-crossing face.

FIFTY

Rad went flying from my simple slap, hit the edge of a
bench with his back, and ricocheted to the floor.

Raising a hand to his wounded cheek, he blinked. "Hey!
What was that for?"

I hadn't meant to hit him that hard, but the anger cruising
my system lessened, so maybe it was a good thing. Working my
way to a standing position, I tugged on my ringing ears and
blinked my eyes to clear away the haze hanging in my peripheral vision.

Cole, Kirill, and Yasmin had now joined our party, Kirill
tending to the witch who lay unmoving on the ground, and
Yasmin hanging on Damon as if he'd been hurt. Which he
hadn't. Bri had released everyone from the crosses, and she and
Di were tending to JR who had passed out. Poor kid.

Maddy stepped in front of me, facing Rad. Her long hair
was tangled and matted with blood. "Don't even pretend you
don't know, pretty boy."

I laid a hand on her shoulder as Rad rose from the floor. His gaze searched mine. "I tried to kill Maria myself, but she was too strong."

He thought I was pissed because he hadn't played the shining knight? Truth be told, it would have been nice if he'd at least kept Maria from hurting my friends, but I'd handled it with Damon and Salmad's help. Neve and Di had jumped in too. Friends who were always there for me, even if I was doing my damnedest to imitate an island.

Maddy set a hand on her hip. "Cut the crap, you back-stabbing two-timing son-of-a..."

"Not here," I murmured. "Not in front of everyone."

Rad looked even more confused, and Maddy, big surprise, wasn't listening. She started in again, and Rad said, "What are you talking about?"

"Parker Burkett." Maddy jeered. "Ring any bells?"

Rad's face blanched. His hand fell to his side. "Kali, it's not what the paps and ezines are saying. I never asked her to marry me."

"I don't want to discuss this now."

He started to take another step toward me, but Di joined Maddy in running interference. "Maybe you should go."

"Yes," Dru stepped to Maddy's side, Bri to Di's. "Kali said she doesn't want to discuss it right now."

Rad stepped up and punched Dru squarely in the nose. "Don't you act like you have a right to her, bloodsucker."

Dru fell back, blood gushing from yet another spot on his body. There were gasps, but I only shook my head. Two guys fighting over me...when had that ever happened?

"Alright, alright." Cole lodged himself between the Master vamp and the Chaos demon before Dru could retaliate. "Take it outside."

Cole turned to me. "Can we get out of here? This place gives me the creeps."

That made two of us. I trudged for the wooden doors, passing Salmad, who was staring at the side of my neck. He pointed to his own, sending me some kind of silent message. Damon saw the action and grabbed hold of my hand, spinning me around. "Your neck. Is that a bruise?"

Most of the candles had blown out when their sconces exploded. Damon drew me toward one that was still lit. I tried to remove his grasp and avoid the light, knowing he'd pull the scarf from my neck and see the matching holes Dru's fangs left behind. His grip on my arm was too strong and I was weak. Tripping over my own feet, I nearly fell into the soft glow of candlelight coming from the stone wall and pooling on the floor. I could only hope the bite marks had healed quicker than the rest of my body.

Neve, Maddy, Di, and everyone except Kirill and the witch fell into a loose conga line behind Damon as he removed the scarf and stared dumbfounded at my neck.

"What is it?" Neve asked, her brown eyes so dark, they looked black.

"Cool." Maddy stared with teenage wonder. "You didn't tell me you got a tattoo."

My fingers instinctively went to my neck, palpating the spot they were staring at. I remembered the feel of Dru's fangs sinking into my carotid artery. The brief pain, followed by the driving pleasure. I raised my gaze to meet his and felt something fall into place. A key locking into place. "I didn't get a tattoo."

He shook his head, his focus on my neck like everyone else's. Even Rad, standing a few feet away, stared openly, a deep crease pinching his forehead.

"Let's get you back to the Institute," Damon said, keeping me at arm's length as he hustled me toward the door. "You've been through a difficult trauma. You need a complete health evaluation."

"What about the witch?" I asked Kirill. "Will she live?"

His head was bowed and I saw him reach for the witch's eyes that stared vacantly at the ceiling. He slid his large hand over her face, shutting those eyes forever. "She did not survive."

Guilt bloomed in my diaphragm, hollowing me out. I shouldn't have jerked the poker back out. Shouldn't have stuck it in her in the first place. She'd been strong—Maria would never have been attracted to anyone weak—but she'd still been human.

I didn't argue as Damon led me out of the sanctuary and took me back to the Institute.

FIFTY-ONE

Being an archdemon's guinea pig has its advantages. Kirill put me through every medical test known to man and a few they don't know about. For every test he ran, I demanded information in return for my cooperation. Information with a side of bacon. Kirill complied without making a fuss, probably because he liked bacon as much as I did. We shared large plates of it while gossiping about Institute employees and discussing my Frankenstein-monster status.

There had actually been a vampire-demon hybrid or two, according to his record books. None of them had been made from a direct descendant of Vlad the Impaler and a demon such as myself, so his best guess about the scrolling silver tendrils decorating the side of my neck and trailing over my shoulder was that they were, in fact, a type of bruise from Dru tapping directly into my carotid artery. How long they would last, he didn't know, but after they hadn't faded in over a week, I had the feeling they never would.

Along with Kirill's in-depth exam, he spilled facts about Damon and Yasmin I had only guessed. Yasmin was doing her best to gain girlfriend status with Damon and lock onto Damon's power, but Damon wasn't interested. He doubted her motives, and from the energy that sloughed off Kirill when we discussed them, Damon and Kirill were both considering ways to send her back to London and the Bridge Institute there.

The few times Damon entered my room in the medical ward, I was hit by a wall of extreme stress and another wall of repressed sexual frustration. Both problems involved me.

I didn't tap into his thoughts—doing so seemed rude and I honestly didn't have the desire to go digging around inside his head. My own head was such a mess, I wasn't sleeping, and when I *did* sleep, I'd wake up somewhere else. Sleepwalking, Kirill assured me, was normal after what I'd been through.

Maria's voice was constantly in my head. I played back the memories of her appearance and disappearance over and over. It bothered me that I had let go of her when I was in the portal, but I hadn't actually seen her go anywhere. One minute, she was there. The next, she'd disappeared into the light.

Hearing her voice combined with the sleepwalking unnerved me. One day, I woke up in the training center, a butterfly katana in my hands and one of the boxing dummies cut to shreds at my feet. I swear I heard Maria laughing when I realized where I was and what I had done. Another time, I woke up in the center's swimming pool, eight feet of chlorinated water above me, as if I had tried to drown myself. Maria's ghostly face floated in the water above me.

Kirill had taken to locking my door round the clock, but it did no good. No matter what mundane locks or magical wards he placed on the doors, I escaped when sleepwalking. I walked in and out of Damon's bedroom one night, leading him, he claimed, to the solitary confinement prison cell where Vicky was held. Apparently, I asked him to lock me inside with her. I had no memory of the event, and when I questioned Kirill if it were possible I was schizophrenic, he confirmed it was a possibility Maria had scrambled my brain. He prescribed antipsychotics, but I refused them, afraid they'd intensify the hallucinations and sleepwalking rather than control them.

Bottles of my blood were sent to Chloe's for Arman and Rad. My friends came and went, all of them except the Chaos demon. Damon even allowed Neve into the Institute to bring me her homemade soup and sourdough bread. We sat for several hours talking and laughing, and for the first time in nearly two weeks, I thought I might be on the mend.

Fifteen minutes after she left, I asked Kirill if I could go to Damon's office and talk to him and Kirill agreed. I put on fresh clothes and brushed my hair, determined to look and act normal, but when I reached the landing outside my boss's office, I overheard him and Neve talking. She told him I wasn't myself yet, and while he assured her I was fine and Kirill was taking excellent care of me, she argued. "Something's terribly wrong with her, any fool could see that. Are you sure Maria's spirit didn't latch onto her soul?"

Regardless of the fact I didn't own a soul, I slunk away, Neve's statement confirming my suspicions. I ended up in the training center, confronting Cole. "Find a piece of iron and drive it through me."

A few vampire recruits were working out with Cole's soldiers. Since Dru was back as acting Master and the European brothers had slunk off to their kingdoms, the treaty between the Undead and the Institute was still in place. The recruits threw suspicious looks my way, having heard all about the psycho vengeance demon who was also their queen. Cole drew me aside, searching my face. "Why would I do that?"

"I think Maria's possessing me again."

He blew out a tired sigh. "Damon said Maria went into the portal. She's gone, Kali."

"Then why am I so screwed up? Why am I acting so weird? I don't even feel like staking any of these vamps." I waved a hand at the Undead recruits. They all took several steps back. "That's just wrong, Cole, and you know it."

"Have you talked to Guitar Boy?"

Unbelievable. "You think this has something to do with my love life?"

He stared at me, his eyes hard but concerned. "Look, I'm not cerebral like Damon, nor am I a pseudo-doctor like Kirill, but you need to clear the air with Beaumont, and then you need to kick the shit out of Dru. You've pent up so many emotions in the past month and a half, you've made yourself crazy. It's not Maria doing this to you, it's *you* doing it."

Emotions. I'd always wanted to be human, so I could feel the way they felt. Now I had too many feelings and sentiments. To compensate, I'd shut down everything inside me.

Maybe being human with all its confusing, overwhelming passions would be too hard for me. Hell, I could barely handle anger, and that was as much a part of my makeup as my demon.

"I need to work out," I said. "You up for a round?"

Cole grinned. "Throw in a steak dinner, and I'll go two."

"You're too easy. I would have thrown in an expensive whiskey for two rounds."

I spent the rest of the afternoon sparring with Cole. It felt good to let loose of everything. The anger, fear, and worry driving me crazy. The deep disappointment. I fed my demon with physical activity and shut off my mind.

After we finished, I was exhausted, but in a good way. I stopped in Damon's office. "Why haven't you reprimanded me yet for injecting Dru with my blood?"

He didn't lift his attention from the enormous book in front of him. The pages were a dull cream parchment, looking as if they were as old as the archdemon himself. He jotted a sentence in a notebook. "What is there to say at this point?"

"You should fire me."

"I should."

"So why haven't you?"

"What is it you want, Kali?"

Was this a trick question? What *didn't* I want? "I want to go home—back to my place. Maddy said your contractor is done making the repairs to the roof, and I'm sick of the scans and tests and the inactivity. If I'm crazy, I'd rather be crazy at home."

Ignoring the pleading tone of my voice, his gaze met mine with a serious lack of empathy. "You took a vow when you joined the Bridge organization to protect and defend humans from supernaturals who would do them harm. Yet, you defy our rules, refuse my guidance. Your latest escapade created a monster."

I'd been lingering in the doorway, but now I stepped inside the office. "*You* created a monster when you let Dru inject me with his blood. How is that different than what I did?"

"I'm keeping you under observation until the Council has sufficient evidence to make a decision concerning your threat level."

"My *threat* level?"

"At the moment, you appear to be a threat only to yourself. We'll continue monitoring you to see if that escalates to include others."

"And if it does?"

He tossed the pen he'd been using to make notes on the desk, sat back in his leather chair, and steepled his hands. The answer was in his eyes. He wasn't going to fire me.

He was going to kill me.

Fat chance I'd let that happen, unless I was a threat to humans.

"What about Dru?"

"He is your mess to clean up."

The flatness in Damon's eyes told me what his version of *clean up* entailed. "You want me to kill him, and then you'll kill me if necessary."

"Consequences are a bitch."

Tough talk from his royal pain-in-the-ass. "Has Dru done anything so far to deserve such consequences?"

"Not yet, but I have no doubt he will."

"Someone mention my name?" Dru said over my shoulder.

I jumped. What was the Master vamp doing there? Why hadn't I felt him sneak up behind me?

My magic reached out instinctively for his, and he responded without missing a beat, curling fingers of support around mine. Our combined blood pumped hard and fast in my veins.

Damon looked unsurprised at the vamp's sudden appearance. He motioned a hand at one of the chairs across from his desk. "Thank you for coming, Alexandru. Come in and take a seat."

"Don't do it," I said, holding Dru back. My instincts were on high alert, and for the second time that day, I felt like my old self. "This is a trap."

Damon rose from his chair. "I'm afraid Kali is still unwell. You'll have to ignore her delusions and paranoia."

I'd show him a delusion. I started to move forward to get in his face when Dru rested a hand on my neck in the very spot where he'd taken my blood and left me with my new tattoo. "I'll be fine," he whispered in my ear. "There's someone downstairs who very much wishes to speak to you. Give him five minutes while I discuss my situation with Damon."

No way. I yanked Dru out of the room and shuffled him down the hall and out of Damon's hearing. "I'm done being queen, and I don't know how to handle my need for your blood, but what I do know is that Damon and the Council will kill you without blinking an eye because of what I did to you. You shouldn't be here, and if you walk into that office, your ashes will be coming out in a box."

"Damon and the Council are right to be concerned. I'm here to offer them my complete cooperation. Meantime," —he pressed a kiss against my forehead—"I apologize for my behavior after you resurrected me. My body was acting on pure instinct, nothing more. I needed blood and you were there."

"And you threw in being an asshole on top of it just for grins and giggles?"

He sighed. "I'm sorry for that, too. I was..."

"An asshole."

"Yes. I was." He held out a hand. "Friends?"

His blood in my veins was going crazy. I needed to protect him. I wanted to do more than that, even if he had been an asshole to me. Stupid blood. "Please don't go in that office."

Something flashed in his eyes. His pupils enlarged. "You're cute when you're worried about me."

I punched his arm. "I'm serious."

"My father's death created an opening in the Undead world, and as you know, there's been a lot of posturing for that position. You're looking at the new Liege of the entire Undead Nation. Believe me when I tell you, no harm will come to me here at the Institute. Damon wants to keep our covenant as much as I do."

"You are shitting me."

"We'll discuss it in more depth next week. For now, your role as queen of the Central Region will play a key part in my administration, and later on...well, let's see just how far two freaks can take the supernatural world."

World domination echoed in my brain. Nudra, Toel, and now Alexandru—all power-hungry vampires wanting to use me to climb to the top of the food chain.

I really *had* created a monster.

Dru grinned as if reading my thoughts. "Don't worry about all that right now. Go downstairs and make nice to your Chaos demon."

Gritting my teeth, I smacked him again. "Why the hell did you bring him for?"

"You need to talk to him before he buries Chicago in this awful blizzard."

I hadn't even noticed the weather. When I shook my head, Dru caught my chin and forced me to look him in the eye again. "I command you to talk to him and straighten out your problems."

Merde. My blood heated uncomfortably, and I tried to break the eye contact, but it didn't work. "Fine. But if you end up staked, don't come crying to me. I'm not bringing you back from the dead a second time."

I stomped away, but by the time I hit the stairs to the first floor, my footsteps slowed.

Rad was in a sitting area off the main foyer. The moment I entered, he rose from a chair. Maddy was there, too, and she rushed forward, grabbing my fisted hand, which was raised and ready to connect with Rad's chin.

"Easy, girl. Hear him out."

First, Dru. Now Maddy. "You're defending him?"

"You need to listen to his side of things."

Rad's eyes were imploring but determined. Seemed I was going to hear his side of things whether I wanted to or not. I turned my back on him and went to stand by a window. The winter landscape outside was definitely blizzard-like, snow rising and falling in waves.

I felt more than saw Maddy leave the room. My nose picked up on Rad's scent, zeroing in on his fabulous salty sea air smell. Warm sand under my feet, Rad's deep, wonderful laughter echoing over the waves. Water smooth as silk against my skin...

Pinching myself, I snapped out of the daydream. Damon was right. I *was* delusional.

When Rad stepped up behind me, his emotions hit me hard. But unlike the others I'd been around that day, his feelings were in tangled disarray. I couldn't separate one emotion from the other. I only knew he was hurting—bad.

"The Hello Kitty pendant went in the trash." I touched my collarbone where it had lain. Had Maria sent that lightning bolt, or had God? "It was ruined after the lightning struck it."

His voice was a low rumble, vibrating against my skin. "It did its job then since you're still alive."

I caught my reflection in the window. Satan's balls, my hair was a mess. Why hadn't I brushed it out after my session with Cole? "Did you put a spell on it?"

"A friend of mine, who happens to be a powerful priest in the Noctifector organization, blessed it with divine protection when I saw him in New York. The major reason I went there."

I chuckled at the irony. "Good thing you didn't tell him who it was for."

"So you brought Dru back to life." His gaze searched mine in the reflection. "Playing God now?"

"So you're engaged. Playing the double-crossing *il pistolino* now?"

His breath left him in a long, Maddy-like sigh. "I'm not engaged. The thing with Parker is over."

"How long has *the thing* with Parker been going on?"

"There never was anything between us on my part. She's been stalking me for months, and I've let her get away with a lot because of who her father is, but she pushed me too far this time."

"You bought her an engagement ring. Not exactly the best way to get her to stop stalking you."

"I went into Tiffany's to get you the pendant. She came in while I was there, and I had to pretend to be in there for some other reason since you won't let me..." He trailed off. "Trying to keep my lives separate is impossible."

"So you *proposed?*"

"She assumed I was there to buy her something. She already had a ring picked out and told the jeweler to put it on my tab. I argued with her and laid it all out. I wasn't interested. I was in love with someone else. No way was I marrying her. She threw a fit, threatened to have her father rip up my contract, and then she stomped out of the store with the ring on her finger, and what do you know? She'd texted her paparazzi contacts before she even came inside, and they were all waiting for us to emerge. I followed her out. She was posing for the cameras and got what she wanted."

"Well, you can always leave her at the altar."

That was low, and I knew it. His gaze cut to the floor. "The other members of the band and I talked it over. We're going to dissolve our contract with Burkett Music and find another producer."

I faced him. "Won't Burkett sue you for breach of contract?"

He shrugged. "Some things are worth the price."

Consequences. Worrying about them wasn't always for pussies. "Thank you for the pendant and the priest's blessing."

The storm outside lessened. His emotions calmed. "I'm leaving the Noctifectors, Kali."

No one left the Noctifectors unless it was in a body bag. "The only reason they've kept you alive all this time is because you're an asset to them. They won't let you leave."

"It won't be easy, but I'll handle it. I want to be with you, Kali. Only you. That's all I've ever wanted, and if that means giving up the other two lives I've been living, then so be it."

The last bits of chaos inside my mind calmed along with Rad's emotions. "Don't give up your singing career, Rad. Never that."

He hugged me to him for a long moment. "What do you say we blow this joint?"

Maddy's voice rang out from the foyer. "I've got her bag."

"What?" I smiled at both of them. "Where are we going?"

Rad took my hand and squeezed it. "We've got a surprise for you."

"I can't leave the Institute. Damon will have a fit."

"Screw Damon." Maddy threw my cape at me. "It's Christmas Eve."

"Excuse me?" Damon said. He and Dru came down the stairs.

"Are we set?" Dru asked, and he and Rad shared a nod of understanding.

Since when were they friends?

Dru shook Damon's hand. "I'll see you tomorrow night."

Damon looked at Maddy, then at me. "Tomorrow is Christmas. We'll expect you on Monday."

Maddy grabbed my hand and tugged me toward the door. I looked at Damon, waiting for him to stop us.

He didn't, giving me one of his nods as if I had his blessing to leave. "Merry Christmas," he said, jogging back up the stairs.

FIFTY-TWO

"What did you say to him?" I asked Dru as we descended the front steps and headed to the parking lot. The blizzard had disappeared, and stars peeked out overhead.

Brianna was waiting for Dru at his car. He patted my arm. "A simple negotiation, Queen. A skill you might want to brush up on."

Under my cloak, I wrapped Volante around my wrist. "Uh, huh. Did this negotiation have me at the center of it?"

"Here we go," Maddy said, but she was smiling. "Everything's about Kali."

"Actually in this case, it is, and on Monday, we'll discuss it further." He dipped his head to me. "Until then, I bid you a joyful holiday. I must get back to Carpathia for the Christmas Eve party."

He left, and we followed suit. A little while later, Rad, Maddy, and I drove into the parking lot at the church. Through one of the windows, I saw a faint glow.

The strong smell of spruce hit me as we entered my house.

A seven-foot fresh tree sat in one corner of the living room, strung with hundreds of white lights. Boxes of ornaments and several large Macy's bags sat nearby. "What's this?"

"Duh, a Christmas tree." Maddy hung up her coat and my cape and skipped into the living room. "We put the lights on earlier, but I thought it would be fun to decorate it together."

"Di and the others will be over in a few minutes to help," Rad said. "And I'll be back before midnight."

I shot him a questioning look. "Where are you going?"

"The governor's. He's having a Christmas ball at his mansion and honoring some of the Chicago military families who have members in Afghanistan and Iraq. He asked me to swing by, do a song or two, and sign some autographs for the kids."

He didn't look too excited about the prospect. "Is Parker going to be there?"

"Probably." He kissed me tenderly. "I'll be back as soon as I can."

After he'd gone, Maddy turned on a movie about a normal guy who got stuck being Santa Claus because he'd stepped into Santa's suit after the real Santa died. Humans. How do they come up with these things? "Want some hot cocoa?" she asked.

I looked at the tree and the twinkling lights and thought about Rad and Parker. The doorbell rang, and Di and JR came in on a gust of winter air. We exchanged greetings, and Di scrutinized my face. "What's wrong?"

JR was helping Maddy hang a Star Wars figurine on the tree. Maddy had also hung the ornament she'd stolen from her parent's tree. "JR, can you make me an invitation for the governor's ball?"

Maddy's head swung around. "You're going?"

"Here, you can have my invite." Di withdrew a cream-colored envelope from her purse. "Why do you want to attend the ball? You hate things like that."

"I thought we were going to decorate the tree," Maddy whined.

"We will." I snatched the invite from Di's hand. "After we take care of some business first."

Maddy saw the gleam in my eye. "You're coming out."

"Out of what?" JR asked, his gaze on the silver scrolls on my neck. "The closet?"

Something like that. "Will you help me pick out a dress?" I asked Di.

"As long as you tell me what this is about."

Maddy squealed. "I cannot wait to see Parker Burkett's face."

Upstairs, Di went through my designer wardrobe and withdrew an Alexander McQueen dress. Sleeveless and body-hugging, it sported a pale pink slip with a layer of cut-out lace over the top. From the shoulders to the outside edge of the hips, another set of cut-out lace in black fanned over my curves.

"Hey, I want to wear that one," Maddy said. "It's better suited to me."

I rimmed my eyes with kohl liner. "Why is that?"

"It's classic gothic princess. That's me. You're more urban warrior. You know, leather, leather, and more leather."

"So I'll wear boots."

"No." Di held up a pair of suede platform peep toes in the same pale pink color. "You'll wear these."

The shoes laced up the ankle and screamed feminine. I tried them on, stood in front of the floor-length mirror in my bedroom. With the gothic lace and dark makeup, there was no way anyone would confuse me with a princess. I was sure Parker had that role covered anyway.

I took off the shoes and handed them to Maddy. "You wear these. I'm wearing boots."

Preferably a pair with wicked heels so I could kick some spoiled princess ass.

JR drove. Di rode shotgun. I flashed my invite at the governor's mansion and Maddy and I were welcomed inside. While we checked our coats, I heard Rad's voice coming from a ballroom on the north side of the house.

"This is going to be so good." Maddy rubbed her hands together. "What exactly are you going to do?"

Ignoring the stares following us, I worked my way through the crush of people, the sound of Rad's voice reeling me in. "Just make sure you get a picture for the tabloids."

The people in the ballroom parted down the center as I strode through the group, my eyes locked on Rad. He was in front of a large fireplace, sitting on a stool with his guitar in hand. The fireplace sported a huge wreath, and not one, but two, giant Christmas trees flanked each side. His eyes were closed, and he was lost in his song. As I drew close, I sent a tendril of magic out in front of me and let it tickle over his skin.

His eyes flipped open, then widened when they saw me. His fingers stuttered on the chord he was playing, and his voice trailed off. Everyone who'd been watching him was now watching me.

Including Parker Burkett. She sat in the front row along with a couple of reporters with large cameras recording Rad's performance.

Rad looked pleasantly perplexed. "What are you doing..."

I walked straight up to him, wrapped one hand behind his head, and kissed him. Long, slow, and deep.

A collective gasp went up behind us. Rad shifted the guitar out of the way, parted his thighs, and pulled me between them.

Tiny lights went off in my peripheral vision...cellphones and cameras capturing the moment.

Perfect.

I broke the kiss, ran my thumb over Rad's bottom lip and turned my head so I was looking directly at Parker. Her left hand was over her heart, the diamond engagement ring shining brilliantly under the ballroom lights. In a room full of humans, I couldn't let my demon peek out, but I sent her a direct challenge. *He's mine.*

Her eyes narrowed, then she made the sign of the cross and murmured what looked like a prayer under her breath. A prayer I'd heard before. *Je vis pour Dieu et seulement pour Dieu.*

I live for God and only for God.

Realization dawned. Parker wasn't just the daughter of a music industry mogul.

She was a Noctifector.

Several of the governor's security personnel hustled in, coming my way. Rad stood, waved them off. "She's with me."

Carrying his guitar in one hand, he grabbed my hand with the other. He nodded to the governor as we passed him and his family, ignored Parker, and together we headed out.

Maddy brought our coats, a large grin spread across her face. Various people I didn't know said things to Rad in passing. Most of them gave me inquisitive stares. To every one of them, Rad made sure to introduce me.

We broke free from the well-wishers, their greetings of "Merry Christmas" and "Happy Holidays" trailing us into the cold night air. JR and Di brought the car around, but they were in a lineup with several cars in front of them, so we waited on the mansion's stairs.

"Who the hell do you think you are?" a woman's low voice hissed from behind me.

I turned and found Parker on the step above me, her hands buried inside a fur coat. "I'm guessing that's a rhetorical question since every Noct in the land knows who I am."

Rad was watching her hands too. "Not here, Parker."

Her eyes never left mine, so I wasn't sure if she was speaking to him or me. "You can't seriously believe you're going to get away with this."

I stepped up and put myself at eye level with her. She was taller than me, but the boots I'd worn had a significant heel. "I'm going to say this once, so listen carefully. If you value your ring finger, you'll return that diamond to Tiffany's and make a statement to the press that your relationship with Radison Beaumont is over. And if you value your life? You'll leave us both alone."

She raised a hand to slap my face, and although I was glad to see it was free of any weapon, I sure as shit wasn't going to let her make contact. I grabbed her wrist in mid-swing and bent her hand the wrong way. Not enough to break any bones, but hard enough to emphasize my speed and ability.

"Go back to the ball, Parker." Rad drew me away from her, put his arm around me. "We're done here."

JR had stopped at the bottom of the stairs and we climbed inside my Land Rover. As we drove away, Parker stood in the same spot, a wicked gleam of revenge shining in her eyes.

I smiled at her. *Bring it, princess. It'll be the last thing you do.*

FIFTY-THREE

When we returned, Cole and Brianna were at my house, checking out the mistletoe Maddy had hung in the kitchen doorway. Neve arrived shortly afterward, still recovering from her ordeal but in good spirits. Another Santa Claus movie was on, and Maddy assured me there was yet a third sequel to look forward to. Rad popped popcorn, JR and Maddy finished trimming the tree, and Di passed out cookies.

JR had brought an Xbox and stacks of games, so after the Santa Claus movie marathon—which was completely corny and yet surprisingly enjoyable—we ordered pizza and played the latest versions of Call of Duty and Final Fantasy. I kicked ass on Final Fantasy.

By sunrise, most everyone had drifted off to their own homes, seeming reluctant to conclude the night but happy all the same. Rad, Maddy, and I braved the cold wind and went up to the castle rooftop. We walked around the area that had been repaired, and Rad declared it up to his standards. I figured as long as it didn't fall in, it was good.

The sun rose milky peach in the east, a few rays forcing

themselves through the ever-present clouds. We sipped hot coffee and munched cold pizza in silence.

My head felt clear, and my body strong. Whatever lasting effects Maria had cursed me with seemed to be gone. I looked forward to a long day of sleep and sex and laughter.

I'm not an island, I told myself. *Just a small country with limited access.*

I yawned, and Rad led me back inside. He and Maddy had bought me a new bed with a thick pillowtop mattress, and before he even got my boots off, I flopped back on the bed, my eyelids too heavy to keep open. "I don't want to sleep," I muttered.

"You're safe," he whispered in my ear, and that was all it took. "I won't leave."

I'd like to say it was a dreamless sleep or that I slept like a baby, but I'd be lying. In reality, my sleep was filled with endless nightmares. Old ones and new. The one that kept recurring involved me straddling Rad's stomach and carving my signature runes into his chest.

I woke in a sweat, remnants of that dream and the haunting ring of Maria's laughter in my ears. *The last one. You did it,* bambino. *The Beast lives!*

Jerking up, I realized I was naked. Rad was next to me. The castle was deathly quiet. I took a couple of deep breaths and massaged my temples.

Rad's fingers touched my lower back. "What is it?"

"Nothing," I said too fast. "Just a nightmare. Go back to sleep."

His lips followed his fingers, kissing their way up my spine, but before I succumbed to them, a loud alarm went off downstairs.

My security system. I jumped out of bed, certain Parker

Burkett had hunted me down. Throwing on my robe, I said to Rad, "Really? You had to date a Noctifector?"

He looked slightly confused. "First of all, I never dated her, and second of all, you don't think that's her, do you?"

Of course, I did. Maddy met me in the hall and together we rushed downstairs and ran into my office, her to shut off the alarm and me to get a look at the security monitor. Rad stood behind me as I tried to make out who was at my front door as the doorbell went off.

"Well, unless Parker has turned into a man who's six-foot-two, weighs at least two-twenty, and," Rad teased, "has facial hair, I'd say that's not her."

Smartass.

Maddy checked out our visitor on camera. "Sure isn't Santa unless Santa looks like Thor. But hey, any guy who looks that good? I'm not complaining. Where's that mistletoe?"

Make that two smartasses.

Maddy and I headed to the entryway. Rad followed. I grabbed the stun baton out of my cape and flipped the switch to activate it. "Who are you?" I called through the door. "What do you want?"

"Name's Shane Wynter." He boasted a heavy European accent. "Belphagor— I mean Salmad—said I could crash here."

The three of us exchanged bewildered looks. "How do you know Salmad?"

"Same way I know you, luv. *Of* you, anyways. I'm one of the sins. You know, as in deadly sins. My demon name is Leviathan."

No. Way. "So much for your Santa Claus theory," I murmured to Maddy.

Unlocking the door, I swung it open, stun baton in front of me. The guy was dressed like a modern-day Viking, his leather and jeans expensive distressed stuff he'd probably bought off the rack at Saks. His chiseled cheekbones and jaw sported a fine layer of beard—not too much, but enough to add a tough air to his smooth skin and pretty-boy blue eyes.

A smile opened his full lips, showing off his pearly whites, and he looked me over from head to foot. "You're a bit shorter than I expected there, Kali girl, but I love the sexy bedhead look. Works for ya."

Rad stepped out of the shadows and cleared his throat. "Why are you here?"

Shane raised a hand in greeting. "*Bonjour*, Frenchman. Didn't my bud, Sal, tell you I was coming?"

"No." I waved the baton at his genitals. "And I don't like surprises."

He stepped back, the grin faltering. "Why, I'm here to help you stop The Beast. A few of the others will be here before sundown as well."

"I sent Maria to heaven...or somewhere. As long as all seven of us aren't walking the earth, The Beast can't rise."

He gave me an incredulous look and chuckled like I was joking with him. "You have no idea what's coming, do you, vengeance demon?"

A memory from my nightmare made me lower the stun baton. In my mind's eye, I saw Rad's chest decorated with runes. Heard Maria's laughter ringing inside my head. For once, I wished for the easy way.

"Would you like some coffee?" I asked, moving aside so he could come in.

"Strong and black." He strode across the threshold, staying out of Rad's way and winking at Maddy. "Better make a big pot. We've got a lot of work to do before the others get here."

Shutting the door behind him, I pressed my forehead against it and sighed. So much for sleep and sex and all that other good stuff. "Merry fucking Christmas," I said to no one in particular.

And then I turned on my heel and headed for the kitchen to make coffee.

Find a special bonus on the next page!

READY TO FIND **out what happens next?**

Click here to get your copy of Sweet Soldier, Kali Sweet Urban Fantasy Series, Book 3 so you can keep the romance and adventure going!

And be sure to sign up for my reader newsletter so you're the first to know about new releases, giveaways, and other cool stuff (including pet pics, crafts, and recipes)!

Yes I want Misty's Newsletter!

WANT MORE KALI, **Rad, and Daemon?** Join my reader community on Ream to read bonus stories not in the books! https://reamstories.com/mistyevans

BONUS FOR READERS OF SWEET CHAOS

Thank you for purchasing Sweet Chaos!
Here is the full lyrics of *Whisper In the Dark* by Radison
Beaumont.
Rock on!

Whisper In The Dark
By Radison Beaumont
© 2010 - 2024

Listen to my music
Listen to my heart
Find the good within
What's lost is keeping us apart

I finally found my way
No words of mine can ever say
How much I miss you...

After all this time

After all the wrongs
I still care...

Listen to my music
    Listen to its heart.
    Listen to the whisper
    Hiding in the dark

The chaos in me rests
    With you I'm at my best
    As I strum these notes

So listen to this song
    Forget those wrongs
    And come back to me

Listen to my music
    Listen to my heart
    Listen to it sing to you
    Listen to me sing to you

Listen to my music
    Listen to its heart
    Listen to these words
    Fading with the dark

GLOSSARY OF TERMS FOR SWEET CHAOS

Bambino – daughter

che cavolo - what the hell? Literally: what cabbage?

Damnat quod non intelligunt - They condemn what they do not understand.

del giorno - of the day

Dio cano - God is a dog

dire o sparare - that's bullshit

faccia di culo – buttface

furor poeticus – a form of ecstasy; or the divine frenzy; or poetic madness

Il est trop malade pour voir qui que ce soit - He's too ill to see anyone.

Il nous est impossible de laisser Alexandru seuls - It's impossible to leave Dru alone.

Il pistolino - dick

Infernum - hell

Je vis pour Dieu et seulement pour Dieu – I live for God and only for God

Ludio demon - excels at sports

Madonna mia – oh, my God; literally: oh, my Madonna

Mai arrendersi - never back down

Mai più - never again

Merde - shit

non arrenderti mai - never give up

Non più - no more

Per Dominum nostrum Jesum Christum - through our Lord Jesus Christ

pseudothyrum - a secret door

Revenants – visible ghost or zombie that shares a number of characteristics with folkloric vampires

Sbagliando s'impara - one learns from his mistakes

VISIT MY STORE

Did you know you can buy directly from me? When you do, the retailer doesn't take a cut and I can pass on the savings to YOU!

https://mistyevansbooks.com/shop

Benefits:
- You can find ALL my books in one place
- SAVE money
- EARLY access to new releases
- Special Collections, Boxed Sets, and Limited Editions
- Support a small business (and support a dream!)

Why Buy Direct?

When you purchase a book by your favorite author, electronic or print, on retailer platforms, the company keeps 30-70% of the sale, leaving the author with little to no profit (after the company deducts delivery fees, taxes, and other fees).

Buying directly from the author means that more goes to them so they can keep turning out stories for you. Every published story, every book, requires cover art, editing, and hours and hours of the author's time simply to create it. Not to mention overhead costs, such as websites, newsletters, writing software, graphics programs, advertising, taxes, etc.

In addition, one of the big-name retailers requires exclusivity, and all of them have terms of service and rules and regulations that make it challenging and time-consuming for an indie author to navigate the publishing world.

Most of us would MUCH rather spend our time creating more stories for YOU, rather than trying to jump through the hoops at the retailers. Buying direct from your favorite authors (where available) helps ensure that an author you love is not subject to unexplained account closures, withholding of royalties, censorship, and other issues that can affect their livelihood.

I've experienced ALL of these. By buying direct, you help put control of my work back in my hands - and I can continue to write more.

Either way, thank you for supporting me! I understand buying direct doesn't work for everyone and even if you use the retailers to buy my books, I appreciate you!

Happy reading,

Misty

https://mistyevansbooks.com/shop

YOU'RE INVITED!

Do you have a passion for my stories?

Want more from my characters?

How about early access to ALL my new releases?

My reader community is for YOU!

Try my **Magic Bites reader community** for a month! It's ONLY $5 - you're buying me a coffee - and in return, you get all these perks:

Writing Updates so you know what's in the works and how soon you can get it

Special Content, including chapters in new and upcoming stories

FREE Access to new books - Read all of my new suspense and thriller releases for FREE before they're available at retailers

Coupons for discounts to <u>my online store:</u> https://www.mistyevansbooks.com/

Don't miss out on this opportunity! Join my Magic Bites reader community today.

https://mistyevansbooks.com/membership-levels

PNR & UF BY MISTY/NYX HALLIWELL

The Accidental Reaper Series

Grim & Bare It, Book 1

Reaper's Keepers, Book 2

In too Reap, Book 3

Killin' It (short story for newsletter subscribers only)

The Vampire's Kiss (an exclusive short story available in Misty's Store. *Intended for mature audiences 17+*)

Grave Girl

Grave Magic

Grim Vows

The Kali Sweet Series

Revenge Is Sweet, Kali Sweet Series, Book 1

Sweet Chaos, Kali Sweet Series, Book 2

Sweet Soldier, Kali Sweet Series, Book 3

Sweet Curse, Kali Sweet Series, Book 4

Witches Anonymous Step 1

Jingle Hells, WA Step 2

Wicked Souls, WA Step 3

Dark Moon Lilith, Witches Anonymous Step 4

Dancing With the Devil, Witches Anonymous Step 5

Devil's Due, Witches Anonymous Step 6

Dirty Deeds, Witches Anonymous Step 7

Wicked Wedding, Witches Anonymous Step 8

Soul Survivor, Moon Water Series, Book 1

Soul Protector, Moon Water Series, Book 2

Cozy Mysteries (writing as Nyx Halliwell)

Sister Witches Of Raven Falls Mystery Series

Of Potions and Portents

Of Curses and Charms

Of Stars and Spells

Of Spirits and Superstition

Confessions of a Closet Medium Series

Pumpkins & Poltergeists

Magic & Mistletoe

Hearts & Haunts

Vows & Vengeance

Cupcakes & Corpses

Tea Leaves & Troubled Spirits

Haunted Honeymoon

Wedding Bells & Psychic Spells

Phantoms Are Forever

Sister Witches of Story Cove Series

Cinder

Belle

Snow

Ruby

Zelle

Sister Witches of Story Cove Complete Set

***

Witchy Candy Shop Mysteries

Tricks and Treats

Candy and Creeps

Gum and Ghouls (releasing 2025)

ROMANTIC SUSPENSE & MYSTERIES

Don't want to miss a single release? Click here to join my reader list!

SEALs of Shadow Force Series

Fatal Truth

Fatal Honor

Fatal Courage

Fatal Love

Fatal Vision

Fatal Thrill

Risk

SEALS of Shadow Force Series: Spy Division

Man Hunt

Man Killer

Man Down

Covert Affairs

Covert Tactics

Covert Obsession

The SCVC Taskforce Series

Deadly Pursuit

Deadly Deception

Deadly Force

Deadly Intent

Deadly Affair, A SCVC Taskforce novella

Deadly Attraction

Deadly Secrets

Deadly Holiday, A SCVC Taskforce novella

Deadly Target

Deadly Rescue

Deadly Bounty

Deadly Betrayal

Deadly Threat

The Super Agent Series

Operation Sheba

Operation Paris

Operation Proof of Life

Operation Lost Princess

Operation Ambush

Operation Contraband

Operation Sleeping With the Enemy

The Justice Team Series (with Adrienne Giordano)

Stealing Justice

Cheating Justice

Holiday Justice

Exposing Justice

Undercover Justice

Protecting Justice

Missing Justice

Defending Justice

SCHOCK SISTERS MYSTERY SERIES w/Adrienne Giordano

1st Shock

2nd Strike

3rd Tango

The Secret Ingredient Culinary Mystery Series

The Secret Ingredient, A Culinary Romantic Mystery with Bonus Recipes

The Secret Life of Cranberry Sauce, A Secret Ingredient Holiday Novella

MEET MISTY

USA TODAY Bestselling Author Misty Evans has published over ninety novels, as well as nonfiction inspirational journals. She loves writing urban fantasy, paranormal romance, and mystery/suspense. Under her pen name, Nyx Halliwell, she also writes supernatural cozy mysteries.

When not reading or writing, she enjoys music, movies, and hanging out with her husband, twin sons, and three spoiled rescue dogs. She's a crafter at heart and has far too many projects to finish.

Visit www.mistyevansbooks.com to check out her online store and sign up for her newsletter.

LETTER FROM MISTY

Hello Beautiful Reader!

Thank you for reading this story! It is an honor and a privilege to write books for you. I'm an indie author and every fan is important to me. I pour my heart into each story and do my best to bring you an escape from the real world.

Readers are the key to my success - not a traditional publishing deal (had four), an agent (had two), or a publicity team (yep, you guessed it, had several of those as well.)

Those of you who read my books, love my characters and worlds, and then tell others about them are the best of friends. I adore you and will keep writing if you keep reading!

If you'd like to learn about my other books, sales, and special promotions, please sign up for my newsletter at **www. mistyevansbooks.com**.

You'll get coupons to download starter packs for FREE, whether you love my suspense or my paranormal.

Support me directly (no retailer taking their cut), grab

special edition box sets, and get new releases before they are out at retailers by visiting my store **https://mistyevans books.com/shop**.

I have sales and offer NEW RELEASES early! Check it out.

Last but not least, if you enjoy clean, cozy mysteries, visit my pen name **www.nyxhalliwell.com** to see those books.

Thank you, and happy reading!

Misty

www.ingramcontent.com/pod-product-compliance
Lightning Source LLC
Chambersburg PA
CBHW020255030726
47499CB00001B/208